Jake Miller's Wheel

by

James Ostby

Other books by James Ostby

Men With Broken Faces: A literary
World War I novel

Jake crawled to the head of the grave, leaned against the stone marker, and pulled his knees under his chin. It was dark and cold, but the inscription on the headstone seared his back: "And know that I will wait for you."

A car passed, but the driver didn't see.

Snow came lightly through the still air, and Jake looked up at the faint moonglow. He sensed he was not alone. A winter-white jackrabbit, on hind legs with front paws folded, stood looking at him. When Jake raised his hand it bounded away, through the graveyard to the adjacent field.

Damn, life had been hard. As in classic Greek tragedy, Jake's life–and his death–had been preordained. That was the only explanation. He had been unable to control his Wheel. With supreme effort he heaved himself forward, sprawled face down on the grave, and prayed for life.

But then, in a divine intervention, he heard an almost audible, "Do not pray for life, pray for salvation," and suddenly he was at peace. A car stopped on the road, then another, and people approached. Hands turned him over onto his back, and lifted him.

PART ONE – 1913

CHAPTER ONE

Jake Miller lay in the slough next to his homestead shack, squeezing his eyes shut against the morning sun. His wool union suit floated next to him. He felt like a hog in a hog wallow, and oh, God, his head hurt! So bad that his mind had abandoned him, to hover somewhere above. It wasn't easy being a melancholiac. Or whatever he was.

"Haw! You're cracked, Miller. All that stuff about your Wheel of Life. Here, give him another drink. We gotta get him normalized!"

Jake wanted to float so that the sun wouldn't be in his face, but he couldn't move. He peeked at a frog, and it was like looking in a mirror. The frog swam off, and Jake's brown-and-white Guernsey milk cow approached. She watched him curiously for a few minutes, drank, plopped a few cowpies into the water, then plodded away, leaving him dismally alone except for the frog that had returned and was squatting on a piece of wood, blinking at him. All of the other frogs were small, but this one was large and intelligent looking, and Jake was surprised at how it could be that large so early in the year. Ah, at one with a frog. Or was it a toad? All in all Jake allowed that he'd rather look like a frog.

"I think he's had too much to drink already, the bartender said. Whew! Lord, almighty Miller, what'd yuh do, shit your drawers?"

He hadn't been drunk since Mable had gotten him straightened out before they were married. Pink elephants–maybe pink elephants, possibly something else–then convulsions. Now he'd have to get himself straightened out. Only two weeks until she'd arrive, and he had poured out all of his spirits. It had been his idea to homestead in northeastern Montana, and from what he'd seen, maybe he'd made a mistake. A big mistake. Nothing but stark, treeless prairie; and sun, and wind. Always the wind. Enough to drive a person batty. What was Mable going to think?

"Out you go," the bartender said as he heaved Jake through the batwing doors.

Jake didn't remember much of anything after being thrown out of the bar, only that he had bounced once on the front step before sliding face first into the dirty street.

The mosquitoes were getting bad, and Jake smeared a layer of mud on his face. It was still spring, but already the water was getting thick and malodorous.

The damn frog smiled at him, but Jake refused to smile back. Actually, Jake had always been lead to believe he was rather good looking. Beatrice Lamont had thought so in fourth grade, and others had too as he had grown older, but he himself hadn't seen it. Didn't see it. His mother had, but that didn't count. Mable did, and that of course counted, but not much.

Horses snorted in the yard: either Lars Nordraak the Norwegian, or Karl Springer the German, his two nearest neighbors.

"Miller! What the hell are you doing in that slough?"

Jake managed to float around to face Lars, and he made himself open his eyes.

"Too long in the saloon in Charity last night, and I ran outta' wash water. And the well driller can't come till next week."

Charity, the closest town–four miles south–had been named by a traveling preacher. Just a dusty settlement along the railroad track, with a mercantile-grocery store, hotel-restaurant, and a bar; but it was growing. A grain elevator and a lumberyard were going in.

"You're a big frog in a small pond. Anyway, it seems like no water at all would be better than slough water." Lars–second-generation American–still had a Norwegian accent. He was tall and handsome, with a Roman-nose profile and a sun-and-wind weathered Scandinavian blush. He and his wife, Caroline, had arrived the year before, from somewhere in North Dakota. They had a little boy named Sexton.

"I had an accident in the saloon. Fouled my pants, and the barkeep gave me the heave-ho. Oh, I think I'm gonna die, Lars. Drinking isn't my strength."

"It's detrimental to your health. My father died from it when he was only forty-eight. Bleeding stomach. Ulcers. Had to pump saltwater into his veins to keep him alive until all the relatives could come to say their goodbyes." Lars hawked up a great, gray glob of phlegm and spat it into the water.

"Hey, watch where you're spittin'!"

"Haw! It's liable to improve the water, not pollute it even more. In fact I should charge you for it. Or better yet, get some little bottles and start selling it. *Lars Nordraak's Miracle Salve. For external use only!* Heh! *Will also enhance and improve your intelligence.* Ha, anybody dumb enough to buy it could use a little intelligence. Might enhance something else too, if you get my meaning." He winked at Jake.

"I had to light the fire one last time before Mable gets here. After that it's gonna be a long dry spell. I guess a permanent dry spell."

Lars slapped a mosquito on his cheek. "Cheer up, I'll sneak you a beer once in a while!"

Jake knew not what to make of him, except that his appearance was deceptive.

"Anyway, I'll haul over another barrel of water," Lars said. "Keep in mind that water's good for drinking too, and it's a helluva lot cheaper than that swill they sell in The Palace."

"Huh."

"In fact, my water's free. I won't charge you a thing for it. Now when I get to selling my miracle salve, that's a horse of a different color. It'll be worth . . . ."

Lars went back to his farm wagon, climbed on, and clicked his tongue to start his two brown mares. As he bounced away along the rough, bone-crunching trail, Jake's headache worsened just watching him.

Jake lay pondering the aurora of his and Mable's fresh start. Oh, mercy, what was Mable going to think?

CHAPTER TWO

Jake and Lars Nordraak stood in front of Jake's one-room, tarpaper-covered homestead shack, braced against the wind, watching Karl Springer dowse for water. Apollo–protector of young men–warmed them.

"Only water he's gonna find is between his legs," Lars quipped in his laconic way.

Karl–short, dark, and portly, wearing his usual white shirt, black trousers with red suspenders, and black derby hat–looked like he was in a trance as he walked slowly back and forth holding the top ends of a Y-shaped willow stick. Now and then the bottom of the stick would dip, and Karl would kick an X in the dirt. Part clown and part conjurer, he had made it clear that he didn't want any interference from Jake and Lars, so they stood at some distance.

"Haw!" Lars laughed. When Karl's back was turned Lars closed his eyes and held out his hands in front of himself, palms down with his fingers spread. He swayed slightly. "Oooooh, ooooh, ooooh," he murmured, softly, so only Jake would hear.

But apparently Lars and Karl were best friends.

Notwithstanding the wind, it was a beautiful day. The first wild flowers of the year–crocuses, that had sprinkled their pretty lavender on the unbroken patches of prairie–were wilted, replaced by yellow sweet peas, and by bluebells. New grass brightened beneath last year's matted stand, meadowlarks sang their spring song–interrupted only by an occasional flight of raucous crows–and the air was fresh with the smell of earth, and of life. One could see for miles, and for miles there was nothing but purity. It was as if the earth were flat, and the only limit was not the horizon, but the acuity of one's vision and the intensity of the viewer's imagination of both the present and of the future. Jake guessed it wasn't so bad there after all. A formation of geese flew north, so high that one could barely hear their honking.

"Haw, haw, haw," Lars laughed, but not loud enough for Karl to hear. "Hee, hee. I wish I had a picture of this. Haw, haw!"

Lars' height and light complexion made Jake feel darker and shorter than ever; somehow inferior, with his flat face and large, dull eyes. Jake started to say something about Lars' intolerance, but he thought better of it. Curiously, it had been Lars' idea to enlist Karl. Lars had a mean streak; a way of getting under people's skin.

But Jake had to concede that Karl was a ludicrous sight, wandering around with his eyes half closed. Anyway, what difference could it make? One place looked as good as another. Or as bad.

"Karl seems to be quite an individualist," Jake said.

"Haw! He's a real mugwump alright! He could just as well dig where he wants it, and be done with it, without all this hocus-pocus. He sure can be a nincompoop if he puts his mind to it."

Karl stopped, and the tip of his stick bobbed up and down. "That's it!" he cried. "Right here." He threw his hat on the ground. "Must be shallow. Strongest pull I ever felt! Good place for a well too. What luck!" He said something in guttural German.

"Ho, ho, ho," Lars laughed. "Why didn't you put it there in the first place? That's where you wanted it all along! Right next to where he's gonna build the barn. Ha, ha!"

Karl gave him a dark look, and Lars stifled himself.

"Good water, too!" Karl called. "I can tell. When you've been at this as long as I have, you know. I could make my living dowsing–I hav'ta turn down people all the time–but I like farming better. Course a guy's not right one-hundred percent of the time, and that's the big drawback. People get so darn mad when they drill a dry hole. Driller doesn't care, he gets his money wet or dry, and he'll drill toward China until they tell him to stop. When it's dry they blame the driller, except for when there's a dowser, then he catches hell."

Karl wiped his forehead and the back of his neck with a big, blue handkerchief. "But I have a good feeling for this one," he said. "I felt a little twist toward the right, and—"

"I hope he's right," Jake said. "Mable will be here Saturday after next." He squinted from under his floppy felt hat at Lars, who was almost a head taller.

"Been married long?" Lars asked.

The wind kicked up even more, and Jake held onto his hat. "Not long."

"What did you do back in Iowa?"

Jake hesitated. From now on there would be questions. For the rest of his life. "Not much. Worked on my father's farm, then for a blacksmith, 'till I got kicked in the head by a mule. Didn't wake up for a week."

Lars studied him curiously, and Jake noticed the deep, Viking, steel-blue of his eyes.

"A week?"

"Still have headaches. First thing I did was slip in at night and give that mule a sledgehammer between the eyes."

"Killed him?"

"Deader than a doornail. Couldn't prove who did it, but they had more than a sneaking suspicion. The smith fired me."

"Kinda drastic, wasn't it?" Lars' steel eyes flashed.

"Well, I don't suppose you can have someone killing the customers' mules, and—"

"Not firing you. Killing the mule!"

"Oh. I wouldn't have done it if I'd been feeling right, but I was a little off for a while. Getting kicked in the dome isn't conducive to good thinking."

"What'd you do after that?"

"Odd jobs."

They watched Karl pound a stake into the ground beside his derby hat.

"Any kids?" Lars asked.

"No."

The sun worked on them through the puffy blue-white clouds. Karl's homestead was on a slight hill, from where he could see for miles. Jake's homestead was on a higher hill, and he felt exposed and vulnerable in the vastness–like a fly clinging to the outside of a windowpane during a storm–and one of the first things he would do–what everyone did–was dig a root cellar, for security as much as for storage.

"So, Iowa, eh?" Lars prodded again. "First rate farm land there."

"Umph."

"Your father still farming?"

"Dead."

"Oh. And the farm?"

"Brother got it. I had decided to leave anyway, what with the mule kicking me and everything. Then there was the . . . well, there was more to it than that. Better to start fresh."

Jake opened the door and peeked in. His father was sleeping in his stuffed armchair, passed out from a three-day drinking binge. Jake crept in and started up the stairway to his bedroom. Not really a room; just part of the loft. He wondered where his mother was. Probably she had taken refuge across the street with the Stivelys. Jake felt his cheek where his father had hit him. It was starting to swell. And again, the guilt. No matter how hard he tried, Jake always felt in his heart that everything was his fault. All he could remember was being beaten down. Told how worthless he was. Being hit and kicked. Once his mother had told him she would take him and his brother away, but there was nowhere to go. Jake was twelve years old

"How did you meet Mable?"

Lord, how long was Lars going to keep on?

"There were some town band concerts, and church. I dunno, it seemed that we had something in common. Not that I ever had any designs on her. She was too far above me. Devil if I know."

"Hmm."

"You mustn't think that I was liquored up all of the time," Jake added. "You know small towns, you burn the candle at the wrong end once in a while, and you've got an invisible sign on you. *Town Inebriate. Village Idiot.* But I guess the sign really was invisible to Mable."

Was Lars so naive as to think he was going to tell him about her slatternly ways? But of course Lars didn't know, so how could he ask?

Jake removed his hat and put his hand to his brow. He nodded at Lars and pretended to listen. Lars was saying something about skunks.

". . . strychnine from Doc Raulsten, and put it in some eggs," Lars rambled. "That fixed 'em. Haven't had a . . . ."

The church was full, and it was hot. Thirteen-year-old Jake and his brother sat between his parents. Usually his mother pleaded with his father to go to church, but this time it had been his father's idea. It was time for them all to repent, his father had said. Jake wasn't sure what for, but as usual he felt it was he who was to do most of the repenting.

Though the windows were open, there was no cooling breeze, and Pastor Martin was only halfway through his sermon on forgiveness. Oh, it was hot.

"Caroline is going to invite you and Mable for supper after you get settled in," Lars said. "Let me know when they get the well dug. I'll help you put up the windmill." A thirty-foot tower lay off to the side, assembled and ready, and Jake had been putting together the windmill blades.

Karl approached them. "You're lucky, Miller. If yuh don't have good water, yuh ain't got nothin'. An if your well goes dry, it's a bad omen. You're finished. Old guy who taught me how tuh dowse told me that. Damn near everybody he knew whose well dried up had nothing but misfortune afterward. Some of 'em even died. It's a dark day when your well goes dry."

As Karl rode away on his mule, Lars said to Jake, "Karl could stand to drink more of his own water, and less of the stuff he keeps hidden in his barn. Emma never has been able to find his stash, though lord knows she's looked. The worst is some kind of firewater that he brought from the old country years ago. I forgot what he calls it–some German name, like gemmervasser or something–but whatever it is, one swig and you can't talk." He held up his hand to quiet Jake's interruption. "No, I'm serious. Your throat's paralyzed. You can't talk, and you have trouble breathing. I learned my lesson, but poor Karl never does. If he only drank beer it wouldn't be so bad, but he hates beer. I thought all Germans liked beer. Emma has her work cut out for her, keeping him straight. Oh well, I guess he isn't so bad most of the time, and on the rare occasions when he, eh, er, gets like you did this last time, she gets me to go in and drag him out of the pool hall, which is no easy job let me tell you. He's usually belligerent. One time he took after me with a pool cue. Another time the bartender tried to interfere because I was bad for business, and I had to mop the floor with him."

"With the bartender?"

"Of course the bartender, you simpleton!"

That evening Jake sat slouched back in his old armchair. The wind filtered through the cracks and slits in the walls, and there would be much to do before winter. Stories had come down from the earlier settlers, and from the Indians and cowboys before them, of the terrible cold and killing wind. Most people banked up their homes with dirt as best they could; some all the way to the top with sod. There were few actual sod homes, and Jake wondered why not. One saving grace was the abundance of coal; either close to the surface to be scooped up, or in small drift mines. Not good coal–blackish-green lignite–but good enough and better than wood. Especially where there was no wood, because there were no trees.

Jake sank deeper into his chair. For as long as he could remember, even as a young child, he had felt the burden of some vague, weighty, hovering, moving, unseen part of him. Like a wheel, or–at its worst–a grindstone, that he could neither cast off nor control. At best the stone, or wheel–as he could only inadequately envision it– moved slowly and regularly, like other people's wheels did, if they had wheels, or some such. However at other times it sped out of control, and the results were beyond all bearing, to the point of madness.

CHAPTER THREE

Mable woke and looked around, bewildered. Her hair was down and slightly matted, and her eyes were on the verge of puffiness.

"Morning!" Jake said. He was cooking a breakfast of fried eggs and bacon. He put down his spatula and came and sat on the edge of the bed. A shaky, saggy old bed with a lumpy, cotton-stuffed mattress, but it had stood the test last night. It had been a long time since they had been together.

Mable smiled. She was extremely attractive, with high cheekbones, a slight olive complexion, and beautiful, soft-brown, languid eyes. She was on the heavy side, but her weight was equally distributed, enhancing her comeliness. "My, the house looks even nicer in the daylight," she said. Her new home was a typical homestead shack; twelve-by-twenty feet, one layer of boards covered with tarpaper to keep out the ninety-five degree summer heat and the forty-below zero winter blizzards. One end of the shack served as the kitchen; the other end was the bedroom. Its only overall distinction was the small, screened front porch Jake had added. There was very little furniture. "Oh, it's grand!" Mable effused. "You've done a splendid job. It's better than I had hoped. I didn't know you were such a good carpenter."

Jake beamed, knowing full well that she was going overboard. There were pitifully few amenities.

Mable continued. "We can get material for curtains, and I brought some pictures and odds and ends. We can use apple boxes for shelves, and I have crepon to hang over the fronts of them. We'll get by just fine."

"Ready to eat?"

Mable padded to the kitchen table, and Jake slid the eggs and bacon onto her plate.

"As soon as you finish, I'll show you the place," Jake smiled. Maybe he hadn't made a big mistake in bringing Mable there after all. "There's not much to show yet, but we have a good well, and the windmill tower is up. I've got the place for the barn staked out, and Lars and Karl are going to help me build it. They're our neighbors. Lars and Caroline Nordraak, and Karl and Emma Springer. Lars is a big, tall Norwegian, and what a humdinger Karl is. He's the one who got so mad when his old Maxwell wouldn't run that he grabbed a sledgehammer and smashed the engine. That night his dog–Trollop– died, and he saw it as some kind of chthonian reprisal. He spent the next three days on a big toot, wandering the hills east of here, until Lars finally talked him into coming home. There sure are some interesting . . . ."

After Mable finished eating, Jake gave her a tour of their new farm, then they stood, hand-in-hand, on their hill. To the south, Charity jutted up like an oasis. Farms had sprung up everywhere, and patches of newly-plowed, rich, dark-brown soil checkered the prairie all about.

"Oh, my," Mable murmured. "What a magnificent view!"

Jake hadn't seen it that way, until now. Not as fully as Mable did.

Mable cried. "How beautiful," she said. She turned into the breeze and smelled the freshness and purity.

The tall prairie grass whispered in the wind, telling Jake everything would be alright. "Come, I'll show you where the barn will be."

For the first time in a long while Jake felt hope and assurance well up inside.

That evening Jake and Mable celebrated their new life with optimism singular to those who have not known much optimism.

"My, how lucky we are," Mable said. She passed the pound cake to Jake. She had made it in celebration.

Jake still didn't know what she saw in him. What she had ever seen. She had literally picked him out of the gutter once. The embarrassment had done wonders for him, and he began going to church with her, and even to Bible study once a week. And yet, why him? A feckless, undistinguished, mostly-reformed sponge. He had asked, but she hadn't answered, except to say that in the several years she had known him, some in the neighborhood had told her of his good side, and of how kind and strong and noble he was when he was sober. But that reply didn't sufficiently mesh with Jake's inner being, and he hoped that before he died he would come to know more, if there was more. And if possible he would determine the genesis and validity of Mable's religious convictions, which were much stronger than his own. Indeed, he was what he self-described as an atheist with some lingering hope, and while he didn't mind going to church with Mable, he did it for her, not for himself.

"There you are again, acting like a philosopher."

Jake wiped his face with his shirtsleeve. He had broken into a sweat.

The wind rose outside as they sat in the yellow light of the mantle lantern that hung on the wall above the table. They would have boxes for cupboards, and little for furniture–and Jake wished he could offer Mable more–but most of their money would go for machinery, and for the barn. They could build on a real kitchen in a few years.

Jake ate quietly, fighting his guilt. Guilt. It had been with him for so long that it seemed alive. Part of reality, as opposed to the conceptions of philosophers. But now his guilt was tempered by a spirit of deliverance.

"This is a grand new start, isn't it, Jake?" Mable glowed with confidence as she sat watching him finish the last of his cake. "Like the next chapter in a book, with many wondrous chapters to come."

That evening, by the light of a coal-oil lamp, Mable wrote in her diary, simply: "I feel reborn."

She showed it to Jake.

"So do I," he said.

Drink thee from the well of everlasting life, ... A snatch of something Jake couldn't remember. He was sure his past could be abnegated, and that his massive, grinding, Wheel of Life could be slowed. His Wheel of Life: that at times had seemed like more than an abstraction. At its worst, palpable in the depths of his consciousness, manifested as a buzzing, sizzling, frying, electrical discharge that he could actually hear. Hear to the point of madness; or was he already mad? Are madmen aware of their madness? Most probably aren't, so, Jake concluded–though somewhat uncertainly– that he was not crazy. But he wouldn't bet the farm on it.

CHAPTER FOUR

Jake leaned his shoulder against the wall, looking out the window, watching the rain. It had rained for two days. Both Lars Nordraak and Karl Springer had said northeastern Montana was good farming country, but when Jake had asked Lars why–if it was such good farming country–there weren't any trees, Lars had snapped at him. Said something about how he was there to raise wheat, not trees.

"What happened?" someone asked. A group of men stood looking down at the man on the floor.

The bartender pushed them back. "There's something wrong with him, Jake."

The penitence that had followed him from Iowa, and that would dog him for the rest of his life.

"What are you thinking?" Mable asked. She was knitting socks. The plain, sturdy, eight-day pendulum clock on the wall across from her ticked. It had been her mother's. The only decent furnishing they had.

"They say this is good farming country," Jake answered. "I hope they're right."

He hoped more for Mable than for himself. Her father had died when she was five years old, and she didn't remember him. Most of what she remembered of her childhood was her mother, working. Scrubbing, washing, . . . , doing what she had to do. Now her mother was dead too, from overwork, cleaning churches and other people's homes back in Connecticut.

"I'm sure they're right," Mable said. She stopped knitting and massaged her eyelids with her fingertips. Then she looked around the room at their sagging bed, Jake's well-worn leather armchair with the horsehair padding coming out, the cookstove, the burned and scarred wooden table covered with a red oilcloth, ... "Karl and Emma Springer can't have children. Caroline Nordraak told me. They wanted children so much–especially Emma–but there's something wrong. Emma thinks it's her fault."

"It's nobody's fault. Things just happen, and we have to face them." Jake took out his handkerchief and blew his nose. "Lars thinks we're in for a three-day rain." He focused on the small bookcase he had made for his collection. Philosophy books, mostly. "Life has bizarre twists and turns," he murmured. After he had quit drinking, he had been lost, then his interest in philosophy had been reignited. He saw himself as a realist. His favorite book was *Critique of Pure Reason*. Kant. None of it meant anything to Mable, though he had tried to explain it to her. How knowledge is limited to what people can experience, but reason is necessary to make sense of that knowledge. The capacity of humans to reason, and where he disagreed with Kant, on realism vs idealism. Not only did Mable not understand, she didn't want to understand.

"Lars is a queer guy," Jake said.

Mable took up her knitting again.

Jake continued. "The other day when he and I were working on his barn, we got into an argument."

"Argument?"

"We were talking politics, and every time I tried to say something, he got mad."

"Oh?"

"It seemed like he always twists things around."

A gust of wind shook the house, then it was quiet again, with only the ticking of the clock and the patter of rain.

"Threw down his hammer and almost hit me."

"Heavens to Betsy!"

"He got over it. One thing about Lars, he doesn't stay angry long." Jake took his Kant book from the shelf. "He and Caroline sure are optimists."

"Don't we all have to be?"

Wind blew through the cracks in the north wall.

That night Jake had a dream.

It was dark, and Jake didn't know where he was. He was afraid to move; afraid that he would fall into some bottomless pit. After a long time, a voice broke the stillness.

"Jake. I knew you would come."

"Where am I?"

"It doesn't matter."

The voice sounded familiar, and it came closer.

"Who are you?" Jake quavered.

"What? You don't recognize me?" A face materialized.

"Lars Nordraak?" Jake faltered. "What are you doing here? And where the hell are we?"

Lars laughed. "Funny choice of words."

"What's going on? How do I get out of here?"

"By waking up. You can leave any time you want to."

"Oh." Jake felt better.

"Any time you want to," Lars repeated, "after the epiphany."

Jake was exasperated at Lars' air of superiority. "What epiphany? What the devil are you talking about?"

"Ha, ha, ha! Another fine turn of phrase. Ho, ho, ho! Well, well, all I'm supposed to do is tell you that trying to be a realist is futile."

"Futile?" Jake sputtered angrily. "What's that supposed to mean?"

"You know very well what it means." Lars stepped forward, and his face brightened.

"You?" Jake rasped. "You and Caroline live in a fantasy world of your own creation."

Lars raised his hand. "We all create our own reality. The difference is, most people know what they're doing, and you don't."

Jake could see only Lars' face and his hand. "I don't? Bullshit!" Jake screeched. "You're the one living in a dream world where things are exactly the way you want them to be. Where everyone is nice, and the crops are always good, and no one is ever sick, and—"

Lars stopped him. "Now, now. Do you really think that down deep inside I'm not really aware? Let me give you an example. Take death. Nobody wants to die, so we try not to think about it. But it's with us every day, no matter what we do. So we do the next best thing. We convince ourselves that there's some kind of life after death."

"You don't seem very devout to me."

"Not the way most Bible bangers are, but I have to think there's something."

"But that's you, not me. <u>You</u> have to believe there's something. As a realist, I don't! I—"

"You? A realist? Ha, ha, ha! That's a good one. You and your philosophy books, and all of your nutty ideas!"

"I may be a bit eccentric, but I do have a firm grasp on reality," Jake wavered. *"Don't you think I know when I cross the line?"*

"No, you don't. Not until afterward, and by then it's too late. The trick is to know before, not after. If you don't know that, you're lost."

"I'll have to think about it."

"Fine. You do that. It's your ass."

"My ass?"

"Sure. You've got a choice. Keep trying to be a realist, or join the masses of humanity who have learned to cope."

"Cope? Your coping is nothing but weakness."

"Haw, haw, haw!"

"I'm getting out of here."

"Good. Don't let me keep you."

Jake got up and put on his clothes. By now Mable was used to his nighttime wanderings.

Outside, under the dark prairie sky, Jake struggled to forget his dream. The dream had been all wrong. In the first place, he hadn't known Lars that long, and there was no way Lars could know about his philosophy of life. Furthermore, neither Lars nor Caroline had any inkling that they were creators of reality. They seemed to hold a somewhat Pickwickian view of life. Pickwickian in the sense that they saw life in its simplest form, dismissing things they didn't want to contemplate, with faith that everything would turn out well. Not stupid, but shallow, living from one day to the next.

The air was cool and fresh, and the stars were clearer then Jake had ever seen. He felt renewed. But he wished the mosquitoes would leave him alone.

CHAPTER FIVE

A MINE OF HEALTH!
By Using the Kickapoo Remedies
Kickapoo Indian Oil, a Quick Cure for All Pains
Kickapoo Salve
Kickapoo Worm Killer,
The Adults' Friend, The Children's Savior, ...

Jake and Mable stood in front of the Gladstone Hotel in Charity, reading the Healy and Bigelow Kickapoo Medicine Company traveling show poster.

Kickapoo Indian Sagwa
For the Kidneys, Liver, and Stomach . . . .

"What does *sagwa* mean?" Mable asked.

A stray plowhorse–strong and gray–walked along the edge of the street, stopping now and then to nibble tufts of grass, working around the wild sweet peas. A lean, brown, short-haired dog that looked like a German shepherd mix was slinking after the horse, keeping its distance, waiting; trying to decide whether to rush in for a nip at one of the horse's hocks.

Jake turned his head to take in the newly-baked bread aroma coming down the alley from the kitchen in back of the hotel. Then he beheld everything around him, and, like God after the Creation, he declared the world good. Of course he didn't believe in God. Better put, he didn't believe in divinity of any kind. Nonetheless, after his bad start in life, now Jake declared the world good, and perhaps he could create his own god. His own religion. Or something that would suffice. Perhaps a secular religion, the first step to working toward a spiritual religion, despite his material bias. Possibly an amalgamation of the best of all religions, except that there was little good in religions, ...

"Don't know what sagwa is," Jake blurted. "Must be some kind of Indian word for medicine."

"Maybe you should try some of it." Mable looked hopefully at Jake.

"Don't need it." He wished she wouldn't worry so much about him.

And by Special Arrangement
Clark Stanley's Snake Oil Liniment
For Rheumatism, Neuralgia, Sciatica, Lame Back,
Lumbago, Contracted Cords, Toothache, Frost Bite,
Chill Blains, Bruises, Sore Throat,
Bites of Animals, Insects, and Reptiles.
Good for Everything a Liniment Ought to be Good For

"Perhaps some of that liniment would be alright though," Mable said. "Seems like you've always got a sore back, and—"

"Jake! Mable! When's the show?" Karl and Emma Springer. Karl had on his perennial white shirt and black derby hat, and Emma–stout and perspiring–wore a faded black dress, and her dark hair was in a bun. Jake guessed she had once been attractive, and she would still be if she lost some weight. And it would help if she got some new dresses to replace the one like she had on; heavy and homespun-looking, similar to what he had seen the Amish women wear. The time he had run away from home. The only time he had been away from his hometown. Should have stayed away.

"Seven o'clock tonight," Mable said. "Did you see the tent west of town?"

"Saw it two miles away," Karl said. "Say, that there sagwa might be just the thing. My stomach's been actin' up some, and I—"

Emma stiffened and glared at him. "Oh, for heaven's sake, Karl!"

"Well, how do you know that it—?"

"You hope there's alcohol in it, Karl Springer. Or that it's mostly laudanum, ..." She was aware of all of his many shenanigans.

Jake and Mable stepped back to let them bicker. "You never can tell," Mable whispered to Jake. She referred to the sagwa.

"Bunk," Jake chuckled.

A fresh, sweet-smelling spring breeze wafted over them, and Jake felt that it carried hope. It had been a long time since he had been able to see past life's evils, into the bottom of Pandora's box, but a box where hope remained. He had confidence that he could forget.

Could focus on the here and now. Be a realist. Or at least a strong pragmatist. Repudiate the snake oil and sagwa of life.

"Could be you're right," Karl conceded to Emma. He turned to Jake. "I had some a' that snake oil once. No alcohol in it at all, far as I could tell. It tasted like coal oil."

"How do you know what coal oil tastes like?"

"Cause I drank some once. Came in outta' the field and saw a cup on the kitchen counter, and took three or four big gulps before I knew it wasn't water. Emma was fillin' the lamps!"

Emma wrinkled her face. "Every time he belched, he held a match up to his mouth. He walked around the house blowing flames like a dragon."

"Lucky I didn't die."

TONIGHT
The Little Merry Maker
Louise Hamilton
in
"Fogg's Ferry"
Produced with special scenery and effects.
Cast of Characters:
Gerald Black . . . .

That evening, after supper, Jake sat in his stuffed armchair with his eyes closed. Mable was disappointed that they couldn't afford to go to the traveling show; nevertheless things were finally going their way. He had been feeling better. No more headaches, surprisingly, after the time back in Iowa when he had been kicked in the head. And thrown by a horse and knocked cold. He wasn't clumsy, more like accident prone. But nothing had happened for a while now. Maybe he had used up his share of misfortune. And Mable hers.

Mable finished the dishes. "Are you alright?" she asked.

Jake smiled at her. "Fine. Just thinking."

"About what?"

"How well things are going. I hope it isn't some divine trick."

"Divine trick?"

"A setup for the kill. Some occult force spreading doom and misery."

"Jake Miller! What a thing to say. Why are you always so pessimistic? Merely because you've had some hard knocks doesn't mean it's going to be that way forever. You have to have faith. You said yourself that past events don't necessarily determine the future. And here you are, talking about divine tricks." Her eyes glowed like embers of coal, as they always did when she was exasperated.

Jake laughed. She always made his worries sound absurd. She wasn't a deep thinker, but she was sensible. That was her best quality, and he wished he had some of it. And he wished he hadn't used the word divine.

"You're right. Down with the past, and up with the future."

"The present," Mable said. "You can't live in the future any more than you can live in the past. You have to live for now."

That was as profound as Mable ever got, but she was right again. He had a tendency to overlook the obvious. He laid his head back and closed his eyes, knowing instinctively that now he had a fighting chance. Best of all, he had had no contact with anyone from his past. Once, in Charity, he had seen someone who had made his heart stop, but the man had turned out to be a stranger. Jake knew he had to stop worrying. The chances of anyone finding him were next to naught. He realized he had to rely on probability. Rather, on improbability. And it was like anything else in life, you can't worry about things beyond your control.

CHAPTER SIX

Jake had insisted that they go to the basket social at Charlie Ingvoldson's place south of Charity, and even before he had a chance to finish insisting, Mable had said yes. She was delighted. Jake didn't like socials, and he didn't like crowds, but Mable's delight more than trumped all of his dislikes. He would do his best to enjoy the evening whether he liked it or not. He would do it for Mable, and for their future.

They sat on the wooden bench along the Norwegian side of the barn, with Lars and Caroline Nordraak and Karl and Emma Springer. In general the Norwegians sat on one side and the Danes on the other, with the rest fitting in wherever they could. The rest were Germans, perhaps a Swede or two, a French-Indian now and then, and those of unknown mix, who usually sat on the Norwegian side. Caroline had always said the Danes were a reserved bunch.

The young single men and the older, bachelor drunks always congregated at the far-from-the-door end of the barn where the musicians normally set up for barn dances.

There was liquor outside if one wanted it, but no one would dare bring it in lest they be escorted roughly back out. In any case Jake had quit drinking, and Lars almost never drank. That left Karl to go outside now and again to "visit John Barleycorn," until Emma decided that Mr. Barleycorn was getting too popular.

Kerosene mantle lanterns hung all about, adding to the gaiety, for such times were gay times; escapes from the humdrum of everyday existence. Someone had hung paper cutouts from strings above the benches along each side–geometric designs similar to snowflakes, but colored–and in front, high on the wall above the low wooden musician platform, illuminated by two extra-bright lanterns with polished tin reflectors, were large, black, paper cutouts of Victorian dancers.

Mable was beautiful in her best dress–a light-tan muslin trimmed in black lace–with her dark-brown hair fixed in back in a bun, and with a blissful smile that Jake had seen too little of over the years. If he had been single and alone, he felt that he would have regarded Caroline as a close second in looks, but as things stood now Caroline was a far second. Besides, Caroline was kind of rattlebrained. One of the most delightful people he had ever known, but there was no getting around her rattlebrainness, though at times her common sense was astounding. A dichotomy that affects most people, and the challenge is to distinguish between the two. Rattlebrain or sensible? Are religious people rattlebrained or sensible? How about those whose entire life is spent contentedly behind a plow; who live to work? And others who purposefully live vacuous lives, unquestioningly accepting whatever comes; or those who . . . There is no in-between in such matters. No gray area, no waffling and no weaseling.

Enough. Why dwell on all that? This was a box social, not a meeting of the local philosophicoreligious society.

The box lunches were stacked on the low stage where the single men and the inebriates had congregated. Some of the young men were both. Every lady had done her best to outdo every other lady's lunch, and after a prerequisite time for visiting, the auction would start. However, Jake's auction was rigged, thanks to Lars. Lars was going to bid on Mable's lunch, and Jake was going to bid on Caroline's. And they were both going to win. Nobody was going to go against Lars Nordraak. Lars was not to be antagonized; that was a community understanding. It was a peculiarity of his, and Jake shared that peculiarity. As for Emma Springer, she was always safe enough to the point of being hopeful for outside bidders, but there never were any.

It was warm and pleasant in the barn, with only a slight scent of manure, oats, leather, cigar smoke, lantern fumes, and of people. Some of the most congenial had assembled in groups of three or four in the center of the open area. In one front corner stood a small, temporary stove upon which sat two large coffeepots, and many were drinking coffee. Someone had also placed a small teapot on the stove.

In the corner of the barn diagonally from the stove sat a small group of single ladies, dressed in their finest. Eight in all, trying not to directly notice the single men, and no doubt hoping that some of the youngest of those single men were decent and reasonably temperate. The ladies, really girls, had all undoubtedly outdone themselves on their box lunches, and in that they had thrown themselves on the mercy of what they would possibly have seen as some form of ancient Greek fate, had they known much of ancient Greece. But by any matter of means regarding ancient Greek mythology, they were obviously nervous. Lars had been known to have also bid on young ladies' baskets whose lunches had no bidders, inviting them to join him and Caroline–rather him and Mable–which case was embarrassing for the young lady, but not as mortifying as eating alone or slinking out the door alone.

"Ain't as many here as last year," Karl observed.

Emma, having prohibited him from any more trips outside, reached over and gently removed Karl's black derby hat and hung it on a nail on the wall behind them. Then she smoothed his hair back with both hands, and smiled as he winced slightly.

One of the men standing in the center of the barn took another lady, evidently not his wife, and began swinging her around in an impromptu dance, until her husband, or whoever he was, tactfully tapped him on the shoulder and broke in to take a few dance steps; then he ushered her back to their bench.

A short, stout middle-aged man with no neck took the platform and rang a cowbell. He was the auctioneer. Jake thought his name was Manfred something or other.

"Ladies and gentlemen, if there, ahem, . . . , if there are in fact any gentleman here," he chortled, and that got a few laughs. "We are about to start auctioning off the ladies' boxes." That brought a few course guffaws, but a greater number of sour looks. "First, this nicely decorated box by, let's see here, Emma Springer. Please stand up, Emma."

Emma was not a shy person, but she stood up shyly, and sat down shyly.

"Do I hear twenty-five cents?" the auctioneer called.

"Twenty-five," said Karl loudly.

"Do I hear thirty?"

Silence, then more silence.

"Thirty!" It was Lars. Karl started, and stared at Lars.

"Thirty. Do I hear thirty-five?"

The auctioneer was getting into his swing.

"Thirty-five," Karl said, glancing curiously at Lars.

"Forty? Who bids forty?"

Silence.

"Come on now, forty?"

Lars stood, laughing. "Forty!"

Karl gave Lars a rather menacing look. By this time Emma was starting to enjoy herself.

Karl now stood. "Verdammt! Fünfzig!"

Emma giggled into the collar of her dress. She was tickled to death.

Lars sat back down. He knew Karl's limits. Jake had heard that once when Lars had teased Karl about something, Karl had taken a poke at him, and they hadn't spoken to each other for two weeks.

Jake leaned back. Ah, peace and serenity. Maybe life wasn't so bad after all.

Emma was still giggling into her collar, and Jake realized once again that Lars had a big heart.

CHAPTER SEVEN

"There," Jake said. He set down his water bucket, and Rudi put the radiator cap back on. They were in Jake's yard, in front of Rudi's black Model T Ford sedan. "You've got to check it. You let it percolate like that, the engine'll—"

Rudolph Prinz was not good with automobiles. He couldn't touch one without lousing it up. "Yeah, alright. Thanks." Rudi took off his hat and glanced at the sun. "Gotta get going. My shift starts at one o'clock." He tended bar at The Palace in Charity, but Rudi wasn't the one who had thrown Jake out during his last drinking binge before Mable came.

"An hour and a half," Jake said. "Why not stay and eat?"

Rudi rubbed his short hair. He was small and wiry, and his nose had been broken more than once in his fighting days. Jake guessed he was in his mid thirties, but he still didn't have an extra pound on him. He kept his hand in too, working out in a makeshift ring behind the bar, where he'd spar with anyone courageous enough to take him on. Take him on wasn't the right phrase though; Rudi never meant to hurt anyone, he just wanted to keep his memories alive. The only time he had hurt someone was when a big railroad worker had decided to make a name for himself. A large Swede who tried to take little Rudi out, and after the first minute of the first round, Rudi started in on him. He didn't knock him out; he punished him for three rounds, till the Swede threw in the towel. It was worse that way. Rudi wasn't the type to do that, but he had his limits.

"Well, if you're sure Mable wouldn't mind," Rudi said. He was a bachelor.

"Not at all."

Mable was grateful for the company. "It'll be a while though. Why don't you two wait on the porch?"

They went back out, and sat watching the flat openness. The emptiness that had become both Jake's assuagement and his unease. He had been planting trees all around the farmstead in an attempt to block out some of the barrenness.

"Nice rain yesterday," Jake said. "We got an inch."

"Um." Rudi had little interest in farming.

Jake tried again. "I heard there was a fight in the saloon the other night."

Rudi waved one hand dismissively. "Didn't amount to much. Couple of alkys."

Two roosters started fighting, but after a little sparring the larger one ran away.

Local gossip was that Rudi had killed a man in a professional fight. Jake had become obsessed with the rumor, and he had to know.

"So you were a prizefighter," Jake said even though he knew sometimes his directness was off-putting.

"Um."

Lars Nordraak had said Rudi didn't like to talk about his fight days, but Jake pressed.

"Where did you fight?"

Rudi leaned forward and spat tobacco juice into the grass in front of the porch. "All over. Took fights wherever I could get 'em."

"Sounds like a tough life."

Rudi took a plug of tobacco from his shirt pocket and bit off another chunk. "It was hard, but I liked it, and we never went hungry. Me and my manager, Ike." He looked vacantly southward. "Old Ike is dead now."

They sat quietly, fanned by the breeze. Then, "I don't mean to pry," Jake said, "but I was wondering why you quit. I heard there was some trouble. An accident, and—"

"That I killed a man?" Rudi straightened in his chair and turned it so that he was facing Jake. He was scarred above both eyebrows, and his two upper front teeth were missing. "I gotta say, Jake, you have a way of getting to the point."

"I just—"

"Nevermind. I'd as soon talk to someone who spits it out, than to most people, who never can say what they mean." He smiled, and Jake saw his remorse.

"Sure, I killed a guy. Down in Texas. I was giving him a pretty good shellacking, but they wouldn't stop it. I eased up, but that only dragged it out. I decided to put him out of his misery, so in the ninth round I clipped him hard with a right hook, and that was it. Except he never got up."

Rudi spat. Then he turned from Jake and sat looking far away again. They were silent for a moment.

Finally, "He died?"

"The next day. He never did wake up. They figured his brain was bleeding." Rudi spat again, and the delicacy of the discharge indicated that he was thinking. "I only saw that happen to one other guy. A heavyweight in Pittsburgh. But, damn, I never thought it would happen to me."

Jake followed Rudi's gaze toward the horizon, where the sky was a panorama of light and dark blue, chartreuse, gray, and dull, turbulent white. Rudi stared intently, like he was looking for something. Some inner chimera.

"What happened then?"

"What do you mean?"

"Well, did they hold you responsible?"

Rudi remained still. "Nobody had to hold me responsible." He spat again through the gap in his teeth. "I assume you have a personal reason for asking?"

"Just curious."

"Seems like you have a mighty strong curiosity."

Jake didn't say anything.

"Anyway," Rudi said, "I finally put it behind me. You have to do that in life, you know. After you've beat yourself up enough, no matter how bad it is, you have to put it behind you. Forgive yourself. Don't bother with going to some priest for forgiveness; you have to forgive yourself."

"What if you can't?"

"You know the answer to that."

"Dinner," Mable called through the screen door.

CHAPTER EIGHT

Sweat streamed down his face. Jake stopped, sat down, and leaned against the south wall of the hole he was digging. The earth was damp and cool on his back. He took off his hat and looked southward, the only direction in which he could look, but there was nothing. Only his plowhorses grazing in the pasture. He stretched and kicked a rock loose.

"How's it goin' on the new root cellar?"

"Ah! Sweet Jesus, Karl, you scared the shit out of me."

"Ha, ha, ha!" Karl Springer, in his derby hat and white shirt.

Jake grasped his right hand with his left to stop it from shaking. "I feel funny out here on the prairie. Like going to church naked. Gotta have a refuge, and there's security and serenity to be found in digging."

"Huh. Reminds me of a big grave."

"My, aren't you morbid today?"

"Quick, lemme in before she sees me." Karl scrambled down.

Jake slid over to some cooler dirt. "What's going on now?" he asked.

"Emma was talkin' about goin' tuh church, and I'm hidin' out for awhile."

"How could she see you all the way here from your place?" Then Jake answered his own question by looking at Karl's white shirt. Karl was a walking flag. A surrender flag when it came to Emma.

"She could drive in any minute."

"Drive? Does she know how to drive?"

"She can if she has to. Hasn't since she backed into Lars' windmill, but you never know." Then Karl said something sounded like "Gimmel wibble waffler." He sat beside Jake. "I can't abide church. I'm not sayin' there's nothin' to it, but I ain't ready yet."

"You might wait until it's too late," Jake laughed.

"Huh."

"Are you going to wait until you're on your deathbed, croaking your last croak, calling for Pastor Vilander? Anyway I didn't think she went to church."

"She usually doesn't. Only when she has too much time tuh think, or when things are goin' bad. Lately she's been moanin' cause we can't have kids. We'd both like tuh have kids, but it I can deal with it better than her. She gets church fever, and has'ta drag me along. Then when she starts feelin' better, she quits goin'.'"

"A lot of people are like that." They watched a salamander slither from a hole and out the front. "I don't think we can have children either."

"No? That's the weeds." Karl balled up a lump of clay and threw it at the salamander. "Maybe we can adopt some orphans or somethin'. I guess if it comes to that we could, then maybe Emma'd forget the church stuff, but I can't decide whether I'd rather get hauled into church once in a while or have a bunch of orphans around. Guess they'd liven the place up." Karl threw another lump of clay at the salamander, then he sat ruminating for a moment. "The rub is, she'd likely start taking the kids to church, and I'd get stuck with both orphans and church. And you could never tell how many she'd get either. I could stand a couple, but lord, half a dozen wunderkinder running around would drive me to distraction."

"Mable wants children more than I do too," Jake said. "Say, do you smell something? What's that around your neck?"

"Poultice. I've got some real busthead whiskey hid under a rock pile, and I sampled it last night when Emma was gone. Did somethin' tuh my throat. Had'a tell Emma it was a sore throat–which it is, so technically I'm not lyin'–and she decided I had'a wear this. Agh!" Karl took off the poultice and threw it in the dirt beside him.

"What's in it? It smells like turpentine and onions."

"That's what it is, and some other stuff she won't tell me. Says if I knew, I wouldn't wear it, and she's probably right. I think it's got camphor in it too."

"Your neck's all red."

"Keeps the mosquitoes away."

"Keeps me away too." Jake slid over more.

"Shush! What's that?"

"I don't hear anything."

"Thought somebody was comin'. Yuh hear about Manfried Gottlieb?"

"No."

"Hurt his back."

"What'd he do, lift too many heavy beer mugs?"

"No, pickin' rock. Ina said he's had a bad back ever since he got bucked off his horse while ridin' tuh school when he was a kid. He's flat on the floor. Can't move."

"Did Ina call Doc?" Jake moved farther away.

"Won't let 'er. Says they can't afford it."

"Must be kind of troublesome, farming with a bad back."

"Ina said if it keeps botherin' him, he could always go back tuh butcherin'. He used tuh be a butcher back in Illinois, but he doesn't like it. And talk about bad luck, a skunk got two a' their chickens the other night. Dug under the wall of the coop. Dog chased it away. Course the dog got skunked."

"No."

"Yeah. And Gunnar Larsen almost got killed helpin' Soren Utlander put up his new windmill. Soren can't stand tuh climb, so Gunnar was up on top, and he told Soren tuh turn it on. About the time Soren pulled the chain, the wind came up, and Gunnar was hangin' on for dear life, tryin' tuh keep from bein' sliced tuh pieces like a salami. He started hollerin' for Soren tuh turn it off, but Soren didn't hear; him bein' half deaf and all. Finally Soren got it shut off, and when Gunnar got down, he took off after him with a wrench. Somebody said Soren may not hear too good, but he sure can run! Haw!"

Karl told the rest of his news, then, "What time is it?"

Jake peered up at the sun. "About ten, I'd say."

"Guess I'll walk down tuh Sheep Crick an' back. That outta' be enough time." He got up and stuffed the poultice into his back pocket. "Don't know which is worse, goin' through all the trouble of hidin' out, or bitin' the bullet an' goin' tuh church. See yuh later."

"Yeah."

CHAPTER NINE

"George Edward Moore," Jake said. A week after their root cellar conversation, Jake and Karl were walking through Karl's lush, green wheat fields. "An empiricist." Jake was aware that Karl wasn't much interested, but he didn't seem uninterested either.

A flock of blackbirds flew over, came back, circled, then landed in a row on the barbwire fence along the road. Karl pulled a wheat plant out of the ground and scrutinized the roots. Someone in a buggy waved. The driver didn't look like a farmer, but he obviously wasn't a salesman either, or he would have stopped.

"He doesn't connect everyday experience with sense experience. To him, what's real is real. Like this rock." Jake kicked a rock, and it rolled a couple of feet. "That rock is a rock, and that's all there is to it, in spite of what some nutty philosopher says about how different people see things in different ways."

Karl went to a huge pile of rocks and sat in the shade. Jake sat beside him.

"He had a great deal of common sense," Jake went on. "An external world, independent of the mind. That's what I . . . ."

Karl pulled another stalk of wheat, and he sat feeling the moist soil that clung to its roots.

". . . for him," Jake concluded. "It makes a lot of sense to me." He supposed he was boring the hell out of Karl, actually. They sat, resting, neither saying anything.

The country school was permeated with the fragrance of children, horses, and coal.

Jake quickly finished his math, despite having no aptitude for it, then he listened for a few minutes to the monotonous drone of the first grade readers.

". . . little dog run," droned Sally Hoffer. "See the dog run to the . . . the . . ."

"House," prompted Miss McGuiness.

"See the dog run to the house. See the little dog . . . ."

It was more then Jake could endure. The Regulator clock on the side wall between George Washington and Abraham Lincoln ticked, and Sally read, interrupted occasionally by a giggle in the back of the room or a pop in the stove. And as usual, Fredrick

Gruber sat on the tall stool in the front corner by the water cooler, wearing the dunce cap that he had worn so many times that it had stretched to fit his large head. Jake felt sorry for him; he wasn't bad, he was just incapable of learning.

Jake sat close to the encyclopedias, the only non textbooks in the school. He reached for volume six, the F's. His marker was still at Fort Sumter. Few others were inclined to disturb any book unless forced to do so.

"Fort Sumter, fort in South Carolina, ..." Jake read.

The youngsters droned, the stove popped, the clock ticked.

". . . was the location of the first action of . . . ."

Another reluctant scholar read on, and Jake paused to rest his eyes.

"The little dog ran back. He ran back to the . . . the . . . ."

Miss McGuiness squelched someone at the back of the room who was giggling. That someone was pressing his luck.

Jake turned back to his volume.

". . . was fired upon . . . withdrew . . . evacuation of the fort . . . . ."

Somebody across the room was mumbling math problems to himself.

"The fort was later . . . and the result of the action . . . ."

A girl in front got a coughing spell, thereby providing the morning's entertainment.

". . . start of hostilities . . . . Union troops . . . ."

Jake looked again at the clock. Seven minutes after nine. The morning would never end. His view from the window–of windswept fields–had not changed in five years, and he had little reason to believe it would now as he looked out for the twentieth time that morning.

"Mumble, mumble, mumble."

The stove popped again.

"Mumble, mumble."

Sally Hoffer was reading again. The clock ticked, desks creaked, children coughed, and feet shuffled.

"Mumble, mumble, mumble."

Miss McGuiness asked one of the eighth grade boys to shake the stove and add more coal.

"Drone, drone, drone. Mumble, mumble, mumble."

But, Jake conceded, it was better than being at home.

"Yeow!" Karl jumped up and put his hand to his left buttock. "I must'a sat on a cactus!"

"Holy shit, Karl, don't scare me like that!" Jake sprang to his feet. "Some cactus! You got bit by a rattlesnake!"

"Rattlesnakes don't get this far from the river."

"Then what do you call that?" He pointed to a snake that was slithering back under the rocks.

"It's a rattlesnake. Oh, my God! I'm bit, Jake! I'm snakebit! What am I gonna do?"

"We have to get you to town. Come on!" He took Karl by the arm, and they started toward the house.

"Oh, I'm snakebit!"

"Settle down, Karl."

"Ah, Gott!"

"Keep walking."

"Mir ist schwindelig."

"What?"

"My head is swimming."

"Poppycock. The poison couldn't act that fast. Keep moving."

"I gotta rest." Karl's knees started to shake.

"No you don't. It's not far."

Jake threw Karl's arm over his shoulder and all but carried him.

As they got to the end of the field, Karl fell to his knees near another rock pile. "Under that flat rock." He pointed. "My whiskey. Fetch it," he panted.

"You shouldn't be drinking—"

"I ain't gonna drink it. It ain't drinkable anyway. I want yuh to pour some on the bite."

"I don't think that will—"

"Pour!"

"All right." Jake lifted the rock.

"Watch out for snakes."

"Don't worry. Here it is. Mercy. John Toomey's Corn Whiskey? No wonder you can't drink it. Good God, corn likker?"

Karl pulled down his pants and went to all fours. "Hurry up."

Jake looked around, thankful that there was no one in sight. He poured.

"More!"

"All right."

"Thanks. Ohhh!" Karl started in German again.

"What are you saying?" Jake smelled the bottle, then sneaked a drink. It tasted like pine oil.

"It's a prayer Grandfather Johann taught me."

"Well don't pray too long, we've got to get going."

"Get out your pocket knife," Karl ordered.

"What for?"

"You gotta' cut an X over each fang mark, then suck out the poison."

"What? What the deuce? You want me to stand out here in the middle of nowhere where everyone can see us, you with your big white German bum up in the air, and you expect me to bend over and suck on it?"

"I'm dying!"

"Well then you're just gonna have to die."

"Is my ass swollen up?"

"Um? I dunno. Let me look. Face the sun. I mean, face away from the sun." Karl crawled so his head was toward the north.

"Hard to tell, but I don't think so."

"Oh! My heart is pounding. Get Emma!"

"She's gone, remember? Went to Cottonwood with Caroline Nordraak."

"Ump." Karl fell flat on his face. "Ow, it's startin' tuh hurt somethin' awful. You got a paper and somethin' tuh write with?"

"No, why?"

"A will. I gotta leave Emma a will."

"Hogwash. You're not going to die, and anyway, who else would get your stuff?" Jake threw down the bottle. "Get up." He grabbed one of Karl's arms.

Karl lay on his stomach on the table in Dr. Raulsten's examining room in Charity. Dr. Raulsten poked the bite marks with his finger.

"Ouch!"

"Lord, almighty, Springer, what's that smell?" Dr. Raulsten was old and round-shouldered, with a bloodless face behind his black mustache. He looked tired.

"Whiskey," Jake answered. "He had me pour whiskey on it."

"Oh, good grief!"

"Am I gonna die, Doc?"

"Not today, unless you drink the rest of that panther piss. Then I couldn't make any guarantees." He turned to Jake. "He should keep still for an hour or so. You'd better sit here with him, and let me know if anything happens. I've got sick people to see."

"All right."

"That must not have been a very discriminating snake," Dr. Raulsten said.

He left, and Jake stood looking at the medicines on the huge shelf along the wall opposite the door. Powders, pills, and dozens of different sized, shaped, and colored bottles. He wished there were something for himself.

"Oh!" Karl moaned. "Doctors are just one step above morticians."

CHAPTER TEN

The summer evolved in pleasant tedium. On the first of July Jake's wheat crop was knee-high, and so thick he could see the ground only by looking straight down. The rich, fertile soil had been blessed by more than enough rain, and Jake spent hours each day walking through his fields, or gazing over them. The land held great promise. The promise of Elysian Plain, the ancient Greek paradise. An earthly Elysian Plain.

Jake stopped to rest on a huge rock he had been unable to dislodge. He would have to dynamite it. He took off his hat and wiped his face with his handkerchief. The air was still, and the sun had driven the mosquitoes down. To the south, Charity shimmered in the heat.

Exciting times, with new and different people arriving every day. A Danish family straight from the Old Country had settled a mile north. Jake hadn't met them, but he had heard they couldn't speak English very well. He and Mable would stop in sometime. Lars Nordraak had said that the Danes were a stubborn, block-headed bunch, but word was that these new neighbors seemed alright.

Mable opened the door and threw out a panfull of dishwater. She stood looking in Jake's direction, shading her eyes with one hand. Jake waved, and she returned his wave and stepped back inside. She couldn't stop fretting, and Jake loathed the part of himself that had made her that way. Some said he had always been a little different. Doubtless she had taken only his good side. She had married him on trust, and she had faith in him.

"Gotta run to Charity for a new shovel." The screen door banged shut behind Jake as he came inside.

Mable started. She turned and smiled. "You startled me." She was making bread.

Jake laughed. He had laughed more lately. "Give me half a cup of coffee, then I'll go. Anything you need?"

"More flour. And salt."

"That all?"

"Could do with some more sugar. Don't really need it though."

Money was tight.

"Flour, salt, and sugar," Jake repeated.

Mable took the dough out of the bowl, plopped it on a floured canvas cloth, and began kneading. She stood with her back to Jake, and as she kneaded, her buttocks moved beneath her dress. But it was her time of month, and Jake knew his attentions would be unwelcome.

Mable had a pot of slumgullion on the stove. Jake smelled the onions and the canned beef, and he lifted the lid to see what else there was. As always Mable did her best with what she had, and as always her best was excellent.

"A salesman came yesterday," Mable chatted. "Selling medicines. He had something for headaches."

"Um."

"Mrs. Pinchon's Pink Elixir. Maybe you—"

"Waste of money."

Mable kneaded silently. Their puppy, Falstaff, scratched on the door, and she let him in. He was a squat, gray, bulldog-looking mongrel. Jake had named him. Mable didn't like the name, though she liked the dog. She pinched off a lump of dough and dropped it on the floor. Falstaff gulped it and looked up, drooling for more.

Jake glanced around at the kitchen. Not a real kitchen. A used Monarch cookstove that he had brought out with him on the immigrant train, a wooden counter with a dishpan and a slop bucket instead of a real sink. Couldn't even afford wallpaper, so Mable had hung magazine pictures all over the walls. Funny, Jake thought. Most people's barns here were better than their houses. It had gotten so cold one winter that an old bachelor had abandoned his shack on top of the hill and had gone down to the barn to live with the animals, sleeping in the straw, wrapped in his body-length buffalo skin robe. The experience prompted him to vow to lay in more coal for the coming winters, but he never did, and neighbors made it a point to stop by with horse-drawn sleds laden with coal every fall.

Anyway, Jake would give Mable a decent house someday. He quaffed the last of his coffee. "I'll be on my way."

Mable wiped her hands on her dishtowel. "Have a good trip."

Jake leaned and kissed her on the cheek.

The road was rough and rutted, and exhaust fumes came up through the floorboards of Jake's Model T Ford. But it was a beautiful day, with the sun shining, and a refreshing zephyr out of the west. When the weather was good, northeastern Montana was Paradise.

Jake basked in the open tranquility, and he had no need for other elixirs, liquid or metaphysical. As he bounced along, he was isolated from all that had gone before, and he knew such isolation would be his sustenance. While he could not assure his future, he could completely and totally abrogate his past.

Birds flitted from in front of the auto, and on fenceposts meadowlarks sang arias to life. Though he could not hear them above the laboring engine, Jake broke forth in song too, loudly, singing with a gusto heretofore unfelt, until he topped a hill and met a German family on their way home from town. Jake waved, and they gaped. Obviously a madman, but Jake–in his exuberance–was undaunted. His spirit soared, and he felt warm inside.

Jake rattled down the main street past The Palace, and stopped in front of Charity Mercantile. As he got out, he turned back toward the bar, and he was thirsty. But he had quit drinking–serious drinking–and he couldn't spend Mable's grocery money, so he forgot his thirst. He nodded at the men on the bench in front of the store, and went inside.

The store was cool before the mid-afternoon heat, and it was busy; mostly ladies shopping while their husbands waited. Jake picked out his few things and went to the counter.

Outside, Jake lingered on the fringe of a conversation.

". . . good soil. Better'n back in Mankato, if we keep gettin' the rain." The speaker stepped to the edge of the sidewalk and spat a dainty stream of tobacco into the dirt. He had a big Adam's apple, and his skin was the color of his spittle.

"Well, maybe that's the rub," Nils Anderson groused. Nils–another of Jake's neighbors–tall and thin, with a big, red drinker's nose, and large, red ears, who had given in to spirits and other dissipations.

"They say you don't need much rain," someone else said. "The clay holds the moisture." It was Claiborne Edwards. He had arrived the week before, from Sheyenne, North Dakota. Jake thought he resembled Falstaff. Not Shakespeare's Falstaff, but Jake's young dog, Falstaff: rotund, gray, bulldog-like.

"Humph! We'll see," Nils answered. His nose and ears got redder. The tobacco chewer spat in the dirt again, and the others shuffled and took turns venturing their opinions. Jake didn't say anything.

"Well, the railroad land man said it was good farming country," John Stokes said. "Said the rails bring rain, and—"

"Haw! Railroad man. What the hell does a railroad man know about farming? All they know is how to farm the farmers!" It was Ludvig Lindburger, another new arrival. They all laughed, even Jake.

"Railroad man. He couldn't tell wheat from barley, and—"

"Who the devil is that?" Jake asked. A lanky, awkward man wearing a white shirt, black wool pants, and black cape, came up the street carrying an open umbrella.

"Walter Grimswold."

The man walked awkwardly, like his joints were about to disconnect. He had dark hair and deep-set, dark eyes.

"Why doesn't he simply wear a hat?"

"Oh, it ain't the sun. He thinks it's gonna rain."

"Rain? There isn't a cloud in the sky!"

John shrugged. "That's Walter."

"What does he do?" Jake asked.

"Nothin'. Moved into that little white shack on the east edge of town."

"How does he live?"

"His father's wealthy. Big lawyer back in Connecticut."

"Why did he come here?"

"Dunno. Not all of the people around here are farmers you know. There's a guy out west of here who's kind of a hermit. Nobody knows where he came from, or anything else about him. He don't do nothin' now, far as anyone can tell. Then there's that old coot and his wife who live in a silo. It looks like a silo anyways. Some say he's running from something; I dunno. Guess it takes all kinds."

"Good night!" As Jake turned to leave, Karl Springer came out of the bar.

"Jake!" Karl was unsteady as he made his way toward Jake's auto. "Emma left me in town. Can I get a ride home?"

Jake nodded, and Karl–with some difficulty–climbed in. Jake cranked the engine, got in, and stepped on the reverse pedal.

"Have a snort." Karl pulled a bottle from his jacket pocket, but Jake shook his head.

"Emma got mad an' left me," Karl explained, and he took a drink. They hit a bump and he spilled, and almost lost his derby hat.

Jake managed a smile. Lars Nordraak had told him that Karl wasn't a true alcoholic, in spite of himself.

Karl sat morosely for the first mile.

Then, "Crops sure look good," Jake said.

"Yeah. Yours especially." Karl tried to concentrate. They hit another bump, and he gave up and screwed the lid onto his bottle. "You said you were a blacksmith's helper back in I-o-way. I got this horse that's always throwin' shoes. Maybe you could take a look, an' . . . ."

They jounced along with Karl doing most of the talking, but as they neared his place, he became quiet again. When they reached his driveway, he had Jake stop.

"I'd better walk," Karl said. "Here." He handed the whiskey to Jake. "You might as well have this." He got out. "Emma's gonna kill me," he said glumly, and he turned and trudged up his driveway.

"Good luck, Karl!" As Jake drove away, he envied Karl for his ability to simply live life.

Life. Wheel of Life. His own version of the Tibetan Buddhist wheel of life. The bhavacakra. The hub of the wheel represents the poisons of ignorance, attachment, and aversion. Jake had mentally skipped out to the sixth of seven circles, that of suffering, but since his hub was not that of Buddha's hub, his suffering was not the same either, and that made it all irrelevant. A bunch of hooey. Still, it was a circle, and all Jake cared about was that he was prone to suffering.

"At least you suffer well."

CHAPTER ELEVEN

Jake stopped in front of Dr. Raulsten's office, tied his horses, and helped Mable from their farm wagon. It was a miserable, windy day, and they would have taken their auto, but it was broken down. Maybe the carburetor. Or the timer.

"Are you sure you don't want me to come in?" Jake offered again.

"No, I'll be fine."

Mable went inside, and Jake hesitated, holding one hand up to shield his face from the sun. Normally Mable was strong, but every once in a while she went off, phrenetically, as if life were too short. Usually it was her health, and she was always vague. Once Jake had pressed her, and she had become hysterical, crying and throwing herself on the bed. But Dr. Raulsten had told him privately not to worry. Just a woman's problem. The *vapors* he had called it.

Sunlight beamed through the bars on the window and woke Jake. He sat up on his cot, and for a moment he was lost. The jailer looked up from his desk.

"How is he?" Jake asked.

Between gusts of wind, Jake squinted up Main Street. A few parked cars and wagons, and two black-and-white, shaggy, mongrel dogs, but no people. One of the dogs lifted his leg on the corner of the hotel. Jake turned his back to the wind and headed for The Palace bar across the street. Best to leave Mable to her wraith.

"Drat!" Jake said as he forced the door shut behind him. "What kind of country is this?" He pulled his handkerchief from his back pocket and wiped his eyes.

An ornate bar ran the length of one wall, and the opposite wall was fronted with round poker tables. The place smelled of cigar smoke, stale chewing tobacco, cheap bourbon, beer, and other indistinguishable saloon odors. Only three customers: a husky part Indian standing at the bar drinking whiskey, and two men in back sitting across a checkerboard from each other, but they weren't playing. They were about Jake's age. One, a little weasel of a man, had a perpetual doleful look. The other was tall and wiry, and his upper lip was scarred so that it turned upward on one end in a permanent sneer. They regarded Jake for longer than was polite. The wiry one resembled a snake.

Max Forbes, the owner, sat on a stool behind the far end of the bar, waxing his mustache. His was hulking and muscular, and usually surly. Jake made a drinking motion, and Max got reluctantly off his stool.

Jake looked out the front window, at the doctor's office. He had ventured to Mable that northeastern Montana could be like Paradise, and he had been right. But it could be like Hell too.

Max plopped down a mug of beer and took Jake's money without a word.

"Goddamn wind," the snake growled. "This keeps up, I'm goin' back tuh Alabama."

"I ain't so sure I shouldn't go back to Tennessee, whether it's windy or not," the sad weasel whined. "Montana ain't what I imagined it to be."

"Nothin' stoppin' yuh," the snake said.

Flies buzzed around the strip of flypaper over their table.

"Huh. Guess one bad place is as good as another."

Jake pushed them from his mind; a device he had learned as a child, when his parents fought. He imagined white-gloved hands sweeping them away, and when they were gone, the gloves covered his ears, and his eyes. Worse than the fighting, though, were his mother's apologies afterward. And her excuses for his father. That his father had been abused by his own father. Beaten, and abused in other ways. A reason, but not a valid excuse.

Jake's chronic malaise was more than ordinary self pity. The self pity had ended when he had left home, after one-too-many of his father's beatings. The lumps had gone away, but an exquisite scar had remained; a scar not only from physical and emotional abuse; but from the randomness of his father's explosions. The damned, irrational unpredictableness. One time his father would be normal–almost joyous–and minutes later he would go into one of his rages. The terrible explosiveness.

"Well quit complainin' then."

"You were the one pissin' and moanin'!"

"I wasn't pissin' and moanin'. I just said I might go back tuh Alabama, and you started . . . ."

Mable hadn't had it so easy either. Her father had been a fisherman, killed–not at sea–but in a bar fight. So liquored up the day she was born he could hardly talk, and instead of May Belle, the doctor had put Mable on the birth certificate. When her mother died, Mable had gone west with a family of Swedes, and stayed with them near Mankato. Then she took a job cooking in a hotel that turned out to be a brothel.

The Indian at the bar staggered and bumped Jake on his way out. A moment later in came Jerome Blodgett. Jake knew him, but only slightly. Jerome had homesteaded the year before, three miles east of Charity.

"Whew! Quite a wind." Jerome slapped his hat on his leg, and dust puffed up. He was tall and thin, with a large head, and his face was creased and colored like a pumpkin. "Must be blowing up a rain."

Jake made another drinking motion to Max, and pointed at Jerome.

The pessimists in back listened as Jerome went on. "Minna's home stuffing newspapers into the cracks in the walls. Dust an inch thick on the table." He held up his hat and swatted it with his other hand. "Blowing up a rain, that's what."

"Huh!" the snake said, loud enough for Jerome to hear.

"Notus and Afer, black with thunderous clouds," Jake said.

"Who?"

"John Milton. *Paradise Lost*."

"Oh." Jerome lifted his beer mug. "To your health." He squinted, his eyes adjusting to the dimness. "Anyway, they say a southwest wind brings rain."

"Southeast," the sad-looking weasel called from back. "Everybody knows that." They were pickled, and Jerome ignored them.

"Lars said the crops were good last year—" Jake began.

"Who?" Jerome asked.

"My neighbor, Lars Nordraak"

"Somebody was just talking about him. Let's see, what was it?"

"Lars?"

"Yeah, but I can't remember . . . Something about a fight in here."

"He doesn't drink."

"Now I remember. He got in a scrape with some guy who said something about you."

-48-

"Said something about me?" Jake asked. He thumped his beer mug down. "Who? What?"

"I dunno."

"About your wife," Max, the bartender, broke in. "What's her name?"

"Mable. What did he say?"

Max flushed. "Well, you know how men talk. About what a tomato she is. That sort of thing."

"I'll bet."

"When he started talkin' about her, well, her, uh, you know, big bubs, Nordraak slapped him down."

"Slapped him down, heck," the snake said. "Beat the bejesus outta' 'im Whaled away on 'im till they had to pull 'im off."

"I don't need anybody fighting my battles for me," Jake grumbled.

"Forget it," Jerome said.

"I don't know who the guy was," Max said, "but he was really boiled. I threw him out, and he hasn't been back since."

"Drink your beer." Jerome slid Jake's mug toward him. "I was gonna say, it's good land here. Rain's the thing. If you get rain . . . ."

The two at the table got up and walked unsteadily in the general direction of Jerome, who had his back to them.

"Buy us a drink?" the snake asked.

Jerome twisted around. "Do I know you?"

The snake stiffened. "That ain't very friendly. Me and my friend were just tryin' tuh be congenial."

"Sorry." Jerome turned back to Jake. "Rain, rain, rain. That's all anyone ever talks about."

"Don't turn away from me like that!" the snake growled. He grabbed Jerome's shoulder and swung him around. "If yuh don't wanna buy us a round, say so!"

"What the hell?" Jerome forced himself free. "You balmy or something?"

"Here we try tuh be friendly, and—" Jerome's antagonist was jerked violently backward, gasping for air. "What the—?"

Max had him from behind, by his belt, and by the back of his shirt collar. "Open the door," Max said evenly to Jake.

Jake hurried to the front door and held it open.

Max, ox-like in strength, tightened his grip on the man's belt and lifted. The man screamed and grabbed for his crotch. "I ever see you in here again, you'll be talking soprano the rest of your life," Max said. He bum-rushed the man headfirst out the door, sending him sprawling across the wooden sidewalk, into the dusty street.

"I was just leaving," the weasel said as he scurried out.

"Sorry," Max said to Jerome.

Jerome nodded.

"Goddamn barflies," Max grumbled. He went back behind the bar and pulled out two clean mugs. He filled them, blew off the foam, topped them off, and slid them down the bar. "On me."

"Thanks." Jake lifted his mug.

Max went back to the dark end of the bar and sat on his stool, staring at the picture on the opposite wall: a stunningly beautiful lady in a long, tight, azure, feather-trimmed dress. Rumors were that she was his ex-wife; a fan dancer.

"Who the dickens were they?" Jake asked.

"Dunno," Jerome said. "Anyway, from what I hear, this is farm country. Only yesterday I was talking to . . . ."

Jerome sure was an optimist.

Jake took another drink. He was worried about Mable, no matter what Dr. Raulsten said.

CHAPTER TWELVE

Jake stood behind the barn, in the stinging, pelting night rain. Lightning struck all about–and thunder crashed from the dark, green-cast clouds–but he was unafraid.

Fear no more the lightning flash, ...

Shakespeare's *Cymbeline*. Jake pulled up the collar of his waxed-linen raincoat, and he felt the dampness penetrate his pressed-straw hat, like cold sweat. Shakespeare, Plato, Aristotle, Homer, . . . , his solace. While other boys his age had done their best to avoid academics, he had taken refuge in the town library. Refuge from the world; refuge from his father. Comfort in Miss Fine, the librarian; in her kindness, understanding, and compassion. An old maid–cynical and bitter–who had seen in him something she had seen in herself when she was young, before she had failed at life.

Another lightning strike–closer–and a clap of thunder. The cleansing rain came harder, and colder, and Jake shivered.

One of Jake's compensations was awareness. No matter how bad things got, he was always aware of his condition. Except after being kicked in the head by the mule, but such indignities should not be taken into account. Aberrations. He took pride in–clung to–being a realist. A philosophical pragmatist, who . . .

"Who are you?" Jake asked. He felt as though he were lying on a cloud, balancing on his back, trying to keep from falling. He sensed that someone was watching him.

"I am The Fatidic Light."

Jake groped for something solid, but there was nothing. He tried to sit up, but there was no purchase, and he floundered backward, floating in a haze of patchy blue and white.

"Who?"

"The Fatidic Light." A point of light appeared overhead. It grew in size and intensity, and came closer. "I am with you always."

"Nonsense!"

"Then who am I?"

"That's what I'd like to know." Jake thrashed around, trying to roll to his stomach and stand up. "I must be losing my mind."

"Not at all. You're merely limited in your thinking. You and those like you. Here, let me help."

Jake stood, unsteadily, like a trained bear atop a huge ball. "Thanks. But I can't help feeling that I'm dreaming. You know, a nightmare, where nothing makes sense, and despite how hard you struggle, it only gets worse. Like sinking in quicksand, or swimming in molasses. And then you realize it's a dream, and you wake yourself."

"Go ahead, wake yourself."

"Alright, I will."

"Jake! Oh, thank heaven! I thought you were gone."

"Mable?" Jake said weakly. He was afraid to open his eyes.

"Yes. Oh, praise be!"

"Haw, haw, haw! Jake Miller, the human lightning rod! Ho!"

It could only be Karl Springer.

"What happened?" Jake opened his eyes. "What am I doing in bed?" His head pounded. He tried to sit up, but Mable pushed him back down, and he lay—as in the dream—wallowing about on his back.

"Jake Miller, I don't know what gets into you," Mable scolded.

"Haw!" Karl stood behind her in his black derby hat and white shirt. He and Mable were soaking wet.

"Standing out in storms like that," Mable went on. "If you hadn't gotten hit by lightning, you would have died of pneumonia. If it weren't for Karl, you'd be dead!"

"What did he do?"

"He saved your life, that's what he did. I was trying to drag you inside when he saw me, and—"

"Flash of lightning as I was driving by," Karl interrupted. He turned up the wick on the lantern he was holding.

Mable took Jake's hand. "As soon as we got you in here, you stopped breathing. If it hadn't been for Karl . . ." She began crying.

"What?" Jake sat up.

"He pounded on your chest." She lapsed into sobs, while Karl stood behind her, beaming.

Jake smelled burnt hair, and he fingered the bare spot on his scalp.

"Couldn't a' been the main strike," Karl said, "or it would'a been all over." He held the lantern closer to Jake. "You look a little pale. Haw, haw! Well, I gotta go. You can thank me tomorrow. Haw!" Then, to Mable, "He'll be alright." He patted her on the shoulder, and she took his hand and held it to her cheek. "Aw." Karl pulled his hand away and hurried toward the door. He stopped in the doorway. "That was a close call. See yuh later, Sparks!"

Jake held his head with both hands. More of his foolishness. And again the guilt. Not only the familiar guilt of his past, but the guilt of having further burdened Mable.

CHAPTER THIRTEEN

Solomon Stein's shivaree was set for Saturday evening. He had proved up on his homestead early that spring, and had gone back to New York to marry. His wife's name was Rachel.

A light came on in Sol and Rachel's house as the procession of automobiles and wagons arrived. Jake parked in front of the barn.

Sol's wide-eyed face appeared in the front window, and he watched in amazement as his neighbors produced tin pans, cowbells, and anything else that would make noise.

"Yo, Sol!" someone shouted. Sol came outside, and the din continued, then Lars Nordraak stepped onto the porch. "Congratulations on your marriage, Sol. It's time to celebrate!" With a few more bangs and shouts, the revelers went to their vehicles and began unloading food and gifts.

Rachel came to the door and peeked out. "What is it, Sol?" She was pretty, with long auburn hair, a strong mouth, and smooth, blushful skin. She and Sol were remarkably alike in appearance.

"Party!" Karl Springer cried as he bounded up the step. "Shivaree!" He thumped Sol on the back. "Everybody has tuh settle down sooner or later," he chortled.

Jake and Mable hung back, enjoying the surprise, and Mable giggled at the look on Rachel's face.

Actually, Sol didn't have much settling down to do. He was by no means a rounder. The first time he had stepped off the train in Charity, he had asked the depot agent where the nearest synagogue was. Billings, hundreds of miles away.

Jake had heard that Sol's only other peculiarity was that he didn't eat pork, and some wag had dubbed him Porkenstein. Sol took it good naturedly.

More cakes, and pies, fried chicken, mashed potatoes, ... And Norwegian and German dishes, some of the names Jake and Mable couldn't even pronounce. The men set up tables in front of the house and began lighting lanterns, and the party was on. It was pleasantly cool, and the lanterns added gaiety to the already-festive affair.

Jake and Mable were last in line. They heaped their plates and sat together on the grass at the edge of the circle of light. Jake was not an extrovert, and he preferred being away from the others. By now he knew most of his new neighbors, and they knew him as well as he wanted them to know him. As well as anyone knew anyone else there, where people from all over the country had come together out of necessity. Jake suspected that he was not the only one with a hidden past, and people seemed to know where the line was. There was no looking back.

Lars and Caroline were sitting on the porch next to Karl and Emma. Caroline, with her statuesque, blond good looks. She and Lars were clearly likes who had attracted each other. Supreme optimists, and in the short time Jake had known them, he had noticed how they carried their optimism to an extreme. For them nothing was ever bad; not in the past, the present, or the future. People were just people, with never a sinister motive or a malicious intent–at worst, they were mendacious–and events simply happened, usually for the best. No one would ever be seriously ill, it would rain, the crops would be good, . . . And if anything bad did occur, there was always a saving grace.

Mable got up for more coffee, and Jake thought he saw a flash of lightning, then he remembered that there were no clouds. First kicked in the noodle by a mule, then struck by lightning. Still, he had come out of it better than he should have.

"Hello."

Jake jerked his head up. "Oh, Johnny."

John Slivohavnick. Necktie Johnny, because he always wore a tie, even while working in the fields. He sat beside Jake. "Some party," Johnny said.

Jake felt a twinge of regret. He and Mable hadn't even had a decent wedding, not to mention a shivaree. "Now you know what's in store for you."

"Huh. Not likely." Johnny was a good-looking bachelor. His dark, sensitive eyes were the most noticeable feature of his youthful handsomeness.

"Don't worry, the right one'll come along."

"Haw. Not around here. Most are married, and the rest are—"

"Not that school teacher south of town. What's her name? Ingrid something or other?"

"Solberg," Johnny said dourly. "She's seeing someone."

"Well then what about Ragnild Gustovson over by—"

"Here's your coffee." Mable sat down. "Hello, Johnny. My, don't you look handsome?"

Johnny blushed.

"He's got his eye on Ragnild Gustovson over north of—"

"Now Jake, cut it out. You leave him alone. Don't listen to him, Johnny, he'll do that all night if you let him. Ignore him."

"But I was just saying—"

"Jake. For heavenly day's sake! You don't know when to quit."

After an appropriate time to show that he was not annoyed, Johnny went for a piece of pie.

"He doesn't like women," Mable whispered.

Jake closed his eyes and tried to lose himself. Guilt: part of the reality that Lars and Caroline had unknowingly renounced. He had lived with it so long, and it never stopped. Then he felt Mable's hand on his.

"There, Jake. It's nothing. You didn't know. Don't be so down on yourself," she said.

A wave of relief descended over Jake, and as always he wondered what he would do without her.

A cloud of dust hung knee-high in the yard where some of the people were dancing, and the moon glowed brighter. Far away a coyote howled, and another answered, then Sol's dog–a small rat terrier–ran to the edge of the circle of lantern light and barked back with a surprisingly deep, resonating yowl. The night air had cooled, and that was one of the things about northeastern Montana that Jake liked. He hated heat. Couldn't stand it, and though there were plenty of hot days, he always had the cool nights to look forward to.

Mable put her head on Jake's shoulder. "It's a new world here, Jake."

CHAPTER FOURTEEN

"Tah, tah, tah, tah-dah; ta-dah, tah-dah, tah-dah, tah-dah!"

Jake stood on the peak of his barn, clawhammer raised, beating time. Lars and Karl were helping him shingle the roof, and Jake looked down at them and laughed at the expression on their faces. "Verdi's Anvil Chorus," he called. "Gypsies singing about wine, women, and life. What a day! You should join me. You can see the ends of the earth from here!" The sky was the same no matter which direction he turned: blue near the horizon, lighter blue farther up, then pale blue; and almost white directly overhead. And cloudless.

"No, thanks," Lars said. "I like to keep one foot on the ground when I'm climbing."

Karl waved his hand and shook his head. Neither he nor Lars could get higher than the eave without getting dizzy.

"Tah, tah, tah, tah-dah; ta-dah, . . . I only remember the first few lines," Jake shouted. "Used to know the whole thing. Heard it on a gramophone. Liked it so much I bought the sheet music, and had an old Italian translate it for me."

Karl started reluctantly up the ladder with another bundle of shingles.

Jake sat in his special place, high in the giant oak tree in the center of Garvey's Grove. No one came there, except during hunting season, and even if someone did, they would never see his wooden platform, painted green and camouflaged with branches.

Jake climbed for two reasons: if his father was drinking, or if his mother was bad. He climbed mostly because of his father, but often because of his mother. Her spells, when she would withdraw and talk to herself, and see things that weren't there. Her "burden" she called it. He could take the lumps from his father, but his mother's deliriums were more than he could bear. And he couldn't help either of them. He could only try to save himself, and hope he would not succumb to their degeneracy when he grew up.

From his tree, Jake could see over the tops of the lesser trees to the green horizon all around, and it was easy to imagine himself as one of the ancient Greek Olympian gods. Sometimes Apollo, sometimes Ares, god of war. And when he was downcast, he became

Hephaestos, born lame and so ugly his mother had thrown him into the Ocean River, where he was rescued by nymphs, and later became a blacksmith. A famous crafter of jeweled ornaments. But never Zeus. Jake knew he could never aspire to that.

"Tah, tah, tah, tah-dah; ta-dah, ..."

Mable came out of the house and walked up behind Lars and Karl. She stared at Jake and slowly, almost imperceptibly, shook her head.

". . . tah-dah." Jake lowered his hammer, teetered at a sudden rush of wind, and sat down. "Well, guess I'd better get back to work." He pulled a mouthful of nails from his pocket. Mable had saved him from his father's drinking inheritance, and she could moderate the legacy of his mother's burden, but she could not heal him. He would have to do that himself. Willpower was the key. Force of will, and optimism.

Mable stood talking with Lars and Karl, and Jake wondered what they were saying. Every once in a while Lars would look up at him furtively. Jake pounded another nail. Damn. Drinking and dementia.

That evening over supper, Mable didn't mention his opera performance, and for that Jake was grateful.

"My, what a beautiful barn," Mable said. "Magnificent." She stood and turned up the lantern wick, then went to the stove for more beans, and outside the wind howled.

CHAPTER FIFTEEN

"Jake! Lars is here!" Mable burst through the barn door. "It's Minerva Lundberg!"

"What?" Jake put down the harness he was repairing.

"She's off on one of her tangents again, and Sven needs help."

"Why can't he take care of his own wife?"

"Lars wants you to go with him."

"He must think I'm an authority on loons."

"Oh, Jake, stop it. He just doesn't want to go alone. Last time, Sven was so distraught he was almost as bad as Minerva."

"Can't blame him. She's buggy. I heard Doc Raulsten wants Sven to commit her to the insane asylum in Warm Springs, but every time they get ready to pack her off, she straightens out."

Jake stood and brushed himself off. "Once she thought she was a Valkyrie. Sven found her riding around naked on one of his plowhorses, waving a pitchfork. Another time she was running all over the place, worried that there was going to be a meteorite attack. He had to tie her up. I'm not looking forward to this."

They started toward Sven and Minerva's house, where they found Sven pacing back and forth.

"What's going on?" Jake asked

Sven–big and blond, with a small, egg-shaped head–pointed to a sidehill several hundred yards away. "She's out there digging."

"For what?"

Sven began to sob. "For diamonds."

"Diamonds!" Jake blurted.

"Said the Lord told her there are diamonds out there. She's been at it all day." He looked mournfully at them, weaving his head slowly from side to side.

"You talk to Doc?"

"Same as always. Told me to take her to the booby house."

Jake surveyed the run-down farm: its unpainted barn, shabby house with the tarpaper peeling off, and crooked, ill-constructed outbuildings. Three hogs lay in the shade of the barn, and a half dozen turkeys strutted about in the grove of young poplar trees down the hill from the windmill. The turkeys were gorging on grasshoppers. Several dozen chickens clucked around the house; all hens but one, a large, white rooster with an enormous, bright-red cockscomb.

"We've gotta think," Lars said.

"Yeah," Jake said. "If she's been at it all day, there's no hurry."

Sven swayed, but he stayed on his feet. "She's been so good. Every time I think she's gonna be alright something like this happens. It's like she has a dam inside, and when it gets full, it bursts, and some kind of bile comes gushing out. After she gets it out of her system she feels better, but in a month or two it starts all over."

"Does she drink?" Jake asked.

"No! That's not it! I don't think she's ever had a drink in her life."

Jake looked at Lars. "What do you think?"

"It's worth a try."

"What's worth a try?" Sven reached out and held onto the corner of his house.

"I'll go to town and get some vodka and a few bottles of sarsaparilla," Lars whispered to Jake.

Jake took Sven's arm. "Come on, let's wait inside."

"I should go out there and—"

"Not yet." They went inside, and Sven fell into his armchair. Jake took the davenport. The interior of the house was as bad as the outside: musty smelling and cluttered, but with almost nothing on the walls. Only Sven and Minerva's wedding photo, and an oil painting of a lake. The lake was surrounded by a pine forest. And in the kitchen a Watkins calendar with a color picture of their famous Red Liniment. Someone had been crossing out the days.

Sven's arms had started twitching. "Are you and Lars gonna do what I think you're gonna do?"

"Sven, sometimes you have to take drastic measures. I don't imbibe much anymore–and I don't generally recommend it–but there are times when it helps. I know that as a fact. Oh, the do-gooders will tell you that you'll go to hell, and it'll pickle your brain and all that, but sometimes it's the only medicine."

"But getting her drunk—"

"Not petrified. Mellow. Worth a try, isn't it? What is there to lose?"

"Nothing. Nothing at all. Not for her, and not for me. I can't take much more. I think I'm the one who should do the drinking."

"It's me," Jake said. He sat on the edge of the bed.

"I'm sorry," the nurse said. She was old and homely, with buck teeth and too many freckles, but she was one of the compassionate ones. "She isn't making much sense today." She patted Jake's shoulder and bustled out.

Jake took his mother's hand. The place smelled of excrement. Someone in a room across the hall was singing; not a hymn, but what sounded more like a prayer. It was not easy to tell, because the door was shut, and Jake had seen a nurse lock it when she had come out.

His mother struggled to sit up, but she didn't acknowledge him in any other way. "That's it," she said as she stared at the crucifix on the opposite wall.

"What?"

She pulled her hand away. "Control. You have to stay in control. What I'd like to know is, when are they coming? They were supposed to come yesterday." She looked out the window, through the bars. "I haven't done anything wrong. They shouldn't put you in jail if you haven't done anything. Is it winter? I love winter. When I was small, there was a hill, and . . . ."

Jake wept, but only inside.

"There were horses, and cows, and white rabbits. There's a fly on top of my head. It's always there, and I can't get rid of it. Sometimes when . . . ."

"Brought you some sarsaparilla, Minerva," Lars said. "Looks like you could use it."

"Oh, my yes! But I can't sit too long. Hello, Jake."

Minerva leaned on her shovel, took the bottle, and drank. Dressed in bib overalls–and with a straw hat on–she looked like a man: large, ruddy, and muscular. She was perspiring heavily, and Jake sidled upwind.

"What are you looking for?" Jake asked.

"Can't say."

"For goodness sake," Lars chuckled, "you don't have to worry about us blabbing."

"Diamonds." She took another drink. She was developing a fuzzy, blond beard.

"Diamonds, eh? Sit down and rest a while."

"Can't. Gotta—"

"Only for a few minutes," Lars urged. He and Jake sat on a pile of gravel she had excavated.

"Well." She plopped down and swigged more of the sarsaparilla and vodka. "Or sapphires, or rubies. But I'm really after diamonds." The pupils of her wide, round eyes were little more than pinpricks.

Jake was chilled. He stole a glance back toward the house where Sven stood hatless in the cruel sun. It was all so futile. There was nothing to be done with Minerva, and he knew it, and Sven must have known it for a long time. Even Lars, one of the master creators of internal reality, had to know.

"You got her drunk?" Mable asked. She buttered another piece of bread.

"Not drunk. Just relaxed."

A dog barked in the distance. Karl Springer's. It was always barking.

"Did it work?"

It was getting dark, and they would have to light a lantern soon, but Jake didn't want to.

"Yes. I don't know for how long, but she's sleeping like a baby. We'll see." Jake dabbed at his mashed potatoes. "I'm sorry, I can't eat." He put down his spoon.

"What is it?" Mable asked.

"She was my mother. Not physically–they look nothing alike–but the demon was the same."

Mable pulled her chair close and held his hands in hers. "You and Lars did the best you could."

"But don't you see? I wasn't concerned about Minerva. I was only worried about myself. Is that what's in store for me?"

Mable put her head on his chest, and he smelled the clean, womanly smell of her hair. "No. It's not at all the same. You're aware, and she's not. That's the difference." She smiled up at him. "Don't worry, things are going to be different for us. Remember?"

Jake felt better as Mable lit the kitchen lantern. Mable was his strength.

CHAPTER SIXTEEN

"Wham!!"

Jake and Mable felt as though they had been levitated from their bed. Mable floated for a moment, then fell back, while Jake gyrated so that his feet hit the floor.

"Mary, mother of . . ." Jake leapt to the front window and peered out. "There's something burning in the pasture! What in the world?"

"Burning?" Mable scurried to his side. "The window pane is cracked!" She buttoned her nightgown to cover her more-than-ample breasts. "What is it?"

"I don't know, but I'm going to find out." Jake took his threadbare work jacket from the nail behind the door, but Mable grabbed it from him.

"No! You might get hurt."

"We can't just stay in here and do nothing."

She backed to the door, blocking it.

"Well what, then?" Jake demanded.

"Go to town and have someone call the sheriff."

"And tell him what? I should at least find out what it is. I know! I'll look at it with my telescope."

"You'll what?"

Jake ran to the old travel trunk in the corner by the bed, groped in the dark, and pulled out a small brass sailor's telescope. He polished the front lens with the tail of his nightshirt. "Uncle Finney's. He gave it to me when I was twelve. I hid it in the woods so my father wouldn't pawn it. Uncle Finney was a sailor in the British Navy."

"Jake Miller, you put on your clothes first. It's bad enough not knowing what's out there, but you don't have to go running around in your nightclothes. It could be a bomb." Mable stiffened her back against the door and folded her arms across her chest.

"A bomb? If it's a bomb, what good would clothes do? And who'd put a bomb in our pasture? If you're trying to kill someone, you don't bomb their pasture!"

"You're the one always worrying that someone is after you."

Jake felt the familiar chill spread from his cheeks, around his neck, and down his backbone. "Oh for Pete's sake, it's probably a meteorite. But all right, if it'll make you feel better, bring me my boots." He pulled on his pants.

Mable lit the kitchen lantern, picked up Jake's field boots and brought them to him, then put on her robe.

Jake buttoned his shirt. "I feel like a knight, suiting up for battle. I'm a little short on armor though. I wish I had my shield, and my trusty sword—"

"Oh, cut it out. You're not funny."

Jake put on his hat, extended the telescope, and leaned to kiss Mable. She winced and smiled wanly. "Life's never dull with you," she said, but her worry showed through.

Jake crept out. He steadied the telescope against one of the porch posts.

"What do you see?" Mable's voice shook as she stood in the doorway. The lantern in her hand shook along with her voice.

"Nothing. The fire went out, and whatever it is is dark now. Maybe I should—"

"No. Don't you dare go any closer! It might explode!"

They sat silently in the dark, waiting. "Fifteen more minutes," Mable ordered. "We'll wait fifteen more minutes."

Jake stiffened. "Now what?" A light came bouncing down the road some distance away. They waited, and as it got closer they saw it was Karl Springer on one of his plowhorses. He was holding a lantern in one hand, and something else in the other. His black derby hat was almost invisible, but his white shirt stood out, ghostlike.

"What's going on?" Karl shouted. "You alright?"

Ichabod Crane. Or Don Quixote.

Karl jumped from his horse, and Jake pointed toward the pasture. "Something landed out there," Jake said. "I think it's a—"

"Holy Jesus!" Karl exclaimed. He ran for the porch, set his lantern down, turned, and pulled back both hammers on his double-barreled shotgun. "Stand back! If it comes any closer, I'll blow it to smithereens!" His hat slid down over his eyes.

An automobile turned in, its headlight beams bouncing. "It's Lars," Karl shouted. "Stop 'im, before he gets too close!" Karl aimed skyward and let loose with both barrels. His horse jumped and began to run in circles, and Mable screamed. The automobile stopped, its headlights went out, and they heard one of its doors slam.

"What in the name of heaven is going on?"

"Keep away, Lars!" Karl shoved two more shells into his gun. "It's something from Mars."

"Mars! What the—?" Lars came toward them, followed closely by Caroline, and by Emma whom they had picked up on the way.

"Mars?" Jake echoed. "It's just a—"

"Yeah." Karl took a practice aim toward the pasture. "Grandfather Johann told me all about the creatures on Mars. I knew this would happen someday."

"It's not from Mars," Jake tried again. "My guess is that it's a—"

"A bomb!"

"Hogwash." Lars stomped up the porch steps. "It's a meteorite, you jackass! Say, where'd you get the blunderbuss? That looks like the one the Pilgrims shot the first Thanksgiving turkey with."

"Grandfather Johann sent it to me from Germany."

"Well stop waving it under my nose."

"Huh," Karl sulked. "Could be a bomb. That's the thing about you, Lars, always so sure about everything."

"Yeah, and I'm always right too. Come on, let's see how big it is."

Mable came out onto the porch, and Jake took the lantern from her.

"A meteorite?" Karl asked.

"A meteorite," Lars answered back over his shoulder.

Karl stayed behind, pouting, while Jake and Lars approached the smoldering rock.

"Still hotter than blazes," Jake said. He kicked dirt over a nearby lump of smoking cow manure. "I tell you, Lars, something like that gets a guy out of bed in a hurry."

"Ha! Only you, Jake. It could only happen to you. You're a pure delight!"

Jake had to agree. He had always been a magnet for disaster. Human flypaper, to which life's annoyances were attracted.

"Look at that," Lars said. "Bigger than an elephant turd."

Jake held out the lantern. He hazarded that Lars had never seen an elephant, much less an elephant turd. The meteorite was a foot in diameter; reddish, with mottled brown-and-gray patches.

"Here comes Karl," Lars chortled.

"Lemme see," Karl said. He pushed between them. "Yeow! Poison gas!" He sprang back and sidled upwind. "Look out!"

"That's burning cow manure." Lars shook his head disgustedly.

"Oh. Say, that thing's big. What are yuh gonna do with it, Jake?" Karl took off his hat and tried to fan the excitement from his face.

"I don't know. Nothing, I guess. As far I'm concerned it's just a big rock."

"Just a big rock!" Karl was aghast. "Just a big rock, eh? Well let me tell you, that there falling star is a good omen. A sure sign of luck. Grandfather Johann knew that. His father had one fall on his house once, and—"

"Here we go with Grandfather Johann again," Lars snorted. "How the hell could it be good luck to have a hot rock fall on your house?"

Karl gave Lars a wicked look. "If you'll shut up for a minute, I'll tell you." He pulled his hat back on, stiffly, with both hands, and growled something sinister in German. "They were gone at the time. That was good luck right there. And when they got home, they found Helmut Schmidt–the village burglar–dead on the floor. Hit by the meteorite. Stoned by the Almighty! Still holdin' a sack full'a their silverware. But the good luck didn't end there. Forever after, on that day, they were blessed. Once Great Grandmother Olga found an old Roman coin in front of their house. Solid gold. Another time five years later an uncle died and left them his farm. Great Grandfather Johann gave up shoemakin' and took up farmin'. And there were lots of other things. Course Great Grandfather died on that date, but the good fortune more than made up for it. And that's what's gonna happen to you, Jake."

"I'll die on this date?" He nudged Lars.

"No. Good fortune. You can expect something auspicious to happen on this day every year!"

Jake was surprised that Karl knew the word, auspicious. "It's almost midnight," Jake said, looking at his pocket watch, "so if something good is going to happen, it had better happen soon."

"You didn't get hit, did you?" Lars asked. "Your luck is picking up already."

"Don't laugh," Karl groused. "I'm gonna be checkin' this date on my calendar every year. Mark my words."

Jake knew that listening to the likes of Karl Springer was sinking to a new low, but he couldn't help being uplifted by Karl's optimism.

Emma approached Karl. "Karl Johann Springer, what have you to say for yourself?"

CHAPTER SEVENTEEN

On a bright and beautiful day, Jake polished the blade of his one-bottom breaking plow and began on the forty acres of virgin sod north of the house. The horses pulled roughly and skittishly for the first hour, then they settled in. Jake savored the fresh smell of the soil. Rabbits, foxes, and gophers ran before the cataclysm that would diminish their lives forever, but for Jake it was another phase of his and Mable's new beginning. Birds sang, and Jake sang along, wildly and spontaneously. Then he raised his voice to the sky. Not in prayer. He never prayed. Rather, in a resonant mantra that only he knew. He had sinned often. Not religiously—he had no religion—but secularly. Now, in his field of hope, he tried to forgive himself.

A hawk plummeted from the sky to take a mouse. It carried its catch to a nearby rock and picked at it, not eating.

Jake stopped at the far end of the field and checked the horses' harnesses and straps, then he went to lie in the grass—not long—only long enough to rest his back. To heck with all illusions. He fell asleep.

———————

Crops were good, spirits were high, and it was time for a community dance. Dances were more than celebrations of good times; they were manifestations of optimism, and Charlie Ingvoldson's barn dance was the most popular in the area.

Jake and Mable arrived as the sun was setting. The Ingvoldson farm was impressive, with its huge red barn; fine, white, two-story house; and rows of small poplar and box elder trees. Jake parked their auto, and they took Mable's baked beans to the table in front of the barn. There was a good crowd, and as Mable put down her pot, Karl arrived.

"Mable! Jake!"

"Karl!" Jake greeted. "Where's Emma?"

"Right over there." Karl pointed to a group of ladies.

"Oh. I thought you'd be dancing. What's the matter, can't keep up to your wife?"

"They ain't started yet. Besides, I ain't much of a dancer."

"That's funny. You look like a natural." Jake clapped him on the back. He liked Karl. They had something in common. An uncommon lack of convention. But there was more. Karl carried a mystique. Lars had mumbled something once about Karl being mixed up with a mob back in Chicago, but that was mere speculation. Karl claimed to have been a piano mover, but other than that, he was secretive about his past.

More people arrived: ladies dressed in their finery, and men in all manner of apparel, from suits to work clothes. Charlie Ingvoldson's son, Virgil, began lighting lanterns, and everyone lined up to eat. Jake and Mable stood beside Karl and Emma.

"I ain't very hungry," Karl grumped.

"Haw!" Jake laughed. "Look at you, nothing but skin and bone." He poked Karl in his ample stomach. Karl didn't see the humor.

Mable gave Jake a stern look and pulled him away. "Settle down now," she whispered in his ear.

Jake felt his face turn red, and he was glad it was getting dark. He had always been somewhat abrasive, but he was–with Mable's help–improving.

The happy throng flowed inside where Halsing Lindefors slouched against the wall in the far corner, tuning his violin. Presently Halsing was joined by someone with an accordion, and everyone was surprised to see another man with a strange-looking stringed instrument that he played with small drumsticks. A hammer dulcimer. The player was from West Virginia.

The first number was a polka, but no one wanted to start. Finally a young man coaxed out a pretty local school teacher.

Jake danced the second dance with Mable–a waltz–and he was restored. They danced again, with grace and ease. Jake knew that Mable felt as he did; free of all fear except one: that of stopping. On and on, until a calm tiredness came upon them.

"Done already?"

Lars. Jake didn't–couldn't–answer. He and Mable sat down.

"Looked to me like you were just getting warmed up," Lars joked.

Jake ignored him. He studied the crowd. There was Nils Anderson sitting on a bench with his wife, Sophie; his big nose redder than ever. And Manfried Gottlieb and his wife, Ina. Manfried had been drinking, as usual. Standing next to the musicians was tall, distinguished-looking J.J. Hill, dressed in a suit and tie. He was an introvert, but his wife–Marguerite–apparently had talked him into coming. Beside J.J., in their finest bib overalls, were two shy young men from Charity. And many others: good, solid, hard-working people.

"I didn't know you and Mable were such good dancers," Lars chuckled. Then he reminisced about the dances he and Caroline had gone to when they were courting.

Jake leaned his head back against the wall and squeezed Mable's hand. The dance hall was a barn, but to Jake it was a grand ballroom, and the people were no longer farmers, laborers, and tradesmen, but royalty. An illusion, but he held to it, before reality overtook him. No. Until he regained reality. That was it.

By two o'clock in the morning most of the dancers were either resting or taking refreshments outside. The children had fallen asleep on a bed of straw in the milking room, and the music was soft and easy. The only ones on the floor were the young bachelor in his white shirt, black tie, and red suspenders; and the school teacher, whose red hair had fallen over the shoulders of her white, silk dress. They moved slowly, holding each other closer than was considered proper. The young man's right hand had fallen low on her back, but not quite to face-slapping level.

The music stopped. Some kind of ruckus outside. Jake got up and followed a half dozen other men to the door.

"What goes on here?" someone asked.

It was a fight, in which one of the participants seemed unwilling. The scuffle went on for several minutes, then a smallish figure stepped up to the troublemaker and hit him under the ear with a left hook. The bully dropped like a sack of grain, and lay crumpled. Two men hauled him away, toward the water trough.

The small man with the short-cropped hair was Rudi Prinz. Only a prizefighter could have dispatched someone so effortlessly. It had been like swatting a fly.

"You better get outta' here, Jake. He doesn't look very good."

"Is he dead?" someone asked.

Always the guilt of the past, that could be disavowed only by forgetting. And always the harshness of life. On the way home, Jake wondered about the coming year. And the next five, and ten, ... Once, he had convinced himself that he could foretell the future, but now he had lost his power. No matter. His compensation would be the stilling–rather, the moderation–of his terrible Wheel of Life.

When they got home Jake went for a walk. He looked up at the night sky, and, as Dante emerging from his Inferno, Jake . . . *beheld through a round aperture . . . some of the beauteous things that Heaven doth bear . . .*

PART TWO – 1925

CHAPTER EIGHTEEN

Jake stood alone in the night, under hell-black storm clouds. Lightning struck close by: Thor's hammer, flung from iron-gloved hand. Cold rain glued Jake's clothes to him, and stung his eyes. Sky lightning laid back the protective night, and the low, rolling hills were void and lifeless. Again the lightning, but now an apparition a quarter of a mile away. A soldier marching? Jake wiped his eyes with the slippery-wet back of his hand, and shivered. At the next flash the figure was gone.

For twelve years Jake had survived by abrogating his past, and by concentrating on the good in life. Then his Wheel of Life creaked, and groaned, and came to life again.

The summer of 1925 was a summer of heat, drought, and discouragement, and the promise of farming in northeastern Montana was false. Life was unsparing. Hard for Mable, but harder–Jake realized–for him, because he was undeceived. Lars Nordraak, Karl Springer–and most of Jake's other neighbors–refused to acknowledge their grim prospects. They had put everything into their homesteads, and they had nowhere else to go, and nothing else to do. They could only hang on, and in order to do that, they were forced to abandon reality. But Jake knew better, and his intellective animus was overwhelming.

Worse, Jake saw a change in himself. While he had always been able to perceive the whole of his life from a higher perspective, on a lower level something else was happening, and he was aware of Mable's concern. The difficulties had started the year before, with his oat diet. He had been suffering from indigestion, stomach cramps, and diarrhea; but two weeks of oat porridge had cured him. Of all but the diarrhea. Then there had been his copper-bar plowing experiments. According to an article in a farm magazine, steel plow blades poisoned the soil, but the effects could be neutralized by dragging copper bars behind each blade. His experiments had been met with widespread skepticism. Derision was a better word.

Jake conceded the extent to which he was regarded in the community as an eccentric, and he resolved again to control himself.

For Mable's sake. Public ridicule meant little to him, but it affected Mable terribly.

And Jake realized that what hurt Mable even more than his peculiarities was Lars Nordraak's sarcasm. She had seen the calumny with which Lars at times treated him behind his back. One day in the mercantile store in Charity, they had overheard Lars.

"He'th a good one, alrighth," a tall, dark-haired, rough-looking man laughed. All of his front teeth were missing, and he needed a shave.

"I hear he's gonna start raising watermelons," John Stokes chortled. He and his wife, Greta, lived on a farm five miles west of Charity. He was even taller than the toothless one, but blond, and better looking. "Whaddya think, Lars?"

"Huh. I wouldn't be surprised. He does act kinda queer sometimes, and . . . ."

Lars had turned red when he saw Jake and Mable, and the next day he came to apologize, but what was done was done.

Thereafter, again, Jake did his best to bridle his eccentricities. At least to resist their manifestations. In doing so, he attempted to limit his activities and perceptions to socially acceptable levels. Also, he worked at maintaining his–and Mable's–optimism. He would never surpass Lars and Caroline in optimism, but he could do better.

As the days wore on, Jake and Mable persevered, working hard; delighting in others, and in simple contentments. Picnics, dances, visits with neighbors, . . . , compensations for their austere life. But often the compensations were insufficient.

The most worrisome insufficiency was Mable's health, which had been tenuous and nebulous. Years of doctor visits and patent medicines, years of ups and downs, but never anything specific.

"Jake, I'm at the end of my rope," Dr. Raulsten said tiredly. He slumped into the chair behind his desk. Mable was still in the examining room. "I'm a medical doctor, not a psychiatrist. I can keep this up as long as she can, but I'm simply going through the motions. Every time I see her, I'm a fraud. A charlatan. It's always the same. She comes in with some vague complaint, I pretend to examine her, then I give her a little laudanum mixed with sugar water–different color each time–and she's happy." He lowered his voice. "But a few months later she's back, and we go through the same ritual."

"I . . . ," Jake started. He backed to the padded-leather armchair in the corner and sat staring across the room at the medicine cabinet from which came Mable's sustenance.

Dr. Raulsten pulled himself up straight. "I could send her to a specialist, but . . ." He hesitated. "But as long as this has been going on, if there were something seriously wrong, she'd be dead by now." Having said it, he fell back again.

Jake looked desperately about the room at the clutter of medical books, Dr. Raulsten's diploma on the wall, ... Then, simply, "I'll have to live with it. We'll have to live with it."

On the way home, Jake knew that the most trying part was not Mable's illness, real or imagined; it was her reliance on him. An underlying faith, despite his flaws. False faith, but it served her well. In the end, however, it would be her unfounded faith that would deal the most crushing blow.

And as for himself, still the guilt.

CHAPTER NINETEEN

The long, severe summer descended like a hot, suffocating, patchwork quilt. At first people jested as a way of coping, but as the crops withered, the joking ceased. Those who had sought strength in the company and commiseration of others turned inward. Those who had never shared their burdens turned even more grim and solitary.

On a hot Sunday morning while Mable was in church–Charity Lutheran–Jake stood in the doorway of his workshop, trying futilely not to think. It had been a sleepless night. Always before, The Fatidic Light had come as a dream, or when he was ill. Yesterday it had appeared in broad daylight, as he was picking rocks.

"Jake."
The Light descended, growing from a small point high in the sky, to a huge ball that hovered several feet above the ground. Its voice was halfway between spoken and understood. Jake threw down his rock and cringed, shielding his eyes, and looking down.
"Who—?"
"You know."
"The Fatidic Light? But what do you—?"
The Light brightened. "You know that as well. Open your eyes."
"That's preposterous! Melodramatic! Anyway, why don't you just tell me? Why . . . ?"
The Light flashed, and, like a bubble bursting, it was gone.

Jake hadn't told Mable. He no longer did; any of it. That left only Lars, and despite Lars' occasional duplicity, it was a relief to see him drive into the yard.

"Hello!" Jake called.

Lars got out of the shiny new Chrysler touring car he had bought the year before. It was big and blue, with a huge rectangular windshield and a cloth top; and people had wondered where he had gotten the money. They soon found out; all but Caroline.

Lars, Karl Springer, and a drifter from Tennessee named Watson had gone into the moonshine business. Lars–the teetotalist–

was the silent partner, Karl was the master distiller, and Watson was the one who told the master distiller what to do.

For weeks the duo fed their still, that for some inexplicable reason they had located on a high hill east of Lars' farm. With smoke belching like smoke signals, they were throwbacks to the time when Indians had sent signals from the hill, which hill later became known by the homesteaders as Indian Hill. The smoke, and Karl with his perennial white shirt and black derby hat, were the main attraction for miles around. They could easily be seen without a telescope, had the law been looking.

After making a little easy money from the first batch, the entrepreneurs expanded their operation, but after the second, larger batch had aged a for few weeks in small wooden kegs, Watson had come in the night and absconded with the fruits of their labor. That abscondment ended the enterprise, but by that time Lars had bought his new car, on which he was making payments.

"Come on over," Jake motioned.

Lars took off his cap, wiped his forehead with it, and lifted his face to the merciless sun. Then, as Jake waited, something caught Lars' eye. Two crows. Norse god Odin's sacred ravens, Huginn and Munnin, Jake guessed. Thought and Memory, flying northward to Valhalla to commune with Lars' Viking ancestors. Lars shook his head at something, then put his cap back on.

"Sit down, lean back, and help me hold up the workshop," Jake chuckled.

Lars sat, and they tilted their chairs against the wall. Half of the shed was a garage, and the other half–the workshop–was Jake's refuge.

"Hot," Lars grouched. His face was red from the heat, and sweat dripped from his nose.

They watched the grasshoppers work on what little green grass was left. Off to the east, dust devils twisted, sucking life from the land. There were no clouds, and the heat shimmered on the horizon. And yet, Jake mused, there was a wayward beauty if one could veil the immediate hardships.

Jake tried to think of something to start a conversation. Not Lars' car; that was still a sore spot. Caroline had not found out about the moonshine venture; and she was angry and confused as to why Lars–usually so frugal–had lost his senses and bought a new car.

It was no use bemoaning the heat. That was getting old. Even less was anyone anymore inclined to comment about rain. Lars liked to talk politics, but Jake didn't, especially with Lars, who was somewhat queer in his views. Some odd brand of socialism as far as Jake could tell.

Lars was not an intellectual, though he was smart enough on a lower level. He was–Jake considered–not dumb, but highly flawed. But then so were most people: good at this, average at that, skilled at the other; but when it came to more elevated thinking they fell short.

"Look who's talking."

"I've been reading an interesting book," Jake said. He was easing himself into a new topic.

"You don't say so?"

"Yes. It's about Gottfried Wilhelm von Leibniz. A German––"

"Was he related to the Kaiser?"

"Kaiser? No. He was a philosopher back in the 1600s. He was a metaphysician, and he was interested in ontology, the—"

Lars turned to Jake. "Ontology?"

Jake felt his face redden and his ears began to burn. Now all he could to was dig himself in deeper.

"The study of reality. He tried to come up with a theory of everything."

"A theory of everything. I do declare!"

Jake tried to swallow, but his mouth was dry. Damn. This wasn't going to help his reputation. However, nothing to do now but to quit digging and try to crawl out of his hole.

"It's not as nutty as it sounds, Lars. He hypothesized that there were basic elements of the universe, even smaller than atoms, that's all. He called them monads, and—"

"Gonads?" Lars chortled.

Jake clenched his teeth. "No, gonads. I mean monads. Jeeze Lars, I'm just trying to tell you what I read! We don't always have to talk about the weather, and the crops, and who's beating his wife, and who's carrying on with his neighbor's wife, and things like that. Don't have to sit and piss and moan about farming. You're no dunce. Don't you ever think about something else than farming? Don't you ever wonder what's real, and what's not? What's real, and what's merely in your head?"

Lars appeared confused and taken aback for a moment, then he reached down and picked up a small rock and held it up to Jake, smiling mischievously. "Here, I just solved your problem. And Leibsnits'. This is real. Look around; what you see is real, Miller."

Lars sat back smugly.

"Leibniz," Jake snapped. "And you certainly aren't the first to use a rock as an example of reality. For Christ's sake, I wish I had never brought it up. I should have talked about the weather, Or about Horace Clapper carrying on with Fisk Flander's wife, Eudora. Lord forgive me for trying once again to rise above the level of the common masses."

Lars glanced back at him, apparently unsure of whether to be offended or to relent and show a little mercy. He chose mercy.

"I didn't mean anything. It's only that when you're out here fighting for a new life, philosophy doesn't mean much, Jake. Philosophy isn't going to bring rain, or protect the crops from grasshoppers, or keep your family from dying of typhoid fever or influenza. We have to be practical."

Neither spoke for a while.

Jake leaned forward with his elbows on his knees and his face in his hands. "I know, Lars, but oftentimes it helps to think that there is a little more to life. More, in quotation marks. And I have a personal interest in what's real and what's not. I won't get into it, except to ask, what would you do if you ever heard a voice you weren't sure was real, or saw something that appeared to be a vision, or an apparition? My guess is you'd do a little reading yourself, that's all."

They sat silently, and Jake noticed Lars's face melt. He had never seen him like that before. Almost like he would burst into tears.

"I'm sorry Jake."

CHAPTER TWENTY

"In the beginning God created the heaven and the earth. And the earth was without form, and void, and darkness—"

"No, no, no, not dat, for God's sake! Not da Old Testament. Nobody above a low-functioning moron would believe dat." He moaned, and closed his eyes.

"What, then?" Jake asked.

"Ohhh, who cares? I'm gonna die and find out for myself."

"Die and find out? Oh for heavenly day's sake!"

"Yust lemme die."

"But what about Sophia?"

His wife, Sophia, was in the back bedroom, sicker than he was.

"Ohhhh."

Halvor and Sophia Berglund had the flu, and Jake and Lars had been helping them when no one else would. Hauling water, washing clothes, feeding the animals, ... Lars was fearless, and Jake, while certainly not fearless, had summoned sufficient courage.

Influenza had been going around, but not as bad as back in 1918. And by now the pest house in Charity had been closed, fumigated, and turned into a boarding house. Not that Halvor would have gone to a pest house anyway.

Fearless as Lars was, he wasn't stupid, and he tried to stay at arm's length from the sick couple, though that was not always possible. Jake tried to stay even farther away, and when he had to do the dirty work–empty the honey pots and so on–he tied a handkerchief over his face and wore gloves. Holding his breath came naturally. He regretted that the pest house wasn't still in operation, but now everyone went to the hospital, or stayed home, and in either case they were quarantined. Both Jake and Lars had broken the quarantine, and each time they went home they took baths outside, then gargled with apple cider vinegar.

Halvor was sure that Death–the fourth horseman of the Apocalypse–would fly through the window on his pale horse to pluck him from his bed. It could have been the fever, or it could have been Halvor's true belief–but in the event, Halvor had asked Jake to read from the Bible.

"Da New Testament, Miller. Anyting in da New Testament. But for heaven's sake get on wid it; I may not have much time left. And when I'm gone, do da same for Sophia. Sweet Yesus!"

"Oh, for . . . You're not going to die. And pardon me–I wouldn't say this to a dying man, but I'll say it to you–if you can't swallow the Old Testament, how can you stomach the New? It's all bushwa and balderdash. Old myths and mysticism carried forward through the ages into the modern time of reason. Believing in some god, any god, pick one; they're all over the place, and if people don't like any of them, some nut invents a new one and tries to push it on others. And if it weren't called religion, those pious and devout followers would be considered to be insane, and would be locked up in the local asylum."

"Ohhh."

"The best part is that when you come around you'll be right back drinking and carrying on with your neighbor's wife, Nellie, down at the willows by your slough in the middle of the night."

Halvor opened one eye and stared at Jake.

"Of course I know, and so does everyone else. Lord almighty, Halvor."

Halvor closed his eye and lifted his hand. "Den I have some atonement to make. Please, Yake, read from anyting in da New Testament. Whatever you tink would be appropriate."

Jake thumbed through Halvor's Bible. Anything would do; the entire Bible was more or less about guilt and atonement.

Jake read.

"And as they were eating Jesus took bread and blessed it, and brake it, and gave it to the disciples and said, Take, eat, this is my body. And he took the cup and gave thanks, and gave it to them, saying Drink ye of it, for this is my blood of the new testament, which is shed for many for the remission of sins."

Halvor sat up. "Stille! Gud for fanden!" He had lapsed into Danish. "God dammit Yake. Dat's off no comfort. Leave off!"

Jake closed the Bible and sat with it on his lap as Halvor fell back on his pillow.

Jake smirked. "You give new meaning to 'Damned if you do, and damned if you don't,' Halvor."

After a little more moaning and groaning Halvor motioned with the back of his hand to a bottle on the stand. It was *Dr. J. Collis*

Browne's CHLORODYNE, Safe and Reliable Family Remedy for INFLUENZA, Colds, Coughs, Catarrh, Asthma, . . .

"Where in the world did you get—"

"Brought it over from England on da way from da old country years ago," Halvor rasped. "I knew der would be an emergency sooner or later, an' dis is dat emergency." He was still in his Danish mode, and he said something else that Jake couldn't understand. "Gimme." He took a long pull at the bottle, hugged it to the side of his chest for a while, then took another big swig.

A good dose of laudanum and goodness knows what else, Jake suspected.

A week later Halvor and Sophia were strong again, Jake and Lars were local heroes, and Halvor was back to his debaucheries.

Jake relished his own heroics, suspecting he would not soon be a hero again. But perhaps he would.

CHAPTER TWENTY-ONE

"Sometimes he just sits there staring, like he's in a trance. I tell you, Nils, he ain't right in the top story. Kinda peculiar. They ought'a put him away, before he hurts somebody."

"Yeah, he's in a helluva shape," Nils said. "Give us another beer." He finished his drink and slid both mugs down to the bartender. "And diggin' all the time. I can't figure that out."

Nils was tall and thin, with a big, red drinker's nose that hung down to his mouth, and he always had his straw hat pulled low over his eyes, indoors or out.

The bartender brought the beer. They had been drinking all afternoon.

"He was locked up, wasn't he?"

"That's what they say, but I heard he was in a hospital."

"I heard he was in a loony asylum." Nils made wet circles on the bar with his mug.

"I heard he was in the pen for killin' somebody, but I don't believe it."

"The hell? I wouldn't be surprised. I guess killing gets in your blood. I'll bet he did in a few of those Krauts over there."

"I suppose so."

"But war's war," Nils said. "Lars Nordraak knows 'im better'n anybody, and he never said anything about him killin' anybody else."

Nils took two cigars from his shirt pocket. They bit off the ends, spit them on the floor, and lit up. The smoke mixed with the blue haze that was already overhead. In the back, a group of noisy onlookers had gathered around a poker game.

"Well what did he say about Morgan?"

"Nothin'. He knows, but he ain't tellin."

"Huh. Maybe he knows, maybe he doesn't. If he isn't telling, it must be bad. I still think he's deranged." Jake down put his mug and started for the back door. "Gotta water my horse." He staggered slightly on the way to the outhouse.

Forever after Jake felt the guilt of that conversation.

"I get queasy in mines," Jake said.

He and Morgan Feeney had teamed up to haul coal early, instead of waiting until fall. The good part was that it was nice and cool in the mine; a drift mine dug into the side of a hill. The bad part was that they had to dig their own coal. Peter Hawkins, the owner, spent more time making white mule than he did tending the mine. He had learned his moonshine skills back in West Virginia.

"Never bothered me any," Morgan said. "I saw the inside of plenty of holes during the war. In fact, I kind of like it down here. Gives me a good, safe feeling." He held up the carbide lantern and looked at the wooden beams.

Morgan was nondescript, in a good-looking way, with broad shoulders, a strong chin, and a calm, stoic look. An intense, natural dignity that was unappreciated by most in the community. Only rarely did he relapse into his trouble from The Great War. Shell shock. The neurasthenia that at times consumed him. Black periods when he sank into total despair. Genevieve–his wife who had been an army nurse in France–had helped bring him back from the worst of it.

"I hope old Hawkins is better at shoring up mines than he is at making mountain dew," Jake said. They were forty yards in from the entrance. One of the seven gates of the underworld. Hell, ruled by Ereshkigal, the Mesopotamian goddess of darkness. Jake was glad to have Morgan with him.

"I drank some of it once," Morgan said. "Hawkins' rotgut. It made me sicker than a dog. Puked my guts out."

People still talked about Morgan when he had first come. How he drank and carried on, how he got the shakes, and saw things. About the army comrade who had come to see him: Lansing Rhodes, with half of his face blown away, who had to wear a partial mask. One of the men with broken faces, as the French artists who made the masks called them. Things like that. Morgan had pulled through, but it seemed like people remembered only the bad. What they held most against him was that he, too, was a realist, now that he was on the right track.

"Sick?"

"Had the shits for three days, and a headache, and couldn't get out of bed except to use the thunder bucket. And to make matters worse, I had to listen to Genevieve harp on me all three days, mostly whenever she had to empty the bucket."

"Lucky you didn't go blind." They passed an air-vent shaft, and Jake peered up through it.

"That's about the only thing that didn't happen," Morgan said. "I had plenty of nasty stuff during the war, but Hawkins' beats all. You could use it to poison skunks. By the way, I wouldn't stand looking up that shaft. You're liable to get beaned by a rock."

Jake pushed the steel cart to the end of the rails and hefted his pickaxe, eager to finish and get out.

"This reminds me of the German dugouts," Morgan said. "They really knew how to dig in. Lotta times their trenches had little rooms underground."

Jake fidgeted. Ordinarily he would have been glad to listen to Morgan, but not now.

"Once, after a big bombardment, we overran their lines, and . . . ."

Jake slouched against the coal vein. Genevieve had once told him that he was the only one–besides herself and Lars–that Morgan talked to about the war. That he and Morgan had much in common. Their outlook on life. No-nonsense, with little regard for artifices.

". . . down in their holes like rats, and . . . ." Morgan put his shovel to his shoulder, and aimed it like a rifle.

Jake shivered from the damp cold, and from Morgan's long and terrible account. It added to the feeling of ennui that had enveloped him for the last few weeks.

"Then we started mopping up. We had to go in with bayonets, and . . . ."

Morgan told a story more horrible than any he had told before.

"No man should have to do that," Morgan said. As he stood with his back to the entrance, haloed by the dim light, he was a ghostly specter. "You can never be the same. It takes something from you." He paused. "But it gives you something too."

Beneath Morgan's haunting reminiscences, Jake saw deep, inner strength.

"Gives you something?"

"Let me try to explain. After I was wounded, in the field hospital I thought I saw—"

"Wounded?"

"In the head. Nothing serious, but it put me out of action for awhile. As I lay in the field hospital, Evangeline came."

"Evangeline?"

"The one I had waited for all of my life. She took care of me, and we pledged our eternal love for each other." Morgan stopped.

"And?"

"When I was better, everyone told me I had been delirious."

"Were you?"

"Yes. But I knew Evangeline was real. Perhaps not there, but somewhere. I knew eventually I would find her."

"Did you?"

"Yes. Genevieve."

Jake was skeptical.

"Let me tell you another story. Once when I was in a field hospital, recovering from shell shock, I had a dream. I was on a battlefield, and I was the only one left alive. Discarded weapons, shell holes, barbwire, bodies, . . . It was horrid. What I remember most is the big, fat, blue flies buzzing on the corpses.

A blinding light descended. It was an angel, exactly like the ones you see in picture books. He told me that I was about to have a great epiphany. I didn't even know what the word meant. He told me he had come to grant me peace."

Jake was speechless.

"He told me I had to renounce all worldly values. I'll never forget; those were his exact words. He said I had suffered too much. He wanted me to abandon love, hope, charity, and compassion. All moral human passions. Only in that would I know true peace. And he wanted me to disavow Evangeline. When I refused, he told me that for every passion I sustained, I would pay a terrible price. Then he was gone. Of course it was only a dream, or a hallucination."

Morgan stopped, and Jake wondered if that was all. "I don't understand."

"Remember, I said having gone through what I went through gives you something?"

"What?"

"Life. You know you've lived. Not like people around here." Morgan waved his hand, palm up. "When you've endured what I've endured, you feel alive. You've lived more in a few years than the average person will in a lifetime."

Morgan looked back toward the light of the entrance. "If you survive, you're alive like no one else is, not languishing in a fantasy world. Most people lead lives of drudgery: working, grubbing, struggling–not only against poverty and tedium–but against the harshness and finality of existence. Desperately seeking some mysterious afterlife. Perhaps contriving it. Then they die. At least I lived, once." He had a faraway look. "Even now I'm more alive than most."

"But those dreams and visions of yours. They don't sound like the inner workings of a realist. They sound like the impenetrable secrets of the mind."

"Afflictions. The mind's attempt to cope. And at the time they were solaces. But I eventually recovered, except for an occasional relapse. Don't you see? You, of all people, should know. You're a survivor, like me. Sure, you've had some problems, but at least you're experiencing life. That's what it's all about, Jake. Living, hard knocks and all. And we're stronger for it; those like you and me. We may have a hell of a time, but we're alive, and we live in the real world."

"I've got to ask, Morgan. One night, during a thunderstorm, I saw a soldier marching. Was that you?"

"We'd better dig," Morgan said.

"Yeah."

Jake hefted his pickaxe and swung, and a pile of coal slid down. The easy part. The grueling work would be the shoveling. He swung again, but this time he heard Morgan shout, and before he could pull back, the ceiling came down. It happened dreamlike, and Jake fell backward with coal and dirt covering him, starting with his legs, then his waist, then his chest. It kept falling, and he cried out.

Then it stopped, and Jake lay in the semidarkness, trying to breathe. Morgan's lantern was only a dim glow in the dust.

"Jake!" Morgan knelt and held his lantern directly over Jake's face. "You alright?" he coughed.

"Ohhh. I can't breathe," Jake gasped. "You've got to get some of this coal off me." The coal covered all but his face.

"I don't dare to start digging. The whole damn thing could come down. I'd better get help."

"No time," Jake whispered. "We'll have to take the chance. I can't . . ." He trailed off, and closed his eyes.

"Alright." Morgan began with the largest lumps of coal, heaving them aside, trying not to disturb the wooden beams. Clunk, clunk, clunk. He worked furiously for a few minutes.

"Hurry," Jake murmured.

Morgan stopped. "Jake, there's a big slab of coal across your chest. I can't lift it. There's only one way. I'm gonna haf'ta break it."

Jake opened his eyes. "Oh, shit," he mouthed as Morgan grabbed the pickaxe.

"Ready?" Morgan asked. He lifted the pick. "Now!"

"Thwack!" Jake felt his lungs decompress, and he gasped for air. "Auuuh, auuuh, auuugh!"

"Anything broken?"

"I dunno."

"Can you get your arms loose?"

Jake wiggled his arms free.

"This isn't going to be much fun either," Morgan said. "I'm gonna pull you out, fast, in case it starts coming down again."

"Wait till I get ahold of Pete Hawkins," Jake groaned; then he coughed, and black spittle ran down his chin.

"Give me your hands," Morgan said.

Jake held his arms above his head.

"Ready?"

"Yeah." Jake felt as though he were being pulled apart. Then he was being dragged, and he heard the crump of more coal falling. At last it was over, and he and Morgan lay exhausted.

"You alright?"

Jake sat up and felt himself. "I guess so. That was a near go." They peered at each other. The dust was thicker than ever, and only their eyes showed. "You look like an owl," Jake said.

"So do you. Whoo! Whoo!"

Jake started to laugh, then he remembered Pete. "Wait till I catch up with Pete Hawkins, I'll—"

"Possibly it wasn't his fault. Could'a been a rotten beam or something."

"Everything about him is rotten. I find him to be very disagreeable."

Morgan's lantern went out. "It's darker than the ace of spades in here."

They fell back against the mine wall and let the earth cool them. Funny, Jake pondered, he had already been indebted to Morgan for helping him maintain his mental equilibrium. Now this.

"Genevieve isn't going to believe this," Morgan said.

"Neither is Mable. Because I'm not gonna tell her." He coughed. "I thought I was a gone goose."

"When your number's up, it's up. That's what the Tommies used to say."

CHAPTER TWENTY-TWO

Jake and Lars Nordraak had grown apart. Not that they had really been together. Not close. But a larger distance had come as a result of Lars' obsession with politics, and when the year before he had been elected to the Montana House of Representatives, that was the last straw. Elected as a member of the Farm Labor Party. But the real distancing had come when Jake had suspected Lars' communist leanings. It wasn't an unlikely suspicion, as for several years previously Lars had been driving thirty miles north to Plainview to attend communist party rallies, and everybody in northeastern Montana knew that the election disguise of Farm Labor Party meant the American Communist Party.

Sure, times were tough, but how could anyone get caught up in such nonsense; the notion that if you pool all of a country's resources, stir them up, then divide them equally amongst the population, you get more out of the process than what you put in? Lars had had only a fourth-grade education, and he was the product of an alcoholic, abusive father who had drunk himself to death by the age of forty-eight. But Lars was smart enough, and even above average. How, then, could he get snared by the communist editor of a newspaper who worked his magic by converting farmers to induce other farmers to further the cause? The cause, under the cloak of desperate farmers fighting hard times, drought, high bank interest rates, . . . Or was Lars a real dyed-in-the-wool communist? Hard to tell, but Jake knew that if Lars lived long enough he would regret it all.

And how did Lars do it? Fall for all of the communist malarkey? He did it by dividing his perceptions into compartments. Everyone does it. Those who are clearheaded in most areas of life can be idiots in others. Consider those running around predicting the end of the world, or the ones basing their lives on the zodiac in the daily paper, or those worshiping some invisible god who is vain and demands constant praise, or . . . . Part of human frailty.

Jake and Lars stood in the barn looking down at Jake's milk cow.

"Looks like she's part Guernsey," Lars said.

"I dunno."

"Where'd yuh get 'er?"

"Milo Jasper. I think I got took."

"How long's she been down?"

"This is the third day."

"Huh."

They stepped back and sat on the wooden kegs that Jake used for milk stools.

"How was she before that?" Lars asked.

"Alright I guess. She's never been much of a complainer."

Lars glanced sideways and gave him a sour look. He had never had much of a sense of humor unless he was the one dishing it out.

"How was her milk?"

"Alright, the last I got, but that's been a while ago."

"Huh."

"Huh? That's your diagnosis? Huh. I thought you knew cows."

"Maybe it's distemper," Lars said. "We had a cat with distemper last year."

"I didn't know cows could get it. Only wild animals. And people."

"It might be rabies. We had a cat with that too. It ran all over—"

"Oh, for heaven's sake!"

Lars studied Jake warily, then he leaned back against a square support post and closed his eyes, and he was silent for a time.

"Cows are like people, Miller. You can never be sure what ails them, even if they tell you. I remember my old aunt Gina. She came down with something she said was the miseries, but she was always having the miseries, so nobody paid her much heed. Well, this time the miseries went on for weeks, but she wouldn't–or couldn't–describe what it felt like, and everybody got disgusted and decided it must have been all in her mind. It went on and on for months, and . . . ."

Lars prattled on, even though he was the last one in the community anybody would label as a blabbermouth.

"Then it got to the point where she couldn't get out of bed, so they hauled her to the doctor. Well, he listened to her heart, and lungs, and so on, and thumped on her, and bent her this way and that, and grilled her until she was in tears. Then he sent her home with a bedpan."

Lars opened his eyes, but said no more.

"Well? What happened to her?"

"Oh she died two months later, and the sawbones never did know what it was. Uncle Olav was sure getting tired of emptying that bedpan."

"Tired of . . . ? Oh my word!" Jake shook his head and looked at Lars curiously.

"What?" Lars asked.

"Never mind."

They regarded the cow. Jake shooed away a horsefly.

"What am I going to do?" Jake asked.

"I'm afraid you're going to have a lot of canned meat this winter."

"Oh for goodness sake!"

They sat in silence again, for a long time.

At last, "For a state representative you sure don't know much," Jake growled, against his better judgment. Lars could be bad tempered, and Jake half expected him to blow his stack, but Lars just sat murmuring to himself for a moment.

"Miller, be careful, if you get any smarter you'll be a moron."

Jake flinched as if he had indeed been struck. He had always known that Lars could be mean spirited and vindictive, but this went beyond anything in all the time he had known him. Jake felt that if he were bigger, and tougher–a prizefighter or something–he would beat the tar out of Lars. But several others had tried that over the years and had come up short; most of them spitting teeth, or walking around all bent over for weeks. Not even Rudi Prinz wanted to get on Lars' bad side, not that he ever would.

Well, Jake considered, he could hire someone to take care of Lars, but that would be a bit drastic. Or he could poison Lars' cows, or some such. But naturally it wouldn't take Lars long to figure out any of that sort of thing.

Lars reached out and patted Jake on the shoulder. "Pay no attention to me, Jake, it's just that I have a lot on my mind. The legislature. You can't imagine the craziness that goes on there."

Lars had a kindness that was the opposite extreme of his abrasiveness.

"And that stuff up in Plainview?" Jake huffed.

Lars recoiled. "What stuff?"

"You know, all of that farm stuff."

"What would you know about that?" Lars asked warily.

The cow groaned and shifted position. She seemed worse than ever.

"They say you're a Pinko. And personally I'm starting to think you're taking on a red tinge."

Jake now had the upper hand, and he was going to play it for all he could get.

"Pink? Red? Who says that?"

"I dunno, a lot of people. You're getting a reputation."

Lars got up, walked to the big front door, and stood looking out. Then he turned. "The banks are charging terrible interest rates, and foreclosing on people, and the federal government is about as bad when it comes to looking out for the little guy. Big business is crushing people. There's no rain, farmers are going belly up and leaving, and some of those who stay are on the verge of starvation. An you sit there and—"

"I don't see anybody starving."

The cow moaned.

"You're nitpicking. Times are tough, Miller, and you sit there and take it, like a cow. Oh, you moo once in a while, and your friends moo back, but—"

"Now hold on Mr. Nordraak!"

"No offense. I'm just saying that if we don't stick up for ourselves, who will?"

The cow moaned again, weaker than before.

Jake looked past Lars, out the door, at the nothingness. "What can we do? And anyway, if you're pink, what kind of answer is that? I've read some of Lenin's Bolshevik stuff, and the Reds call for the overthrow of government. Is that what you want?

"No, but we have to do something. It's more of a farm movement—"

"Farm movement, farm schmovement. Lars, communism is either or. There's no half way. It's like poker, either you're in or you're out."

Jake raised the bet. He was playing his hand for all it was worth.

"You don't understand," Lars started. "If we can get the attention of the—"

Jake held up his hand. "Stop. Now I'm going to give you some advice, and you'd better listen. Think twice. You'll live to regret it."

"Some advice, coming from you."

"Be that as it may, whatever I am I'm not stupid. And what you're doing is just plain stupid. God almighty Lars, you're my friend, and all I'm doing is trying to save you from ruin. You could be charged with sedition, and sent to prison."

Lars walked over to the cow and looked down.

"What does Caroline think of all this?" Jake asked.

Lars nudged the cow with his foot. "She thinks you should put her out of her misery. The cow, I mean. As for me, she thinks I'm nothing more than a toady for the higher ups."

CHAPTER TWENTY-THREE

Work. Backbreaking work. Jake knew it was one of his few roads to salvation. Salvation not in the religious sense, but earthly salvation. Work, and living neither in the past, nor in the future. Accepting the present. The Buddhist *thus* of life and the universe; trying to live the right way.

Clunk . . . clunk . . . clunk, one rock after another onto the stoneboat, then get on the tractor and move to the next hill and start again. Clunk . . . clunk . . . clunk.

Cars passed a quarter of a mile away, just out of waving range. Clunk. Mable hadn't been feeling well, but how could one know? Dr. Raulsten had said it was all in her head . . . .

Clunk. But no thinking. Only work. Clunk. Mercy, the heat. Jake spat, and the glob of phlegm hit the dry dirt, rolled, and disappeared. Clunk. Mable's religious faith sustained her, but he and Mable had an understanding: she would not proselytize him, and he would not abase her for her beliefs.

Clunk. A whitetail deer leaped from a thicket of weeds in a dry slough and bounded away. It stopped on a far hill and looked back, apparently satisfied that Jake wasn't following. A meadowlark on a nearby rock warbled its summer song of hope. Clunk. Jake felt he was losing control.

"Please, sit down Jake." Pastor Martin indicated the chair in front of his desk. He was emaciated, with a rough, smallpox face. His fine, white hair floated in all directions, and he had the sickly-sweet smell of an old man.

Jake sat looking at the religious artifacts and icons on the walls of the church office. A two-foot-high wooden cross; a framed Bible verse; the obligatory portrayals of Biblical characters, both Old and New Testament, ... Behind the pastor, a large bookcase, shoulder high, running the length of the wall. And through the open window the breeze stirred a bouquet of fresh violets on the pastor's desk.

"I want to thank you for coming," Pastor Martin said.

"My mother sent me."

"Mother. Yes, mother's love. Indeed." He put his elbows on the desk, and folded his hands. He closed his eyes, and lowered his

head. Jake thought he was praying, but perchance he was just thinking. After several minutes Pastor Martin took a deep breath, and looked up.

"I feel the utmost compassion for your mother," he said softly, "but lately I have been more worried about you. I never see you on Sunday."

Jake felt his face redden, and he tried to find the right words. He chose truth. "I have no faith."

Pastor remained still for a minute, then he shuddered. "Have you ever had faith?"

"No."

Jake felt the heat of Pastor Martin's searing eyes.

"Never?"

"No." Jake waited, but apparently Pastor Martin expected more. "I don't mean to offend you."

Pastor Martin's left cheek began to twitch. "I'd like to hear." He rubbed his cheek, and the twitching stopped.

"Even as a small child, none of this," Jake waved his hand, "made any sense. None of it. I'm sorry, I didn't believe a word of it, and I still don't. To me, it's mere mythology. Nothing more." He paused to judge the effect, but Pastor Martin only frowned. "Isn't that what faith is?" Jake continued. "You either believe, or you don't?"

"It isn't that simple."

"To me it is." A bumblebee flew in through the window, circled the violets, and flew back out.

The pastor's cheek began to twitch again, and a film of sweat welled up on his forehead. "So. A heathen."

"I—"

"You have joined the legions of the eternally damned." His face had turned to a shade of magenta.

"You can't intimidate me," Jake shrieked. He stood to leave. "For centuries religious leaders–priests, prophets, pastors, abbots, and other malignant insensates, whatever they decide to call themselves–have intimidated and enslaved humanity with their superstitions. But no more. And certainly not me. You and demagogues like you have no power over me. This isn't the Middle Ages, where you can force piety on people."

"Out!" Pastor Martin jumped up and seized his cane. He came around the end of the desk. "Blasphemy! Blasphemy, here in *this holy place!" He raised the cane. It had a carved ivory grip, and the bottom third appeared to be of solid brass. "Out! I won't listen to this! Out!"*

Clunk. Backbreaking work. Jake stopped picking and got on the tractor. He sat for a moment, head bowed, shoulders sagging, with the sun beating down on the back of his neck. He wanted nothing to do with theism–except maybe Buddhism, and that was more of a philosophy than a religion–but damn, the guilt. It wasn't easy being an atheist-realist.

CHAPTER TWENTY-FOUR

Minerva Lundberg had been unwell from the fifth month, and Dr. Raulsten had called Mable to assist with the delivery. Jake waited in the shade of the barn with Minerva's husband, Sven. Mable had chased them off the porch.

"I hear Jasper Cornwall got a new car," Jake said. "Ford Model A coupe. Where he gets his money is anybody's guess."

Sven sat holding his egg-shaped head in both hands, staring at the house. He wasn't to be distracted, but Jake kept on.

"First thing he did was run into his chicken coop. Didn't hurt the car, but raised hob with the coop. Killed three chickens. Guess just before he hit, he hollered whoa! Ha, ha, ha! Wish I could'a seen that. Whoa Nellie!"

Sven seemed not to hear. Still, he was stoic enough. The only time he really lost his nerve was when Minerva was having her mental disorders, like when she had dug for diamonds. But she had been good lately.

"Spent the next three days rebuilding the coop, haw, haw, haw! Carrie was sore as hell. Didn't want a new car in the first place, heh, heh. Said they were fortunate it was just a few chickens. Told him he was lucky he hadn't killed himself, and her too. Ha, ha! And he ran through a barbwire fence the day after he got the coop rebuilt. Har, har. If anyone ever calls him a moron, he should take it as a compliment!"

Sven smiled faintly. Jake pulled a stalk of grass and started picking his teeth. They listened to the wind. The sky was cloudless, and it was warm even in the shade. Jake had to keep talking.

"Randall Norris hit his thumb with a hammer yesterday. Bloody mess. Doc doped him up with laudanum and fixed him the best he could. Said he wouldn't be able to bend it anymore. Asked him if he hurt the anvil. Haw, haw, haw."

Sven stared dumbly at the house again.

"Randall was pretty woozy from the laudanum, but the next day his thumb swelled up to the size of a carrot, and hurt like hell. Same color as a carrot too. Said he'd like to put Doc's you-know-what on the anvil. No sense of humor."

A dozen crows flew over, cawing, intent on something. Funny about crows, Jake considered. Always so solemn. Always preoccupied.

"Maybe I should check," Sven suggested.

"Naw, I don't think so. Doc's kinda grumpy today. They'll let you know. Did you hear about Goofy Grimswold? Walter?"

"No."

"He's building an ark. Says there's going to be another big flood. Can you imagine? Poor guy."

"Huh."

Jake ran out of gossip, and they sat in silence.

A car turned in. Lars and Caroline Nordraak. Jake and Sven met them in the yard.

"We've come to see the new baby," Caroline smiled.

"Too soon," Sven murmured.

"Go on in," Jake told her. "Maybe they can use some help."

Caroline hurried away, and Jake led Lars and Sven back to the barn.

"I've seen 'em go on for days," Jake consoled. "Let's have a nip of that special stuff you keep."

They found Sven's bottle under the hay in the manger. They each had a drink–even Lars–then Sven had another. After Sven's third, Lars put the cap back on the bottle and put it away, and they went back outside and sat down. The wind had subsided. Sven's mangy dog–Topper–came and licked Sven's face, then he went to the house and curled up on the porch in front of the door. Topper looked worried. Maybe he sensed the worry in Sven. Or more than likely he looked normal and sensed nothing. He was, after all, a dog.

Lars began telling, yet again, about the fight he and Karl Springer had almost gotten into in The Palace. He had been teasing Karl about losing at poker, and Karl had taken after him with a pool cue. Lars grabbed a chair, and it was a standoff.

Jake stretched out in the grass and put his hat over his face to keep off the flies, and he pretended to nap. He tried to think about nothing, by using his imaginary white-gloved hand to wipe away all thought, but the images remained, swirling before him. Images of the past, and again he tried to wipe them away, only to have them reappear. He saw himself on a cliff, high on a mountain above the clouds. He was dressed in a white robe, and he had long, white hair.

In his right hand he held a bright, flaming sword. Behind him was a cave.

Something distressed him, and Jake was compelled to enter the cave. It was dark, and he felt his way. There was a light in the farthest recess, and he was drawn to it. Rounding a corner, Jake came upon Mable seated on a bright, crystal throne, clutching a glowing staff. All about lay flowers, and the walls were draped with lavender tapestries. To one side was a long table laden with food, and on the other side was a giant chest overflowing with treasure. Despite it all, Mable wept piteously. Jake understood there was no consolation.

Back outside on the cliff, Jake gazed heavenward, then down in fear at the impenetrable fog. A familiar green face emerged, leering. Jake stepped forward, and with a mighty stroke of his sword he severed the head from the body. Both parts sank, the head still smiling. Another specter rose from the mist, more horrible than the first. Again Jake struck, and as more figures loomed he fought furiously. Then, exhausted, he fell back in defeat. But no more came.

Rested, Jake stood, and all was calm. He looked heavenward again, sword raised, and for a time he stood in prayer. Then he heard Mable's heart-rending cry, and again he entered the cave.

Mable got up from the throne and moved toward the table. But, as she approached, the table disappeared. Dispirited, she floated in the direction of the treasure chest, and it also disappeared. Overcome, she returned to her throne, sobbing in frustration, and the table and the treasure both reappeared.

"Mable, take heart! We will prevail," Jake cried, but she didn't hear.

"It's a test of our will," he called. "Be strong!"

Still she did not hear.

Mable's sobbing continued. Jake took the hat from his face and sat up.

"I couldn't stop the bleeding . . . ," Dr. Raulsten trailed off. He was old and tired, and his face was pale from overwork.

Sven's face contorted and he leapt to his feet. "No!"

". . . never had anything like that before . . . ," Dr. Raulsten tried again.

Caroline stood with one arm around Mable. Sven worked his throat, trying to speak, but nothing came.

"The baby's alright," Dr. Raulsten said.

Sven collapsed. Dr. Raulsten stood rigidly.

"Sven!" Jake croaked. Sven lay with his eyes open, staring at the sky. Jake knelt and straightened him. He leaned forward until they were face to face. "Sven! Can you hear me?" There was no response.

Jake looked up at Dr. Raulsten. "What wrong with him?"

Dr. Raulsten shook his head. "Dunno." He walked away.

After Minerva's death, Sven sat alone in his barn for a week while Caroline and Mable took turns with the baby. When it was time, they brought Sven his daughter. Two weeks later Sven sold his farm and left.

CHAPTER TWENTY-FIVE

Painting the barn. Work. Both sustenance and palliative. On a fundamental level Jake found satisfaction in covering the ravages of time. Masking the sun-blistered south side, concealing the hail-chipped north, camouflaging the dirt-scoured west, ... Barns, like life's constructs, that can never be undone; only added to and covered over, or destroyed. That was why starting over in Montana had been so difficult.

Jake moved his ladder and climbed to the top again. The obvious strategy was to work on the south and west before the heat of the day, and in the shade of the north and east later on. Jake twisted and looked toward the garden where Mable was hoeing, then he gazed out over his dry wheat fields. Rain–the only topic of conversation–in churches, in bars, and over kitchen tables. Rain, rain, rain. Jake looked up, hoping, but the only clouds were small, white puffs, and staring at them for too long made him dizzy.

Then, as Jake stretched to reach a bare spot he had missed, it happened: a heat-driven gust of wind pushed him backward. "Oh, God, no!" He dropped his paint brush and grabbed for the eave, but missed. Just before he hit the ground, he heard Mable scream.

"Don't feel anything broken," Dr. Raulsten said. "Could be some bleeding inside though. Can't tell yet."

Jake kept his eyes closed.

"How did he fall that far and live; that's more the question," Dr. Raulsten muttered. He poked and prodded, then Jake felt the coolness of the stethoscope.

"Will he be alright?" Mable quavered.

"Dunno. I'll come back tomorrow. We should know by then. In the meantime, keep him still."

"He ain't goin' anywhere."

Jake recognized Karl Springer's voice.

"He got kicked in the head by a mule once," Mable said. "And then the lightning."

"Well, this isn't going to help any," Dr. Raulsten said. "Guy fell off a ladder the other day, up north of here. Joe Singleton."

"How is he?"

"Dead."

"Jake ain't gonna die, is he, Doc?" Karl asked.

Jake opened one eye just enough to peek without anyone noticing. Dr. Raulsten straightened and took off his stethoscope. Mable and Karl loomed at the foot of the bed. Curiously, auras emanated from them, like angelic glows; especially from Mable. Similarly, the room itself seemed to radiate energy.

Dr. Raulsten put his stethoscope into his bag and stepped back. He looked tired, but he was always tired. He didn't answer Karl.

"He don't look so good," Karl persisted.

Dr. Raulsten pulled his shirt sleeves down and adjusted his garters. "Springer, I'm glad it wasn't you," he growled through his mustache. "There'd have been nothing left but a grease spot."

Karl looked like he had been struck.

Dr. Raulsten's face reddened. "I . . . , why all I meant was—"

"I know what yuh meant," Karl said. He put on his derby hat and stomped out.

Jake closed his eye and remained still. He didn't think he could move anyway, because of the pain.

"Mable, I didn't mean that. It's just that I've been so busy lately, and I . . . , I don't know if I can keep it up."

"He'll get over it."

"Tell him I'm sorry. I'm better than that. Tell Karl I'm sorry."

"I will."

The next day Jake was better, and the auras were gone. A week later he got out of bed, but his head ached. Unfortunately, it seemed like every time he started to recuperate, something happened to his head. And he saw a change in himself: a change that apparently no one else could discern. He hoped it was only a temporary setback.

CHAPTER TWENTY-SIX

"Haw, haw, haw!" Ludvig Lindburger laughed, wiping tears from his eyes. Ludvig was big, dark, and mean looking; but he wasn't mean. He had a kind, almost childish disposition.

Randall Norris continued. "Unloaded his gun, put his hat on, went back to his car, and drove away. Didn't say a word." They were sitting around the cold, unlit stove in the grain elevator office. Randall chuckled. He was cockeyed, so that when he held his eyes level, his head was always tilted to one side. He had just told how Chester Sorrels had blasted his own duck decoys. "So mad he couldn't talk."

"Serves him right for shooting sitting ducks out of season," Jake said.

"Yeah," Randall said. "He and Wilfred still ain't speakin' to each other."

Wilfred Gross had stolen Chester's decoys and set them up the night before, then told Chester where the good hunting was.

As so often happened, Jake felt his attention drift. Just a dim, dusty room with a roll-top desk in one corner. Above the desk was a calendar with a picture of a movie actress lying on a couch with her white silk dress pulled above her knees. A huge walk-in safe took up the rest of the wall. Jake had never seen the safe door closed. In the corner opposite the desk was a shelf of wheat samples in canning jars, and a door beside the samples led to the unloading area. Cobwebs hung from the center of the ceiling.

"Ain't that right, Jake?" Ludvig said.

"Huh?"

"I said, it looks like rain."

"Oh, yeah." Actually, it didn't look like rain. Sunny and hot, and it hadn't rained significantly all summer.

"I heard Sam Skinner got a quarter of an inch the night before last," Randall said.

"That's what I heard," Ludvig said. "The crops don't look too bad, considering."

Jake brushed a fly from his nose, and he felt the bitter loneliness swell within him. The crops were all but dried up, yet here was Ludvig insisting that they didn't look bad. It was like living in Alice's Wonderland, where nothing—and no one—made any sense. An insane, lunatic place, where everyone was oblivious to reality. No. Worse than that. They recreated their own reality precisely the way they wanted it to be.

"It's gonna rain," Ludvig said. "I can feel it in my big toe. Every time there's a rain brewing, my toe aches."

That was too much even for Randall. "Haw! Big toe! But there might be something to it at that. Every time it rains my ass acts up the same way. And everyone knows that an ass is more accurate than a big toe! In fact, I challenge you to a rain-predicting contest. Your toe against my ass, and . . . ." Randall was just getting warmed up, and obviously Ludvig didn't know he was joking.

It brought to mind, for some strange reason, an argument Jake had heard long ago, between a realist and a nonrealist. The realist–the ass–wins every time, Jake opined. Unfortunately, in the long run the winner loses.

Jake's head still ached from his ladder accident. Mostly to stay busy, he broke another forty acres.

"Ka-whoom!"

Jake knew Mable hated it when he dynamited boulders. Not so much the danger, but that he enjoyed it so much. The gleam in his eye scared her, she said.

"Ka-boom!"

The funny part was, the blasting made his headaches go away. Better than any elixir.

Jake laid a stick of dynamite on top of a huge rock and attached an ample length of fuse, then he poured water on the ground, made mud, and packed it over the dynamite. He looked around for a place to hide, lit the fuse, and ran carefully, knowing that if he fell and hit his head or broke a leg, he could kiss himself goodbye. As he ran, a bizarre mental image came to him: that if he ever wanted to end it all, dynamite would be a good way. Kind of a mess to clean up though. Like Morgan Feeney's war friend in France–Jake Hermann–who had blown himself up with a Mills bomb.

Jake dived into a depression. He waited.

"Ka-wham!"

Rock chips rained down around him. He stood to size up the damage, and it was sufficient: the largest piece was smaller than a milk pail. Out of the corner of his eye he saw Mable in the window. She had more reason to worry about him than other women had to worry about their men, but she never complained. He did the best he could, and he would try harder.

Jake picked up his burlap bag full of dynamite and fuses, and plodded to the next boulder. Only three more, then he could start picking rocks again. He liked the blasting more than the picking. Rocks were the nemeses of the plains farmer, and they always would be.

The last rock. Jake packed mud over the dynamite and rolled out the fuse. The nearest hiding place was farther away than usual, but he could make it. A strange, self-pitying musing came to mind. So what if he did fall and get blown to bits? No big deal. But he immediately thought of Mable. She deserved better. She didn't understand him, but that wasn't her fault. She had stuck by him through everything, and she needed him. Perhaps now that he had begun to care about himself again, he could be strong for her.

"Ka-wham!"

Jake shook his head. Funny how much better dynamiting rocks made him feel. If only he could avoid blowing himself to Kingdom Come.

CHAPTER TWENTY-SEVEN

"It's the end of the world!" Mable cried.

Jake finished putting the horses and cows in the barn, and he ran toward the house where Mable waited on the porch.

They stared westward at the approaching storm. Jake had been uneasy all day, and so had his animals. The morning had been beautiful, but unusually heavy and humid, with a high, sultry haze.

"My garden," Mable cried.

"Forget your garden. To the root cellar!" The wind increased, and Jake looked around for tornadoes. A fat raindrop splatted on his forehead. "It's bad," he said.

They paused at the cellar door, mesmerized. Lightning flashed, dark clouds roiled low overhead, and the wind increased. Then Jake saw the white swath of hail.

Ka-boom! They shuddered as great sheets of lightning illuminated the sky. Shee-thumm! A cloud of steam rose from the ground near the barn. "Get in!" Jake shouted. He opened the trapdoor and followed Mable down.

"Make sure it's latched," Mable said. They moved to the back where it was dark, dank, and secure. "Which way was the hail moving?"

Jake tensed. He thought she hadn't noticed. "Don't know." He put his arm around her. The hail was moving toward them.

Kraaak! Lightning flashed through the cracks in the door, and the ground trembled.

"Hope that wasn't the house," Jake whispered.

He felt Mable stiffen, and he regretted having said it. He hadn't been doing well with her, and he decided to keep quiet. They sat on a large wooden crate and waited.

The storm reminded Jake of those back in Iowa, and of one in particular, when he was twelve years old. He had always been terrified of storms, and he had been caught in the open on his way home from fishing. As he ran through the fields, lightning played all around, and though he was in no way religious, he prayed. His hair felt as if it were vibrating, and he heard something sizzling, but he made it home safely. His prayer had been answered. But by the next morning he had again abjured religion.

Wind shook the trapdoor, and Mable tightened her grip on Jake's hand. A rivulet of rainwater ran down the steps. Jake flinched at another close hit. Thunderstorms conjured images of the Napoleonic wars: the flash and thunder of artillery, smoke, blood running on the ground, bodies strewn about, wounded horses screaming, ...

"Jake?" Mable shook him. "Jake, are you alright?"

"I'm fine."

"What's wrong?"

"I, uh, I was thinking about something."

"What?"

"War. Storms always remind me of war."

"War? You never told me that before. You weren't in the army. How curious."

"Not really. Cannons, smoke, rifle volleys—"

"Um. Well, I think the storm is letting up."

They listened.

"Let's wait a bit," Jake suggested.

Rain still pelted the door, but there had been no hail.

When it was safe, they went out. The house and the barn were undamaged.

In the morning the sun shone brightly between the scudding after-storm clouds, and the wind was cool and fresh. Jake checked his fields, then he went to town to see how others had fared. On the way he dropped Mable off at the Nordraak's. Lars and Caroline were also unscathed.

Jake went into The Palace.

"How are things up your way, Sparks?" Soren Utlander asked Jake, in reference to his lightning accident. Soren, standing at the bar, was shaped like a fifty-gallon oil drum.

"Sparks, eh? You've been talking to Karl Springer. God, I hope that doesn't catch on."

"What?" Soren couldn't hear very well.

"Never mind."

Now, because of prohibition, The Palace was a blind pig. Or, a not-so-blind pig. Not like the back rooms and secret door knocks in the bigger towns. A new guy named O'Malley owned it. It still looked like a bar, and smelled like one. Worst of all was the chewing tobacco in the spittoons. The only concession to prohibition was the sign above the mirror: *No Alcohol Allowed.* And there were no bottles visible.

"Crops came through, but not much rain," Jake said. "Lars Nordraak's alright too, and Karl Springer. You?"

O'Malley glared at Jake. For years–except in times of dire need–Jake had been drinking water, and O'Malley knew it.

"Same. Lot'a wind, not much rain." Soren's scaly skin gave him an unhealthy look.

"Hellova scare," Jake said. Now he didn't even drink water. Last spring Soren had told him he had seen a barkeep spit into Jake's water glass as he was filling it.

Others gathered around, and they had the same stories about the storm. Jake caught some of them glancing nervously past the dark end of the bar to where Otto Ostberg sat at a table. Otto was drinking.

"He get hailed?" Jake whispered.

They nodded. "Bad," Sam Skinner muttered. "Everything. Wiped 'im out."

"Them's the hazards," Soren said.

Otto ordered another malt, and they tried not to see him pull a bottle of tickle-brain from his boot top and pour a goodly dose into his mug. He looked old, and tired, and gray. He was only thirty-five.

"Poor devil," Soren murmured. "But without any more rain than that, what does it matter?"

No one moved. There was no more to say.

That night Otto tried to hang himself in his barn, but he was too drunk, and his wife cut him down. He couldn't talk for weeks.

While Otto Ostberg lay in bed recovering from his self-imposed quinsy–but mostly recovering spiritually–those who had not been hailed continued to pray for rain.

———

Jake turned his car in to Morgan's place. He felt that he had much in common with Morgan, but he hoped Morgan wouldn't start reciting war poetry again. He had told Jake that he knew Siegfried Sassoon's anti-war poem, *Aftermath*, by heart. "Look up, look down," and so on. He said he had had enough sense not to admit to poetry, except to his wife, Genevieve, and to a few friends. And he had confided to Jake that he knew what horrors the secular soul was forced to endure. That he, as in the poem, would never forget. Sometimes Jake suspected that he didn't want to forget.

Jake got out of his car, and Morgan emerged onto the front porch. Fine, powdery-gray dust whisped low over the yard, and a cow mooed by the water tank in front of the barn.

"Mornin', Sparks," Morgan greeted.

Morgan didn't look good. That was the way with him: either good or bad. No in-between. But he still possessed his intense, natural dignity.

"Huh." Jake wiped his face and the back of his neck with his bare hand, and started toward the porch. But Morgan met him in the yard.

"Let's go down here and sit in the shade." He put his hand on Jake's shoulder and turned him toward the barn. "Genevieve's on the warpath," he whispered. As they walked, grasshoppers flew up in front of them.

"What happened?"

"Little too much firewater last night."

"You don't drink. Not seriously."

"Well I did last night. Got lit up like a store window. Have I got a head."

Only a big head. Usually when Morgan looked bad it was the other kind of head, and he'd start rambling on incomprehensibly about the war.

Jake lowered himself into the soft grass in the shade of the north side of the barn. The only soft, green grass on the farm. Morgan sat beside him and closed his eyes, and they both slumped against the barn wall, and were quiet.

Then, "Genevieve knows that I have to take the cure once in a while," Morgan said. "When I get bad, it helps. The trick is not to do it too often. That's why she's on me. She worries that I won't stop."

"You always do."

"Sure, but it would be easy not to." Morgan felt the back of his scalp where he had been wounded. "Sometimes I think I should just give up."

"You've got to keep going."

"I know. But you can't explain it to someone who wasn't there. You simply can't, Jake. How can someone like you know what it's like to lose every friend he had; blown to bits, gassed, or gut-shot? Dying like dogs. How do you explain what it's like sitting in a hospital with people looking at you like you're mad, and the harder you try, the worse it gets? How do you tell someone what it feels like to walk down the street knowing everybody thinks you're balmy? And it's the same old thing: the harder you try, the worse it gets. And you wanna know the worst? It's that while you were over there getting the hell blown out of yourself, everyone back here was going on with their lives like nothing was happening. Then after you get the crap beat out of you, you come back, and this is what you get. That's the worst of it. You want people to have to go through what you went through, so they'll understand. But you don't really, because no one should have to endure what I've endured. So you go on, living day to day, not caring whether the next day comes or not."

"I didn't know it was that bad. Now, I mean."

Morgan sagged. "Well I guess it isn't, usually. But when it is, it seems like it's always been bad, and always will be."

"Is there anything I can do?" Jake asked. He had come to Morgan for help, and here Morgan was in worse shape than he was. The cow by the windmill mooed again.

"No."

They watched the last of the morning clouds scud away to the east.

Jake knew he shouldn't, but he had to try. "Morgan, I know this isn't a good time, but it always seems like we're in the same boat, and—"

Morgan opened his eyes and scrutinized Jake.

Jake went on. "It's Mable. I think she's sick. In her head. In other ways too. Brainsick, and I don't know what to do. I'm at wit's end. The pity of it is, she took care of me, and now I can't take care of her when she needs me. I just . . . And then there's the other."

"Other?"

"From my past. I'm afraid they'll catch up to me someday."

Morgan held up his hand to silence Jake, and a bit of the old madness flashed in his eyes. "We aren't in the same boat, Jake. I used to think we were, but we aren't. We're both balmy, and we can't even take care of ourselves. But you don't know my demons, and I don't know yours. And even if I did, I couldn't help. My reserve of charity is low, like the water in my well. That old cow will just have to wait until the water level rises. Trouble is, my charity level will never rise. Shit, Jake, I don't even have enough for me and Genevieve, let alone you. You're barking up the wrong tree."

"At least there's usually plenty of wind for the windmill," Jake tried to joke.

"Don't you see? I can help you fix fence, or dig rocks, and things like that, but I can't help what ails you inside. Dammit, Jake, you ought to know by now that when we're born, we're born into family and friends, but when we get older, we're on our own, and when we die, we die alone. I don't care if you're on your deathbed with wife and kids and the local preacher and everyone else gathered around, when your time comes, you leave them behind. They can't help." Morgan slumped back and closed his eyes again.

Rejected and defeated, Jake sat unable to move.

In a low, terrible voice, Morgan spoke again. "And when you die, nobody's gonna be up there waiting." He pointed at the sky, without opening his eyes. "When you die, that's it."

The cow mooed again.

"I can put the rod in myself," Lars said.

"You sure?" Jake asked. He had helped Lars put new pipe in his well.

"Yeah, you go on. You've probably got things to do." Lars leaned one leather-gloved hand against the galvanized frame of the windmill tower. His face had become creased and old looking, and he was sweating.

"So, what do you think?" Jake asked. While they worked, he had presented his problems to Lars, much the same as he had to Morgan. But he could tell from Lars' indifference that his appeal had been futile, like he had been speaking some language that Lars didn't know.

"About what? Oh, Mable, and how you don't feel right, and all that? You gotta try to pull yourself together. You think you're the only one with problems? Last week the Simms baby got diphtheria and almost died, and just the other day Randall Norris' bull did die. Life goes on, and bawlin' about it doesn't help."

"I suppose not."

"I hope my well isn't going dry," Lars said.

———————

The summer was agony for Jake and Mable. They thought about leaving–starting over somewhere else–but Jake knew that if they couldn't live in northeastern Montana, they couldn't live anywhere. Leastwise that's what he told Mable, but the real reason was that he just didn't know what else to do. He had considered offing himself, but without him Mable would perish. So they stayed.

CHAPTER TWENTY-EIGHT

As the summer of glorious tribulation unfolded, farmers hung on. Heat, drought, grasshoppers, . . . , all manner of privation . . . . The phantasms that haunted Jake most were, still, the specters of guilt. Yet, was it not guilt born of weakness; a failing for which he could not be held morally responsible? At the low ebb, when there was no deeper despondency, Jake found strength in the conviction that life could only get better. Thus he again found the resilience to face life.

With his resurgence of strength, Jake again resolved to strive for whatever normalcy he could attain, but before he could begin anew, there was another trial.

"What is it, Jake?" Mable asked. She stood anxiously by the bed.

"Oh, my head. I don't know. I thought if I waited it would pass."

Mable felt his forehead. "You're warm. Let me take off one of these blankets."

Jake felt ill all that day, and the next. By the third day he couldn't get out of bed. That afternoon Caroline and Lars came. "He's warm, and he won't eat anything," Jake heard Mable say from the porch.

"Let's take a look," Caroline offered. As they approached the bed, she glanced at Lars.

Jake knew how bad he appeared–wan and shrunken–and he knew how bad he smelled, too.

"Time to get up, Jake," Lars boomed, but Caroline shook her head.

Jake managed to acknowledge them with a murmur. Caroline felt his face.

"How are you feeling?"

"Uhhh. Alright." He squeezed his eyes shut.

Caroline withdrew her hand and they moved to the kitchen end of the house. "Lars, you'd better get Doc Klause," Caroline said. "I think it's typhoid fever." The screen door slammed.

Jake guessed from the way he felt that he would be lucky to last a few more days.

Hours later, Lars returned. "He can't come right away."

"Can't come?" Caroline all but shouted.

Jake rolled his head on the pillow and blinked to clear his eyes. Lars looked like a mirage.

"He's working on a boy who stepped on a rusty nail. He cut the boy's foot open with a scalpel, and pus squirted all over. You should'a heard that kid holler! I had to help hold him down, and it was all we could do to—"

"Alright!" Caroline said. "When can he come?"

"Tomorrow."

"Tomorrow!" Caroline's face turned livid, and her neck bulged. "That's outrageous! Why, Jake could be . . . ."

Jake managed to turn away from them, toward the wall. The yellow roses on the wallpaper made him even sicker, but he hadn't the strength to roll back, so he put his hand to his eyelids and closed them. All he wanted was for everyone to go away.

"Tomorrow?" Mable sobbed. "Didn't you tell him how bad Jake is, and—?"

"He said there was nothing, er, that one more day wouldn't make any difference. Anyway, maybe it isn't typhoid."

Jake was aware of short, heavy Dr. Klause hovering over him. Dr. Klause had taken over for Dr. Raulsten.

"He isn't good," Lars said.

"Is that so? Well, Dr. Nordraak, since you're so sure it's typhoid fever, you ought to know there isn't a damn thing I can do about it."

Dr. Klause–muscular and shaped like a beer barrel–looked more like a blacksmith than a doctor. Lars glared at him.

"What kind of well do they have?" Dr. Klause asked, ignoring Lars' irritation. "How deep?"

"Thirty feet. I helped him—"

"Where is it?"

"Down by the barn. It's—"

"Aha! Quit drinking the water. Keep him cool, and give him plenty of liquids. I'll be out in the morning."

The next day Dr. Klause returned, but he didn't stay long. The fever persisted, and the following day it was worse.

Jake writhed. He didn't know how long the pain had been with him–deep in his gut–but it seemed like an eternity. He felt a presence, and above him floated a figure in a black robe. It raised one hand, and the pain was more intense. Jake tried to speak, but he couldn't. Nor could he open his eyes, though he was able to see.

The Fatidic Light, though in the form of a black-robed being, was somehow radiant, and as it descended an incomparable dread enveloped Jake. Again Jake tried to speak, and again he was unable. Nonetheless, his questions were answered.

"Trust in me, for I will be with you always."

Trust? Jake knew that was a crock of warm bull piss; nevertheless he tried to ask if Mable would be alone.

There was no answer. The figure ascended and faded.

Again Dr. Klause came, and Lars and Caroline were there.

"Typical," Dr. Klause muttered. He pulled down Jake's nightshirt.

Jake could see only dimly.

"He's not worse is he?" Mable pleaded.

"No, but he's not better either."

Jake's eyes cleared, and he saw a wave of self-reproach come over Dr. Klause for the harshness in his voice, and for his jaded heart. And somehow Jake understood what Dr. Klause was feeling: that he should never have become a doctor. That it was too demanding. Dr. Klause moved beside Mable and put his arm around her.

"No, it's no worse. That's a good sign. I'll come back Wednesday."

Mable kept vigil as Jake alternated between lucidity and delirium. He hovered near death, and for a time he preferred death.

"Why do you struggle so?"

Jake could not answer.

"Have I not sustained you?"

The Light receded.

"Remember, I will be with you always."

Jake felt Mable washing him with cool water. He tried to make her stop; to let him drift away.

"There, Jake, it's only me," Mable soothed.

She finished washing him, and covered him with a clean sheet. After throwing out the water, she resumed her watch. She sat by the bed, humming hymns and knitting.

By the second week Jake's lucid moments were more frequent, and he could see encouragement in Dr. Klause's demeanor. Now Jake fought for life, and on the morning his temperature returned to normal, he knew that–if given another chance–he would quit procrastinating and get to work on his Unified Theory of Life. To hell with The Fatidic Light.

CHAPTER TWENTY-NINE

After Jake's illness he came alive with a new intensity. The first thing he did was confide in Lars his intention to develop his Unified Theory of Life.

"Unified theory of what?" Lars asked.

Jake had had a new well dug, farther from the barn, and he and Lars had moved the windmill tower, and they were putting in the pipe. Lars put down his wrenches and wiped his hands on his overalls. Jake sat on an upended bucket. There was the smell of burnt grass in the air, but they could see no smoke.

"Unified Theory of Life," Jake repeated. "I'm like a lot of people. I'm not religious, so I don't get answers there. Still, I believe I have a philosophy of life, but if you put my feet to the fire and make me tell what it is, I can't. That's because most of us have a few ambiguous ideas, but when somebody calls us on it–put up or shut up–there's nothing there. Most people's notions of life are just that: notions. Oh, sure, some pretend to have secret, profound beliefs, and I suppose they really think they do, but usually it's just hot air. When you ask them to explain, they get evasive and incomprehensible. And that's when you know they're nothing but gasbags."

Lars sat in the grass and looked quizzically at Jake. Then he smiled.

Jake went on. "I was always going to quit equivocating and set down what I believe, in black and white. Then, when I was sick, I knew the time had come. I may not have another chance."

"Unified Theory of Life?" Lars giggled.

"Yes."

"Haw, haw, haw! Unified Theory of bullshit! Haw, haw, haw!" Lars took out his handkerchief and dabbed the tears from his eyes.

Jake bristled. When he had told Lars of The Light, Lars had gotten furious. Now this.

"Go ahead and laugh."

"Thanks. I will. Haw, haw, haw! Unified Theory of Life! Ho!"

Jake sat sullenly, waiting for Lars to wind down. He wished he had never told him. Finally Lars stopped.

"If you know so darn much, what do you believe in?" Jake asked.

"Whaddya mean?"

"I've noticed you and Caroline don't exactly wear out the front pew in church. So what? What do you believe in? And none of that mysterious 'I've got my own religion' crap either. That's just whiffling."

"I dunno. It could be there's something after we die."

"That's it?" Jake asked derisively.

"Yeah. That's it, because nobody knows, including you. Anybody who claims to know is full of applesauce."

"Well even if a guy never knows, that shouldn't keep him from trying."

"Yes it should. It's a big waste of time."

Jake stared abstractedly past Lars, at the beauty of the setting sun. He saw he was getting nowhere.

―――――――

Jake also began working on an anti-gravity machine. Against his better judgment, he again confided in Lars.

". . . so the worm gear drives this, and it turns . . . ."

He had brought Lars out to his workshop, where he was showing him the drawings he had sketched. All about them lay pasteboard boxes full of mysterious components.

". . . then the pendulum provides momentum for the—"

"But I don't see how that's going to—" Lars broke in, but Jake interrupted.

"Wait. I'll get to that. It's all in the gyroscopes. They're electric, and they're attached to eccentric wheels. When the wheel on each gyroscope gets to its apex, its axis shifts as it comes down. Then, at the lowest point, the axis shifts again, and it starts over. Each wheel is ninety degrees out of phase with the others, so there is always an upward thrust. For every reaction there is an equal and opposite reaction. I've had this in the back of my mind for years, but now's the time to . . . ."

Lars' mouth hung open.

"The only thing I'm going to have trouble finding, or making, are the gyroscopes," Jake said. "But the rest will be easy. Can you imagine, a drive that will make airplanes obsolete? The batteries will be heavy, and I won't know how that'll work out until I get the first model built. But . . . ."

A large, yellow butterfly fluttered in and landed on the drawings, and Jake gently brushed it away. It flitted toward Lars, who clapped it between his hands, crushing it.

CHAPTER THIRTY

Charity Lutheran Church was three miles west of town, on the edge of a wheat field. Warm air wafted through the windows, and birds sang until organ music drowned them out. Babies cried along with the songs and people coughed, murmured, and fanned themselves. Pastor Vilander came out of the chancel and arranged his notes on the pulpit, then he disappeared.

Jake had let Mable inveigle him into coming. He felt he owed it to her, though he could never understand how people assume they can change someone's beliefs through moral intimidation and the laying of guilt. Making someone feel cheap. Harping and carping. Not that Mable was so bad that way, but the essence of intimidation and guilt was always there. She meant well, but she was too limited to know that it wouldn't work. Couldn't work.

Jake's shirt was soaked beneath his suit coat, and everyone else looked as wretched as he felt. And from what he had heard about Pastor Vilander, the flock would be even hotter after the sermon. Good, stodgy farmers, most of them. Seemed like they always clung to the old ways.

Mable appeared satisfied. Evidently her main goal had been getting him there, and she assumed any spiritual gains on his part were now out of her hands. She sat nodding and smiling at friends and acquaintances, while Jake cleaved to his philosophy of verisimilitude. Resigned to an hour of misery, Jake stared at the icon behind the altar.

Right after they were married Jake had tried to talk religion with Mable, but she had been uninterested, and she remained so. For her it was enough to go to church–and to try to get him to go–and for him it was enough to avoid going. On a higher level, while Jake recognized Mable's limitations, he knew his own intelligence. And because he had known it for so long, it was no special conceit.

Across the aisle, old Luke Griggs began to snore. Usually he waited for the sermon. His wife, Agnes, woke him by pinching his nose shut while holding her hand over his mouth. There were guffaws and snickers.

Jake squirmed. The germ of Mable's religious inclination had begun about a week after they were married. He guessed it had been brought on by her hard life before they had met.

Luke Griggs started to snore again. He must have had a long bout with Demon Rum the night before, for which he was in need of repentance.

Jake squirmed again. Someone behind him didn't smell very good. He turned and looked. Old Inez Stolz, who had always been allergic to water. A not-very-refreshing effluvium radiated from her, but mercifully, a puff of fresh, warm air came through the window.

Even Mable was beginning to suffer. Jake reached over and took her hand. The flies were getting bad, but closing the windows would have been suicide. Fortunately the flies preferred Inez.

Jake glanced around at the assemblage of the faithful. Most, he guessed, were like Mable, basically normal people. And most–even the dullest–nurtured high opinions of their native intelligence. There are myriad self deceptions in life. How, then, Jake wondered, did he know his opinion of himself wasn't a self deception? He had pondered that before, and it had always come out the same: he just knew, and the probability that others held exaggerated views of their potential was irrelevant. There was some guilt, however, for a mental habit he had fallen into: that of regarding others on a continuum, from the most intelligent down to the mental deficient whose cerebral facilities are comparable to those of higher animals. Jake was always aware of that continuum, and therein lay the validity of his intellectual acumen. But the baseline of Jake's pomposity was the fact that everybody else just seemed to be so god-damned dumb. Abject mental pygmies.

Pastor Vilander came out again. He was tall, thin, and big boned. He reminded Jake of John Brown, the abolitionist. The music stopped, and the service began.

". . . all of you here this fine morning, blessed in the Lord's presence, partaking of his . . . ."

Jake settled in.

". . . the grace of our Father, ..."

Mable nudged him, and they stood for the first hymn. Jake focused on the hymnal, but he didn't sing. He wasn't a good singer, and he was thinking. Something about the boy in front of him took him back to his own childhood. It had not been a happy time, but Jake was not the kind to feel sorry for himself. He had gotten that out of his system long ago: an alcoholic father, an unstable mother, the poverty and punishing work, ... Still, he had managed to finish school through the sixth grade. Any more had been out of the question, and college was the realm of rich people.

They sat down, and Pastor Vilander read from the scriptures. Jake looked out the window at the stunted wheat in the field across the road.

Another hymn, then it was time for the sermon. Pastor Vilander took to the pulpit, rearranged his notes, and gazed over the crowd, fixing every soul with a look of wrath and indignation. At the point of maximum discomfort, he began.

"I find it hard to imagine how anyone can yield to the bottle." He paused to let it soak in, so to speak. Jake relaxed. He was off the hook, but he noticed some of the drinkers twitching.

"How can anyone . . . ?"

Pastor Vilander started slowly and ominously.

". . . and let their families suffer the humiliation and despair of . . . ."

He was building.

". . . the depravity . . . ."

Jake tried not listen. He was on his own as far as redemption was concerned. Mable, Lars, Morgan, preachers, . . . , no one could help. Jake looked out the window, and he saw two crows flying northward. Odin's sacred ravens yet again? No, just two damn, dumb crows.

CHAPTER THIRTY-ONE

Jake and Lars stood looking at the huge, camel-colored tent in Lionel Murphy's pasture on the east edge of Charity.

"Too bad it's a temperance lecture," Lars said. "Even a medicine show would'a been better than this."

"Yeah."

Despite their disappointment, no doubt the fire and brimstone would be interesting. Neither Lars nor Jake drank–except in emergencies–but Lars always took some satisfaction in the misery of those who did. A manifestation of his callous side.

"Emma's been trying to get Karl to go," Jake said.

"He doesn't drink. Much."

"Yeah, but when he does—"

"Um," Lars agreed.

He had been around Karl a time or two when he was drinking. When Karl binged, his personality changed. And he had been drinking more lately.

"Last time he was on a bender it lasted for three days," Jake said. "Emma stayed with us. He's never hurt her, but she was afraid. You know how he gets."

"Um."

They watched the tent canvas ripple in the breeze. Behind the main tent were several smaller ones where the temperance people stayed. A number of local people were milling around.

"Speak of the devil," Lars said.

Karl came bounding toward them. "Lars! Jake! Guess what? I'm gonna be in the program! Me an' Philo Barnes." He took off his derby hat and wiped his brow with the sleeve of his white shirt.

"In the program?"

"Yeah. We was helpin' 'em put up the tent, an' afterward we was havin' a few drops with one a' the temperance people, an' he asked us if we'd like tuh help get the ball rolling."

"You were drinking with the temperance people?"

"Just one drink. Anyway, after they get everybody all worked up, they ask for drinkers tuh come forward and take the pledge. You know, go on the wagon. When he gives the signal, I go up and cry and carry on, and he sort'a blesses me or somethin', and I

-125-

repent and all that. Then he calls for more boozers tuh come up, and that's when Philo steps forward. He goes through the same thing. Primin' the pump. Gonna pay us each three dollars!"

Jake could smell whiskey on Karl's breath.

"Kinda crooked, isn't it?" Lars grumped.

"Hell no! They do it all the time. What's the difference how yuh save people? Nobody wants tuh be the first tuh be saved."

"You mean nobody wants to be saved?" Lars asked sarcastically.

"You were back having a drink with them?" Jake pressed.

"Well, yeah, but don't get the wrong idea. They ain't drinkers. They limit themselves. It's the people who can't control themselves that haf'ta worry. Say, keep this under your hat, will yuh? Could ruin everything."

By eight that evening a huge crowd had assembled in front of the main tent. Jake and Mable stood off to one side, near a gas lantern. Jake had not told her of Karl's complicity.

"My, look at all the people," Mable said.

The lantern was attracting millers and other insects.

One of the temperance people came outside. "Come on in, folks," he announced. "Show starts in a few minutes. Move to the front. Right this way."

Jake held Mable back. He saw Lars and Caroline and their thirteen-year-old son–Sexton–go in, and Karl and Emma, and Philo Barnes. Frog Barnes–squat with protruding eyes–was a bachelor, and he was an unrepentant drinker. Jake knew where Philo's three dollars would end up.

Jake steered Mable to the back row of benches. He couldn't wait to see the look on Emma's face. And Mable's.

The air was ripe with the smell of unwashed bodies, and Jake was glad he and Mable were near the entrance. At the front of the tent stood a low wooden platform, on which was a podium. A banner above read, *Demon Whiskey!* Near the podium was a wooden travel trunk with brass fittings. The temperance man who had invited everyone in was busy urging them to fill the front rows. Jake guessed there would be a money collection, after everyone was good and worked up.

Lars, near the front, turned and looked around. He saw Jake, and winked. Jake smiled back.

"My, it's hot," Mable said.

She fanned herself with her bonnet. Jake pulled out his watch and giggled to himself. Ten after eight. As he put his watch back, the other two temperance men entered and stepped onto the platform. One of them moved to the podium and began shuffling papers. He was tall and thin, with dark hair and a beak-like nose. The other–also tall and thin–positioned himself beside the trunk. He was pale, and his forehead was beaded with sweat. The speaker looked up and the crowd quieted, but just as everyone thought he would began, he stepped toward the other man and whispered something. They opened the trunk and peeked in, then the speaker moved back to the podium and shuffled his papers again. Playing it for all it's worth, Jake observed. He noticed Philo across the aisle, nervously twisting his cap.

The man with the beak nose put down his papers and stepped back three paces. As he did, there was a loud crash, and three ladies in long black dresses came through a side door. The first carried a set of cymbals, the second a drum, and the third a cornet. They circled the audience, playing something unrecognizable, then they marched up the aisle and onto the platform. The cymbal player and the drummer did their best to drown out the cornet player, a short, fat, elderly lady with a red face made redder by her exertions. When they had finished, they bowed to polite applause. To everyone's relief, the speaker stepped to the podium again, and from the look on his face, he was ready.

"Ladies and gentlemen, the Ladies of the Light Ensemble!"

Another smattering of applause.

"Thank you, thank you. And thank you ladies."

The three ladies sat down behind him. His assistant stayed by the trunk.

"First of all, I want to thank you for such a warm welcome. It's people like you throughout this fair land who make our mission worthwhile. As we were setting up our tent, I . . . ."

Jake settled back, knowing he was in for a long wait. He sneaked a glance at Philo, who was still twisting his cap. Philo obviously needed a drink. The man who had ushered everyone in sat behind Philo, in case he should bolt, Jake assumed. A good judge of character.

". . . and as we talked with some of you fine people today, we got the sense that all is not well. Some of you told of . . . ."

The speaker was starting slowly. Jake could tell by the deep resonance of his voice that he had much in reserve.

"When I asked that good lady how long it had been going on, she said as long as they had been married. Can you imagine? She has been suffering for years, and . . . ."

Jake was curious about the trunk.

"Lo! The Dark Angel of Ruin, hovering above us, ..."

Up front, Lars was squirming. Jake smiled. Lars was a man of little patience. Jake felt like squirming himself. It was suffocating, and the flies were bad. They weren't supposed to be out at night, but they were attracted to the light and the warmth inside the tent. And to the people. Jake wondered why they didn't congregate around those more odoriferous than he, but tonight they were indiscriminate. It would have been easy to make some philosophical connection between the flies and the audience–or between the millers that had been drawn to the lantern outside–but Jake decided that analogy would be unfair to the insects.

"How many times have you seen lives ruined? How many wives have suffered the untold . . . ?"

The man by the trunk stood impassively. Sweat ran down Karl's neck as he sat waiting for his part. Philo seemed to have calmed down.

"The first is the liver of a man who drank for fifty years."

The man by the trunk opened it and took out a huge jar.

"Pass it around. Look at it! Twice the size of a normal liver! Take a good look!"

Women shrank as the jar was passed in front of them.

"If you think that's bad, what do you suppose happens to the brain?"

Out came another large jar, with half of a brain floating inside.

"Notice the number of small cavities, the direct result of a lifetime of alcohol consumption. There, but for the grace of God, could be you, unless you . . . ."

Most of the audience passed the jar quickly, but some examined it. A lady fainted, and her husband carried her outside.

"In the name of the Almighty, I beseech those of you who are in the grip of Demon Whiskey to fight with all of your strength! Fight hard, for it is the fight of your life. If you will only . . . ."

He had a head of steam now, jumping and dancing about, waving his arms. The audience was spellbound.

"Who will be the first to step forward to take the pledge? Who?"

The speaker eyed Karl, who seemed frozen.

"There is no power great enough to hold the repentant! Who will be the first to renounce drink forever, and free himself from the grip of death? Who?"

He pierced Karl with his stare.

"Who has the courage?"

No one moved.

The speaker stepped up to Karl and leaned to look him directly in the face. "I said who!" he bellowed.

Suddenly Karl leaped to his feet and ran to speaker's platform.

"Ah, my friend. Are you caught in the clutches of evil? Does drink have a grip on you? Are you ready to be saved?"

Jake peeked at Emma and suppressed a giggle. She was sitting with her mouth open, and everyone could see the redness rising on the back of her neck. More of her neighbors were staring at her than at Karl.

"Is it time, brother?"

Karl had fallen to his knees, and he was crying and carrying on. The speaker put his hand on Karl's shoulder.

"Then repeat after me. I–whoever you are–do solemnly swear . . . ."

Karl played it perfectly, and when he was done, Philo came forward. Though he was not in Karl's league, he did a creditable job. Throughout, the Ladies of the Light Ensemble kept up a chorus of "Praise the Lord!," "Amen!," and "Hallelujah!"

Karl and Philo had earned their three dollars. Soon there was a small group in front of the stand; each man waiting impatiently to swear off. Something to his left caught Jake's eye. It was the usher, with a silver collection plate.

"No need to push, men, we'll get you all in. Steady now."

Karl made his way back to his seat, but Emma was gone.

Jake wanted a drink.

———————

Jake had been on his rolled-oat diet for almost two weeks, and he hurried toward the outhouse. He saw Mable watching him through the kitchen window. She said she thought it had affected his mind as well as his innards.

Jake got there in the nick of time. No matter how he tried, he always got caught as far from the outhouse as possible. Anywhere out of sight would do in a pinch, but of course there was no toilet paper, and the grass was dry and scratchy. Anyway, only two days and he could get back to normal. He didn't know if he could do the diet four times a year though, like the magazine article said. He always felt better, but four times a year was too much. Possibly twice a year, but not four times.

Jake peeked through a crack in the door and saw Mable shake her head. She had pleaded with him not to tell anyone. If Lars found out, they could just as well put it in the newspaper. Lars had a perverse streak. But–Mable had guessed–the end result would be the same regardless of who found out. She had smiled at her accidental choice of words *end result*. Anyway, Jake knew her too well, and it was easy to see what she was up to. Hoping he would suffer enough to where he would give up his diet.

Jake settled in on his throne. Much of his best thinking was done there, oats or no oats. The outhouse was where he had decided that whatever travails he and Mable had endured, he would not give up. Perhaps he was not destined to be totally happy, but he would settle for whatever small measure of contentment he could attain. For him life was not happiness, but the absence of suffering. And if he could make Mable happy, that would be enough, though he conceded that his oat diet wasn't making her very happy.

A hornet flew in through the quarter-moon hole in the door. Jake shooed it out with his hat. He had been bitten by a hornet once, when he was a child. He could still feel it on the back of his neck. His mother said he had almost died.

Jake knew Mable thought he was balmy at times, but he couldn't help that. He loved her dearly, but she had her intellectual limitations. That was what made him so lonely: no one to talk to, now that Morgan had pushed him away. The best he could come up with was Lars. Lars was no clod-hopping nincompoop, but he was so prosaic; always talking about hogs, and cows, and farming, with no interest whatsoever in anything on a higher plane.

Jake's hornet bite when he was a child was still vivid in his memory. He had run to the house and collapsed in front of the kitchen door. He was unable to speak, and it wasn't until that evening that his parents and the doctor knew what had happened. It was worse for them than for him. He was in a dream world: a place he did not want to leave; a place he took to be Heaven. There were no angels or anything, and it was nothing like he had been led to believe, but he knew it was Heaven, and he knew there was a higher power. But, as always, when he regained his equilibrium he dismissed his divine perceptions as nothing more than metaphysical claptrap.

It was hot, and Jake cautiously opened the door a crack, looking for the hornet. Apparently it had gone away. He left the door partly open.

He and Lars had little similitude, yet neither of them had any inclination to carry on the futile search for the traditional more. But of this world, Lars and Caroline were not uninventive. They found their *more* in everyday life, by changing and rearranging things the way they wanted them to be. Building skycastles. Impossible optimists and obfuscators. Jake resented them for the way they were, while–paradoxically–wishing he could be like them, taking life as a phantasmal facade.

The hornet returned, and Jake gave up. He wiped, pulled up his bib overalls, and relinquished his domain. He would have to do something about the hornet. Where there was one, there were more, and one bite could kill him.

It was a bright, sunny day, the air was fresh and crisp, and the clouds–when there were any–had changed from early-summer blue to late-summer gray. And people quietly worried about their crops.

CHAPTER THIRTY-TWO

"Pretty strong medicine," Jake said.

They were sitting on Jake's front porch. Lars had come to enroll him as a member of the Workers Party.

"It's time for strong medicine. You know Garf Landon up in Plainview, don't you?"

"Sure. The one you've been hobnobbing with all this time."

Plainview was a sizeable town thirty-some miles north. Garf Landon had been a communist organizer for years.

"It's always the little guys doing the work, while the big guys get rich," Lars said. "Guys like you and me, working our hind ends off. If we get together, we'll have a voice. And that's what Garf's trying to do: get us all together. It's time for tough action, and . . . ."

Jake listened patiently. Once Lars got started, there was no choice.

". . . and Garf said we have to . . . ."

Jake concentrated on Lars' mouth.

"No reason why we should get poorer while the rich get richer. We're carrying them on our backs . . . ."

Lars' mouth was more interesting than what he was saying, the way it moved and formed the words. Lips together, then round, with his tongue flapping up and down inside. And he still couldn't say his J's right.

"It's time for those like you who have been riding the fence to take a stand, Jake. You can't keep letting the rest of us do the strong-arm work for you."

Jake didn't answer. He had read some of the material Lars had given him, and when it came to the forceful overthrow of the government, that was too much. And while Lars didn't go as far as to advocate violence for its own sake, there were some in the organization who did, and Lars would eventually have important decisions to make.

Lars started in again. He had good teeth, and Jake wished his teeth were as good. Never could afford to go to the dentist.

At last Lars talked himself out. Now it would be easier to say no. But what most struck Jake about the conversation was Lars' lack of insight. It had always been that way: on everyday things he was usually sensible–even if he was a hopeless optimist–but on a higher plane he was consistently inadequate. He was incapable of conceptualizing wholes; only parts. And–Jake had long ago observed–in addition to being a hopeless optimist, Lars possessed a unique something-for-nothing mentality, manifested in the belief that wholes could be greater than the sum of their parts. Jake wasn't thinking of simple constructs, like manufacturing an automobile, wherein it could be legitimately argued that the whole was indeed more valuable than the parts. It was a defect of perspective. Lars' overall logic was flawed, and his involvement in the communist movement was a good example. Throw the fruits of people's labor into a communal pot, stir things up, muddle and rarefy everything, and, *voila*, out comes more than went in! Lars didn't see that communism wasn't natural; that it stifles people's initiative, ambition, and creativity.

"I'll have to think it over, Lars." He didn't want to get into another row with Lars. He had tried to warn him about communism once, and that was enough. Lars would have to sink or swim on his own.

Lars' face fell.

After Lars left, Jake ruminated on their conversation to make sure he hadn't missed anything, but he knew he hadn't. He and Lars were philosophical opposites. No wonder they had grown apart.

The next day Jake felt he should be doing something, but as always there was nothing to do, and no money to do it with, so he sat on the porch, looking over the wheat field in front of the house. He could almost physically sense Mable behind him, inside. She hadn't been feeling well.

An eagle soared high above the ragged field, then it swooped down, looking for prey. Apparently there was none, because it flapped away, south. Jake didn't know what kind of eagle it was. He didn't know anything about birds. It could even have been a large hawk.

The crops weren't good, but with luck there would be enough of a harvest for people to get by for another year, if they wanted to stay. Even some who had attempted to ignore reality had begun to leave. There was desperation in the air.

Now Mable was rustling around in the kitchen, and Jake felt guilty for sitting, but if there was nothing to do, there was nothing to do. He was glad she was trying to stay busy.

Desperation. Some in the community clung to each other more than ever, but most turned the other way: hard, and bitter, clinging to their animosities. The week before, a country school had burned in the middle of the night. Everyone knew it was George Binns, but nobody could prove it. He had been squabbling with the school board for years. And someone had shot Baxter Sondheim's bull, but again, no proof. Then there was Albert Stull.

Albert and his wife, Gina, lived on a farm east of Charity, along the railroad branch line. Jake barely knew them, but they had come from Illinois, where Albert had worked as a dray-man, hauling garbage up and down the alleys of his small hometown. Later he had worked on the railroad, as a brakeman.

One day when Gina got back from town, she found her husband on the kitchen floor–stabbed to death–and what little money and valuables they had were gone. It didn't take long for the sheriff to find the killer–their nearest neighbor, Hugo Blatz–but Gina had ceased living. She left for Illinois a week after the trial.

Jake leaned sideways and spat into the dry grass. Grasshoppers jumped out of the way, then they re-converged around the spit. Heat shimmered above the wheat fields.

The Light came. Jake had learned to acquiesce, and ride with it. Sometimes it was a recognizable figure, often not, but always now it spoke. "Jake."

Jake stared as it hovered in front of him. "What?"

The Light said something that Jake could not understand. Then it beckoned, and Jake left his body. He floated, dreamlike, until he was in a bright room with indistinct, cloud-like walls. The Light was still with him, and in the middle of the room an ill-defined form hovered in repose. There was nothing else.

"Where are we?" Jake asked.

The Light motioned Jake closer to the reclining figure. As he approached, Jake saw it was Mable. Her eyes were closed, and there was a look of peace on her face.

"Why is she here?"

"You know," The Light said.

"No! Not before her time!" Jake fell to his knees and pleaded. "Please! Not Mable. Me, instead!"

The Light touched him, and he was calmed.

"Look at her face, Jake. When have you seen her that way? So peaceful?"

Jake stood, and hung his head.

"Never. I have never seen her that way. She has known nothing but adversity and pain."

"Then take comfort."

The transmigration had not lasted long. Perhaps only seconds in real time, but the impact was profound, and Jake found solace in the fact that it was only an aberration. Behind him, in the kitchen, Mable was still busy, banging pots and pans.

Then it was quiet–as quiet as a monastery–and the quietness, formerly Jake's friend, was his enemy. Some thrived on quiet, but the loneliness ate at Jake's soul, gnawing like a Norway rat.

A coyote crossed the wheat field. It stopped on a rise, panting, its head hanging. It was thin and mangy, and despairing. After a few minutes it loped away, slowly and aimlessly.

The Light had been a part of Jake for so long that he accepted it, but the other voices were new and worrisome.

CHAPTER THIRTY-THREE

"It's almost one o'clock," Mable said.

She had talked Jake into going to the circus in the nearby town of Cottonwood.

"Ready," Jake replied, as he wet his hand and smoothed the cowlick on the back of his head. He wasn't keen on circuses, but Mable had wanted to go, and it didn't cost much. Mostly they had to get off the farm. He forced a smile. He was trying to claw his way from the abyss. Trying, through sheer willpower, to achieve a bit of equanimity.

The circus had set up on the west edge of town: a colorful contrast to the stark prairie. The red-and-white big top, and the sideshow tents with the bearded lady, the contortionist, the human pincushion, the fire eater, ... People milling around, with noisy children running and shouting.

"Oh, my," Mable said as they approached. "How I remember the elephants. Once we were sitting in the front row, and one almost stepped on my foot. My mother pulled me back just in time. I was only five years old, and . . . ."

They stopped in front of a lemonade stand. Mable's words echoed, and the sideshow tents began to undulate, as images do in distortion mirrors.

"But the best part was the clowns. Mostly I remember the clowns, all painted up, ..."

The tents were dark within, and as they swayed back and forth, they grew, and Jake felt something pull him toward a red one on the end.

"Jake, where are you going?"

Mable's voice sounded far away as she followed him. "What is it, Jake?"

He stopped. The sign over the door read, *Madame Venezanio, Fortunes Told.* A dark, Gypsy-looking lady in a red-and-gold dress sat inside at a table, filing her nails. She put her file away and beckoned.

"I . . . ," Jake started, but Madame Venezanio gestured toward a chair, and he sat. She pointed to a sign: *Your Destiny - 25¢.*

Jake felt in his pocket for a quarter. He put it on the table and slid it across. Madame Venezanio ignored it as she whipped a red-and-gold Florentine scarf off her crystal ball.

"Now," she said. Her eyes were close together, and she had a pubescent beard.

Jake noticed Mable still standing, and he took her hand and pulled her to a chair beside him. Then he glanced around at the tent walls. After a period of silence Jake went rigid as Madame Venezanio began to speak. It sounded like Spanish, or Italian, and her half-closed eyes rolled upward. For more than a minute she intoned–and all Jake could make out was, "la muerte," then she stopped, and her eyes closed all the way. She sat still for another minute. Mable put her hand on Jake's forearm.

Madame Venezanio opened her eyes, and focused on Jake.

"Ce ti-e scris, n frunte ti-e pus."

Jake mouthed, "What?"

Waving the back of her hand to quiet him, she peered into the crystal, and so did Jake.

For an eternity Madame Venezanio concentrated. A fly landed on her cheek, but she ignored it. Then, without looking up, she pushed the quarter back toward Jake, shaking her head.

"What?" Jake asked.

"Leave," she whispered.

"Why? What is it?"

"Do not ask."

Jake felt Mable tug at his arm.

"But what?"

Madame Venezanio looked away, past Jake's head, and she muttered something. Then, "Take your money and leave, or if you must, double it. But beware the truth!"

Jake flinched. He dug for another quarter. Mable tugged harder.

"What?" Jake asked again.

Madame Venezanio shook her head.

"I had hoped you would leave. Give me your hand."

Jake put out his hand. It was shaking. Madame Venezanio turned it palm up, glanced at it, and flung it away.

"As I thought!"

She swept the quarters from the table and put them in a pocket in her dress.

"But—"

"Go, now, before you put it on me!"

"Put what? I—"

Madame Venezanio stood and pointed at the door. Then she whirled and disappeared. Jake tried to follow, but Mable held him back, and forced him outside.

The fresh air revived Jake, and he heard Mable scolding him, ". . . fell for the oldest trick in the book. You know we don't have money to waste like that."

They found shade beside the big top.

"You don't really believe in all that, do you?" Mable asked.

Jake shook his head.

"Then why in heaven's name did you go in?"

"I don't know. Something happened. I got dizzy, and there was a frying noise in my head, like radio static."

Mable scowled. "Something's always happening. I don't know what gets into you. Why can't you just be normal once in a while, Jake? Would that be so difficult? Why can't you . . . ? "

As she lectured, Jake grew numb. He was the last to believe in sorcery, or anything like it. What, then, had compelled him? He was confused, and ashamed. "Don't tell Lars," he interrupted.

"Lord knows, I won't. But you've got to promise not to go off like that again, Jake."

Jake looked up. The sky seemed brighter blue than usual, and the sun purified him.

"You don't believe in all that hocus-pocus do you?" Mable asked again.

"No."

People began buying tickets for the main show, and Jake and Mable got in line. Jake saw two elephants pass behind the row of sideshow tents. They didn't look very big. A fat, dour-looking man behind Jake blew cigar smoke, and children frolicked.

"Jake." Mable tugged at Jake's collar. He leaned, and she whispered. "Did you see anything? In the crystal?"

"No."

She seemed relieved.

The line moved slowly. Jake looked again at the tents. They were faded and tattered, not bright and new as they had first appeared. The fat man blew more smoke, and when Jake grimaced at him, the man turned and smoked in another direction. The sun was hot, and the children kicked up dust.

"I told her she should use turpentine on it, and . . . ." Mable had found someone to talk to.

Jake felt a trickle of sweat run down his spine. Fortune tellers were pure charlatans. Why, then? What had happened?

A lion roared, and everyone peered through the door of the big top, but it was too dark inside to see anything. The lion roared again, and children's eyes widened. A gust of wind cleared the dust.

At the second roar, Jake understood. It had been something primal. Something passed down over the ages.

CHAPTER THIRTY-FOUR

On a Sunday, early in the morning, Robert Brewer hanged himself.

"Where'd he do it?" Jake whispered to Karl.

They and Lars were standing in the shade of Charity Lutheran Church. It was hot, and they wanted to wait as long as possible before going inside. The hearse had just arrived.

"Barn. Where else?" Karl answered loudly, and everyone stared. "They always do it in the barn."

Lars edged away, embarrassed, and Jake was sorry he had asked.

"Botched it up too," Karl continued. "When we got there his hands were raw, and there was blood on the rope. When he kicked the barrel out from under himself, the rope stretched, and there he was, dancin' on his tiptoes. Tried tuh hold himself up by grabbin' the rope. Must'a hung on a long time from the look of things. Kicked around so much he dug a little hole, and that only made it worse."

Nils Anderson and several others gathered around. Jake, like Lars, sidled away, but he stayed within hearing distance.

"Found his jackknife on the ground. He got it open, then dropped it."

"Libby know what time he got up that morning?" someone asked.

"Dunno. She was carryin' on something awful, and nobody could make much sense out of her."

"I heard five o'clock," Nils said. His nose and ears were bigger and redder than Jake remembered.

"Well, then he hung onto that rope for a long time, cause when we got there he was still twitchin'," Karl concluded. "She'd cut 'im down, but it was too late."

Jake felt sick. "I think I'm gonna throw up," he said.

"Me too," Lars said quietly.

They looked at Morgan Feeney, but he was impassive.

"You ever see anything like that?" Jake asked Morgan.

Morgan shook his head and mumbled something about machine guns.

"Guess we better go in," Jake said.

It was stifling inside. Jake and Lars joined their wives near the back.

Throughout the service, Jake tried to block everything out. Then Pastor Bjorkland delivered the eulogy. Pastor Bjorkland had replaced Pastor Vilander. He was young, dark, and handsome–in a flabby way–and not as scalding.

". . . can't know what went on in Robert's mind in the days before the tragic event. What we want is the assurance that . . . ."

The plain wooden casket had remained closed. Someone had put prairie flowers on top.

". . . things we can't understand. Things beyond human comprehension."

Robert Brewer's wife sobbed.

". . . we can only pray for grace, and . . . ."

Jake felt lightheaded, and the rest of the service passed in a haze of morbidity.

"Amen."

The pallbearers solemnly lifted their burden and followed Pastor Bjorkland down the aisle, then came the family. Jake was glad to leave, but it was a good lesson if he ever decided to hang himself.

————

Jake was determined to pursue his Unified Theory of Life, despite recent doubts. Not long after Robert Brewer's funeral, he went to see Pastor Bjorkland. As life had unfolded in all of its asperity, Jake had adhered to his anti-religion position, but he was driven by desperation.

"So, what can I do for you, Jake?"

Pastor Bjorkland folded his hands on his desk. He was younger than Jake, and there had been rumors about him and some of the ladies in the congregation, but only rumors. He was married.

Jake didn't know how to start. He couldn't come right out with his Unified Theory project.

"Well, it's not easy to explain. I've never been very devout, but I'm open-minded, and . . . . I guess I'm looking for answers."

Pastor Bjorkland smiled.

Jake pushed on. "So I thought I'd come and talk to you, and try to make some sense of things."

"What sort of things?"

Jake felt himself flushing.

"Things like faith. And afterlife, and . . . ."

Jake and Pastor Bjorkland talked all afternoon. On the way home Jake was disquieted. He had wanted answers, and all he had ended up with were more questions. His religious inquiry–as part of his Unified Theory of Life–had been a great disappointment. He hoped that when it was time to tie in the non-religious philosophies, science, and the rest, it would go better.

CHAPTER THIRTY-FIVE

To take his mind off things, Jake resumed work on his anti-gravity machine.

"It'll take a while to get it set up, so sit down and relax," Jake said.

He had invited Lars to his workshop again. This time Lars would see his invention in action.

Lars sat in a rickety chair in the corner.

"Let's see," Jake fussed. "Did Mable take the scale? Nope, here it is."

He pulled a bathroom scale from a box on the floor and set it on the workbench. Then, from another box, he produced his invention.

"There she is," Jake exclaimed. "What do you think of that?"

He held it up. It was a cubical steel framework the size of a large hat box. Inside were all kinds of gears, weights, wheels, gyroscopes, and small electric motors. Two wires dangled out.

"Well, what do you think of that?" Jake repeated. He couldn't tell anything from Lars' expression.

"I dunno. Does this whatchamacallit work?" Lars hedged.

"Sure. Well, I haven't perfected it yet, but I'm almost finished. Just needs a little fine tuning." Jake went to the door and peered around to make sure no one was coming. Caroline was in the house with Mable, looking at Mable's new window curtains. "Now remember, I swore you to secrecy on this," he reminded Lars.

Lars held up his hand as if taking a vow.

"No blabbing around town," Jake said. "My reputation has suffered enough. Anyway, they'll soon be laughing out of the other side of their mouths."

He put a flat, heavy weight on the scale; then his anti-gravity machine. After fastening them down, he connected the wires to a car battery underneath the workbench.

"There! All set. Ten pound weight, and the machine weighs ten pounds."

Lars got up and approached the mysterious apparatus. He leaned and squinted at the inner workings, while Jake made adjustments, poking and prodding with a screwdriver.

"Ready?" Jake asked as he peeked out the door again. There was only his old dog, Falstaff, who had outlived his time on earth.

"Unh," Lars replied.

Jake flipped a switch, and Lars twitched. The machine hummed, and its gears started turning. When it got up to speed, it sat, growling, rattling, clanking, and jiggling up and down. Lars drew back as though it were about to explode, but Jake leaned closer, examining its innards. Then he checked the dial on the scale.

"There! Look at that, Lars." He pointed to the dial. "See that?" he cried gleefully. "Ten pounds! Ten pounds of upward thrust!"

Lars leaned over and squinted.

"See?" Jake persisted.

"It's kinda hard to tell."

"Whaddya mean. Look here! It was right on twenty before I turned it on. Now it's only ten!" He was getting sick of Lars' skepticism all the time.

"The needle's jiggling all over."

"Look again. You've got to average the highs and lows."

"Um. I guess it looks like ten," Lars said.

"Yeah, ten pounds," Jake exalted. "Now all I have to do is—

"

"But how are you going to lift the batteries?" Lars cut in.

"Well, that's what I was gonna say. I'll have to iron out the wrinkles, but that's just twiddling. Imagine what this is going to mean! It'll be a new era in . . . ."

Two days later everybody in Charity knew.

CHAPTER THIRTY-SIX

Jake's anti-gravity machine came to naught, and the failure caused him to re-evaluate his life, yet again. To regain control. It wasn't that he lived in a dream world. He possessed self-awareness, but only in retrospect, and that was the conundrum. He could never project himself into the future, no matter how hard he tried, or how much he thought things through.

Solitude. The condition most necessary for Jake's reflections. Yet, in excess, it had become his bane. Often he and Mable went days–even weeks–without encountering another soul. Sometimes longer. But every so often they broke free.

"Fine day," Jake said to Monroe Jackson.

Everyone had gathered for a picnic in Ole Grande's trees, south of his barn by a dry slough. The trees were not yet six feet tall, but they were trees in a treeless land. And indeed it was a fine day: sunny, and the wind had subsided to a caressing breeze. A day to rest, and to forget.

"Nice day," Monroe agreed as Jake sat down beside him with a full plate.

Monroe–short and heavy, with blond hair–was getting a drinker's blush. He seemed sober now though.

"Get that north twenty broke?" Jake asked.

"Naw. Lot'a rocks, some as big as a house. But I'm workin' on it."

Everyone knew that Monroe worked more rigorously at his drinking than at farming. Pity, Jake reflected, as Monroe was such a nice person. That was the way of it. Most of the drinkers he knew were nice. Maybe not so nice if you really got to know them, though. Not so nice if you were their wife. Jake had heard the usual rumors. That Monroe whacked his wife, Irma, around once in a while.

"Where's Irma?"

"In the outhouse."

"Oh."

Jake concentrated on his fried chicken. He noticed that Monroe's hands shook slightly as he ate.

"Good chicken," Jake said.

"Uh."

Monroe wasn't very talkative. Obviously he needed a drink. After fifteen minutes of half-hearted conversation, he excused himself and went to his car. Jake could see his head bobbing up and down as he slugged from his bottle.

Jake put down his plate and lay on his back looking at the blue nothingness above. He was not tired; he was still thinking about his Unified Theory of Life. To hell with Pastor Bjorkland, he would have to get his answers elsewhere, through some common sense, and through some good, old-fashioned Aristotelian deductive logic.

Small white clouds materialized directly above, and Jake lost his train of thought. One cloud was a rabbit, and another a small child wrapped in a blanket. Then an angel. The angel was followed by a knight in white armor. Then a sailboat, then . . . . Not The Fatidic Light, but the voices again. Jake sat up, horrified. He hadn't heard them for days. He looked to see if anyone was watching. He was shaking, and he couldn't stop.

"Did you eat too much."

Jake jumped. Monroe had come up behind him.

"I was—"

Monroe, well fortified, had become talkative. He sat beside Jake and started in.

"Or maybe you was too long in The Palace last night. I know guys like you. Always tryin' tuh make everyone think yuh never take a drink. Always so upstandin'. Hell's bells, never was a man that never took a drink. In fact I don't trust anyone who don't. Sometimes a man has'ta . . . ."

Monroe's voice faded, and the voices came again. Jake threw down his plate and tried to stand, but his legs failed him.

"What'sa matter, I hit a nerve?" Monroe chortled. "Come clean. You can't fool me, I . . . ."

Unable to get up, Jake leaned forward and put his head on his knees, with his hands over his head. Monroe was delighted. "See there, I knew you was one a' them hippo-crits. Well don't worry, your secret's safe with me. Nothing to be ashamed of, life's too short to . . . ."

Monroe was still talking when Jake revived. ". . . , so I said tuh Irma, we can't always have what we want, and . . . ."

Jake looked around. He turned toward Monroe. "Have I been sitting here long?" he asked.

"Oh, 'bout fifteen minutes I reckon. I was gonna—"

"Once in a while I have these spells. I—"

"I have 'em too," Monroe consoled. "Don't worry, they always go away. Once I was out pitching hay, and . . . ."

Jake flexed his legs and got up. He felt somewhat better, but all he wanted to do was go home. A dozen years ago Monroe would have been right; he would have needed a drink. Maybe he still did, but now he possessed self-control.

Mable came up to him. "Jake, some of the men are going to get a baseball game going. Are you going to play?"

Jake couldn't tell her. He had been too rough on her already. He lied. "I don't think so. I must have eaten too much. I can barely walk. I think we'd better go home."

Mable's disappointment showed, but not as much as if he had told the truth. She went to collect their things. Jake picked up his plate and utensils and started toward the car.

"So remember what I said," Monroe called. "Yuh haf'ta take life the way it comes. That's the only way tuh . . . ."

Jake was quiet as he drove, and evidently it still hadn't occurred to Mable that his condition was other than physical. When they got home, Mable found her bottle of *Lydia E. Pinkham's Vegetable Compound* and gave him a double dose, then she helped him to bed.

As Jake lay trying to sleep, he worked at keeping the voices away. He knew it was the guilt again. The guilt that had waxed and waned ever since they had come to Montana. The guilt that would ultimately defeat him, unless he found some way to defeat it. Survival lay not in those like Pastor Bjorkland, or Lars, or Morgan, or Mable, or in anyone else. It lay within. And it didn't help when others blamed him. A story came to mind—one that Karl had told—about the guy whose farmhouse was burning down. The guy called the fire department, but they wouldn't come. They told him to piss on it. The next day, when he confronted the firemen, they told him it was his fault for not pissing hard enough. One of Karl's silly stories, but despite how desperately he tried, Jake suspected he would never be able to piss hard enough.

Mable came and sat by the bed. After a while Jake smiled, squeezed her hand, and bravely waved her away. She smiled back, and he wondered at his ability to cover up. Always before she had been able to see through him, but the last few years had been different. His deceptions were more subtle. Or perhaps she was trying not to see.

Jake stood before a throne, and he wanted to laugh. There were clouds all about, and he knew he was at the gate of Heaven, but he also knew it was a dream. Heaven wasn't really like in children's picture books. It was all so ridiculous. There were angels, and cherubs, and saints, and Jake sensed a higher being behind a wall of darker clouds. Just as he decided to wake up, he looked down into the netherworld. He shrank back, but the cloud on which he was standing disintegrated, and he fell. Down, down, down, and as he fell, he became hotter, and hotter.

Jake woke himself. He had known all through it that it was only a dream.

CHAPTER THIRTY-SEVEN

"Makes me think of Dr. Raulsten's stories about the flu of 1918," Dr. Klause said.

He and Jake had stepped outside so Mable couldn't hear.

"The Spanish flu?"

"Dr. Raulsten said he never slept. Lost ten people in one month."

"What about Mable?" Jake followed Dr. Klause to his car.

"Hard to say." He threw his bag into the back of his Oldsmobile sedan. "I'll be back tomorrow. Should know in a few days."

He looked strangely at Jake. Perhaps despairingly, but Jake couldn't tell; he had always had trouble reading faces.

"Plenty of fluids, and keep her cool."

Jake nodded. "How are the others?" He was interested in their prognoses more as in indicator of Mable's fate than out of compassion.

"Same. Too early to tell. Nola Steele seems better."

Dr. Klause was tired. He was always tired like Dr. Raulsten had been.

"Thanks," Jake said.

Dr. Klause drove away, and Jake felt more alone than he had ever felt. He watched the trail of dust from the car, then he gazed past for a moment, at Lars and Caroline's place a mile away. They had wanted to help, but he had warned them away. Lars had been a hero during the 1918-1919 epidemic, tending to those who could not take care of themselves; doing their chores, keeping them going, with disregard for himself. Some thought he had saved J.J. Hill's life; all the more surprising because most of them believed it hadn't been worth saving. What would make someone do something like that, Jake wondered? He couldn't. Except for Mable. Or for their children, if they had had any. But not for anyone else. Then he remembered helping Lars take care of the Berglunds, and that had taken some courage.

Dr. Klause's trail of dust stretched for two miles before the first of it started to drift. Jake lingered, reluctant to go back inside. Not afraid for himself, but helpless.

Jake turned again in Lars and Caroline's direction, and again he was ravaged by his inner desolation. Alone, beleaguered, destitute of any supernatural virtues and of any other well of strength, he felt himself going under. He sank to his knees in the parched dirt, and slumped forward. He could smell the dust. Always the dust. He had not cried since he had been a boy, but now he did, sobbing, trying to catch his breath.

A crow flew over, noisily. Jake straightened and raised his eyes, and it seemed to be speaking to him. It stopped its northward flight and circled, agitated at something. Then it swooped and settled on a nearby fencepost, eyeing him, still cawing. Jake felt lightheaded, and he swayed in the heat. Why was he always so susceptible to crows? They bedeviled him.

"Caw, caw, caw-whah!"
"What?"
"Caw, caw, caw! Cuw-ah!"
Jake's vision blurred. He shook his head and attempted to get up, but he felt himself falling sideways. As he lay, unable to move, the voice of the crow became clear.
"Persevere."
"Persevere?" Jake quavered.
"Have courage. Take heart."
"Take heart?"
"And have courage. Courage, courage, courage—"
"But I—"
"Courage, courage, courage."
"How can I—?"
"Courage, courage."
Jake struggled to sit up.
"Who are you?"
"What's the difference?"
"You're not a crow."
"Without doubt!"
Jake couldn't tell if the retort was acknowledgment or mockery. In any case, the crow smiled.
"Look at you, lying in the dirt like a dog, feeling nothing but self pity. Where's your backbone? When will you learn to put your past behind you? When will you learn to—?"
"Sometimes I can't stop thinking."

"Try harder. Harder, harder, harder—"

"I can't."

"Of course you can. Perseverance is all you have. It's all anyone has."

The crow fluffed its feathers and prepared to fly.

"Don't leave," Jake pleaded.

"I must." The crow kicked itself from the post. "Harder, harder, harder," it cried as it flew away.

The sun fell. Jake crawled to the porch. There, he pulled himself to his feet and staggered inside.

All night Jake sat beside Mable. He slept off and on, and in his half sleep he communed with the crow.

Every hour Jake got up and fussed over Mable. And each time, as he stood wiping her with cool water, he knew that if he lost her, he lost himself. And when he sat down, he relived his and Mable's life together, and he wished, again, that he could make it easier. Or maybe it wasn't his fault, if some kind of fate controlled him. Still, he wanted things to be easier.

Mable moaned, and Jake reached for her. He took her hand, and sat listening to her deep, restless breathing. He squeezed, but there was no return. He murmured something, and as he did he felt how hot she was.

"Jake. Jake."

Mable was sitting up in bed, gently shaking him.

"Um."

"Are you alright?" she asked.

"Oh, yeah, fine."

"I'm sorry, I wouldn't have woken you, but—"

Jake straightened in his chair and felt her forehead. "Better. You're better." He leaned forward and put his head on her lap, and cried.

"Certainly I'm better. I had a good doctor. You."

Jake wiped his eyes on her gown, embarrassed. "You'd best lie down again. You shouldn't overdo it."

"I'm fine. Jake, I want to tell you—"

"Dr. Klause said that even if you did start feeling better, you shouldn't—"

"Listen to me. I had a dream."

Jake saw her seriousness. "Dream?"

"About a wonderful place. It was . . . ."

When she had finished, Jake stood and smiled down at her. "You look hungry. One bowl of graveyard stew coming up. Oh, I didn't mean—"

"I know."

He fixed her a concoction of warm milk, butter, salt, pepper, and lumps of bread.

"I had a dream too," Jake said as he sat by the bed to make sure she ate. "Just before you woke me."

"Another of your nightmares?"

"No. It was magnificent. I was walking across the fields to Lars and Caroline's place, and halfway there I came across a pond surrounded by huge trees. Like an oasis. And there were fancy houses all around. Not a town. A settlement, I guess. Anyway, the houses were mansions, and I felt that one of them was ours, but I didn't know which one."

"My!" Mable dabbed at her graveyard stew, intent on Jake's dream.

"It was beautiful. Cool, with lush grass and lovely flowers. And there were ducks and swans. Tame ducks, not the wild ones like around here. And in the middle of the pond was a fountain." Jake smiled. "I didn't want to leave."

"Sort of like my dream."

"Strange, though. There weren't any people."

"That is strange."

"I've been having good dreams for months now, mixed in with the bad ones."

"That's a good sign."

"I hope so. But I think part of it is a longing. The good dreams are all of blooming, colorful places, or of fine houses and things like that. I come across them unexpectedly, out in some field or patch of dry prairie. And when I'm awake–when I walk or drive by those places–I can still see the dreams, like mirages."

CHAPTER THIRTY-EIGHT

Mable was away visiting her aunt in Sioux Falls. Jake appreciated her absence, but he would appreciate her return more. They had not been apart since she had joined him in Montana.

On the fourth day after Mable left, Jake got up early and went to his workshop. There, in the corner, covered with dust, sat his anti-gravity machine, now only another forlorn symbol of failure. Oh, well, time to get on with things. His IHC 15-30 tractor had been acting up. He was sure it was the magneto, which sat defiantly on the workbench.

Jake had not mastered all of the intricacies of farm machinery, but he was more competent than most of his peers. He felt that his competency lay in his disposition. As with any of life's challenges, where his friends and neighbors tended to dive right in, he would hold back. Only after he understood fully the nature of the problem would he begin.

Light beamed through the window directly onto the magneto. Jake sat on his stool, chose a screwdriver, and began. As he removed parts, he carefully set them aside in order. Over his head, unnoticed, a spider spun its web.

Falstaff hobbled in and nuzzled Jake's leg.

"Good morning old and faithful Falstaff," Jake said, but he was absorbed in his work, and the dog left.

It was uncomfortably cool, but there was no use starting a fire. It would warm up soon enough. Birds chirped outside, but he took no notice. He was hoping for something simple, like a loose wire.

Jake paused, brushed an ant from his hand, and looked out the window. A green Chevrolet went by. In the back seat a small boy peered out, and then the car was gone, past the trees, heading north. Jake bent over his work again. He didn't see anything wrong, and he hated to keep going, but there was no choice. He rubbed his eyes, knowing he needed glasses.

Jake recalled his father. Long gone now, and good riddance. An awful thing to think, but that was the way he felt. Nothing but an odious drunkard. He had killed Jake's mother. Not directly, but over the years. Worse than if he had taken a gun to her. People had talked when Jake missed his father's funeral. He had considered going, as a way of rejoicing, but there would have been no real point to it.

"Jake Miller?"

Jake jumped from his stool and spun around.

"Uh! God, you scared me." He threw down his screwdriver. "I didn't hear you come."

The man stood in the doorway, blocking the light.

"Who are you?" Jake asked.

The man twisted his mouth into a smile, but the rest of his face was set. He had dark hair and a thin mustache, and he wore shabby work clothes. "Mind if I come in?"

Jake motioned him in, toward a chair. The man remained standing.

"You know me?"

Out of the corner of his eye Jake located the screwdriver on his workbench. Not much of a weapon. He began to sweat. "You look familiar."

"Oh, really," he sneered. "You know why I'm here."

"I thought it was over," Jake said. He was surprised that his voice was so steady.

"Things like that are never over."

"But it was so long ago, and—"

"Time heals? Is that it? Just a matter of time?"

"It wasn't my fault!"

"Fault! Ha! Ha, ha, ha! Fault? Don't talk to me of fault. Talk to me about morals, and ethics. That's what I want to hear. I want to hear how you have resolved your moral and ethical quandary, if indeed you have recognized it. Let me hear your reasoning, so that I may know how you have repented and rationalized it all away. Give me some reason to grant mercy."

Jake backed up a step, but the figure didn't move.

"Nothing to say? I should think you would have plenty to say after all these years of penance. No apologies, no explanations, no excuses? Speak up, Jake!"

Jake felt faint. "Is there no mercy? No Christian compassion? No clemency at all?"

Again the sinister half-smile.

When it was over–as Jake lay on the dirt floor–waves of remorse washed over him, one after another. Then he felt Falstaff licking him, and he was able to get up. He went not to the house, but to the barn, and there, alone, he drank from his hidden bottle until it was empty, and he slept where he had drunk: on a pile of straw.

CHAPTER THIRTY-NINE

As the dog days of summer closed, time slowed.

The dance at the Sonner om Norge hall in Charity was supposed to be a celebration, but now dances were part celebration, part solace. Yet everyone went. There was nothing else to do, and they lived on hope.

"I'm ready," Mable said.

She said it with resolute cheerfulness, and Jake replied with equal resolve.

"So am I. Let's go then. Don't forget the cake."

The hall was full of dancers, even those who cared nothing about the Sons of Norway. Those not dancing gathered around the picnic tables outside. No one went hungry, even in the worst of times; even as people were giving up their farms and leaving. Some left because they had to; some because they had weighed the rigors of staying against the uncertainty of what lay ahead, and they had decided to gamble.

Mable put her cake with the others, and she and Jake sat on a makeshift bench. They sat alone.

"Big crowd," Mable said.

"Yeah. Always a big crowd," Jake agreed.

He was watching Ludlow Manheim fill kerosene lanterns.

"Look, there are Lars and Caroline!" Mable said, pointing. She waved, and Caroline waved back.

Lars and Caroline had been even more distant lately. Lars had a soft spot for underdogs, but Jake supposed there were limits.

Ludlow finished filling the lanterns. He pushed the potato plug back into the opening in the kerosene can, and set the can aside. There would be daylight for another hour, so he put the lanterns aside also.

The wind had died, and the sun was reddish-orange, casting an ominous glow in the dusty western sky. A pack of dogs barked and yapped their way through the crowd, then they swarmed past the mercantile store and down the alley. The flies disappeared for the day, to be replaced by hungry mosquitoes. The music ended, and a few dancers came out of the hall.

"That looks like Lola Hagen," Mable said. "I haven't seen her in ages."

Lola caused Jake to think about his Unified Theory of Life. He didn't know what the connection was.

"Lola!" Mable greeted, but her friend only smiled and went on by.

Jake got on his Unified Theory again. Was it a waste of time? What's the use? You live, and you die, and you do the best you can. Trying to know the unknowable? Is there an unknowable, or do people only think there is, always looking beyond the temporal? Are we just animals who grew out of nothing, and is meaning simply one of the terms we use to delude ourselves into thinking there is something more to life? Are philosophy and religion indeed only panaceas for those too weak to face reality?

James Ostlund sat next to Jake; and his wife, Clara, sat by Mable. James was tall and wiry, with long gray-white hair and a matching beard, and Clara was heavy, with dark hair and warts all over her face. She and James had loaded their plates.

"Delightful evening," Clara observed.

As Mable agreed, Clara worked on a chicken drumstick.

"Did you hear about poor Wolfgang Muller?" James asked Jake.

"No. What?"

"Got dragged to death by his horse."

"Wolf got dragged? No! Dear me, I never heard that!" Jake said. "When did it happen?"

"This morning. Piper Stone found him. The horse had stopped by a fence. Wolfgang was still alive, but he died ten minutes later."

Mable had stopped eating, and was listening wide-eyed. Wolfgang was a young bachelor who had recently arrived from somewhere in Illinois.

"He had his jackknife in his hand when Piper found him. Couldn't get it away from him till after he was dead. Didn't see any cut marks on the stirrup strap though."

"How far was he drug?" Jake asked.

"After they hauled Wolf away, Piper followed the trail. At least a mile. All the way from Johnson's corner."

"When's the funeral?" Mable asked.

"Day after tomorrow. His people wanted to ship him home, but you know how it is in hot weather. Figured they should take care of it the sooner the better."

Mable blanched and put down her fork.

"He told Piper a wolf jumped up in front of the horse," James went on. "I haven't seen a wolf in years. In fact I've never seen a wolf. But that would spook a horse alright." James put his plate down on his knee and looked at Jake. "What a hellova deal," he said.

Jake agreed. It seemed like everything was a hell of a deal.

Some rowdies staggered in. There were four of them, all young men who worked on the railroad section crew.

"Hey, free lunch!" one of them shouted. He was good-looking, but his eyes were owlish from drinking. The others were in similar condition, but more odious. "Well, don't mind if I do!" a burly, long-armed, short-legged one said as he grabbed a piece of pie and began stuffing it into his mouth. While his friends followed suit, people watched, bemused. Some of the ladies were outraged.

"What's this town coming to?" Jake heard someone gasp.

It was Marceline Hemmings. Her husband had died two years ago, and she was making a living cooking and baking at the hotel restaurant.

The revelers made a mess of several of the pies and cakes.

"Hey, let's dance!" one of them cried. He was dark and bowlegged, with a body like an oil barrel. His short arms stuck out on each side like fenceposts, and his nose was bent to one side. He spotted Marceline. "Well, hello Marcy. How 'bout a dance?"

Marceline was an attractive redhead in her mid thirties. She was used to advances. "No, thank you," she said coldly.

"Oh, c'mon!" The man's name was Bond. Something Bond. He staggered forward, pulled her up from where she was sitting, and put one arm around her waist.

Instantly Lars jumped up, but before he could get there, Rudi Prinz stepped in. "Let her go," he said.

"Who the—?"

"Let her go." Rudi–the former prizefighter–was no longer young, but he was still in good shape.

"Forget it, Bond, let's get another drink." The least piffed of the four tried to pull his friend away.

"Who the blazes are—?" Bond started to say, then his eyes refocused on Rudi. "Well, just wanted tuh dance. No harm intended.

Sorry." He let go of Marceline and backed up. "Guess we ain't wanted here. Let's go."

The drunks weaved back outside, and Rudi limped slowly away. Rudi didn't move as fast as he used to, and he drank too much sometimes, but it wouldn't have been much of fight. Lars helped Marceline back to her place on the bench.

Jake had watched it all with congenital detachment. He saw the incident as a confirmation of what he had just been thinking: that life is a constant struggle. That there are no positives. That anything good in life is only the absence of negatives.

Lars and Caroline came and sat down.

"Hello, Jake," Lars smiled. "What's the matter, aren't yuh talking to us tonight?"

Jake couldn't help laughing. That was Lars' way. A perverse sense of humor, and his mendacity.

"How are those new Herefords doing, Lars?" Jake asked.

"Alright. If I get through the first year, ..."

It was good to have a friend again, if only for a while. Others gathered.

There was a flash in one of the windows.

"Hey, was that lightning over there?"

"Wouldn't be surprised. Jasper Cornwall said the ants have been digging. Sure sign of rain."

"My dog's been chewing grass," Stygg Larsen said. Jake thought *stygg* meant stinky in Norwegian, but he wasn't sure. A nickname, perhaps.

"These dry spells go in cycles, and—"

They went outside.

"Yeah, it's lightning," Lars said.

They were quiet, as if in prayer. A low rumble followed another flash. From behind a car, off in the dark, Barney Elmo–one of the town soakers–shouted something to someone. Then, another flash, and the roll of thunder.

Jake shuddered, reaching for hope, but afraid to grasp it. Mable had told him it would rain, but her optimism was the assurance of unthinking religious faith.

"Gonna rain," Stygg said.

"I don't think so," someone said.

Most of the men went back into the hall, while Jake and Lars tried to hold the mood.

"I'm afraid he's right," Lars said, letting go. "Looks like more dry lightning to me."

Lars and Caroline left, James and Clara had already gone home, and Jake and Mable were alone. Jake led Mable inside and found a place to sit, where they could savor their forgetting. They and all of the others worked diligently at it; at inducing oblivion. And when they could not forget, they worked hard at remembering the good times, and at anticipating the good times that would return, if they could somehow last long enough.

Jake rested, physically and spiritually. He looked vaguely around the hall, and succumbed to his own objectivity. He had always been objective. More like an observer of life than a participant in it, and as always he would have preferred to participate. Nevertheless, he was an observer. He couldn't help it.

As the last dance ended, it came to Jake: Lola Hagen was every unthinking person. That was it. Everyperson. Every average, unthinking person.

That's it, Jake thought, I'll work hard at not thinking so much. Not about anything more than everyday things. I'll re-join humanity!

He took hold of Mable's hand, and peace overwhelmed him.

CHAPTER FORTY

Jake sat at the kitchen table, poking at the beans on his plate. Mable had gone to visit a sick friend in Charity.

Mable's friend was Minnie Place, who had suffered from tuberculosis for years. She had been in a sanitarium in South Dakota, where she had been pronounced cured. Then, a month ago, the coughing spells had returned. She didn't want to go back, and it was Mable's job to help her husband, Olav, convince her. Olav worked as a butcher, and it was troubling for him to leave her alone each day. And, people were beginning to boycott Olav's meat counter.

Jake heard a car go by. He went to the window and held the white lace curtains aside. Stuart Simpson, the banker, in his black Packard. Jake sat down again. He didn't have any notes with Simpson's banks, or with any other banks. He distrusted bankers. They were the only ones getting rich, while everyone else struggled and went broke. Jake viewed himself as an intelligent person, nevertheless here he was, struggling for a living with the dumbest of them. Intelligence certainly wasn't synonymous with successful farming.

Jake wiped his plate with a piece of bread. The only sound was the ticking of the clock. The clock was taking on a new and obvious implication, and Jake hated it for what it represented.

With much effort Jake refused to hear the clock, and the quiet was bearable only because he was accustomed to it. He got up, poured a second cup of coffee, and sat down again, staring blankly through the window. Outside a flock of sparrows twittered by.

Jake's one confidence had always been that whatever happened–no matter how much he lost control–he knew something was happening, or at least that it had happened. Gradually, however, that confidence had weakened. Now there were disturbing lapses. Periods that he could not account for, and the only way he could judge them was through Mable. Her reactions, mostly, but sometimes she would come right out and tell him.

"Jake? Are you alright? Wake up!"

Jake smiled–almost laughed–at the way Mable had put it, like he had been asleep.

"How's Minnie?"

"Worse. She's coughing blood again. They're sending her back next week."

"Oh."

"Each time she goes, she knows she may not return. That's what's so unbearable about it."

Jake shuddered. That was the worst of it with him, too; knowing that sometime he might not come back.

CHAPTER FORTY-ONE

Jake couldn't sleep. He got up, pulled on his pants and boots, buttoned his shirt, and slipped outside, leaving Mable to her gentle slumber. Her nights were better than her days.

Jake stood looking south, toward Charity. He held his pocket watch to the moonlight. One o'clock. For three nights he had not slept. Or if he had, not much. He could blame Nietzsche. And farming. But mostly Nietzsche.

From beside the house Falstaff growled in his sleep, and a light flashed three miles away. Jake walked to his workshop. When the car was two miles away he could hear it. No doubt someone coming home from The Palace.

As the car grew closer, the beams from the headlights swept up and down through the night; probing, searching. Jake stepped to the dark side of the shed. It wouldn't do his already-eroded reputation any good to be seen standing in the yard at one o'clock in the morning.

The car groaned slowly by in second gear. Old Cecil Kamp in his dark green Studebaker. He would have hell to pay when his wife, Ella, got after him. Jake smiled. At least he didn't have Cecil's problem. Not that he didn't take a few good, stiff drinks once in a while. Sometimes it helped. That, and reading.

Morgan Feeney had never struck Jake as being much of a reader, and it was a total surprise when one day Morgan loaned him The *Complete Works of Friedrich Nietzsche*. Jake had read Nietzsche, but he accepted the book because of Morgan's enthusiasm.

Jake started Nietzsche all over again. At first the reading went slowly, then he could not put the book down. All of his suspicions and inner convictions were reconfirmed: religions– especially Christianity–are conceptions that renounce life; the strong are responsible for human advancement, and . . . .

Jake had tried to read carefully-selected passages of Nietzsche's book to Mable, but she professed not to understand. Then, one day after another reading, she boiled over, and Jake knew she understood all too well. It was religious faith that had delivered her from her own spotted past.

"He's too biased," Mable complained. "He goes too far."

"How can you be too biased on Christianity?" Jake argued. "Either you believe all of the myths and inventions, or you don't. Either God exists, or he doesn't. It's not a case of bias. How can you be biased on an either-or belief? It's not a question of degree."

"Nietzsche's intolerant. Don't others have the right to their beliefs?"

"Certainly, but you're berating me for agreeing with him. Don't I have the right to my beliefs? Don't you see, you're the one who's intolerant. The standard tactic of religious people: demand tolerance and obedience, but show none to those who disagree. To those who are capable of rational thought. What hypocrisy!"

They had gotten into a terrible argument, and Mable persisted in demanding tolerance, while showing none. None whatsoever. And the worst of it was, she refused to think. She had accepted religion unquestioningly, and that was that. On second thought, Jake decided, that was not the worst of it. The worst of it was that she reproached him personally for thinking objectively. For casting off the shackles of the ages: the myths, the ridiculousness, the intolerance, ... Jake realized that he could never again talk to Mable of religion.

The sound of Cecil's car faded, and Jake was fatigued, but he knew he still could not sleep. Damn Morgan Feeney, and damn Nietzsche.

An owl hooted. There weren't many owls.

What is it about people? Stupidity? Certainly, for most of the masses of humanity. But what of people like Mable, who are intelligent enough? Those who approach life rationally, except when it comes to religion? Moral weakness, he supposed. He shouldn't be so self-righteous. Weakness is to be pitied as part of the human condition.

Jake looked up at the stars. He didn't know one constellation from another, and he didn't care. Stars were stars. He guessed if he had to depend on them to navigate he would be more interested.

Jake hearkened back to his childhood. Because it had not been a pleasant time, his recollections were incomplete and chaotic. He remembered his dog, Joe; and his cat, a large, gray tomcat. He recalled yet again his mother, but most of all he remembered his father.

A cow mooed a half mile away, and in the opposite direction a fox yipped. Damn, life was merciless.

And was he too down on religion? Could it be that he wasn't as smart as he thought he was? Welcome to the Brotherhood of the Eternally Disenchanted.

CHAPTER FORTY-TWO

There had been a time when Jake had tolerated farm work, but not anymore. Now it was tedium; all of it. And rock picking was the worst. He had a tractor and wagon instead of a horse and a stoneboat, but it wasn't much of an improvement. Pick, move, pick, move, ... Go to the end of the field and dump. Then start over, and the rocks never ended. Prevailing wisdom was that rocks were a sign of good soil. The stock response was that there was a lot of good soil.

As Jake picked, he worried. Mable had been losing weight, and not eating right. Nothing serious Dr. Klause said, and he had given her a bottle of something cherry-colored. A teaspoonful every morning and every evening. Jake couldn't see that it did much good, but Mable thought it helped.

A dark cloud came over, and large drops of rain pelted down. Jake threw off the last rock and crouched on the downwind side of a tractor wheel. The air was still hot.

Jake had assumed he would be the first to go, but life had not been kind to Mable. Which would be best, him first, or her? Morbid. Best not to think of it. What comes, comes.

Down the road in his dilapidated Chevrolet truck came Nils Anderson. He saw Jake and pulled over, and the rain stopped. Hardly enough to wet the ground, but dark clouds were moving in from the west. Nils got out and started across the ditch, waving, his large red ears flopping.

"Jake, yuh hear about Jerome Blodgett?"

Jake stood. "No. What?"

"Robbed the bank in Cottonwood, then when they caught up with him, there was a standoff, and they shot 'im!"

"Shot Jerome? The hell they did? Where?"

"Right between the eyes." Nils sat on the edge of Jake's wagon.

"No, I mean where was he?"

"They found him in his barn, then they—"

"When?"

"Yesterday afternoon. In the first place everybody in the bank knew who he was, even with a sack over his head. He told 'em not tuh come outta' the bank or he'd blow their heads off. He was carryin' a 30-30. Well, 'course the first thing they did was call the sheriff, and they all followed him home. Can you beat that? Lord have mercy. What gets into people?"

"Holed up in his own barn?"

"Yeah. Before Minna knew it the yard was full'a guys with guns."

Jake was stunned. He had known Jerome well.

"Minna tried to talk him out, but he kicked her outta' the barn. Said he'd sooner die than spend the rest of his life in the state pen. And he'd rather spend the rest of his life in the pen than farming. Well, Minna carried on so much they had tuh tie her up."

"Couldn't they have just starved him out?" Jake asked. "A guy can't go without water for more than a few days."

"That's what they were gonna do, but he made a run for it on a horse, and some a' the young bucks got all hopped up and started shootin', and for chrissake, they got 'im right between the—"

"Eyes."

"Yeah."

A sickness grew in Jake's stomach.

"Don't you see? That's what he wanted, and getting it quick like that was the best he could have hoped for."

"Why not just shoot himself or something?"

"Dunno." Nils sat with a sad look on his face, gazing over the hill toward Jerome's place. "He went out with a bang," he sighed, completely oblivious to his unintentional pun.

"Wonder what Minna will do?" Jake asked. He was thinking of Mable.

"God, I dunno."

It began raining again, and this time it didn't stop, but neither Jake nor Nils moved. It was the kind of rain without thunder and lightning; a dull drizzle that could last for days. Jake felt he should have been glad for it, but he wasn't. It was too late.

"There's something else," Nils said.

"What's that?" Jake asked flatly.

"Jerome robbed a bank before he came to Montana."

"He what?"

"Told me about it years ago. Bragged about the money."

"You're shitting me."

"No siree."

"Why would he tell you a thing like that? They'd never stop looking for him."

"He was ossified when he told me. The next day, after he got sobered up, he came over and made me swear. Said if I ever told anyone, he'd get me if it took the rest of his life."

"Jeez. Jerome Blodgett? I can hardly believe it. He never even cheated at cards. Sat in church every Sunday."

A cold wind started from the northwest, driving the rain. Nils got up and squinted at Jake through the rain. "Gotta go."

As Nils waded through the wet weeds and grass to his truck, Jake looked again in the direction of Jerome's farm.

On the way home Jake worried about Mable.

CHAPTER FORTY-THREE

Dr. Klause insisted there was nothing wrong that a few good doses of calomel wouldn't cure, and Mable believed him because she wanted to believe him. Jake wanted to believe too, but he couldn't. How, then, could he take hope from someone like Karl?

"Yup, I never thought I was gonna get over the gout, but after three days in the spring water, I was as good as new. Better than new, and it fixed Emma's back too! Now we go there every fall. You outta' try it," Karl said. His hat was getting worn, and sweat stained the underarms of his shirt.

They were in the middle of the road, leaning against Jake's Model T. Karl was talking about Flandrum Hot Spring. Flandrum was a small town a hundred miles west of Charity. Jake had never had much faith in such things.

"Minerals," Karl persisted. "All kinds of different minerals. Don't try tuh drink any of it though! An old guy from South Dakota talked me into drinking a cupful of it. Damn near killed me. Had'a stop every twenty miles on the way home. Had the trots for a week. Thought I was gonna die. Lost fifteen pounds before it was over. Doc Klause finally gave me something, but he sure was touchy. And him with a bad back. Wouldn't hurt him tuh soak for awhile . . . ."

The wind swept the road, blowing grit into Jake's face. It was worth a try, and it would be good for them to get away for a few days. It could be that Mable's problem was mental, and . . .

"That old guy from South Dakota–I think his name was Simms–was gonna bottle the stuff and sell it as a tonic," Karl continued. "Lord almighty, he must own a toilet paper factory. If he does, he's gonna clean up!"

Karl beamed, proud of his joke. Jake smiled. Another gust of wind, and Karl pulled his derby tighter. Sure some interesting characters. Karl. And Johnny Slivohavnick. Necktie Johnny. Then there was old Theodore Grant. Stinky Theodore. Didn't believe in taking baths. Was convinced that it lowered his resistance. And Mary Hogworth from over west of town, who farmed like a man. Chewed and cussed and smoked and drank like one too. And Goofy Grimswold. Lately he had been getting plastered and taking off his clothes in the middle of the street. Now the rumor was that he thought there was something wrong with his teeth. Some outside force was using them, through the roots, to control his brain. And Micky McDuff, who made a living soliciting for his wife, and . . .

"Take 'er out and have 'er soak in the water for a few days," Karl said. "I guarantee it'll cure whatever ails her, and it'll do you good too."

Jake noticed the chewing tobacco stains on the front of Karl's shirt.

"Gotta go," Karl said. He clapped Jake on the shoulder and turned to leave.

After they made sure each other's car would start, they waved and drove off.

Two days later Jake and Mable were on their way to Flandrum Hot Spring. Mable had been reluctant to go, but Jake had prevailed.

"Don't worry, the car's running great. We'll have a splendid time," Jake said as they drove out of the yard. He had been looking at the new Chevrolet coupes. He guessed they'd have to wait though.

"It looks like rain," Mable said.

They had packed a lunch, and the only real expense would be two nights at the hotel. Jake had brought tools, and plenty of tire patches.

"We'll get by all right," Jake said, but out of the corner of his eye he saw Mable look back apprehensively, as someone leaving forever might.

An hour later they turned west at Cottonwood, and soon they were on the Fort Peck Indian Reservation, with the trees of the Missouri river on their left, and the dry, clay prairie on their right. The going was slow, but Mable seemed to enjoy the ride, and Jake realized he had done the right thing. They passed a log cabin. An old Indian and his wife sat in front. Jake waved, but they didn't wave back. Funny how they are; never try to adjust. People from all over the world–Norway, Germany, Sweden, Finland, Russia–learn the language and the customs, and do their best to get along. But it seemed like the Indians fought it all the way, like they'd rather die than adapt. Most didn't take any interest in farming. Some ranched, but not many. Lost in the past.

They passed through Poplar. Not much of a town. Part white and part Indian, coexisting.

On the other edge of town, more of the same: scrub prairie to the north, and the river on the south. And more log cabins, and an occasional white man's ranch or farm. But mostly nothing but sun, and dust, and space. Jake slowed for a flock of sheep. He waved at the young Indian boy tending them, and the boy waved back. The boy was skinny, and his face was expressionless. Then they were through, and Jake reached down with his left hand and pulled the high-gear lever.

By the time they reached The Regal Hotel in Flandrum, Mable was spent. She needed help up the stairs to their room, and she collapsed on the bed with her clothes on. Soon she was sleeping, and Jake covered her, and sat watching over her.

The room was well furnished, with an oak dresser and a chest of drawers, and an iron bed that was decorated with ornate cast-iron floral fixtures. A huge crystal chandelier hung from the high ceiling, and there was a fancy lace-fringe lamp on the stand beside the bed. An oriental rug embellished the floor.

Jake looked out the window, at the town's main street. It had been years since he had been higher than first floor. The bustling people seemed preoccupied, and it was nice not to know any of them.

Mable hadn't stirred since falling asleep, and Jake got up to see if she was still breathing, then he sat down again, embarrassed. He was aware that he had lost his equilibrium; his facility to distinguish abnormal behavior. A facility that–as he grew older–he wasn't sure he had ever truly possessed.

Across the street two men tumbled out of the Grain Growers Hall, and resumed fighting. Not the clean fighting of professionals, but the down-in-the-dirt kicking, gouging, biting kind. From their clothes Jake could tell they were cattlemen. For several minutes they rolled around, then one stayed on top, beating the other in the face with both fists. The town constable came and rapped the top man over the pate with his billy club. While the recipient of the blow lay kicking and screaming, the constable grabbed the underdog by the back of his shirt collar and dragged him away. Presently he came back for the other man, who by now was lying still, moaning, and holding his head. As the constable dragged the second man away, someone opened the Grain Growers Hall door and threw out two cowboy hats.

It was getting dark, and the street lights came on. Piano music floated from somewhere. Jake considered waking Mable to go downstairs for supper, but he decided she needed the sleep more. He reached into the paper bag on the floor beside his chair and found a soggy butter-and-onion sandwich. It was difficult to swallow without anything to drink.

Mable began to snore, gently. The shadows on the walls brought a chill to Jake, across his shoulders. Then a light appeared, high in the corner of the ceiling opposite the window. Jake watched as the familiar glow brightened–The Fatidic Light–but this time it burst into thousands of tiny, sparkling pinpoints that disappeared, leaving him alone again in the darkness.

When Jake opened his eyes he was in bed with his shoes off, but with his clothes on, and someone had covered him. He heard Mable in the bathroom, softly singing Rock of Ages. He got up and started toward her, but she heard the floor creak and came out, brushing her hair. She was radiant.

"Good morning," she smiled.

"Well, look at you. How long have you been up?"

"Hours. I thought you were going to lie there and mumble all morning."

"Mumble? Was I talking in my sleep?"

"Something. I don't know what."

"Umm. Well, I'll get ready."

Jake shaved while Mable packed their bathing suits in her carryall.

The hot spring was two miles west of town. There was a big sign, *Flandrum Hot Spring, Rest and Recuperation*, and an arrow. The spring was a half mile off the main road.

"Did you bring the towels?" Jake asked.

He parked with the other cars in a graveled area. On the edge of the parking lot stood a shack–apparently an office–but it was closed.

"Towels and a blanket, in case we want to sun ourselves," Mable answered.

The pools were enclosed by a high board fence, painted blue. There was a ticket booth at the entrance. Someone had scrawled a note: *Admission, 10¢ (each).* Jake dropped two dimes through the slot in the top of the can, and picked up a pamphlet. They went in.

The spring water ran through a galvanized pipe into a concrete pool, and from that pool into another, thus providing both hot and warm water. On one end was the women's dressing room, and on the other the men's. There were wooden reclining chairs scattered about. A dozen people–mostly elderly–were soaking, and several lay on blankets. A couple with two young children sat eating a picnic lunch. The woman was thin and ashen-faced, and she had red blotches on her skin.

Jake read the pamphlet:

ENJOY THE WATERS OF EUROPE, RIGHT HERE AT HOME!!
The same water as the famous baths of
Wiesbaden, Germany!
The 83-degree mineral-rich . . . .

The spring had resulted when a wildcat oil rigger had drilled a test hole. No oil, but plenty of hot water. Cowboys began bathing in it, and later a rancher built a wooden tub so that his son, who was stricken with paralysis, could soak. The treatment was so beneficial that others came, and over the years the facility had been enlarged and improved by the local American Legion Post.

"See you in the pool," Mable said.

She put the blanket on one of the chairs and went to the women's dressing room. Jake watched her walk away. She seemed young again.

Jake went inside and self-consciously put on his bathing suit. He had not undressed in front of anyone–except Mable–since childhood. The only other person in the dressing room was an old man who could have been in his nineties. He was having difficulty getting his clothes on–all tangled up in his suspenders–and he paid no attention to Jake.

When Jake came out, Mable was already sitting on the edge of the pool, dangling her feet in the water.

"In you go!" Jake joked as he pretended to push her.

"Oh, my, no, it's too hot. I don't think I can stand that. Let's try the other one."

They eased into the other pool, and after a few minutes Jake felt himself relax. He floated as he had not done since he was a boy, swimming in the warm, muddy water of the creek at the edge of town. He could almost hear the voices of his friends, shouting and splashing. Oscar Hess, Billy Harvey, Jack Hamilton, ... He wondered what they were doing. He hadn't heard a thing about any of them. Except Jack, who had supposedly died in a forest fire in Idaho, but that was just a rumor. Funny how things go.

Jake peeked sideways. Mable was lolling in the shallow end of the pool, leaning back, eyes closed, face skyward. The lady with the skin blotches bobbed serenely next to her, and Jake hoped she didn't have anything contagious. She was saying something to Mable.

Jake stopped floating and stood in the water. The old man from the dressing room had finally gotten his clothes on, and now he was looking for his glasses. Then Jake saw why he had been having such a tough time getting dressed; one hand was missing. A farmer, or a veteran of the Civil War. One of the thin lady's children found the old man's glasses on a chair, and the man put them on. "Time to go home for a shot of knock 'em dead," he said to Jake as he walked by.

So he was a Civil War veteran. Jake waded toward Mable.

"My, this is relaxing," Mable said without opening her eyes. Jake wondered how she knew it was him.

"Don't drink any," Jake warned.

On the way home, and for several days, Mable was cured.

CHAPTER FORTY-FOUR

Jake threw three large lumps of greenish-brown lignite coal into the stove, then he went to the window and looked out at the blizzard. "Can't see a thing." He returned to his chair and sat restlessly. Now, more than ever, they needed their Zenith radio, but it stood cold and lifeless. The batteries had been dead for weeks.

Mable brought him a cup of coffee, then she sat on the other side of the stove. Her pain came and went. Dr. Klause had been giving her a dozen bottles of laudanum every two weeks. Luckily she had stocked up; they had been snowed in for three days. The only time Jake had been outside was when he had crawled to the barn to feed the livestock, but after the first two days he had given up. People had died in lesser storms.

The wind shook the house, and even with the chimney damper all the way shut, the stove roared and belched, and at times the door turned cherry red. Jake took some comfort in the coal shed he had built onto the back of the house. It was full. And they had plenty to eat.

Occasionally snow filtered through a crack in one of the walls, and Jake would stuff the opening with newspaper. He and Mable each had on two sweaters, and he wore a cap. And they both wore galoshes. At night the drinking water in the pail froze unless Jake got up to stoke the fire. He had put layers of newspaper under their thin mattress, and they slept with every blanket they had.

Jake suffered unspeakably. Perhaps more than Mable, but in a different way. He looked at the clock. Three in the afternoon, but it was like night. Then, as he began to read again, there was a thump on the wall behind him. Then another, near the corner. Then two more from the kitchen. Jake leaped across the room and pulled open the door.

"Auugggh!" Mable cried.

There, in the doorway, was a dark, shaggy figure covered with snow.

"Yuh gonna let me in or not?" Karl demanded.

"Why, uh, yes. Karl, what in thunder—?"

Karl stomped in and whipped the wool scarf from his face. He was wearing a buffalo-skin robe.

"Karl, what in the world?" Mable echoed. "Are you alright?"

"Fine."

"What in the name of heaven are you doing out in this?" Jake choked. "Are you off your rocker?"

"It's a nice day for a stroll." He took off his fur cap and threw it on the floor beside his scarf, then he pulled off his mittens and cast them down as well.

"But how could you see?"

"Don't have to. Followed the fence lines."

"But—"

"Help me get this thing off," Karl huffed as he struggled with his robe. "Heavy darn thing, but yuh could sleep all night in a snowstorm if yuh had too."

Jake and Mable were dumbfounded as they draped his outerwear over chairs near the stove.

"Wanted to check on yuh," Karl said as he sat down at the table. "Just came from Lars and Caroline's. They're alright. Lars was afraid tuh go out to the barn, but I told him not to be such a ninny. Yuh have tuh . . . ."

Mable recovered enough to put on another pot of coffee, and she dug in the pantry for the cookies she had made before the storm. Jake sat looking across the table at Karl.

"Lars got kinda grumpy when I called him a ninny. I was afraid he was gonna . . . ," Karl went on.

As Karl talked, drank coffee, and ate cookies, Jake ruminated. Perhaps Karl was eccentric. Some even thought he was unhinged. But how many would walk through a blizzard to check on his neighbors?

"Well," Karl went on, "I couldn't stand for that, so I told Simon that if he was so damn, er, I mean darn smart, then he should go out and buy a bunch a' them kinda chickens he was talkin' about, and show us how it's done. So he says . . . ."

Jake relaxed a little.

"Well, then Ludwig took out a revolver, and that's when the bar man got out a baseball bat and hit him over the head. Didn't wake up for two hours, and . . . ."

When he had worn himself out talking, Karl got up to leave.

"But it's getting dark," Mable protested.

"Haw! Haw, haw, haw!" Karl responded. "What's the difference if yuh can't see your hand in front a' your face anyway? Haw, haw! Don't worry, if I made it over here, I can make it back."

"But—"

"Here, help me with this robe. Friend gave it tuh me when he heard we were moving to Montana. Said I'd need it."

Jake helped Karl bundle up.

"Sure wish you'd stay, Karl," Jake tried one last time.

"Can't. Gotta get back tuh Emma. Thanks for the cookies." With that he was gone.

Jake and Mable exchanged glances, then they held each other. They would have called Emma, but the telephone was down.

On the last day of the blizzard–in the evening as the storm blew itself out, and as Jake had come to terms with himself yet again– there occurred a foretoken of his fate; a foretoken that was more than a premonition.

"It's easing," Mable said, without looking up from her knitting.

Jake didn't answer. He didn't know if she meant the pain or the storm. He sat staring at the window, listening to the wind. Something had happened that had never happened before. Always he had been the master of his own destiny. He had reconciled his past sins, his weaknesses, his eccentricities, and his departures; and he felt he could deal with them no matter what. Then, his composure was extinguished.

It had come swiftly, and Jake didn't know how long it had lasted. Not The Fatidic Light, or the voices, but something else. He had reached a new depth; an abasement that had left him weak and empty; unable to think of anything but the terror he had just experienced.

Jake knew he could never explain it to anyone. It was like he was drifting, with waves of something indescribable washing over him. It was a bright place–a place of nothingness–but it was the very nothingness that alarmed him. A void. No people, nothing; only fear. And always the waves, increasing and subsiding; pulsating; on, and on, and on.

"It's letting up," Mable said.

Jake made himself look at her, to see if she knew, but she didn't.

More than anything, Jake was afraid of being alone.

CHAPTER FORTY-FIVE

When Jake could no longer care for Mable, he took her to the hospital in Charity. As he carried her to Karl's sleigh, he felt how light she was, and her feeble protests cut him.

Jake held Mable while Karl drove. Karl stared straight ahead, and he was uncharacteristically quiet. A quarter of a mile from home Mable struggled to look back. The horses snorted, and the only other sounds were of the leather, and the runners slicing through the powdery snow. It was a beautiful day; not a time for dying.

The tears froze on Jake's cheeks, and the sun made them glisten. Mable again protested, then she saw Jake's tears, and she quieted herself. She took his mittened hand in hers, snuggled close, and put her head on his shoulder.

In a corner of a spare, white-painted room on the second floor of the small hospital, Mable lay still, and Jake lay beside her. They talked of everyday things.

Mable worried about Jake until two days before her death, then the pain was too much, and she pleaded with Dr. Klause to end it. Jake pleaded too, but on the morning of the day he would do it himself, Mable died.

The grave diggers had to thaw the ground with coal fires.

Jake remembered little of the funeral, and nothing of the cemetery, except standing in the cold with Caroline by his side holding his arm.

CHAPTER FORTY-SIX

On a Tuesday morning two weeks after the funeral, Jake plodded through a foot of snow to the mailbox. The air was calm, and the late-morning sun reflected the frosty magnificence of the day, mocking his grief.

Jake stopped in the middle of the road. Only one track: Daniel Fabian, the mailman. Jake unbuttoned his pants and urinated, watching the yellow stream cut the powdery whiteness. When he was finished, he felt that he had defiled nature, and he stirred the stain with his foot.

As usual there was only the newspaper, but when Jake pulled it out, a letter fell to his feet. He picked it up; a large, white business envelope with no return address. It had an Iowa postmark, but the town was blurred. His long-familiar inquietude gripped him, and his hand trembled.

A car fought through the snow a mile away. Jake put the letter in his coat pocket and started back. By the time he got to the yard the car was almost to the mailbox, and Jake ducked around the corner of the house. He waited. It was Nicholas Sprague, probably stocking up on panther piss in case of another storm.

Jake brushed the snow from the bench along the wall. He sat and closed his eyes, letting the sun warm his face. He and Mable had spent many hours there, in their place of tranquility; the place they had chosen for the good times. Over the years, however, there had been few good times, and their special place had become one of bitter disappointment.

Jake took out the letter and laid it on the bench beside him. Then he dug in his pants pocket for his jackknife. A sparrow fluttered to rest on top of one of the clothesline poles. It watched him, unafraid, cocking its head first one way, then the other. Jake had to squint against the brightness to see it.

The knife was warm, and Jake held it in his clenched fist. He focused on the letter beside him, where Mable should be, and he wept, quietly, without tears. There had been no tears since the funeral. The sparrow fluttered away, and a jackrabbit peeked from under a bare box elder tree.

Jake opened the knife and slit the envelope.

Jake,

When I knew there was no hope, I entrusted this letter to my old friend, Amelia Evans.

Dear, troubled Jake. By now we have said our goodbyes, but I want you to know forever that I love you with all of my being, and that I never regretted any part of our life together, not even the bad times.

We have each had our secrets, though they never really were. There is something in my past, however, that you do not know. Long ago, after my mother died, I became involved with a spiritualist. I won't go into the details, but on two occasions she enabled me to communicate directly with my mother. I know this will be hard for you to accept, but you must. Whenever you need me, I will be with you. When you are alone in our special place, reach out for me. In the quietness of the night, open your heart, and I will come.

And know that I will wait for you. Be brave and true,

Mable

There was another page. A poem.

My life on earth is done;
> *Lord, give me peace,*
> *And peace to the one I love.*
And from my place in Heaven;
> *From by your side;*
> *Allow me one last wish:*
> *Until we are together,*
> *Here, to dwell with you,*
> *Please grant my darling Jake your grace.*
And if you will, my Lord;
> *On that fateful time,*
> *Let me be with him forever.*

Jake read the poem again; and again the letter, and the familiar whirl of nonsensical images came. He looked up, and the rabbit was still watching. It seemed to be leering at him. Jake closed his eyes.

The rabbit was gone. The sun had put the bench in the shade, and Jake tried to stand, but everything about him was a swirl of white.

He fell to his hands and knees and crawled through the snow toward the front of the house, around the corner, and onto the porch. He reached up for the knob and swung the door open. Warm air cloaked him, and he crawled in. As he lay, exhausted and broken, he kicked the door shut behind him, and the swirling receded into a melange of images of Mable. When he spoke, she didn't answer.

Jake woke, shivering. He stood, and though it was difficult to tell in the darkness, he thought the dizziness had stopped. He fumbled for a match from the holder on the wall and lit the coal-oil lamp on the table. Then he shook the ashes in the stove and refilled it with coal. He paused once to feel his pocket for the envelope, and when he had finished with the stove, he took off his clothes, extinguished the lamp, and went to bed.

In the morning Jake reached for Mable, as he had every morning. Then he remembered. He got up, stoked the stove, dressed, and made coffee. Two cups instead of four.

On a Sunday evening Jake began. First he re-read Mable's letter. Then he turned down the lamp and sank into his stuffed chair, and as he sat in the semidarkness he recalled what Morgan Feeney had told him, of parents of soldiers killed in The Great War. Some claimed to have contacted their dead sons. At the time, Jake had scoffed. Morgan, too, was skeptical. He had told Jake it was only those at home who believed in that sort of thing. Most of the men in the trenches knew damn well that when people were dead, they were dead, and they were unlikely to communicate with anyone.

Jake listened, and he could almost hear Mable in her rocking chair, humming to herself as she knitted.

There had been one exception to Morgan's skepticism. An exception that Morgan could not explain. An army comrade's mother, who said that on the first Sunday of every month she communicated with her dead son. Morgan told of how there were things she could not otherwise have known. Innermost thoughts shared before battles. And a secret so shameful that–on his deathbed in the field hospital–Morgan's friend had made him swear never to tell.

Jake had read about Arthur Conan Doyle's investigations into the possibility of messages being transmitted from the otherworld.

The great writer eventually claimed proof of life after death, and after the war he attended a seance where his dead son spoke to him. Other well-known people had had similar experiences. The usual: dimly-lighted rooms, flickering candles, trances, books jumping off shelves, table turnings, ...

Jake reasoned that–if it were possible to communicate with the spirit of those departed–psychological accouterments like candles, hand-holding, and mediums, were unnecessary. If one could commune with the dead, one could do so without the mumbo jumbo. Still, he turned down the lamp.

Clenching Mable's letter, Jake endeavored to put himself into the mood he imagined would be conducive to a trance; the kind induced by a spiritualist medium. Not knowing what kind of mood or state that was made his exertions difficult, and the result was a keen effort to concentrate on Mable, and on the content of her letter.

Outside the wind rose–rattling the front door–then it died. A mouse poked its nose from behind a box of groceries on the floor in the kitchen; groceries that Jake had yet to put away. Mable had always done that.

Jake ignored the mouse and concentrated, but nothing happened. He read again, in the dim light, Mable's letter:

. . . reach out for me. In the quietness of the night, open your heart, and I will come.
And know that I will wait for you. Be brave and true,
Mable

Clutching the letter to his heart, Jake concentrated, as if resolve could summon Mable. As if, should he fail, it would be a failure of will, not of reason. He had had visions before, why not now? The wind came again, and this time it stayed, howling and swirling, seeking cracks in the walls; trying to force its way under the door and around the windows.

In the morning Jake slept, exhausted and defeated.

PART THREE – 1936

CHAPTER FORTY-SEVEN

"I was just over at Morgan's place," Lars said.

"How is he?"

"Hmmph! Still stuck in the war, but he manages."

Jake had a commonality with Morgan.

"He's counting on his hogs to get him through till next year," Lars continued.

Word was Morgan had been in an asylum before coming to Montana.

Jake hadn't felt right since the last Fatidic Light. He, who had always been at least tolerably sane, going balmy. A realist who had repudiated the fantastic speculations and psychical creations of metaphysicians and religious architects. But the Light had had the gall to tell him he was anything but a realist.

"It'd be nice to have hogs," Jake said, brushing a fly from his ear. The fly kept coming back. They sat watching Jake's chickens feast on grasshoppers. Chaucer, his dog, ambled across the yard from the barn and nuzzled Lars. Falstaff had died years ago from eating poisoned eggs that someone had put out for skunks. No doubt Lars had put them out. Falstaff had been very old, but he should have died naturally, not in agony from poison.

"Hello Chaucer," Lars said as he scratched behind the dog's ears. He said it like *Chaser*, and Jake knew he had no idea of who the real Chaucer was.

Jake had gotten Chaucer from a neighbor. Chaucer–the runt of the litter–was barmy-looking, but he had turned out to be not only a good dog, but intelligent. Jake was sure he understood some of what was said.

"Oh, have I got a head," Jake said. He massaged his temples with the heels of his hands.

"Too long in The Palace?"

"Huh." Jake considered telling him more about The Fatidic Light, but if Lars started blabbing . . .

"It isn't Mable, is it?" Suddenly Lars seemed troubled. "You aren't going off on her again are you?"

"No. She's gone," Jake shrugged.

"Well what, then?" Lars pushed.

"That, um, situation I was in, before we moved here. That's part of it."

"You've been moaning about that for years, whatever it was. What else?"

"Oh, alright." Jake weakened. "But you've gotta keep this dark, Lars."

Lars sat straighter in his chair. "Yeah, sure. What?"

"Now, dammit, I mean it."

"Yeah, yeah. What's going on?" Lars's jaw tightened, and his eyes glinted.

"This gets out, I'm all done—"

"Alright! For Christ sake!"

"Um. Well yesterday I was picking rocks, and I had kind of a, um, . . . , well, kind of a vision." Jake waited for Lars to explode in laughter, but Lars merely sat, staring. "A light came down, and got bigger, and bigger, until it was as big as–oh, I don't know–as big as a tractor, but it was round, I guess, and it hovered about three feet above the ground. I think it was round. It was so bright it was hard to see, and—"

"A light?" Lars croaked. "A light came down from the sky?"

"Now, remember, you swore to—"

"A light as big as a tractor came down from the sky?"

Jake felt his face turn blood red.

"Then what?" Lars asked.

"It said it was The Fatidic Light again." Jake wished he had kept his mouth shut.

"Again?" Lars stammered. He sat, gaping, while a gust of wind passed over them.

"Yeah. A bright white light, but sometimes it's red, or, I dunno. What's the difference? It's been showing up for years. Maybe it's all in my head. Anyway, it spoke to me, or somehow the words came into my head."

"What did it say?"

"That there's something I'm supposed to find out for myself."

"What else?"

"Nothing," Jake said, almost whispering. "But I think it's evil."

"It must have been a dream."

"Well, I . . . , I used to dream about it. But I was awake." Jake slumped in his chair, expecting the worst, but Lars sat stone-like.

"And?" Lars asked.

"That's it." Jake expected gales of laughter, but Lars was silent. He appeared stricken.

The wind picked up again, and this time it stayed steady from the west. There would be no rain. The chickens kept eating, and Chaucer nuzzled Lars.

"But I'm fighting it," Jake said. "I don't expect you to understand. People like you don't have a firm grip on reality."

Lars, whose gaze had shifted to the west, jerked back around and glared at Jake. "Horseshit!" he shouted. "You go off your beam, then you tell me I don't have a grip on reality? Kicked by a mule, hit by lightning, and God knows what else; and you accuse me of walking around in the clouds? What gall!"

CHAPTER FORTY-EIGHT

"Mable?" Jake sat up in bed.

"Yes."

"But it's been so long. Eleven years. You're young. And look at me. I'm an old man."

She came to the side of the bed and put her hand on Jake's cheek. "You're not old. You're my age. To me you haven't changed. Only—"

"Only?" Jake held her hand to his lips and kissed it.

Mable looked vexed. "Inside you're the same."

"Yes."

"I want to help."

"How?" Jake kissed her hand again, and pulled her down on the bed beside him.

"Dear Jake, always so sensible. Don't you know by now?"

"Know what?"

In the spring of 1936 life was good. Life was good, but farming was not. The drought and the economic depression would never end; however Jake had, in spite of himself, mastered the art–the unconscious ability–to repudiate reality. An innate characteristic common to all of humanity.

"Jake."

It was The Fatidic Light.

"Oh, it's you again." Jake said. "You—"

The Light silenced him. "Poor Jake. A cerebral man, but so ingenuous. Don't you know?"

"Know what?"

The Light materialized. "Who I am?"

"My spiritual essence?"

"A part of you that you refuse to acknowledge."

"You're so clear. So lucid. How do you know things? Like that Mable would die? And—"

"You knew."

"No, I—"

"You knew it all, Jake."

"Then if I knew, and didn't do anything to help her, I'm to blame!"

"There was nothing you could have done."

Jake studied the apparition. His face contorted in fear. "If you are part of me, I'm insane!"

"No. But you are an extreme realist, and that is your ruination."

"Extreme realist. Then I am doomed to an eternity in some form of purgatory?"

"Doomed? Not necessarily. To be redeemed, all you have to do is accept the creation of reality."

"Accept the creation of reality? Here I am sitting on a patch of the worst land in the country–nothing but drought, hard times, and pestilence–my wife is dead, I have no friends, my past haunts me day and night, I'm demented, . . . , and you tell me to create my own reality?"

"People do it all the time. All babies are cute, all troubles are soluble, all affronts are forgivable, ... All people are by nature redeemable; all are created equal. All gods are true–humanity has worshiped them for centuries, in one form or another–in the search for order and reason in the chaos of the universe."

"But, Jake retorted, religion was only a way of trying to understand what would later be explained by objective knowledge and science. Surely you don't want me to regress into the world of ancient talismans, parchments, idols, myths, deities, and crackpot prophets and sermonizers? That's lunacy! I may as well start seeing fortune tellers and clairvoyants. Worshiping Zeus, or some magic rock!"

"Do what you have to do. Isn't relief from suffering the main goal in life? Sometimes you have to put reality second. Perhaps you should start by seeing Pastor Bjorkland."

The Fatidic Light began to float backward and up.

"Wait!" Jake cried.

The light was never a voice; more like a murmur. Even less than that. A reverie. Actually, more than a reverie or a dream. It was inexpressible.

Jake sat in the second pew from the front, right side, where he always sat. People joked about his spiritual waffling. Furthermore, some considered engraving his initials on the seat, where the letters would eventually mold his buttocks into a pattern, the same as how barflies' butts were molded into the shape of their favorite barstool. He had never wanted to sit in the front pew, as that would be too flagrant an indication of his devoutness. Devotion that had come despite his having been a devout realist.

Fanny Ward had once called him a devotionalist. He guessed she meant that he was leaning toward religious excess; she who sat behind him in church every Sunday morning, wearing either her gaudy blue-and-white dress, or her thin, solid-red one through which her bloomers showed, blubbering at the sermons, waving her white silk handkerchief, praying loudly above all others, and singing in a clamorous forte. Jake knew the reason she sat behind him: she had her eye on him. Fat Fanny Ward, who had chased Morgan Feeney after he had gotten back from the war. She lived with her mother on the edge of town, and she made a precarious living concocting wild-rose perfume. She had never given up on finding a man, but that man sure as blazes wasn't going to be him, Jake reiterated, and he wasn't going to relinquish his place in the pew either. Better to roll up small bits of paper and plug his ears, and ignore her. Which he did. Every Sunday.

Pastor Bjorkland continued his sermon: ". . . no matter who or where we are, or whatever our trials, we will be comforted by the Lord. He will take upon himself our burdens, and . . . ."

Across the aisle at the far end of the first pew, Gina Stradby sat in her wheelchair quietly dabbing away tears. She was old–probably in her early nineties–thin and bent, with long white hair, and she had been in the chair for as long as anyone could remember, and no one knew her affliction. Rumors had circulated–some kind of nerve disease, a horse-and-wagon accident, a beating at the hands of Olav, her husband who had died decades ago, severe lumbago–but nobody knew, and she would never say. Whatever the ailment, Gina was in church every Sunday. Once they had had to carry her in, lay her on the floor, and prop her up with pillows.

Jake had to admit that Fanny's rose perfume did smell good.

On the way out Jake felt a hollowness. He never felt like rejoicing.

CHAPTER FORTY-NINE

Jake stopped in disbelief. The sign over the door was the same: *Madame Venezanio, Fortunes Told.* It was the same circus as back in the mid-twenties, and the same Gypsy-looking lady in a red-and-gold dress sitting inside at her table. She looked older, but not much.

And again, as when he had been there with Mable, Madame Venezanio waved him in and motioned toward a chair. Her sign still said *Your Destiny - 25¢*.

"Hello Jake Miller," Madame Venezanio said.

"You remember my name? It's been years."

"I remember all of my supplicants, especially you."

"Supplicant? I wouldn't call myself a—"

"All of my supplicants. Not only their names, but their, ah, may I say, petitions. Their afflictions."

Jake slumped in his chair. He felt silly, and he hoped nobody had seen him come in. And he would try to sneak out the back of the tent. Yet he meekly placed a quarter on the table.

As before, Madame Venezanio pulled the colorful scarf from her crystal ball. She closed her eyes and sat silently. Her fuzzy stubble-like beard had thickened and turned mostly white. Maybe she was really a man; Jake couldn't be sure, but he didn't think so.

"I don't know why I—"

Without opening her eyes Madame Venezanio held up her left hand to silence him. She put her right hand on top of the crystal. Thus she sat for several minutes.

Jake started as Madame Venezanio began to speak. He understood nothing. She opened her eyes and regarded the crystal somewhat curiously, Jake thought. Then she leaned slowly forward in intense concentration. That went on for many minutes as from time to time she muttered something to herself.

Madame Venezanio raised her head and eyed Jake. She smiled beneficently, and muttered something that sounded like *Tutti-fruity*.

"What?"

No answer. Only the smile.

"What?" Jake repeated.

"You have a bright future ahead, Jake Miller. You have persevered."

Jake flushed. "Persevered?"

"Yes. You have learned that reality is only a question of perception."

Jake tensed. "How the hell can you tell that?"

"Hold your tongue, you clod-hopping blockhead!"

Jake was taken aback. Moreover, he thought he had detected a Brooklyn accent. "What the—?"

Madame Venezanio calmed herself. "Ignore that," she exclaimed. "Sometimes I speak in voices."

Jake sneaked out the back of the tent.

CHAPTER FIFTY

From the knoll behind his house Jake could see the Eternal. God. Or the essence of some deity. He felt as though Demeter, the ancient Greek goddess of harvest, marriage, the sacred law (whatever that was) and the cycle of life and death, watched over him. Demeter, who held out hope in life, and in the afterlife. And who helped her supplicants control their cycle of life, which cycle was much like Jake's Wheel.

Northeastern Montana was often unbearable. But at times it was Elysium, even when it was unbearable.

The spring sun shone, a breeze ruffled the grass, and the smell of life emanated from the fresh earth. The near horizon, at least ten miles away in every direction, was as clear as Jake had ever seen, and the farthest horizon, some twenty-five miles to the west, was gray-blue and shimmering. West was the direction fixed on by the eye of every farmer during the trying times, in entreaty to whatever deity he held dear. If there were no such deity, then to whatever hopeful belief, conceptual talisman, mental crutch, or variation of hope he could summon. Birds twittered and called, and insects that had survived the unsurvivable thirty-degree below zero winter crawled or flittered about. An occasional gopher popped up, and a coyote hurried along several hundred yards away. The only human sound was a far-off tractor. And Jake felt unified with them all.

And, in the glory of newfound life, Jake was overwhelmed by the hope of once again finding Mable. He had always suffered his ups and downs, but maybe this time would be different. And perhaps the ends of the drought and the depression were nigh.

CHAPTER FIFTY-ONE

Jake sat with Walter Grimswold on the bench in front of the Gladstone Hotel. Walter, who had never been seen outdoors without his umbrella deployed–sun, rain, snow, or wind–was showing his age. He retained his lankiness, but his dark hair had grayed, and his deep, dark eyes had dimmed somewhat. His apparel remained unchanged however: white shirt, black wool pants, and a black cape.

"Gonna rain," Jake remarked. "Keep that umbrella handy."

He could joke with Walter, for whom he had a soft spot, and Walter took it easily, knowing that Jake meant nothing by it, unlike most of the other jesters in the community.

Walter smiled without looking at Jake. "If it does, let me know. It's been so long I wouldn't know what rain looks like."

"Heh."

"As far as that goes, I wouldn't know what a dollar looks like either. I know the paper ones are green, that's all. To be sure the silver dollars are silver, but I'm pretty vague about those too. All I know is, I'd like to have a few of them. The silver ones. The green ones never appealed to me. Too insubstantial. I'll have a thousand silver dollars, if you please, then after I bury them in a secret place, I'll stand in the village square, salute Roosevelt for the New Deal, and sing *Happy Days are Here Again!*"

"Haw! Don't you think your reputation is shaky enough without that? In any case, there is no village square."

Walter turned to Jake and smiled. "My dear sir!" he said. He pulled a cigar from his shirt pocket and bit off the end. "Reputation? Who cares about reputation?"

"Not you, obviously."

"Then you and I could both stand in the middle of the street. You could sing backup." They both chuckled.

"You are a real delight," Jake said. He longed for a cigar, but they upset his stomach. "A credit to knaves and jesters worldwide."

They watched Lars Nordraak chug by in his clunky Chrysler touring car, followed by a dust devil and two scruffy-looking brown-and-white shorthair dogs. He had bought the car new back in 1924. Jake and Walter sat for a long time, neither speaking.

Then Jake leaned back and looked vacantly at the eastern sky above the machine shop across the street. "Walter, I have to ask. Now don't get owly, I'm simply curious."

"Ask what?" He lifted both eyebrows in surprise, or in suspicion.

"Two questions. First, were you ever married?"

"Yes. A beautiful full-of-life girl named Volusia. We were very young and very happy, but she died."

"I am sorry. What was it?"

"We never knew. It was something like the flu, but not that. She got up one morning not feeling well, and in two weeks she was gone."

"Mercy."

"I almost went batty, but in time I recovered enough to keep on living. You're never the same though. What else do you want to know?"

"Why do you carry that ratty old umbrella around all the time? And did you carry it before your wife died?"

"That's four questions. And you aren't the first to ask," Walter responded equably.

"I'm sure I'm not, but as far as I know, if you tell me I'll be the first to find out."

"And the last."

There was a crackling silence.

"Well?" Jake prompted.

Lars pulled his car to the side of the street, got out, and kicked the flat front tire. He took off his floppy felt hat and chased away the dogs with it, then he got out his jack.

"It's hard to explain, Jake. I suppose it's a feeling of security in a bleak and inhospitable world."

Walter finally lit the cigar he had been fondling, but he merely sat and smoked.

"That's it?"

Walter turned. "Why yes. What were you expecting, some long, philosophical explanation?"

"Well, I dunno, I guess I was . . . , just assumed there was more to it than that. I mean, considering it's such a singular—"

"We all have our quirks and foibles, Mr. Miller. I could mention a few of yours if you want me to."

"But my word, walking around with an umbrella?"

"No worse than getting polluted on corn liquor, communing with fortune tellers, or—"

"Alright!" Jake snapped.

Lars' car slipped off the jack, and the fender came down on his head. He staggered around in circles for a while, holding the back of his neck, then he sat down on the wood sidewalk, spit on his handkerchief, and pressed it on the back of his head.

Jake and Walter watched Lars.

"Aren't you going to help him out, Jake?"

"Naw. Why stop him when he's putting on such a good show?"

Lars lay back with his eyes closed.

"There isn't that much distinction between us, Jake. We do what we have to do. All of us. We do it to get through life. Especially the older and more frail we become. We go to church, we worship this god or that–Thor to Zeus, on through the ages; this icon, that rock, or the nitwit who claims divine authority–we immerse ourselves in our work, we find comfort in philosophy, we do good works for others. We work ourselves to death for work's sake. We find comfort in family and friends—"

"If we have any," Jake interrupted bitterly.

"We go into denial, we hit the bottle, we carouse, we—"

"But that's all Irish bull! Tommyrot!"

"It works, Jake. That's what's important. You're turning into a real croaker."

Lars got up, found two rocks, and chocked one of the rear wheels so the car wouldn't roll again.

Jake watched Lars resume changing his tire, then he stared back at the sky, gritting his teeth, but he had to get it out. "I know we all have our devices, but Lord in Heaven, an umbrella? I might be able to believe a lucky charm, a cross, astrology, voodoo, stuff like that, but an umbrella?"

"For pity's sake, Jake, that's not it and you know it."

"What about my other question?"

"What other question?"

"Did you carry the umbrella before you wife died?"

Walter winced. "No."

Jake coughed, and spit off to his side into the grass. "Couldn't you at least get a new one?"

Two weeks later Jake presented Walter with a fine, new, shiny black umbrella. It was apparent that Walter appreciated the sentiment, if not the gift. Withal, he carried his new umbrella from then on.

CHAPTER FIFTY-TWO

If Walter Grimswold weren't enough, there was Ichabod Klopper.

Ichabod—who looked nothing like his namesake Ichabod Crane from Sleepy Hollow—had come from a stodgy German family in North Dakota, and Ichabod was without doubt stodgy. Reserved in manner as well as in looks: not tall, he was round-faced, pudgy, blond, and quiet to the verge of disablement. And, curiously, he was always surrounded by a vague miasma that hindered his social intercourse. Ask him a question, Jake would say to others, and you'd have to squeeze his private parts on a downhill pull for an answer.

But Jake had learned that Ichabod's father had been a baker, and Ichabod had taken up the profession; and though he farmed south of Charity, he baked as well as farmed, and his baked goods were the talk of the area. As were his sausages and other special meats, which he prepared and delivered to the Gladstone Hotel whenever he had the time. Most felt that he could just as well quit farming and take up baking and sausage making full time.

On the occasions when Jake sat between Ichabod and Walter Grimswold on one of the street benches in Charity, he was even more conspicuous, as all in the community recognized, and about which none of the trio of sitters gave a shit. Jake sat to assuage his loneliness. He couldn't tell why Walter sat, and if Walter was an enigma, Ichabod was a brick wall. An even greater mystery was the thread they shared. "Lost souls," Walter had once murmured, and Ichabod had gone as far as nodding in agreement. "Rudderless boats. We're boats without direction, and without the prospect of direction."

"I heard that Milo Jasper's milk cow had twins," Jake said. He held his regular spot on the bench, between Walter and Ichabod. Neither of his fellow sitters had anything to say.

"Guess the Jaspers are gonna be a little short of milk," Jake added.

"Umph," Walter muttered.

"Umph? What the deuce does umph mean?"

"Umph means umph. Don't you know that? What else could umph possibly mean? Everybody knows what umph means."

Jake swiveled his neck so he could stare directly at Walter, at whom he directed his best scowl. "What, then, does buffoon mean?"

Walter folded his umbrella and delicately leaned it against his end of the bench. For a second Jake feared he was going to challenge him to a fistfight.

"And a delightful day to you, too, Mr. Miller. I was just thinking, 'tis a wonderful, bright, sunny day; a great day to be alive."

"Careful, Walt, you might catch a sunburn without your umbrella of life, or what'err you call it," Ichabod piped up.

"As a matter of fact I was thinking of abandoning my umbrella of life, as you so cleverly call it. I suspect that at some point in life there is no further need for metaphysical supports. We age, we weaken both physically and mentally, and we are resigned to our end. Resigned, Ichabod. Not that a spring chicken like you would appreciate what I'm talking about."

They were interrupted by a commotion in front of The Palace. Two strangers–Jake hazarded that they were railroad workers–began shouting and shoving each other, but after a short while they tired of it, and, arms around each other's shoulders, they re-entered the bar. A few seconds later one of the men flew back out the door, over the sidewalk, face-first onto the dusty, manure and tobacco-spit stained street. He moaned, got to his knees, found his railroad cap, and regained his feet.

"I ain't no spring chicken either," grumbled Ichabod. Yet he seemed to be in a tolerably good mood, and he had opened up more than he had in years.

"All I'm saying is," Walter went on, "that in the end all that matters is what helps you get through life. That's it. The meaning of life. The meaning of life is muddling through!"

"Poo!" Ichabod smiled.

Ichabod's left eye was lazy. Apparently he had no control over it, as it was wont to roll in any direction at any time. Jake first thought it was a glass eye, but after he had tested it by various devices such as waving his hand at it from Ichabod's profile, he had concluded that he could see as well with the loose eye as with the good eye. But which eye was dominant was yet to be determined. Face to face it was instinctive to concentrate on the good eye, but one could never be certain which eye was better, though it was almost inconceivable that the rolling eye could be of much use simply because it could not be controlled and coordinated.

"By Jove, I daresay you're right!" Jake said. "The meaning of life is muddling through.

"Thank you," said Walter.

"You're very astute," Jake added.

"Thank you again."

All three relaxed on the bench, and gazed, without seeing, straight ahead. Or whatever passed for straight ahead for Ichabod.

Ahhh, Jake mulled, whatever gets you through life. Friends were part of the approach, even if they were eccentrics.

"Athos, Porthos, Aramis!" Walter blurted out. Jake and Ichabod jerked and stiffened.

"Whaat?" Jake quavered.

"Here we are, the three musketeers. Forever friends. One for all, all for one!" Walter waved his closed umbrella like a sword.

"Good god, Walter," Jake quaked as he slumped back against the hotel wall. "You're turning into a real cackler. Control yourself. Anyway, I want to be D'Artagnon."

After he had collected himself, Jake looked up at the blue-white clouds; the type of clouds that hold some moisture, but promise no rain. Rain, rain, rain, the topic in every home, on every street, and in every field where farmers stopped their tractors to visit and commiserate with neighbors. A week before, Jake had been nonplused by an elderly man who had gotten down on his knees in front Lars Nordraak's tractor to pray for rain. And pray he did, for onwards of five minutes, hatless in the scathing sun, and loud enough to be heard for a half mile. He alternated between pleading and cursing, and concluded with a crying jag.

Clouds. They brought Jake some alleviation. Now, he concentrated on a medium-sized pinkish-blue puff that stood out from the others, and he brought forth Mable, as a conjurer performs magic tricks. He tried to look past the clouds to whatever celestial place she was, and he willed her to descend and to again be a part of him. "Silly, silly, silly," he moved his lips inaudibly. Yet, and still, he felt better, and he could almost hear Mable's soft voice of comfort. At infrequent intervals over the years he had actually heard her voice, not in his head, rather as if she had been across the kitchen table from him as they had their morning cup of coffee, or as when she used to sit on the edge of their bed at night calming him after a bad dream. But that had happened even less often lately–the real voice–and he attributed it to his greater perception of life, and death, and to his ability to hold the damnable Wheel in check. There was, he knew, a fine and fragile line between communing with Mable, compared to actually hearing her and talking with her; and crossing that line meant the difference between sanity and insanity. As it was, most of his friends and acquaintances couldn't abide the communing, so he had had sense enough not to mention it anymore. Another element to retaining what friends he had, and his modicum of dignity, was to never speak of anything of any particular meaning or importance. No philosophy, religion, . . . , nothing of the supernatural, or mystical, whether he believed it or not.

Upward. Upward were his obsessions. There was no use looking down. Nothing but dry dirt. Nor was there any percent in scanning the horizon. The only way to look was up, past the dust, past the clouds–if any–past the moon, the sun, the planets, the stars; beyond even Einstein's space, to where there was real light, and hope, and . . .

Ichabod had hawked up a big glob and had proudly spat it almost to the street.

Real light, and hope, and solacement, and . . .

"Mercy," Walter said disgustedly to Ichabod.

Solacement, and, and perhaps Mable. Nonsensical? Desperation? Creation of reality? All of those things, or perhaps plain-and-simple lunacy, but after all, if people can create religion, why can't they create their own conception of what they really want? If they write a book–a novel–and the story is plausible–and within the bounds of history–in the reader's mind's eye what is there to distinguish between whether the characters are or were real? Or if someone is so devoted to an occupation or preoccupation that it absorbs them and insulates them from the real world, to that person what is the difference? Their perception is their reality. We create customs and traditions, we create religions, we create cultures, ... And therein lies the key; each individual's perception is, to them, reality.

And what's to be lost? If there is a *more* to life, hallelujah, and if not, one is no worse off. Nothing to lose. We win or draw, but in no way do we lose. A poker game of life in which one never loses.

Walter spat again.

"Goddammit Walter!" Jake barked. He closed his eyes and conjured up Mable.

CHAPTER FIFTY-THREE

In the summer of 1936 Jake's Wheel of Life began spinning out of control.

Jake plodded through the field north of his house, alone except for his good-and-faithful dog Chaucer, contemplating his vicissitudes of life, and his present downhill slide.

Already, by the first of June, the heat was unbearable. The sky was cloudless, and the air was hot with the desert-like dryness that had turned the fertile prairie into a wasteland. Every day farmers walked through the desolation of their fields, haunting the land like spirits, scanning the western horizon, willing rain to come, the price of wheat to go up, and the good times of their youth to return. There, under the scorching sun, some prayed, and some blasphemed. And each day some surrendered, packing their meager belongings and leaving. Those who left were the weak, the desperate, or the sensible. The same could have been said of those who stayed.

Jake had known for years his condition. The ridicule behind his back, the scorn, the pity. Even–sometimes–overt laughter. His few remaining friends were distancing themselves even more.

Jake came to a pile of rocks, evicted a fox, and sat in the shade, planting himself in the dry dirt, knowing that at least the land was still his. He had lost it a few years earlier, but he had managed to get it back. Lars and his communist friends had seen to that. In their desperation many had flirted with communism; many with socialism. For some it was more than a flirtation.

The rock pile was not high enough to shade Jake's head. He stood, brushed the dirt from his pants, and licked his chapped lips. A ridge of clouds materialized in the west, but the wind was wrong for rain. He started up the hill, toward home.

Jake had to get away, if only to Charity. Sometimes it helped to sit on the bench in front of the mercantile store and try to forget. To see what was going on in the community. To hear a new joke or a fresh bit of gossip, or to try to believe that it was not too late for rain. And most of all, to firm the conviction that there were better years ahead.

Jake slowed for a rut in the road. The engine of his Model A Ford coupe needed work, but he couldn't afford it, so he disregarded the knocking.

The main street was almost deserted. Jake parked in front of Charity Mercantile, but he didn't go in. Instead he joined old Knute Arhus on the bench outside. Knute couldn't hear very well, but he was a good talker. When he saw Jake coming, Knute picked up his hearing horn. He sat rigidly, staring straight at Jake.

"How are things?" Jake asked loudly.

"Things? Oh, can't kick." Knute had the annoying habit of holding his horn like a trumpet and talking through it as well as listening through it. "It's a great life if you don't weaken." He was stocky, with a pale face and red, watery eyes, and tobacco juice ran down his chin into his white beard.

"Any news?" Jake asked.

He almost wished he had stayed home. A man had to be desperate to listen to Knute. He didn't know much about Knute; only that he had come from Denmark with his parents years ago. He still had a thick accent that sounded like a lisp. He couldn't say his *v's* right. They came out kind of like *w's*. Most of the old timers from Denmark never got the *v's*, or the *th's*. They left out the *h*, so *thumb* sounded like *tum*. And they couldn't get the *j's* either. *Jim* always sounded like *Yim*, and so on. Funny how they . . .

". . . my well went dry," Knute rambled. "That's when I rented my place out to John Cornelius and moved to town. With my share, and what I make swamping out The Palace and working at the lumberyard, I get by fine. Keeps me in chewing tobacco, heh, heh, heh!" Knute spat in the dirt close to Jake's feet.

"Um."

"Never was much for drinkin', or women either," Knute continued on. "Don't take much to keep me goin', heh, heh, heh."

Jake was getting thirsty. Knute had that effect on people.

"Course I used to drink too much, and . . . ."

It was hot even in the shade. Jake watched dust swirl down the street and disappear across the railroad tracks, then he saw Goofy Grimswold come out of his house and start working on his ark. He had been piking away at it for years, and people were making bets about whether he would finish in time for the flood. Jake smiled grimly. At least Grimswold was taking some of the heat off him.

"Then one time I got so corked I thought I was gonna die, and after that . . . ."

Jake looked past Knute at The Palace.

"There's a lesson in that," Knute offered. "By gum, if yir gonna drink—"

Jake got up. "Gotta get going, Knute. See you later."

"No use tuh hurry off," Knute yelled through his horn.

Jake headed toward The Palace.

It was cooler inside, with the usual smell of stale tobacco and fresh whiskey. There were a half dozen men standing at the bar, and some at a table.

"What'll it be?" O'Malley, the owner, spoke with a low, Irish brrr. He was a hefty, round-faced man with a large, indistinct nose. He was from Boston. Jake asked for a Schlitz beer.

As O'Malley filled the mug, Jake looked around. Several of the men at the bar glanced back curiously. They hadn't seen him in there much. Then they ignored him.

O'Malley put the beer in front of Jake, and Jake paid. After the obligatory small talk, O'Malley went to the other end of the bar. Jake brushed a fly from the rim of the mug and took a drink. Two men came in and owled him with wide eyes unused to the dimness.

The first half of the beer went down fast and easy, and Jake savored the rest. When it was gone he ordered another. He always felt better after a few, but he knew the relief would be short lived. With luck someone would make a tonic, or a pill; some kind of medicine that would make people feel good, without the aftereffects of alcohol. And if they could do that, maybe they could make a pill for whatever else got into people's heads. A pill for the deranged. Jake knew it would have taken quite a pill for his mother.

"Haw, haw, haw!"

The men at the table laughed at a joke. Jake wished he could join them.

"Ho, ho! Hee, hee, hee!"

They had apparently been in there for some time. Jake felt guilty for spending good money on beer, but he couldn't help it. It helped him think. When he finished, he ordered still another. O'Malley gave him a free shot of house whiskey to go with it, and Jake knew it wasn't out of generosity. O'Malley wanted to get him tanked; get every dime out of him that he could.

The two who had just come in left, eyeing Jake again on the way out. Jake nodded, and they nodded back. Jake turned toward the mirror behind the bar. He was not as old looking as he had thought when he had first come in.

Jake tried to forget his mother. A year she had been in the asylum. He had visited her as often as he could, but she didn't seem to care whether he came or not. He was glad when she died. Glad for her. Well, on with life.

Drinking alone. Jake pondered his perspectives. Things were bad, but not as bad as they seemed. He was hanging onto the farm, and the drought was bound to end sooner or later. Others were worse off. At least he had a roof over his head, and enough to eat. That was some consolation, and . . .

"Haw, haw, haw!"

Jake had always tried to put the past behind him. And he reckoned he wasn't as crazy as he had thought. Maybe people were standoffish because of their own peculiarities, not because of his. And due to severity of their lives.

"Haw, haw! Heh, heh, heh!"

Lars had stuck by him, till the going got rough anyway. And Morgan, the best he could. And Mable always. Sure, living with him hadn't been easy, but her background was a little tainted too. He had forgiven them all, but he couldn't forget. Not much to forgive Mable for. She had had her past, as do we all, and if he couldn't forget, at least he didn't have to keep dredging it up.

"Har, har!"

The men at the table were getting wound up, and O'Malley glowered at them. Not that O'Malley had much to worry about. Once word had gotten around that he had thrown out three of the toughest drunks in town–all at the same time–he had had little trouble.

Mable. Jake guessed they had deserved each other all right. If one of them had gotten the short end of the stick, it was her. Still, there was something . . .

"Wah-hoo!"

One of the men had jumped up on the table and was doing a jig. O'Malley walked over and jabbed toward the door with his thumb. The dancer a total reprobate–stopped, got down, gave O'Malley a stern look, picked up his hat, and left.

Jake was first aware of the clock ticking. He opened his eyes, and a sharp pain cut through his head. After it passed, he slept again, and by mid afternoon he regained semi-consciousness. He remembered little; only a melange of people, and snatches of conversation. Through it all came Mable, and something was wrong. He tried to push her aside, but she reappeared, again and again. Instead of diminishing, she became more vivid, and he tossed in bed, too ill to get up, too tormented to sleep.

That evening Jake got up and cleaned himself, then he went for a walk. As the sun set, the coolness came. Jake stopped at the well for a drink, pumping with one hand; scooping with the other. His head felt large. He splashed water on his face, then he went to the barn for a little hair of the dog from his hidden bottle. Hidden out of habit.

Jake walked eastward, down a path between two fields. He recoiled at the anguished cry of a hungry fox; a human-like scream. If only he could sleep that night he would be all right. Maybe he would be all right. He was sure of it.

CHAPTER-FIFTY-FOUR

Jake–and Lars and Caroline–were in Karl and Emma Springer's yard where they had been so many times before. Only this time it was different. Karl and Emma were leaving. People had been leaving for years, but it didn't seem possible that Karl and Emma would ever leave.

Karl had been the first person Jake had met in Charity back in 1913. Jake had unloaded his things from the train, and after hitching two of his horses to his farm wagon, and tying the third behind, he had started up the main street.

In front of the hotel restaurant, Jake had found himself standing next to a short, heavyset man in a white shirt and a black derby. The man didn't look like a farmer.

"Hello."

Jake thought it sounded more like a statement than a greeting. "Hello."

"Where yuh from?"

"Iowa."

"This your outfit?"

"Yeah."

"Where yuh headed?"

"I got a relinquishment north of here about four miles. Used to be owned by a guy named Sullivan. Know where it is?"

The man's face brightened. "Yeah! You bet I know where it is. Looks like me an Emma are gonna have neighbors! Name's Karl Springer."

They shook hands.

"Me an Emma live right across the road and down a little. We been wonder'n who was gonna take over Sullivan's place. He got killed yuh know. Shot tuh death in a saloon fight. Funny guy. Never did get to know 'im. Say, can I could ride home with yuh? I hitched a ride to town, an' now I'm sort'a stuck here."

Jake's curious new friend talked all the way home.

Karl had piled everything of value that had not been sold or given away into their broken-down Chevrolet truck. He was off to make his fortune at Fort Peck–a hundred miles west–where a huge earth-filled hydroelectric dam was being built. He had scratched up enough money to start a small hardware store.

Emma had been in the kitchen all morning with Caroline, crying; and now–after all of the stalling–they were ready.

Jake was not an emotional person, but Karl's leaving was painful. He and Karl were as different as people could be, and they had quarreled from time to time, but they were friends. Lars had tried to convince Karl and Emma to stay, but Karl had made up his mind. Karl's main strength, and his biggest weakness, was his determination. Besides, he had confided to Lars that the last several years had been too much for him. He was wearing down–worn out all the time–and he needed a change; something easier. Should never have been a farmer.

"You've got time to stop at our place for a cup of coffee before you leave, don't you?" Caroline offered.

"That would be—" Emma began, but Karl cut her off.

"Like to, but if we're gonna go, we'd better get going."

Jake remained silent while Karl took off his hat. A new, tan dress hat, to replace his tattered old derby. They shook hands as they had in Charity so many years before. Jake had a catch in his throat. He hated to see his friends go, but there was more to it than that. Failed dreams of youth.

"Well, you all take care of yourselves, and come and see us once we get set up. Fort Peck ain't that far, yuh know."

Jake knew he would never see Karl and Emma again.

Caroline and Emma embraced, and they both cried. Karl came over and gave Caroline a hug.

"Take anything that's left," Karl said. There wasn't much left; only an empty, ramshackle house and a run-down barn. Karl put his hat back on, and for a moment he struggled, trying to get it to fit right. He helped Emma into the truck, then he came around to the driver's side and got in. He started the engine.

"Don't take any wooden nickels, Karl," Jake said quietly.

"Take it easy!" Karl waved, and with that he put the truck in gear and they slowly rattled and swayed out of the yard, onto the road. As they turned south, Karl waved again, and Jake could see Emma trying to get one last glimpse of them, and of her house.

Jake and Lars stood watching, and soon all they could see was a trail of dust two miles away; then nothing. Caroline cried on Lars' shoulder, then she and Lars walked, hand in hand, toward home.

Caroline stopped once and looked back. "I can still see Emma in the kitchen window," she called to Jake.

Jake lingered, remembering Karl's meteorite. This was the auspicious date that Karl had marked on his calendar as Jake's lucky day.

CHAPTER FIFTY-FIVE

Red Farmer. That's what many of the neighbors called Lars behind his back. The communist movement was all but over, Lars had been defeated in two elections for the state House of Representatives, and times had changed. Lars had changed too, from a strong young man to a corpulent old man–older than he should have been–who regretted not his involvement in the farm movement, but who felt shame and remorse for his communist activities. He had much to be remorseful for, because he had been one of the higher-ups. He had been a communist when he was a state representative, he had been sucked in and used, he had done much of the dirty work, and now it was all fading into local history. Finished. And for all that, nothing was accomplished that couldn't have been accomplished through regular Farm Labor Party involvement, protests, and normal political means. In any event, and ironically, what had the biggest impact was a change in the spirit of the times. That's what Jake saw, and what Lars had not seen coming. That and the preposterousness of communism in the first place. Jake had known for quite a while that Lars' activities in the Communist Party were backfiring. Inevitable. Communism was a fraud. An elaborate something-for-nothing scheme. Served him right. Such a know-it-all. And who would fall for it? Communism? Fourth-grade-educated guys like Lars Nordraak. Not stupid, but ignorant.

Lars' recent indignity was hearing that his effigy–a scarecrow-like dummy in bib overalls and a straw hat, with a *Red Farmer* sign on its front and back–had been hung from a pole in the middle of Main Street in Plainview, doused with gasoline, and burned.

Jake and Lars had talked about the burning only once, and Jake had been unable to resist saying *I told you so*, and a few other not-so-tactful observations that he had been bottling up for years. Lars was as tough as ever though, and Jake had expected anything from a punch in the nose to a tongue-lashing. But he received neither.

Now they were sitting in Jake's barn, on the same wooden kegs on which they had sat eleven years ago when Jake's cow was dying; when he had warned Lars about turning pink.

Lars was subdued. Eleven years ago he had had the fire of his convictions, and had gone on about banks, farmers, and starving people, and all. Now there was nothing but a placid, lackluster, cloudy look in his eyes.

They sat quietly on the kegs, and it was like deja vu, only real. But this time as Jake gazed past Lars out the big barn door, instead of sun there were dark storm clouds, and far-off thunder like that which always reminded their Great War friend, Morgan Feeney, of heavy artillery, and of death. All about them in the barn everything was the same, except for themselves; still, as they sat, they could conjure up their younger days, despite everything. At times Jake felt a youthfulness and hope in himself, and he even detected occasional flashes of light in Lars' eyes, and a quiet sense of humor. They talked quietly, of farming, weather, local gossip, and of nothing. They were at peace, with each other, and with life.

But outside, through the door, everything was different. Mable was gone. Karl and Emma Springer had left–along with many others–and times were changing. Morgan Feeney and his wife, Genevieve, were still there, though Morgan was an odd sort. Walter Grimswold was still around, but he was even odder than Morgan. And Ichabod Klopper, his other eccentric friend and fellow bench sitter, had managed to hang onto his farm. Aside from those stalwarts and a few others whom he considered friends, all was different outside that almost-mystical barn door. All but the dry barrenness; that was the same and always would be. But the country was different–politics in particular–and the people seemed changed, . . . Times were changing. Karl Springer, in his own simple German way had called it *gestalt*, and Jake ventured that Karl had been right. Jake hated change.

Jake was tempted to say something about his ruminations to Lars, but he knew better. No use breaking their reverie, and besides, Lars probably had a similar feeling.

"Bent Larson's wife chased him down Main Street with their car the other night," Jake said.

Lars raised one eyebrow, as he always did when curious. "Why?"

"She came to town and peeked in the front window of The Palace, and there was Bent, boiled as an owl and in the arms of some floozy. Ingaborg picked up a big stick and charged into the bar like Carrie Nation. She chased Bent out the door and down the street, but polluted as he was, he outran–or I should say out-staggered–big, fat

Inga. Well you know Inga, that wasn't enough, so she got into the Essex and tried to run him down."

"I didn't think she knew how to drive." Lars whisked away a fly.

"I didn't either, but she had made it to town, and then took a good stab at running over him."

"All he'd have had to do is turn up an ally or something."

"He was slobbering drunk, and all he could do was run down the street like a rabbit in the headlights. Guess I shouldn't even call it running; it was—as I said—staggering."

"What happened?"

"Well, she'd have done him in for sure except a bunch of guys converged on the car. Most of them grabbed onto it and were dragged along, but one of them managed to grab the controls and stop the car."

"What then?"

"They dragged Bent into the back room of The Palace and threw him onto a pile of gunny sacks. Two others took Inga home, and took away her car keys. Just to make sure, they pulled the spark plug wires loose when she wasn't looking."

"Well I never," Lars chuckled.

Jake looked past Lars again, out the door. He wished he could stay in the barn and never come out. The house evoked remembrances of Mable, he was a bit of an eccentric in town, he had no relatives and not many friends. His Wheel—he had come to see it, envision it, feel it, or whatever, as his Grindstone—had ground to a near halt. Ha! There was no future in farming, and as far as all that went, he had no future at all. He'd have to invent a future, or perish. And the way things were going, if he perished, they'd have to put up a wrought-iron fence to prevent people from dancing on his grave.

But there was always the barn.

CHAPTER FIFTY-SIX

As Jake dried the last dish, there was a knock on the door. He hung up his dishtowel and peeked out the window. He didn't care anymore, yet he was afraid. But it was just an old man. Jake pulled open the door.

"Good day, sir." The man bowed slightly. He had wild, white hair, and at first Jake thought he was wearing a robe, but it was a long overcoat.

"What can I do for you?"

"That's what they all ask! The first thing you can do is invite me in."

"What?"

The stranger's eyes flashed in the dusk. He held a black book in one hand.

Jake stepped back. "But what do you—?"

The man picked up his carpetbag and entered. "Obadiah, named after my father, who was . . . ." He was tall and dark skinned.

"Yes, but what are you? What do you do?" Jake asked again.

The man touched a chair, and Jake nodded for him to sit. Jake remained standing.

"I can take your coat."

Obadiah held up his hand. "This coat is my penance, Mr. Miller. I never take it off." His face was wrinkled and sunburnt.

"How did you know my name?"

"I asked. Big, drunk man offered me a ride. Drives a black Packard. No divine revelation there, Mr. Jake Miller."

"Never take off your coat? But it's over ninety degrees. How can you—?"

"A small price to pay. That, and my work."

"Where are you from?"

"That changes."

Jake was getting uncomfortable. "I don't mean to be nosey, but what do you do?" he asked again.

"I do the Lord's work."

Jake relaxed. Yet another traveling preacher, only a little more crackbrained than most.

"Psychogenic game playing," Jake murmured.

"Ah, I see! Psychogenic, Mr. Miller? My, I am about to be challenged!" Obadiah leaned his chair back and hooked his thumbs in the pockets of his coat. "It's not often that I am challenged," he went on. "With you it's going to be different. Different indeed." He sat smiling.

Jake knew he was going to have to pay the price, unless he threw the old fart out. "Why did you stop here?"

"I stop everywhere." He leaned forward, with his hands folded on the table, over his Bible.

"Well, if you talked with Ben–the guy with the Packard–you should know I don't have much to do with people. Especially preachers."

"Oh, I'm not a preacher. Not at all. I'm an evangelist. Big difference you know."

"No, I don't know. All the same to me," Jake said good naturedly, but he was still considering throwing his visitor out.

"I beg your pardon, but it's not the same. I don't take kindly to being lumped in with preachers. Not that I have anything serious against them. Only that they live in their own cloistered little worlds. That's so, isn't it, almost by definition? Their ivory towers of religion? They never see the real world like I do, and while the dictionary definitions of preacher and evangelist may be the same, there's a vast differentiation. When I go out into the world, I see . . . ."

As Obadiah talked, his hair floated upward, reminiscent of someone who has had the wits frightened out of him. But other than his hair, he had the appearance of one who had never been frightened in his life. Not only was he unafraid, he appeared to welcome whatever fate could deliver.

". . . the decay that has consumed our land. Spiritual and moral decay that will only end when each individual seeks atonement. And like the prophets of old, I have been called to . . . ," Obadiah continued, patting his Bible with his left hand, and pointing to the ceiling with the other.

"If I remember correctly, Obadiah was only a minor prophet," Jake interrupted. "A few short passages in the Bible about how the Israelites were put upon by their enemies?"

"The Edomites. But indeed he must have been a significant prophet. It's reasonable to assume that if he spoke against the

Edomites, he was! But we're quibbling. In Jerusalem at that time . . . ."

Obadiah's hair stood out even more, and his eyes flashed brighter. This is too much, Jake grumped inwardly. A parody. Or was Obadiah an apparition?

Two hours later–after Obadiah had finished his standard spiel–he glared sternly across the table at Jake and asked, "Now, how may I help you?"

Jake, lulled by the two-hour sermon, had been fighting to stay awake. "Help me? That's a good one. Nobody can help me. You have met your match, and perhaps it's time for you to—"

"I have never met my match, Jake Miller. Never! Now let's get down to it."

For a half hour, Jake summed up his life, and presented to Obadiah the skeleton of his now-abandoned Unified Theory of Life.

"So that's how I came to be the miserable wretch before you," Jake concluded, with sarcastic melodrama.

Obadiah sat studying him, and for a full minute he was silent.

"You are in desperate need of salvation," Obadiah finally said. "Are you ready to repent the sins you have just recounted, and all of those untold?" He glared at Jake, more as an adversary than a saver of souls.

"Repent? Yes I repent. I have repented nearly every day of my life, but not in a religious way. And that's the rub. I'm not a religious person. I don't—"

"I sense you have been in church many, many times over the years, Jake Miller."

"Well, I've had my struggles, but the spirit never really moved me. As I was about to say, I don't expect you to see it–those like you never do–but no matter how tough life gets, I can't weaken. To me religion is nothing but mythology. In fact to my way of thinking, there is no religion. If none of the hocus-pocus of religions is true, then how can there be something called religion? It would be the same as if there were no pipes, how could there be plumbers?"

He paused, expecting an outburst, but there was none.

"So that's it," Jake concluded. "No more long-winded philosophical arguments, nothing. When it comes right down to it, you either believe, or you don't, and I don't."

Obadiah sat stone-still, piercing Jake with his eyes, then he stood and held his Bible high above his head. "I have met my match, and he is evil," he said. He picked up his bag to leave. "You're crazier than I am!"

"Evil?" Jake shuddered. "How can you call me evil? I couldn't help—"

"I pray that God will save your soul, Jake Miller." Obadiah moved toward the door.

"That's just it, I have no soul. Nobody does, therefore there is no such thing as religion."

Obadiah walked out the door.

"Wait! Come back here, you pious sonovabitch!" Jake cried after him.

The screen door slammed, and Obadiah was gone.

CHAPTER FIFTY-SEVEN

Jake rattled his way over the hills in his Ford Model A coupe, driving aimlessly. Anything to get out of the house. He made it to the top of the high ridge that separated his place from Tunney Hunmann's, and started down the other side. The transmission gears whined now that he was coasting, and he touched the brake to keep from building up too much momentum. Several years ago he had missed a gear coming down the same hill with a load of wheat, and had nearly wrecked his truck. A north wind buffeted him through the open window, driving the stale engine fumes out the other side.

By the time Jake got to the bottom of the hill the wind was kicking up dust in the fields. He turned north and waved at Tunney's wife, Fern, who was gathering clothes from the clothesline. Tunney and Fern were from Virginia, where he had been a sharecropper, raising tobacco. Nice people, but Tunney hadn't taken to farming on the plains. Too different from what he was used to, and he seemed to do everything wrong.

Jake passed a rock pile in the near corner of a quarter section of pasture that Tunney was breaking up. Tunney's tractor was at the other end, and Jake assumed he had gotten off to visit with whoever had parked a blue Dodge sedan on the road nearby.

Halfway to the far end, Jake still couldn't see anyone, but they were probably sitting on the other side of the tractor, out of the dust, solving farm problems. The car looked like Morgan Feeney's. Jake took off his hat and shooed a bee out the window. He didn't know how a bee could fly in that kind of wind. Funny, the tractor was parked at an odd angle.

The wind strengthened. Jake still couldn't see anyone, and he shifted into low. The tractor, a Hart-Parr 12-24, sat with both front wheels against a big rock.

Jake got out, walked to the rear of the tractor, and studied the disk harrow. Something wasn't right. Then a chill gripped the back of his neck. He turned and saw that the tractor seat was missing; broken from its spring-steel support.

Jake was sick, and he felt his legs work to hold him up. He steadied himself against one of the huge steel wheels, and looked down at the disk again. There, stuck to part of the frame, was a piece of cloth.

The wind blasted dirt into Jake's face. He lifted his head and wiped his eyes, but he couldn't see past the first rise. He pulled himself away from the tractor and followed the disk path, plodding numbly, wondering how he would tell Fern.

The path was surprisingly straight, then it curved southward. Jake couldn't understand why the front wheels hadn't jackknifed until the tractor had come to the rock. He squinted into the dust and walked on, until he topped a small hill. On the back side of a pile of dirt, lying face down, was Tunney. Morgan was kneeling beside him. Jake stopped for a moment, then approached. "Tunney?" His voice sounded like that of a stranger.

Morgan nodded as he brushed the dirt from Tunney's back and rolled him over. Tunney flopped loosely onto his back with his eyes open and his mouth packed with dry soil. Jake gagged, fell to his hands and knees, and threw up. When he was done he covered the vomit with dirt and crawled over to Morgan.

"An awful way to go," Morgan said. He sat, broad-shouldered and seemingly calm.

Jake tried to talk, but only gibberish came out.

"Settle down, Jake. Nothing we can do for him now."

"But we can't simply leave him here! We gotta—"

"I'll straighten him out as best I can. You get some of the neighbors. Have them come and load him up. And get Lucy and the other ladies to help you break it to Fern."

Lucy was Fern's best friend.

"Okay." But Jake couldn't move. "I could stay with him," he said.

"If it's all the same, I'll stay. I saw it all in the war, and it doesn't bother me. Often I can deal with death better that with life, and I don't think I could stand it when you tell Fern."

"Give me a few minutes."

"Sure."

Morgan gently closed Tunney's eyes, cleared his mouth of dirt, and forced his jaw shut. He took off his hat and put it over Tunney's face. "I can hear artillery off in the west," Morgan said.

"Artillery? "

"Not really. Not actually hear it. But almost. I don't know. At odd times I guess I can." Morgan reached out and patted Tunney's leg.

"Why Tunney?" Jake asked. "If there's a God, why would he do this?" He looked past Morgan, and he couldn't see over fifty feet in the blowing dust.

"If you had been in the war, you never would have asked that question. You live, the guy next to you gets blown to smithereens. The sky pilots used to talk about divine intervention, and how there are no atheists in the trenches, and all that rot."

"Sky pilots?"

"Chaplains. Easy for them to say, they weren't on the business end of a howitzer. There's no faith like that of a noncombatant. There were plenty of atheists in the trenches, and the longer the war went on, the more there were. There is no divine intervention."

"But they say you've been going to church lately." Jake wiped a bit of dried vomit from his lower lip.

"They're right."

"What about all of your talk about living in the real world, like me? All these years of being so cynical?"

"What about you, trying to communicate with Mable? Kind of the same thing, isn't it?"

"Uh, I don't know. I guess." Jake hung his head.

It was getting dark, mostly from the dust. Morgan closed his eyes, shuddered, and mumbled something about star shells. Then he looked somberly at Jake. "When Genevieve and I got married, I was pretty beat up, but she helped bring me back. Part of it was her religious faith. Sometimes I believed her; most of the time I didn't, no matter how hard I tried. But now I do. Simple as that. And one of the things I know is, God doesn't intervene. He at most winds the clock once in a while. And holds our hand."

"Quite a reversal," Jake murmured.

After telling Lucy, Jake couldn't go straight home. Something drew him to Mable's church. He parked in back as the sun went down, hoping no one would see him. One good thing about country churches, you could sneak in.

Jake groped his way to the front and sat down. He waited for his eyes to get used to the gloom, and after a while he could make out the altar, and behind it the traditional icon of Jesus knocking.

The worst of it had not been Tunney's open eyes, or his dirt-filled mouth. It was something else that had cut to Jake's heart.

Whatever it was had gone deep into his soul. Soul hell. He didn't believe in souls and eternity. No afterlife; nothing. Yet here he had come crawling to church, like the wounded dog his mother had told him about. Her dog, that had come home one day, cut and bleeding. Her father was going to put it out of its misery, but before he could get his gun, it had crawled into a pig sty. There it lay in the mud, and they assumed it had died, but a week and a half later it came out, and it lived for ten more years. Jake felt like that dog: crawling for salvation when things got bad.

Jake heard a car, and he was irritated that someone would disturb him. No doubt it was only passing by.

The altar seemed to glow, and the urge to pray took hold of Jake. He was chagrined at his weakness. He viewed all religion as wishful thinking, but at the same time he wanted to believe. Sitting in the semidarkness, before the glowing altar, Jake longed for a sign. Nothing new in that. People throughout the ages had wanted signs–some so desperately that they had experienced them–and again he was embarrassed at his moral frailty.

The car slowed. Nosey busybodies. Jake felt woozy.

The altar shimmered, and the Jesus icon was clouded by a nebulous form. The form took shape, and Jake apprehended it to be the Archangel Uriel: fire of God, most radiant of angels, leader of the order of Seraphim. Uriel–archangel of salvation–in heavenly glory, his open hand holding a red-and-gold flame. Jake bowed his head and awaited his redemption, but he felt nothing. He steeled himself and looked up, and as he did, the archangel clenched his hand, extinguishing the flame.

Jake sprang from the pew and fled down the aisle to the back door, and as he descended the outer steps, he bumped into someone.

"Ow! What the . . . ? That you, Miller?"

Jake ran through the dark until he collided with his car. He got in, started the engine, and roared away in a fog of disconsolation and fear.

CHAPTER FIFTY-EIGHT

"Professionals. Had tuh be, the way they blew the vault."

Gabriel Dyken was talking about the branch bank across the street. He and Jake were sitting on a bench in front of Charity Mercantile. Henry Norton stood beside them, leaning his shoulder against the wall.

"Last night?" Jake asked.

"Night before last." Gabriel's big, owl eyes blinked into the glare of the sun.

"Nobody heard 'em?" Henry asked.

"Naw. Too busy with the fire."

There had been a fire in Jan Olson's barn on the north edge of town.

"The burglars start the fire?"

"Sure. I told yuh, they were professionals."

All three surveyed the bank. It was closed, and there were two out-of-state cars parked in front.

"Yuh know, it's kinda funny," Gabriel said. "They went tuh all that trouble, and they didn't get nothin'. There wasn't over a hundred dollars. They did more damage tuh the vault than that. But the worst of it is, people are startin' tuh talk. They're worried there's gonna be a run on the bank."

"Stuart tell yuh that?" Henry asked.

Stuart Simpson was president of the First State Bank of Cottonwood, and the branch in Charity.

"No, but I got it on good authority, yuh can bank on that."

Jake smiled at Gabriel's pun, intended or not.

"Stu's a worried man," Gabriel said.

A fight broke out in front of the hotel; a Great Dane and a part wolf. Mrs. Jorn, the restaurant cook, came out to empty a pail of dishwater. She threw it on the dogs and went back inside.

"That Morgan Feeney's wolf?" Henry asked.

"No," Jake answered. "Morgan's dog stays home." Always Morgan. Morgan had suffered enough in the war, but people never let up.

"I'd a' bet on the wolf," Henry said.

"The Great Dane was doing alright."

Jake didn't have a pick. He was worried. About the voices. The Light he could live with, but not the voices. The Light only came once in a while, but the voices came almost every day now, mostly when he was alone. Occasionally an intonation, a word, or a phrase would pop out, and that was what concerned Jake the most. And he had noted a correlation between the frequency of the Light and the speed of his Wheel.

"Gettin' so there are more dogs than people around here," Gabriel said.

Jake felt his forehead. Pernicious utterances too appalling to bear.

"I had an egg-eater once," Gabriel went on. "Used tuh dig into the chicken coop at night. Well, I filled some eggs up with red pepper, and . . . ."

Jake tried to settle himself. The only thing that kept him from coming apart was that he was used to it by now.

"Lousy dogs," Henry said. He went into the store, and came out with a pouch of Red Man chewing tobacco. He stuffed as much of it as he could into his mouth, poking it in with his index finger. Jake and Gabriel stared at the bank.

"Wonder when they'll reopen," Gabriel said.

"Opun wun therr ruddy thu opun," Henry said. "Whuds thu duffurunce?" He put the rest of the tobacco in his pants pocket.

Another gust of wind swept the street, and the puddle of dishwater was almost gone. Sun and wind.

"Hear about that fight in the pool hall in Cottonwood?" Gabriel asked.

Jake shook his head.

"Two miners from Butte. Damn near killed each other. Fought till neither of them could move. Bartender had tuh swamp the place out after they were through. Blood, teeth, hair—"

"What a fright," Jake said.

"Yeah, Rudi Prinz never saw anything like it, in or outta' the ring. He was a prizefighter, yuh know. Said both of 'em were half dead by the time it was over. Old Doc Whaddyucallim's tryin' tuh patch 'em up. Had tuh move their beds apart in the hospital. They was still tryin' tuh get at each other the next day."

Neither Jake nor Henry said anything. Someone in a dark blue suit came out of the bank, got into one of the cars, and drove away. Stuart Simpson lingered in the doorway, squinting, following the dust of the car. Then he backed up and slammed the door shut.

"Stu don't look very happy," Gabriel chortled. Henry laughed.

Jake gritted his teeth. He could tell it was coming, and when it came all he could do was hang on and ride with it until it passed. This time it wasn't bad–a rush of thoughts and feelings–then it was over. Maybe that was it for the day. Usually he didn't get two in one day.

"He never looks happy," Henry said. "Say, you're kinda' quiet, Jake."

"Bad stomach."

"Oh. In The Palace too long last night, eh?"

It was their standing joke.

"You know me."

"Haw!"

At first Jake had fought the voices with such ferocity that he couldn't remember what they said. Now he was starting to remember, but they made no sense. Today, for instance. Something about taking a journey. And about his Unified Theory of Life. He couldn't remember what, only that it was uncomplimentary. And a laugh. He had definitely heard a laugh.

"Yuh hear about Alice Martingale?" Gabriel asked.

"No. What?"

"Aloys chased her all the way up the street," he indicated in front of them, "with his double-barreled shotgun the other night."

"Must not have caught 'er," Henry said. "I saw her this morning."

"Wasn't tryin' tuh catch 'er. Just scarin' the shit outta' her. And he did scare it out of her, literally. But that's not the best part. The best part was that she didn't have a stitch on."

"No!" Henry said. "Well that couldn't a' been the best part. I'll bet Alice looks better with clothes than without."

"How do you know? You seen 'er with 'em off?"

"What happened?" Jake asked.

"Nothin'. Chased her around the block and back home, and that was it."

Henry seemed skeptical. "How do you know all that?"

"From Sidney Franklin. He was comin' outta' The Palace when they went by."

"The heck," Jake said.

"Yeah, and he said . . . ."

Jake lost track. He was thinking about Mable.

"That must'a been some sight," Henry said. "Haw, haw, haw!"

"Wish I'd a' seen it! Haw, haw, haw! Hee, hee! Sidney said she's built for comfort."

"Here comes Diggs."

Orion Diggs. Jake had heard that he and his wife worked for a mysterious character named Hirshmann; a retired doctor from Germany who had arrived recently, built a mansion on a hill northwest of town, and lived the life of a recluse. Few people even knew what Dr. Hirshmann looked like.

"Every Thursday Diggs comes for supplies," Henry said. "Otherwise–unless there's somethin' tuh pick up at the depot–yuh never see 'im."

Gabriel waved, and Diggs waved back but didn't come over. "Diggs never says anything about the doctor. Said if he did, he'd get canned, an' he's too old for that. Some a' the boys got him ossified once, but he still wouldn't talk. All he'd say was that Hitler is making it rough on the Jews, and that Hirshmann's wife is dead."

"What happened?" Henry accidentally swallowed some tobacco juice, and he went into a gagging spell.

"Dunno. But it sounds like Hirshmann got out while the gettin' was good. And he kept goin' on about a guy named Sigmund Froid, or Frued, or some such."

"Freud?"

"I guess. He's kind of hard to understand. He's not German you know, he's from Austria." Gabriel looked up at the sun. "Suppose I should be gettin' home," but he didn't move. "Old Hirshmann's a talk doctor."

"A talk doctor?" Jake said.

"Yeah."

CHAPTER FIFTY-NINE

Through his workshop window Jake saw a man with a suitcase walk into the yard. Jake quit what he was doing and went outside.

"Afternoon," the man called. He was a negro. He put down his suitcase.

Jake waved.

The man was dressed in wool pants and shirt; incongruous in the ninety degree heat. "Could I trouble you for a drink of water?"

Jake beckoned him toward the well, took the enameled tin cup from its nail on the fence, handed it to the stranger, and began pumping. "Wait 'till it gets cold," he said. He pumped for a minute.

The man drank, and Jake pumped him another cupful.

"Oh, mercy. Thanks." He finished the second cup. Jake started to pump again, but the man stopped him. He was about thirty-five, medium height, well built; and what struck Jake most about him were his eyes. A look of exceptional intelligence. And of something more.

"Mind if I rest a while?" His southern accent was new to Jake.

"It's about suppertime. Could you stand something to eat?"

"If it's not a great inconvenience."

"No trouble at all. Nothing fancy, just meat and potatoes."

"Meat and potatoes sounds good when you haven't eaten in two days."

"Two days without—?"

"I'm used to it."

"Good lord, I—"

"Can't pay you. I could work, if there's anything you need done."

"Let's get you fed."

The man held out his hand. "George Goodman."

"Jake Miller."

Their eyes met straight for the first time.

"Let's eat," Jake said.

They ate, and Jake had to cook more. He was glad to do it.

"Dothan, Alabama, eh?" Jake said as he fried more potatoes and opened another jar of canned beef.

George nodded. He hadn't said much.

"Grew up on a farm?"

"You could call it that. Wasn't ours anyway. Left when I was fifteen."

"Been back?"

"Never been back."

Jake turned to him. "Don't mean to pry. I don't get much company, that's all, and—"

George flicked the back of his hand toward Jake. "You're not prying."

Jake poured the beef into the pot, then he went to the window and opened it wider. The evening heat made the horizon ripple. Close by, the leaves on the caragana trees were curling prematurely. Jake returned to the stove and added another lump of coal.

"Don't mean to eat you out of house and home," George said. "Can't seem to control myself."

"I'll keep it coming as long as you can eat it," Jake said. He chuckled, and George smiled back. While George ate, Jake talked, abashed at his own blithering, but unable to stop.

"When Mable died, I thought it was the end. I guess it was. Here, let me get you another cup of coffee."

As Jake poured, he noticed George's knuckles were raised, like he had arthritis.

"I can put on some more potatoes, but damn, I'm afraid it'd kill you," Jake said.

George laughed, and he pushed away from the table. "No, thanks, it probably would kill me!"

Later they talked into the night.

"What then?" Jake asked. "After you worked on the railroad?"

George had worked on a section crew in Colorado, repairing track.

"Then I rode the rails, instead of working on them. Traveled the country, but ended up picking fruit in California. That's when I got into fighting."

"Fighting?"

"Prizefighting. A friend I was picking with used to fight. His name was George too. George Pendleton. He had to quit because of his eyes, but he carried gloves in his suitcase. We sparred every night after work. He touched me up pretty good at first. I thought he was giving me hell, but later I knew he was taking it easy. After awhile I began to catch on, and then he really started working with me. Guess he saw something." George gulped the last of his coffee.

"Then?"

"He took me to see his old manager. The next day they put me in with a heavyweight to see how I'd do. Big Swedish palooka from Wisconsin."

"How'd you do?"

"Got beat. He was no slouch, and I only weighed a hundred and fifty pounds. I must'a passed the test though. Old Fisk, the manager, took me on."

Jake took the mantle lantern from its hook on the wall and pumped it up. He put it back and sat down again.

George gazed dreamily at the window over the sink. "The picking season was over, so they had me working out in the gym, and running, and all that. I never worked so hard in my life, and just when I was going to quit, they scheduled my first fight. Four-rounder with a guy from Chicago."

"Who won?"

"I did. Knocked him out in the second round. Fought again two weeks later, and knocked another guy out in the first round. Then they didn't want to give me any more fights."

"Why?"

George seemed amused. "Why? Hell, I was beating all the white guys, that's why. They weren't looking for me to win; they were looking for a villain. Wouldn't schedule me unless I'd lie down."

"Did you?"

A coyote howled far away, and both men sat quietly for a moment.

"Yeah, but only once. It was an obvious barney, and everybody wanted their money back. I got another fight though, but when they found out I wasn't going to fall down anymore, they let me go."

"Then?"

"Another trainer took me. Not out of the goodness of his heart. He was a promoter, and he knew the more I won, the more they'd hate me, and the bigger the crowds would be. He was right. Well, after I beat everybody there was to beat, we went on the road."

George told of fights won and lost, dirty hotels, swindlers, . . .

"Then I got too old. One morning I woke up in a hotel in some little town in Idaho. My manager and my trainer were gone. There was a note and twenty-five dollars on the dresser, and I never saw them again."

Jake fixed a bed for George in the workshop.

George stayed. He and Jake picked rocks and did whatever else they could that didn't cost money. In their spare time they talked, and in the evenings George taught Jake to box.

"No, when you throw a left hook, you hold your thumb up, and turn on the ball of your left foot," George said. "Like this. But you've got to be in position. Bend your knees, crouch, then when you swing, twist at the waist, ..."

They were in a makeshift ring: a rope strung between two fenceposts and the clothesline poles. They had been at it for three weeks, and at first Jake was ready to quit. He was too old, and too slow, and mostly he didn't like getting hit in the face. But George wouldn't let him quit, and after the first two weeks, Jake started liking it. It took his mind off things, and his headaches were not as bad.

"No! This way," George said. He slapped Jake with a left hook, with just enough force to get his attention.

They rested in the evening shade of the house, and Jake brought up his Unified Theory of Life. George listened politely.

". . . so I figured if I could distill the quintessence of the great philosophers, and the foundations of the world's great religions, I'd have . . . ."

George said little, but once in a while he would ask a question; an indication that he knew what Jake was talking about.

"So if Plato's forms were . . . ," Jake continued.

George grunted.

"But," Jake said, "I gave up on my so-called Unified Theory of Life. I was getting nowhere."

Then it was back into the ring until dark.

"You have a bad habit," George said. "You're telegraphing your punches. Look, instead of holding your arms way out in front of you, and pulling back for every punch, tighten up. Here, right hand beside your chin, left hand out a little. Then, when you punch, don't draw back first. Drive your arm straight, and twist."

Jake tried it.

"That's better, but rotate your shoulder into it."

Jake threw a left jab and a straight right.

"Good, but you're still pulling back. Look, I'll show you."

He held up his gloves.

"The instant I pull back, even an inch, you're going to duck, right? So if you start ducking before I even throw the punch, I don't have a chance. You're going to have to work on that."

Jake parked in front of Charity Mercantile and got out of his car. He had only a few things to get. It was cool inside, and dim, and it took him a moment to see. He was the only customer. The predominant odor was that of cheese.

"Morning, Jake."

Jake nodded. Alexander Small worked at the store part time. The rest of his time was spent next door at the bar.

Salt, sugar, yeast. Only the staples. It didn't take long.

"That all, Jake?"

Alexander tried to be congenial, but Jake could tell his heart wasn't in it. Jake had never liked him. He didn't know why. Likely his indolence.

Jake walked to his car. As he was putting his groceries in, Frazer Mullins approached.

"Hello, there, nigger lover!"

Jake closed the car door and turned. Behind Frazer stood Wilbert Uhlman. They were both unshaven and bleary-eyed drunk.

"I said, hello there, nigger lover!"

It was over in less than thirty seconds. Then Jake got into his car and drove off.

"I think yuh hit 'im too hard Jake! He ain't gettin' up"

The next day the county sheriff came. His name was Smith. He was tall, lean, and solid looking; and he had been a sheriff for most of his life. He and Jake talked on the porch.

After the sheriff left, George came out. "I couldn't help hearing," he said. "Sounds like I taught you too well."

"It was nothing."

"Well, thanks, but you don't have to fight my fights. I wouldn't want you to end up in the can on my account."

"I've been in jail before."

The sheriff's car disappeared over the last hill.

"I'll be leaving tomorrow," George said. He seemed tired inside, Jake thought.

"No need to leave, it was just a—"

"Nothing to do with that. Time to move on, Jake."

Early the next morning George left. Jake cooked ham and eggs, forced twenty dollars on him, and watched him go. He could see him for two miles, and no one stopped to give him a ride.

CHAPTER SIXTY

Jake suspicioned that his persistence would be his undoing. In many others, persistence was a strength. In him it was a debility. And so it was that he could not relinquish Mable. After his first unsuccessful attempts to intercommunicate with her had failed, he had fallen into a general state of dolor. Sheer folly, trying to revisit the dead. Nothing more than the refusal to accept the unacceptable. Desperation. But over the years the need had grown, until it had become an obsession. Until all logic was rejected; all dispassion cast aside; all reality denied.

Jake devoted every evening to the divination of Mable's immortal part. He would sit in the semidarkness—with the gas lantern hissing and the wind moaning—listening desperately for a sign. Loneliness permeated every cell of his body, and when he had endured more than any normal human could endure, he would look yet again at Mable's chair, hoping to see some aura of her. Always he was disappointed, with only the flickering shadows of his memories. Then he would fall asleep where he sat. Conditions were never right.

"Please sit down, Mr. Miller."

Jake balanced carefully on the front edge of a Victorian chair. The sitting room was small, and filled with decorative furniture. The walls were draped with extraordinarily colorful tapestry, and there were beautiful and mysterious art objects all about. A black cat lay on the floor beside his host's feet, and not until Jake had sat for a good many minutes did he realize it was stuffed. The cat reminded Jake of his childhood cat, only his cat had been gray, and . . .

"All the way from Montana, Mr. Miller?"

Mrs. Averagado was dressed in a black gown stitched with swirling red designs. An attractive, middle-aged, foreign-looking woman with straight black hair, she smiled from behind a Chinese fan. "All the way from Montana to New York City. I suppose you expect me to say I knew you would be here today?"

Jake nodded noncommittally. It had been a long train trip, and there was every chance the whole deal was a flim-flam.

"Then, Mr. Miller, I am so very sorry, but you misunderstand the function of a medium. Only a false medium would have said that. You do see my meaning?"

"Yes, I—"

"The raison d'etre of a medium is solely to assist. I would be deeply offended if you were to expect more."

From behind a curtain an elderly lady emerged carrying a silver tea service. She was short and dumpy, with graying hair and a round, wrinkled face. She put the tray on the tea table, poured, and left.

"Tea time, Mr. Miller. Sugar?"

Jake shook his head and clumsily took one of the small, delicate cups. Mrs. Averagado held her cup gracefully.

"All the way from Montana because you read of me in a newspaper. My, that is interesting."

There was an aspect of Mrs. Averagado's demeanor that Jake found disconcerting. Her refinement. And he was uncomfortable with the theatrical aspect of his host's quarters. Beaded doorways, frescoed ceiling, boldly-carpeted floor, . . . , all manner of ornamentation and furnishing. Such an atmosphere could be the concoction of a charlatan. Indeed, the air reeked of fraud. Jake had come prepared. One hint of chicanery and he would be gone. He was sure of the foundation of what he was about to undertake, but charlatans abounded.

"And now, Mr. Miller, the delicate subject of fees. As with any professional–doctor, lawyer, accountant–I have set rates that I . . . ."

That evening Jake lay on the bed in his hotel room, preparing himself for the next-day's seance. Unfortunately there would be other clients. He had hoped to be alone. And the maid. He wasn't sure of her function. Perhaps to help lift the table and rattle the walls.

Jake took Mable's letter from the inside pocket of his suit coat that lay on the bed beside him.

Whenever you need me, I will be with you. When you are alone in our special place, reach out for me. In the quietness of the night, open your heart, and I will come.

He folded the letter and put it away, and turned off the reading light beside the bed. He lay propped up, looking out the window, watching a red light flash from the top of the building across the street. He thought back to his and Mable's hotel room in Flandrum when they had gone to soak in the mineral spring. Now, in the dark, the dingy room receded, and he pretended for a moment that the dim form of his coat was Mable, sleeping. He tried to suppress a long, low sob.

The following evening, Jake returned to Mrs. Averagado's residence. On the outside it was plain, like all of the other row houses. He grasped the knocker and rapped.

Three others were already in the sitting room: a man and two women. They were all elderly and well dressed. The man was bearded and distinguished looking—he resembled Tzar Nicholas II—and Jake took him for a banker. The women were both heavy and matronly, and they wore what Jake supposed was the latest in fashion for the wealthy: long, black dresses and wide-brimmed feathered hats. One had makeup caked on her face. The other was very handsome: delicate, with dark, short hair and a kind smile.

Mrs. Averagado entered, followed by her housemaid.

"Come, it's time to start," Mrs. Averagado said. "Into the drawing room, if you please."

She led them to a smaller room. Precisely as Jake had envisioned: a round table surrounded by straight-backed wooden chairs. The floor was covered with an oriental carpet, and the ceiling had been painted with cryptic symbols. On each wall hung a lithographic portrait. Jake recognized the one on his left as that of Sir Arthur Conan Doyle, but the other three men were unfamiliar as they glared at him from beneath bushy eyebrows and from behind shaggy beards. The only other fitment of note was an ornately-carved corner cabinet that reached almost to the ceiling.

"Please," Mrs. Averagado said, indicating for them to sit. "First, I want to introduce you. Mrs. McCarvel, from Schenectady," she indicated the lady with the painted face, "Mrs. Ivanovich, from right here in New York, and Mr. James Dougan, from Savannah, Georgia. And all the way from Montana, Mr. Jake Miller."

They all murmured greetings, and Jake and Mr. Dougan leaned across the table and shook hands. Jake was self-conscious about his clothes.

"Before we begin," Mrs. Averagado said, "I want to tell you that Mrs. Ivanovich and Mr. Dougan are old friends of mine. Mrs. Ivanovich has been with me for, what is it, seven years? And Mr. Dougan for almost as long. So as you would assume, we have developed a firm, and if I may say, efficacious relationship."

She smiled seriously at the two newcomers. "It is most important that you are in an undisturbed state of mind. There is no magic in what we are about to do, and please rest assured that no harm can befall you."

As she spoke, the housemaid–by now Jake knew her name was Miss Higgins, and that she was more than just a maid–turned off the ceiling light.

"We always start and end with a prayer," Mrs. Averagado said. "Our Holy Father, please be with us this evening. We pray that you will bless . . . ."

Jake bowed his head; something he had vowed never to do again. He was restive–eager to get on with the seance–and the room was stuffy.

". . . in our attempts to reach those in the realm beyond. Please let us . . . ."

Jake sneaked a glance around the table. All of the others had their heads down and their eyes closed, except Mrs. Averagado, who sat with her outstretched arms slightly raised, staring vaguely at the picture on the opposite wall as she prayed.

Jake cleared his throat to suppress a cough, and he pondered the inconsistency of his apostasy–on one hand–and his spiritual beliefs on the other.

". . . , in your holy name, Amen."

Mrs. Averagado let her arms fall gracefully to the table, and she gestured to Miss Higgins, who went to the corner cabinet and took out something. It was an irregular, pellucid crystal, mounted on a pedestal of burnished oak. Not the traditional orb of sideshow fortune tellers, but a jagged, brilliant formation of unmistakable beauty that glittered and radiated even in the dim light.

"Now," Mrs. Averagado said as her assistant placed the crystal in front of her. "No mumbo jumbo. I use this to help me concentrate, you see?"

Miss Higgins went to a chair in the corner by the door and sat down. Mrs. Averagado quietly gazed into the crystal. Mrs. McCarvel started to say something, but Mr. Dougan quieted her.

Jake became restless, and he slipped out his pocket watch and peeked at it. Miss Higgins saw him, and frowned. Jake poked the watch back into his pocket. He sat looking down at the table, at nothing. A huge grandfather clock in the sitting room ticked. He couldn't see it, but in several minutes it would chime, and Jake wondered how that would affect his host's concentration.

Then Mrs. Averagado spoke. "Thank you for coming so soon." She was looking at Mrs. Ivanovich.

"Dear Johnny," Mrs. Ivanovich replied. "I only wish I could come more often. It's troubling, you know. If only . . . ."

Jake struggled to breathe. He didn't know what he had expected: something more dramatic, perhaps, with a mysterious flair, like levitations, and incantations. As it was, all apprehensions about fraud and falsity evaporated. Mrs. Averagado held up one hand to silence Mrs. Ivanovich.

"Don't talk like that, Mother. You do the best you can."

"But I should do better, Johnny."

"Everything is ordained. We've been through it all before."

"Yes." Mrs Ivanovich slumped slightly in her chair, and hung her head. "It's just that it's so difficult, and your father—"

"Someday he will come."

Jake was surprised that Mrs. Averagado spoke in her own voice, and that she showed such little emotion, much as would a matron conversing with a close friend over tea. As he listened, he was soothed by the conversation. Then he checked himself, and the possibility of fakery again welled. There was nothing in the dialogue that indicated any special clairvoyance. Only small talk. But why, then, had Mrs. Ivanovich returned for all of those years? Certainly she would have been aware of . . .

"I have waited so long, Jake."

Jake jerked. Mrs. Averagado had turned to him. "Mable?" Jake stammered.

"Dear heart. Didn't I tell you I would wait for you?"

Now that she was speaking to him, Mrs. Averagado's voice had an unearthly tone. Neither her locution, nor Mable's. Rather, a ghastly quality that caused Jake to lose all sensibility, including his degree of skepticism.

"I—"

"Calm yourself, Jake. You have no reason to be distressed."

"But, I—"

"You, who were always so disbelieving," she continued. "Aren't you going to ask me questions only I can answer?"

With that, a warm, soft hand brushed Jake's cheek. The room grew darker, and it was like he was in the center of a carousel, and those at the table were circling him. He grasped the seat of his chair with both hands and tried to keep from falling.

"Jake!"

Mrs. Averagado reached out, and Jake took her hand as one would a lifeline. He held on until his head cleared.

"Mable, if it is you, what is your favorite color?"

He was embarrassed at asking, but Mrs. Averagado didn't seem to mind. She smiled serenely, and without pause she answered, "Why, green, of course, silly! The dark green of the spring grass beneath the dry stems of last year's growth. The fresh green of newly-planted wheat, and the shiny green of my . . . ."

Jake heard people talking. Then he knew he was lying on the floor, staring at the ceiling. Someone had turned on the overhead light, and the brightness hurt his eyes.

"Lie still for a few more minutes, Mr. Miller, and don't worry. This happens frequently."

Jake's head felt like there was a large barn fly buzzing around inside. His only other concern was that he seemed to spend an inordinate amount of time conked out on floors, or on the ground.

Jake attended two more sessions. After the last, he spoke with Mrs. Averagado. ". . . , so, considering the distance, it would be difficult for me. Is it possible for someone—?"

"To be his own medium? Very rarely. It is a special gift. I wish I could be more encouraging, but . . . ."

The train ride home was a kaleidoscope of images of Mable, Mrs. Averagado, and of all of the events of Jake's past.

CHAPTER SIXTY-ONE

After the trip to New York, Jake was heartened. He knew beyond any doubt that he had communicated with Mable. Not some vague, self-induced trance, or a catalepsy, but an actual communication, in which Mable had said things that only she could have known. Now, alone again, he prepared to meet his strongest challenge.

For two weeks Jake disposed himself. That he took so long was not due primarily to any tangible preparations; rather, it was fear of failure. He had failed for years, and Mrs. Averagado had not been encouraging. There were few true mediums, and in her life she had known only one individual who had been able to do her own channeling, and even that lady had to have a trusted friend present to interpret. Jake was neither sure of any special channeling ability, nor did he have a friend whom he could trust. The prospects were not great.

Still, Jake had hope. Would it not be a compensation for his lack of psychic endowment to have already contacted Mable through Mrs. Averagado? To have greased the skids, so to say.

The hot days of early autumn passed with their usual monotony, leading Jake to his self-appointed time. The crops were poor, and people continued to leave, looking for better lives. Jake, and others with minimal requirements–or whose tenacity was ingrained to a greater degree–struggled on. Perhaps if he could succeed in his spiritualistic quest, life would be easier.

At last the time had come. The time Jake had both dreaded and anticipated. Sunday night. Sunday seemed portentous, and midnight even more so. It was time to exceed the boundaries of the human condition.

Jake prepared. First, he took out Mable's favorite dress, brushed the dust from it, and draped it over her armchair. He put her best pair of shoes at the foot of the chair and set her flowered hat on the magazine table. Then he took her photograph from the wall and placed it beside her hat, facing his chair. He went to the console radio, tuned in Mable's favorite station, and turned the volume down so that the music was barely audible. Last of all he made coffee. At five minutes before midnight he set one cup on the table, beside Mable's photograph, and settled into his armchair with the other cup.

Jake reasoned that the key to success was concentration, and he rejected the absurdity of his preparations by viewing them as aids to that concentration. Nothing more. The only variable was the degree to which mental effort is focused. Not intelligence–though Jake supposed it would be impossible for a dullard to succeed–not faith, not mystical incantations, but total absorption. And, he grudgingly conceded, perhaps a bit of faith in something higher.

At midnight, as the wind sang along with the music of the radio, Jake took a last sip of coffee. It was time. He began by attempting to reconstruct the same state of mind that he had had during Mrs. Averagado's sessions. He imagined Mable with him, and he listened for her voice. He concentrated on her photograph, and waited.

———————

After weeks of frustrating attempts, Jake admitted defeat. He wrote to Mrs. Averagado, and the reply was another defeat.

Dear Mr. Miller,
I am sorry to inform you of the death of Mrs. Averagado. She passed away in her sleep after a particularly trying session. As you would assume, we are devastated.

Most sincerely,
Miss J. Higgins

Mary Magdalene Madison. Her maiden name had been Mary Magdalene Madison, and she had come from Massachusetts in 1915 as a newlywed. Her husband was Sterling Golden. Was. He had died two years ago; conked out right in the middle of a field one hot summer day. By all accounts he had been a decent, hard-working, good man.

Jake did not yet know the origin of Mary's middle name; she didn't seem very religious. Mary Magdalene–that's what everyone called her–was a few years younger than Jake, and she was almost beautiful. Long raven hair, smooth white complexion, smiling blue eyes, a fine figure, and a cheerful disposition that had carried her through the tribulations of her, and Sterling's, lives. After Sterling's death she had reclaimed her maiden name, and had worn black for a year–except when farming–for she had taken on farming with the strength and determination of a man. Her innate cheerfulness was subdued but not vanquished, and at the end of the year of black–to the very day–Mary came out, and seemed her complete self again.

People said Mary Magdalene had money, or leastwise her parents had had money. That was apocryphal, and in any case she continued to live frugally, as she and Sterling had always lived, and the hard work strengthened her, within and without. Some wits and cynics had taken to calling her Muscles Madison.

Every year Lars and Caroline had dragged Jake to the box social. And every year Jake had gone, against his will and pouting; but he had gone, mostly because Caroline had been so very kind, and persistent. The plan was always the same: there were single women who attended the social out of loneliness, and Lars was very good at prodding Jake to bid on their boxes. He had once even gone so far as actually twisting Jake's arm to the point of sharp pain. In the event, the ladies were pleasant, and Jake had to admit it was better than sitting at home mooning.

The thing was, Jake always had his suspicions that sooner or later would come the setup. He trusted Caroline, but Lars was capable of anything. All in all, however, he would maintain his trust in Caroline, while keeping up his guard.

The barn was festively decorated and brightly lighted, and the extraordinarily large crowd was in fine spirits; and outside the spirits flowed to those who were in the habit of imbibing. To start things off, a fiddler, an accordionist, and a banjo player struck up a tune that sounded to Jake like an old Norwegian gammaldans, an old dance; and a more-than-usual number of couples took to the floor in fine fettle and form. Some were not following the gammaldans steps, rather they were dancing as they felt like dancing as long as they kept to the rhythm of the fiddler. All were dressed in their finest, which ranged from very fine to not so fine. Jon Svenson, a middle-aged bachelor, tried to keep up his reputation as a rake and rounder–though he would not describe himself that way–by dancing with the best-looking of the youngest of the single ladies, and as such he was, to them, a scourge: the Attila the Hun of the dance. Jake relaxed and enjoyed the evening, resolving to get out and about more in the future without being pushed. Nonetheless he was on edge because of an occurrence a week before.

––––––––––

Jake sat alone on the bench in front of the hotel watching people, dogs, stray cats, and automobiles. He had splurged and bought a dime cigar that he was savoring and trying to keep lit for as long as possible. It was an art. And he was also practicing spitting, because in addition to not inhaling, he was averse to swallowing tobacco juice. It was a beautiful day.

"Jake!" Caroline called. She had approached as he was leaning the other way perfecting his spitting.

Jake twitched and sat up. Caroline was accompanied by Genevieve, Morgan Feeney's lovely wife.

"Oh. Good morning." He lifted the front of his hat in greeting.

"And a very good morning to you, too," Caroline cooed. She sat on one side of him while Genevieve, never a slave to convention, pushed him to the center of the bench with her ample bottom, and sat down on the other side.

Jake smiled weakly and confusedly as it dawned on him. Here we go, he thought. And he was right.

"Mr. Miller," Caroline began. Neither she nor Genevieve were the least bit shy. "You have been moping around for far too long. Languishing in self pity, and it's time you did something about it. Life is too short."

"She's right," Genevieve chimed in. "Jake, I can speak with some authority. You are aware of some of Morgan's war afflictions, though you could never know all of them. Not nearly all. But perhaps what you don't know–or have never thought of–as you are so immersed in your own, ah—"

"Self pity?"

"Call it what you will, I'm not here to dwell on that. However it is time for you to get on with life. So as I was saying, I have had some experience with inner afflictions, and I have come to know that there is life after inner, spiritual, death. I know what I'm talking about, Jake. Life can go on, perhaps not as before, or as perfectly as we would wish, but it can go on."

Jake took a puff on his cigar and flicked the ash on the board sidewalk in front of him, refusing to look at them.

"Well?" Caroline prompted. "We think we can help, if you will only let us."

"How?" Jake croaked. There was no stopping them.

"There is this lady. Her name is Mary."

"Mary Madison," Genevieve continued. "You must know her; Mary Magdalene?"

Jake clenched his teeth and stared straight ahead.

"She's a wonderful girl, eh, lady," Caroline added. "She's not looking for anyone, but who knows, a decent, handsome fellow like you would—?"

"Handsome?" Jake barked. "Me, handsome? What kind of nonsense is that? Have you come to ridicule me? Is this some sort of joke? I would never have thought it of either of you! Maybe decent, and certainly troubled, but handsome? Shame on you both!" And still he refused to look at them.

Caroline and Genevieve sat, rigid and stunned for a long moment, then Caroline jumped up and stood directly in front of Jake. "No, shame on you, Jake Miller, to think that we would joke about something like this. For shame!"

Jake raised his eyes to her.

"What in heaven's name is wrong with you?" Caroline went on. "Is it possible that you don't know?"

"Know what?" Jake murmured.

"Impossible," Genevieve cried. Now she too had gotten up and was standing by Caroline. "Is it possible?"

Both ladies studied Jake, then looked at each other incredulously; and at last it sank in.

"He doesn't know," Genevieve said weakly. "Lord have mercy, he doesn't know."

Tears came to Caroline's eyes. She sat back down beside Jake, and Genevieve sat on the other side, and they each put an arm around him.

"Dear, sweet Jake," Caroline whispered, "how can you not know? You are a handsome man. I would never say it if it weren't—"

"Please," Jake interrupted, "Don't pretend. That would be too cruel."

"We are not pretending," Genevieve said. "We are realists. Jake, have you gone all of your life believing you are homely?"

"Of course. I am. All of my life people have told me otherwise, but I knew they were only trying to be kind."

"Oh, god." Genevieve took her arm from around Jake's shoulders and leaned forward with her face in her hands. "When I was in nursing school I read something about this sort of thing, where there are those who are unable to interpret faces and emotions. In some cases they even have trouble distinguishing people. At its worst they can't tell one person from another."

"Is that true?" Caroline asked.

"Yes, but how rare it must be." Genevieve sat up and wiped her eyes with her kerchief.

Jake was stunned. He felt his face turn to stone. It was all he could do to speak. "I don't believe it," he said. "I can tell people apart, for chrissake."

"Alright, but what about their emotions. Have you ever had difficulty telling when people are happy, or sad, or angry; things like that?"

"Um. Well I guess I wasn't so good with Mable. Seemed like she was always in a huff about something I should have known. Yeah, come to think of it."

"What about, oh, Lars for instance," Caroline put in. "Have you ever had trouble figuring him out?"

"Sure, all the time." Jake worked up a smile. "But with Lars it's easy, he's either one way or the other; no in between." He scrutinized Caroline to see if he could tell what she was thinking, but as far as he could tell, she was thinking nothing. "Then again, there were times when Lars blew up at me when I had no idea it was coming. And the same with old Walter Grimswold. We'd be sitting here and all of a sudden he'd chew me out, then get up an walk away, and I never saw it coming. Damn. But what does all this have to do with the fact that I look like a frog?"

"God dammit, Jake!" Genevieve jumped to her feet as if she had been sitting on a cactus. "It has a lot to do with you thinking you look like a frog, you idiot! I'm sure there's more to it than what I've been talking about, reading faces and so on–you obviously have other afflictions–but you are no longer going to be able to console yourself with the notion that you look like a goddamned frog! Now I don't know what else ails you, but no more frog stuff. We could parade a hundred people down this street, and not one of them, man, woman, or child, would say you look like a frog. To the contrary, they would probably say you were more than agreeable to the eye. Put that in your pipe and smoke it! Furthermore, I don't know about all of the other woes you have, but I know the answers to those woes. How do you like that? I don't give a hoot about what your trials and tribulations are, but I can fix them."

Caroline got to her feet, approached Jake as closely as she could, snatched his now-cold cigar from his fist, and threw it out into the middle of the street. "Quit smoking those stinky cigars, get some decent clothes, get cleaned up, er, tidied up, and stop looking in the mirror and thinking about frogs, and you could yet have a good life."

"Think it over Jake," Genevieve said. "And after you do some soul searching, we have ways of helping you. Farewell for now."

After they had left, Jake was confounded to the point of both mental and physical paralysis. It would be painful to admit that they had been right, but it would be even more painful not to admit it. He would go home and think through it all, but for now he was aware that what Caroline and Genevieve had presented to him would explain a lot in his past, starting with how Mable had taken up with him when they had first met.

CHAPTER SIXTY-THREE

Jake had quit cigars–he had smoked them only occasionally anyway–he had bought some new clothes, and he had made it a point to improve his cleanliness. He knew what was coming.

The only thing of particular interest to Jake was that both Caroline and Genevieve were on the other side of the barn in conversation with Mary Madison, and while none of them were looking in his direction, he was sure of what was transpiring. Surprisingly he was not panicked, and moreover he was almost–but not quite–flattered.

Caroline and Genevieve crossed the dance floor, walking slowly and satisfiedly without so much as glance at Jake. The fix was in. Behind them Mary was in conversation with a youngish middle-aged man of decent looks and demeanor, and it seemed to Jake that the man had a more-than-casual interest in her.

The lead player tuned his eight-string Norwegian hardanger fiddle, then led off with another dance number. Hardanger fiddles always sounded harsh to Jake, and he much preferred traditional violins. The only thing worse than a hardanger was more than one hardanger, the sounds of which resembled the yowling of cats.

But here he was, thinking about fiddles, when if he had any reservations about what was to come he should be thinking about running like the devil. Strange, however, he didn't feel like running; he was looking forward to staying. Besides, if he ran, what then? Back to sitting alone, depressed and slovenly? The only dark thought was, what would Mable think? After all these years, and despite his skepticism of the validity of religion and as to any afterlife. Would she be hurt, or would she be happy for him? And what would be her . .

Jake's thoughts were interrupted by the accordion flourish at the end of the dance. Now for the time of reckoning. The baskets. The plan was for Jake to do his own bidding, and for Lars to quash any high bidders. Jake's hands began to shake, and the auction hadn't even started.

The first basket went quickly, then another, and before Jake had the chance to either compose himself or to fall apart completely, Mary's basket came up.

"Twenty cents," someone called.

Jake felt Lars kick him in the ankle.

"Twenty-five!" The man with whom Mary had been speaking had bid even before the auctioneer had called for more bids.

Lars kicked again.

"Thirty," from the first bidder.

This time Lars kicked so hard Jake nearly cried out in pain. But Jake stood and bid higher.

"Forty!" called the one who had spoken to Mary. The first man had dropped out.

There was a pause. "It's not the money," Jake whispered to Lars, "but that guy is getting irritating." Jake stood and called "Forty-five," and as he did so he was surprised at seeing Lars get up and stride across the floor.

"Fifty." Then Lars had him by the throat. "I said fif-they," the bidder croaked before finding himself bum-rushed to the wide front door.

Jake calmly bid sixty, and it was over, and both Caroline and Genevieve gaily escorted Mary and her lunch basket to a place alongside Jake. Mary seemed happy, and given that, Jake was happier than he had been in years.

Lars came back inside and sat by Caroline. He had a scratch under his left eye, but Jake's competitor did not return.

———————

Weeks passed, and Jake was renewed. He and Mary had seen each other nearly every day. It seemed that they had been destined for each other, and they shared their life stores, their highs and lows, and their hopes and aspirations. They had much in common, and often they talked late into the night, tongue-wagging gossips be damned. They agreed that if there was no spiritual Heaven, there was a temporal one to which they had been admitted.

Jake was cautious, however. He made no amorous physical advances. Surely that would come later, when–perhaps even if–Mary was ready. He was content with whatever life presented, from now on and forever. If he could manage his memories—his lingering unity—with Mable.

Jake and Mary's happiness lasted for a month, until Jake's bliss began to fade. Mable—more and more of Mable—their love, their youth, Jake's memories of her, their good times and their adversities; and in the end it was too much, and Jake realized he had to end it with Mary. Sweet, blessed Mary; what had he done to her? And his guilt returned.

Mary cried, and when Jake lamely said something about being friends, she sobbed even harder, and when she had regained her self control she told him that after all they had shared, friendship was impossible, and that they must go their own ways, difficult as that would be in a small community.

―――――――――

And so it was that a week after Jake and Mary's parting, Jake was sitting again on the bench in front of the hotel. He had lost his last chance for true happiness. Or had thrown it away. Whatever he called it, the loss had been, in some strange way, out of his control. And there was a slight irony: that of finding out that not only was he not bad looking, he was a tolerably decent person, though he had suspected the decent part all along, and his discovery in that regard was more of an reaffirmation. The crux of the irony was: what did it matter now? That he would fade into old age as a good-looking eccentric? It was all over, and here he was back on the bench with Walter Grimswold.

Jake and Walter had little to say to each other. Everything to be said had been said.

After some fifteen minutes of silence, to Jake's astonishment Walter asked him a simple, straightforward question.

"How's your Wheel?"

Jake went rigid. "What wheel? On my car?"

"No! Your Wheel of Life."

CHAPTER SIXTY-FOUR

Jake down-shifted. Why Dr. Siegfried Hirshmann had retired to the godforsaken plains of northeastern Montana was a mystery. Getting out of Germany was obvious, but why Charity? Nonetheless, there he was, ensconced in his white, three-story house, high on a hill overlooking nothing but dry pastures and fields. A heavyset, fierce-looking solitary, living with his daughter.

Jake and Dr. Hirshmann had met several times while walking. The first time, circumstance imposed on them a desultory exchange, but at each successive meeting their conversations had become more lively; even animated, and the doctor was less aloof. At last, one day as they shook hands and parted, Dr. Hirshmann insisted that Jake visit him.

Dr. Hirshmann's daughter answered the door. She was compact, like her father, with curly, auburn hair. She appeared to be about thirty-five. Her straight, thin nose, puffy face, and large eyes made her unattractive, and she augmented her unattractiveness with a dour countenance. Spinster material. She drew Jake in without speaking, and closed the door behind him. After he had stood uncomfortably for a moment, she stepped in front of him and took his hat.

"This way, please, Mr. Miller." She led Jake into the parlor.

"Jake, if you don't mind. Call me Jake. I—"

"Be seated. I'll announce you to father." She indicated a straight-backed armless chair in a corner of the sitting room, then she disappeared behind a curtain.

Jake sat looking around the room. It was reminiscent of Mrs. Averagado's sitting room: raised wallpaper, colorful tapestries on one wall, exotic floor rugs, ornate furnishings, ... In one corner was a shelf full of medical books, and in another corner stood a large roll-top desk. On top of the desk was a metronome; the wind-up kind, with an inverted pendulum. Curiously, there was no piano or other musical instrument. Perhaps in another room. The Swiss clock high on the wall ticked. It was a chalet, with a small door in the peak, presumably for a cuckoo bird. In the center of the room was a huge oak desk, and a microscope stood on a small table beside it. On a table on the other side of the desk was what Jake could only guess was some kind of world globe, though there were no recognizable representations on it. Movable brass rings encircled it, and on the rings were etched some sorts of inscriptions and pointers.

The truly remarkable thing was that on the outside, the house–except for its large size and the fact that there were few outbuildings–was extraordinarily unremarkable.

Jake heard someone talking, but no one came. It was warm, but not hot. There were no windows, but Jake noticed a grilled opening in the ceiling, and he could feel a draft coming through the door. The incongruity of his plush surroundings made him feel hundreds of miles from home. Rumors about the eremitic Dr. Hirshmann and his mansion had circulated freely, and if what Jake had already seen was any indication, the rumors were true; all of them.

Someone came down a stairway. Dr. Hirshmann entered wearing a dark suit and a tie. "Mr. Miller!" He held out his hand.

Jake had worn his best trousers and a white shirt, but he wished he had put on a tie. Dr. Hirshmann, however, seemed not to notice.

"Mr. Miller!" Dr. Hirshmann repeated. "How nice you could come." His daughter reappeared in the doorway. "Allow me to introduce you to Abigail, my only child. Abby, this is the man I was telling you about, Mr. Jake Miller."

"We have already met," she smiled. It was a tired smile.

"It was my pleasure," Jake said, bowing his head slightly.

"Well, then, tea, Mr. Miller?" the doctor asked. His accent reminded Jake of Karl Springer.

Tea, as with Mrs. Averagado, Jake noted. "Yes, thank you, Dr. Hirshmann."

"Sig. And I shall call you Jake, if you don't mind."

"Please."

"If you will, Mrs. Diggs."

Through another doorway came an old lady carrying a tea service. Her resemblance to Mrs. Averagado's maid, Miss Higgins, was singular: short and stout, with graying hair and a round, wrinkled face.

"Make yourself comfortable." The doctor indicated for Jake to sit.

Mrs. Diggs poured.

"Now, Jake, suppose we get to know each other a bit better," Dr. Hirshmann said. "Where are you from? You don't mind, do you?"

Jake was perplexed. The doctor's unfriendliness was an established part of local lore. The only time others ever saw him was when he was riding his fancy horses–Tennessee walkers–and then he would only nod and lift his riding crop to the brim of his queer-looking cap.

"Not at all," Jake said, though he did mind. "Small town in Iowa. I homesteaded here because there was no room on our family farm. Decided to start new."

He hoped that would preempt any further questions. He would talk about his life in Montana, but not about his past.

"I see, so you . . . ."

They drank tea, and more tea, and Dr. Hirshmann probed. In response to Jake's corresponding questions, the doctor was evasive.

"A hypnotherapist. A psychiatrist specializing in hypnosis therapy," was all he would say. "I'm from Austria, but I practiced in Germany for most of my life."

"What a change; Germany to the plains of Montana."

"Um." Dr. Hirshmann changed the subject.

Abigail said not a word, and after a half hour she excused herself.

Dr. Hirshmann's interest in Jake continued. They talked on, and Jake stayed late into the evening.

———————

Over the next several weeks Jake returned often. That Dr. Hirshmann's interest could have been mostly professional did not escape Jake, but it had been a long time since anyone had shown him any consideration. Dr. Hirshmann had offered his services free of charge. Forced them on him so to say.

"Now, I want you to concentrate on the pendulum," Dr. Hirshmann said.

He spoke quietly and calmly. The room was unlighted, and Jake was resting in a deep, soft armchair. Before him, on a stand, stood the metronome, ticking slowly. The weight had been painted blue.

"Relax, and watch the pendulum. As you do, your eyes will become tired. Concentrate on the pendulum, and on my voice. Put all of your worries aside, and relax. Your eyes are becoming tired, and soon they will close. Follow the pendulum, and . . . ."

Jake was more tired–indeed torpid–than he had ever been, and his eyelids began to droop.

". . . tired, and now you are closing your eyes, and concentrating more and more on my voice. Closing your eyes and . . . ."

"There you are, awake and feeling refreshed," Dr. Hirshmann said.

"Awake?"

"You were in a hypnotic state for quite some time. We had a good talk, but don't worry, as I said, I can't–even if I wanted to–force you to do or say anything that goes against your moral, ethical, or religious beliefs."

"But I wasn't—"

"You were. You just don't remember."

"Oh." Then, "How did it go?"

"Well, you don't get to the root of things in one session. It takes weeks, even years to—"

"Years? But I don't have years. I mean . . ." Jake sat up straight and looked desperately at Dr. Hirshmann. "I may not survive—"

"Now easy does it, Jake. It looks promising, and I would like to see you the day after tomorrow."

He said it with such professional command that Jake was calmed.

"Jake, I am perplexed. Nearly every other day for three weeks we have met, and I must confess, I have never encountered this . . . , this kind of, eh, problem."

Dr. Hirshmann reached over and put his hand on Jake's shoulder sympathetically. He and Jake had finished another session.

"I'm stumped," Dr. Hirshmann said, shaking his head.

Jake had nothing to say. He sat uneasily in the armchair, looking at the metronome. He had had hope, but now? Better to have never had hope at all.

"It is your past, Jake, as you told me. But I can't seem to . . ." He faltered. "There's something . . . , I don't know. Repression like I have never . . ."

Dr. Hirshmann got up and went to his desk. He stood for a moment with his back to Jake. Then he turned. "With your permission, I would like to confide your case to a former colleague. He may be able to advise me."

Jake lifted both hands, and let them fall back to his lap. He stood and thanked Dr. Hirshmann.

"I don't deserve your thanks yet. Someday I may, but not now. I will contact you after I have consulted with Dr. Manheim. He lives in Germany, so it may take a while. In the meantime, I want you to feel free to stop by any time, as a friend."

Jake nodded and left.

Jake returned to see Dr. Hirshmann a month later, and that was his last visit.

CHAPTER SIXTY-FIVE

Jake did his best thinking in two places: in his outhouse, and on his tractor. There was no accounting for the validity of his outhouse ruminations–he couldn't see how bowel movements could be conducive to lofty thoughts–but the efficacy of his tractor was obvious due to the tedium. He was his own captive audience.

Jake could gauge his life according to the rhythm of his tractor. His McCormick 15-30 with its steel-lugged wheels and flat-spring supported steel seat. Ups and downs interrupted by periods of what for him passed as normality. He bounced over a rock, then settled back into the ups and downs as the tractor pulled the disk harrow easily, then harder, then easily . . . . He had always meant to add some kind of brace to the seat support in case it broke and he wound up being run over by the disk like Tunney Hunmann had, and he wished the tractor had rubber tires, but he couldn't afford to have the conversion made. Steel wheels weren't so rough in the fields– they were only a problem when he had to move down a road–but he didn't have to take to the roads much. The main problem with steel wheels was the big lugs that kicked up so much dirt. Sitting on a tractor in the heat and insects was punishing enough without being sandblasted in the face. Furthermore, he wasn't young anymore, and the bouncing and jolting was ruining his back. Sometimes, after a long day, he would feel an ague coming on, and he was starting to worry about his kidneys.

Jake stopped at the end of the field, got off the tractor, and went to a big rock in the shade of which he had put his burlap-wrapped crock water jug. He took a long pull, then re-wetted the burlap with some of the water. *Keep in mind that water's good for drinking too, and it's a helluva lot cheaper than that swill they sell in The Palace. Lars, so many years ago.*

Back on the tractor, Jake settled in. His goal for the day was to quit blowing hot and cold. He intended to settle his religious beliefs once and forever. For years he had struggled, and for years he had come up short. And over those years the only light he had seen was in the faces of the believers, despite and withal their foibles, weakness, intellectual deficiencies, and hypocrisies, including the eleventh commandment: *Thou shalt not be found out.*

He had long since given up on his fruitless Unified Theory of Life, and now it was time to change course.

Jake started at the beginning. "In the beginning . . . ." Religion, a vestige of the ancients, when humanity could account for the unknown in the only way possible at the time: in terms of the three *M's* of mystery, mysticism, and mythology, which views had persisted into modernity, to be clung to by those of lesser intelligence and intellect. But, Jake conceded, what if–in defiance of all logic and higher faculty of reason–and by some slim and overriding possibility, there were some sublime hope? Hope, notwithstanding all of the unhappiness, misfortune, evil, and depravity religion had visited on humankind. Hope, Jake acknowledged, was all there was inherent in any vague confidence in the mystery of a divine mover.

A cloud of dirt blasted Jake in the face and he stopped the tractor. One of these days he was going to extend the fenders out to the sides and to the front.

Faith and hope, with logic to be damned. Desperation. "The mass of men lead lives of quiet desperation . . . ." Thoreau's famous observation. And, Jake conceded, he was at the center of that mass, and was at the point of total logical and mental collapse. But would faith and hope necessarily be bad? What would be the alternative? It was a nominal, either-or choice. Continuing as he was was unbearable, and if he acquiesced to belief in a prime mover, what would he lose? It was a choice between his present, unendurable, vacuous life; and a possible–though admittedly improbable–existence. The only other conceivable choice–and he had pondered it often throughout his life–would be living a lie; knowingly caving in to claptrap, but maybe that wouldn't be as bad as he had thought either.

Jake put the tractor in gear and let out the clutch, and as he did the sun brightened–though he had to admit that maybe that was just his perception–and he felt a measure of peace. Were peace and hope not the most common of human aspirations, and if so, were they at the core of existence, so to speak? Furthermore, if they are, is it not possible that there could be some grand design, not in the traditional sense of some guy out in space somewhere pulling the strings, or of gods and goddesses, and the like? Perhaps some inconceivable force beyond comprehension.

Jake was astonished at the feeling that his gloom was lifting. As he returned to the water-jug end of the field he stopped and shut down the tractor so he could hear the birds singing, or squabbling, or whatever they were doing. The gentle breeze, now free of dust, wafted over him, bees and butterflies went about their daily tasks, a dust devil twisted its way across the field, and even the grasshoppers that were the bane of farmers seemed less pestiferous. As Jake sat, the lassitude that had been part of his life for so long lifted, in great part, if not totally. He cried, not audibly, but silently with his head bowed and his red handkerchief covering his eyes. He knew now that regardless of what ups and downs he would encounter, he had hope, and nothing from then on would ever be as hard to endure as before.

CHAPTER SIXTY-SIX

But sometimes hope was not enough. It came and went, and it helped when it came, but it was not enough.

Jake took to walking the fields and prairie again. Now the meadowlarks sang their soft, apprehensive, leaving song. Jake wondered where they went in the winter.

When he wasn't walking, Jake withdrew. His religious hopes and expectations were all but dashed, as were his attempts to be reunited with Mable. His desperation had been displaced by an inner gloom. Once again he was heartsick.

"You down there, Jake?" Lars asked.

"How'd you find me?"

Lars stood with the sun to his back, holding the door open, and despite everything, he laughed.

"You weren't in the house or the barn. Or your workshop. Where else but in your root cellar?"

"Wonderful logic. Only you would look for someone in a root cellar."

"Only you would hide in one. Can I come down?"

"Umph."

Lars laid the door open and descended. "Phew! It doesn't smell so good down here. How long have you been sitting here, anyway?"

"If you don't like it, you can leave. Go home and mind your own potatoes."

Lars sat on a peach crate. "What are you doing?"

"I always felt safe down here."

"I thought your safe place was the barn."

"This is safer."

"I've been expecting you to stop and see me," Lars said.

Jake said nothing. It cut both ways: Lars seldom stopped to see him.

"What else you been up to?" Lars asked. "Besides sitting down here like a gopher."

"This, that, and the other." There had been a time long ago when he would have confided in Lars.

"Pastor Bjorkland says you've been staying home."

How would Lars know? He was, if not a confirmed atheist, a strong agnostic, and between that and his strange political beliefs, most ministers stayed well clear of him. He was a torment to them.

"Not much to do if you're a widower, and if you don't hang out in the bars," Jake said. He knew what Lars was doing. He wished he would just leave.

"Well, you don't have to hang out in bars to have a good time. There are picnics and things. And you used to play baseball, maybe you could . . . ."

Maybe if he kept quiet. But Lars started telling about an attempted murder north of Charity. A man who had tried to poison his wife.

". . . she woke up just as he was about to throw her down an abandoned well. He was so surprised he fell in himself. Well, she went for help, and it took them all night to get him out. Had to have an old coal miner from Kentucky show them how to tunnel down from the side, then they sawed away the casing and pulled him through. Any farther down and he'd have been finished."

"Why'd she go for help if he tried to poison her and dump her down a well?" But Jake had little interest in the story. Just more of humanity's eternal lunacy.

"She was too sick to think things through. Anyhow, some of the neighbors got checking around and found a bottle of formaldehyde."

"Then why isn't she dead?"

"That's what Dr. Sparks would like to know."

"Huh."

"She isn't out of the woods yet. Got her in the hospital up in Plainview. When the miner found out about the formaldehyde, he wanted to find her husband and throw him back down in the well!"

"Should've."

"I guess."

Lars was still, like he was groping for something to say. Then, abruptly, he looked sick, like he had the flu, or a severe hangover. "Did you hear about Karl Springer?"

"Umph?"

"Went blind. Emma died, then he went blind. Sugar diabetes
. What a heckuva deal." Lars looked like he was going to cry. "He
can still run his store though."

"Um."

"The Bible was Emma's solacement during her dying. Karl
said she practically slept with it."

"That's good."

"Karl, too. He took up Emma's Bible after she died."

"I'm glad. Maybe there's something to it. I've been re-
reading the Bible."

"You?"

"Yeah. When you think about it, it's no less plausible than
some of the nutty philosophies I've studied. And the other esoteric
stuff I've dabbled in. Possibly I'm not as smart as I thought I was.
Too structured in my thinking."

Lars leaned forward and stared through the gloom at Jake.
"Level with me, Jake. What's going on? I gotta say, you don't look
too good."

Suddenly the years melted, and to Jake it was like their
younger days, before he had gone completely off, and before both he
and Lars had grown cynical.

"Not so good, Lars. God, I don't know how much longer I
can go this. When I think it can't get any worse, it does. And it's
been getting worse for years. Ha, ha, ha! It started out bad, and it's
been getting worse ever since. Ha, ha, ha!"

Jake saw that Lars was perspiring, and gripping his hands
tightly together, but he went on.

"Then there were the phone calls. I never did tell you about
those. Phone would ring, but when I'd answer, there was nobody
there. I took the phone out, and I told the mailman not to bring any
suspicious-looking letters, but he said he had to deliver everything.
Gives me the screaming meemies. I can't help it. No matter; nothing
you can do anyway. They—"

"They?"

"The past, Lars. Ever since we moved to Montana. I thought
they'd stopped, but then they started again. After Mable died, I didn't
think I'd care anymore, but I do. Funny how that goes. Instinct I
guess. Self preservation. It's a curse. A joke on humanity. Ha, ha,
ha—"

"Some joke. What's going on, Jake? If you tell with me, I can—"

"Telling nobody. Too dreadful. Only one who knew was Mable, and when I go, it all goes with me. Dead men tell no tales, and all that. And neither do dead women, Lars. Ha, ha, ha!"

"You need to get outta' here. Why don't you come and stay with us for awhile? Nobody'd know where you were, and—"

"No use. You can't hide from perdition. Unsound mind. You can't . . ." Jake sagged, and he felt like he was melting.

"Stop being such a chump, Jake. Nothing's so bad you can't live with it. If I can't help, someone can. Let's get Pastor—"

Jake silenced him with a look.

"Or we could—"

The moment evaporated.

"Go home, Lars. I appreciate what you're trying to do, there's nothing for it. Please, just go home."

Lars was not a man to give up easily. "You've got to keep a stiff upper lip, Jake. You have to—"

"Go home, Lars," Jake pleaded. He felt like asking Lars to throw him live upon his own funeral pyre when the end was near.

Lars' fumbling attempts to help had only made things worse. That evening Jake prepared. Where else, but in the barn? It was tradition.

The familiar smell of manure wafted over Jake as he sat on a wooden crate, tying the knot. The hempen necktie. Seven turns, or thirteen? Thirteen was too many. The Montana vigilantes had been particular, but he wasn't, and he decided on eight. Just so the job was done right, and eight looked the most efficient.

Jake set the noose next to the lantern on the galvanized steel barrel beside him. Not much to do but kick the cow outside so she wouldn't starve before someone found him. He didn't have a dog anymore. Chaucer had died the week before, and the irony of it brought a bitter taste to his mouth, like he had been sucking on a lemon; that the only ones depending on him were a cow and a horse.

Moths fluttered around the lantern. Jake leaned against a support post and looked up at the hayloft. No time to louse up, like Robert Brewer had. He had died, but not easily. Should've jumped from the loft. A ten-foot drop would do it all right, unless the rope was too long, or if it broke. Jake guessed anyone could have second thoughts if their neck didn't break, and they were dangling at the end of a rope, slowly strangling. He took his jackknife out of his pocket and threw it out the window. The cow mooed outside, wanting back in.

No need for a note. To whom? Jake stood in the center of the barn and looked up again. It was going to be easy. As he lowered his head he sensed someone behind him, but when he turned there was no one.

Jake hesitated in order to strengthen his resolve. His throat ached from the thought of hanging. He threw down the rope and went outside for a drink of water, but his well was dry, and Karl Springer's words from years ago rang through his head: "It's a dark day when your well goes dry." He went to the house and found a bottle of warm beer, and by the time he had quenched his thirst the urge to dangle from a rope had passed.

CHAPTER SIXTY-SEVEN

He had come every Sunday evening for weeks. The trick was to wait until it was almost dark, and to park in a coulee in Jason Merchant's stubble field. He got out and started walking. Some nocturnal animal ran in front of him, and he felt a kinship to it. A moment later, as he passed a dry slough bed, two deer bounded out of the tall weeds, coughing in fright.

Jake stopped at Mable's grave, knelt, and spoke to her. When he was through, he ran his fingers over the cold inscription on her granite marker. Then he went inside and sat where they had sat when he had come to church with her. He wished that he had come more often. Moonlight–filtered by one of the arched, stained-glass side windows–painted the Jesus icon at the front of the church in blue, green, red, and yellow, and the musty smell of the church basement wafted up through the heat registers in the floor. Outside the wind rose, whistling under the eaves and rattling loose shingles.

Jake's life had consisted of ups and downs, as to religion, reality, philosophy, . . . Now his serenity had matured, so gradually that its germination was indeterminable. Certainly the seed had been sown before his encounter with the Archangel Uriel. Perhaps during his first pathetic attempts to commune with Mable's spirit, or later, with Mrs. Averagado. Or maybe it had always been there. How does one know? And what difference did it make? All that mattered now was that he had achieved–or bungled onto–serenity, and that it wasn't too late. And he hoped that his serenity would be his final up. Or if not that, his final down.

Something flew close to the ceiling. A bat, no doubt from the belfry. Bats in the belfry.

A realist. An insentient, lifeless realist, and it had cost him nearly everything. Still, Jake understood that whatever he had done to squander his and Mable's lives, he could attain grace here, where the staid members of Charity Lutheran met to confess their sins, and to quench their guilt. But he had little unity with the religious community and their conventional conceptions. For him religion was an amalgam of all religions, of some of the most benign philosophies; and of all locations of the spirit: within each being, residing in the community of humanity, in nature, and far beyond the heavens. How could he know his insights weren't the very self deceptions he had derided in others? There were many tests. One was the benediction of tranquility. The only tranquility he had ever known, except for the temporary anesthesia of drink. And the other tests. If one held, they all held. If the result of any one was valid, that was enough; they weren't mutually exclusive.

Jake prayed, then he got up to leave. As he descended the front steps, he felt the need for a good, stiff drink. A half dozen good stiff drinks. He had been imbibing too much over the last five or six years, and the thirst had continued, notwithstanding his newfound religious convictions. A paradox he had not yet resolved. If he had found spiritual peace, why the lingering urge to drink?

When he got to the road intersection a mile west of Charity, Jake had a decision to make. To The Palace bar, or home. He couldn't decide, so he pulled over, shut off the engine, and turned off the lights. Like so many things in life, sometimes there were no good choices. If he went home, there would be nothing to do but sit alone, reading the newspaper he had already read, listening to the radio, or reading the Bible. Or, if he went to the bar, it would be the same old thing: listening to a bunch of drunken assholes, then becoming one of them. And afterward he would have to go home anyway.

Some kind of dove, or loon, or something cooed out in a field. Jake wiped a tear from each eye. God, he missed Mable. She had been his life. He should have listened to her, instead of being so self-righteous. Oh, how he had underestimated her.

The bird cooed again. Jake kicked the starter switch, backed up, and headed for The Palace. Life is a farce.

CHAPTER SIXTY-EIGHT

Jake's desolation–there was no ameliorating word for it–had bottomed. His serenity had not lasted. He had to do something. But what? Mable was gone. Leastwise he thought she was gone, but to be sure he himself would have to die to find out, and he wasn't quite ready for that. At other times, in moments of what he could only call weakness, he was certain she was with him, up there, or she was part of him in some other sense. Nonsense, to be sure, but the awareness seemed very real.

Then–as in an ancient time, or as transcribed in a religious tome–on a bright, peaceful morning as Jake walked out of his front door to greet the day–indeed saying to himself in jest, *Hello, day*, he was struck out of the clear, light-blue sky by a revelation. A revelation that could only be proverbial, and which came as a proverbial bolt of lightning, proverbially out of nowhere, to proverbially change his life. And to make it all the more surprising, he had not even been thinking of religion, or of Mable, or of anything in particular. Only *Hello, day*.

The essence of Jake's revelation was that while most of the members of the religious masses succumb to the arguments of faith–that they just know–and the defunct and equally preposterous assertion that if so many people believe in something, that something ipso facto must be real; Jake's flash of inspiration was: If there is any more to life, and to death, it is not in the conventional religious sense. If there is any more, it will not come from the three *M's* of mythology, magic, and mysticism, or from blind, groping faith in some vain, vengeful, deity, or from any other such nitwittery. Like bad dreams, when we confuse the dreams as happening to us, when of course we cause the dreams. We confuse religion as happening to us, when in reality we invent–or propagate–the religion.

Jake fell back and sat on his wooden front step.

What, then?

Well, what if the faith of the common masses were valid, but instead of emanating from belief in a vain god who insists on being worshiped, or in a sun god, or any other balderdash; what if faith in an afterlife were inherent in all of us as a part of whatever force that created the universe? Or perhaps the universe was not created at all; it has always existed. No matter; what if we were to throw away conventional religion altogether, and ascribe our theism to a cosmic force? A cosmic force that people of lesser intelligence and intellect can only interpret as some sort of god. That would explain everything, and it would give us hope.

Jake breathed the fresh air and said again, *Hello, day.* And this time he meant it not as a joke.

If all this were true, Jake reasoned, then he could start his own religion. What to call it? The Non-church of the Non-religious Believers? The Congregation of the Unholy? The Temple of the Cosmos? Assembly of False Hope? Whatever it was, it was more rational than current religions. He had heard it said that if you want to make real money, start a religion. He could build a stone church on the forty acres behind his house. Then he would . . . .

He was being silly, and it felt good to be silly. He felt better than he had in years. Now there was a rock on which to cling, precarious as it was. He was giddy.

Moreover and best of all, his Wheel had slowed, and was grinding less execrably. It had its variations. But, like dreams, the fact of the matter was, the Wheel had never influenced him; he had controlled the Wheel, for better or for worse.

"You've re-invented the Wheel. Get it? The Wheel?"

"I get it. What's your point?"

"All of your stuff and nonsense about the Cosmos. You've re-invented Buddhism."

"No, not at all. I'm talking about something larger; more vast. A concept beyond what the average person can appreciate. A dimension far beyond anything that has ever . . . ."

PART FOUR – 1937

CHAPTER SIXTY-NINE

"I just happened to be coming home from doing a sick friend's chores," Morgan said. "He's down with lumbago."

Morgan and Sheriff Smith were standing in the Charity Lutheran Church cemetery, waiting for the undertaker. Morgan and some others had discovered Jake's body.

"Good thing you didn't tramp all over the place," Smith said. He was steely-looking, he needed a shave, and his mustache needed trimming. He pulled out his makings and rolled a cigarette, one handed, like cowboys did when they were on horseback.

"You think there's something fishy?" Morgan asked. "You're starting to sound like Sherlock Holmes."

"I dunno."

"What's your feeling?"

"Sometimes they like to go out with a flourish." The sheriff took out a match. "What do you think? I hear you've seen a few stiffs in your day."

"Most of the ones I saw in the war were obvious." Morgan kicked at the snow with the toe of his boot.

"But what do you think?"

Morgan watched Sheriff Smith light his cigarette. "I was going to mention that—"

"Undertaker better get here pretty soon or it'll be dark," the sheriff grumbled.

It was cold–almost twenty below–but there was no wind. The snow continued, and Morgan took off his cap and whisked the snow off the coat that covered Jake.

The sheriff stood quietly smoking, watching a car go by. The driver gawked. "You were his friend?"

"Friend? I guess so," Morgan replied. "I tried to help him out whenever I could. He could be somewhat stultifying though."

"Help him out? Whadd'yuh mean?"

"Oh, you know, he was an odd duck to begin with, then his wife died and that set him back even more. He was . . . , I don't quite know how to say it. Strange. Really strange. Smarter than hell, but always going off on some tangent. He kept having hallucinations.

And then there was his Wheel. He claimed to have this imaginary wheel–actually a grindstone–always grinding away at him, and—"

"An imaginary wheel?" The sheriff flicked his un-smoked cigarette off onto a snowbank, and his face contorted slightly on one side.

"Yeah. I guess it was his way of visualizing hardships. After the war I, well, you know, we all have different ways of coping. The thing is, it always seemed to me that for Jake that grindstone was nigh onto real."

"Huh. Was he suicidal?"

Jake propped open the barn door with a wooden fencepost, stepped onto a wooden crate, and mounted his old gray mare. He had never known why he had kept her, but now he knew. Riding bareback, he headed out the driveway. The milk cow and the chickens would be alright for a few days, till someone found them. Jake pulled down the ear flaps on his cap, turned up the collar of his coat against the wind, and went in the direction of the church.

Morgan stomped his feet. "I don't know. What's does it matter now?

Neither of them spoke.

"I thought I felt some life in him when we rolled him over," Morgan said.

The sheriff stubbed out his newly-lit cigarette on the gravestone.

"I don't see any blood or anything," Morgan mumbled. "If there was something funny going on, why'd they do it here, in a graveyard?"

"Dammit Feeney, is that all you can tell me about him?"

"Kinda queer. Always was. Then, like I said his wife died," Morgan nodded down at the grave, "and he got worse. He was really down in the dumps. Turned into a hermit toward the last." Morgan felt the war-wound lump on the back of his head. "I wouldn't be surprised if he froze to death on purpose."

"Anything else unusual about him?"

"Everything about Jake was unusual. He came here from somewhere in Iowa, and the story was that he had been in trouble back there."

"What kinda trouble?"

"Some thought he had killed a guy, but you know how the rumors go, and if he had, you'd think they'd have tracked him down by—"

"Who else could I ask?"

"Let's see . . . You might want to talk to old Pastor Vilander. He's been retired for a long time, and he's getting kind of forgetful, but he might know something."

Sheriff Smith reached under his coat, took a notebook and a pencil stub from his shirt pocket, and wrote down the name. "Anyone else?"

"Yeah, try Lars Nordraak. He and Jake were neighbors. Good friends too."

The sheriff wrote it down. "Who else?" He blew on his writing hand to warm it.

"Dr. Hirshmann. You know where he lives? Big house on the hill." Morgan pointed. "You could see it from here, if it weren't snowing."

The sheriff scribbled the name, and something else, in his notebook. "I've heard about Hirshmann. Mysterious character."

Morgan fastened the top button on his coat. "Old Hirshmann's always been kinda highfalutin. Jake was about the only one he ever had anything to do with. Jake went over there regularly for a few months last fall. Then the neighbors said he stopped going. Hirshmann being a head doctor, I'll bet he could tell you what was going on. If he'll let you in. They say sometimes he doesn't answer the door."

"He'll answer," the sheriff said. "What town in Iowa was Miller from?"

"Jake never would say."

Sheriff Smith put the notebook back into his pocket and started to make another cigarette. They watched a jackrabbit stare at them from under a frozen Russian thistle at the far end of the cemetery. Sheriff Smith lit his cigarette and threw the match back over his shoulder. The tobacco smoke went straight up.

Morgan stomped his feet again. "Stiffer 'n a board," he said, looking down at Jake. "Wish I could have helped him more. Guess I was too busy taking care of myself."

"Um."

"Oh, I started to say," Morgan murmured, "when I first got here and found the body, I saw horse tracks over by the church. You can't see them now."

CHAPTER SEVENTY

The next morning Sheriff Smith went to see Pastor Vilander.

"He was a tortured soul, Sheriff," Pastor Vilander said. He put a plate of Norwegian fattigmann cookies on the table. The pastor was tall and thin, but despite his age, he sat straight in his chair, and his blue eyes were clear. "Any counsel I gave remains private, and—"

"He's dead." Sheriff Smith's jaw tightened. "What difference does it make?"

There was a clock on each of the four walls, all of them ticking loudly. On the north wall was a cuckoo clock, on the south wall a Regulator. A huge, maple grandfather clock with carved tree branches, vines, and birds, stood against the west wall; and opposite was a cube-shaped cut-glass work of art that ticked the loudest of all.

"Dead only in the temporal sense, and I'm sure you realize he has gone on to . . . ." Pastor Vilander started into a discourse on the afterlife. ". . . so anything Jake said to me must be held in—"

"Pastor, he's dead, and I've got to find out what happened to him, and frankly I don't give a hoot in hell about all of your religious prattle. Confidentiality doesn't apply to dead people. Now I don't care how old you are, or whether you're a preacher or not, you can either tell me what was going on with Miller, or I'll haul you down to the county jail for hindering an investigation. Think it over, but don't take too long. I've got other people to see."

Pastor Vilander glowered at the sheriff. "You don't intimidate me. If there were anything significant to tell, I would never divulge it, and you would have to haul me off to jail. But you won't. How would that look, throwing an old man in—"

"I think it would look just fine; you sitting in the clink like a monkey in a zoo. Darwinists could come and feed you bananas."

"I don't think you'll find many Darwinists around here."

"You're looking at one, and I know plenty more."

They sat at an impasse for a while.

"After all this time who would care what Jake may or may not have done?" Pastor Vilander asked.

"Could mean a great deal to someone. If he committed a big crime, like murder, there would be people who should know; family members and so on. You seem to take me for a hard case, and I suppose I am, but not as hard as you think. I'm doing my best for—"

"The truth is, I don't know. Something back in Iowa. Whatever it was, it consumed Jake. I tried to tell him that the Lord forgives, and I wanted to help him. At first he wouldn't listen."

The pastor leaned sideways in his chair, selected a piece of wood from a cardboard box, and threw it into the field-rock fireplace. Ashes and sparks flew up the chimney, then the fire settled down again.

"At first?"

"Yes. Then, this last year, Jake and I became quite close. Indeed, I think I was the only one he saw much of. I assigned him Bible verses to read, and he would come over, and we would discuss them. Afterward, we would pray. And though Jake never confided in me about his past, I helped him find peace and forgiveness." Pastor Vilander leaned his head back and half closed his eyes. "The last time I saw Jake, he said he had found ataraxis for the first time in his life."

"Ataraxis?"

"Peace of mind." Pastor Vilander opened his eyes all the way and smiled up at the ceiling. "Jake liked to use big words."

"Peace of mind, eh?"

"Yes, true peace, and I was blessed to have been able to help him. And that's all I know."

"Hayden Smith." The sheriff shook hands with Rudi Prinz, the ex-boxer. They were standing in front of the mercantile store in Charity.

"You here to pinch me?" Rudi joked.

"Just a little information. Wasn't Jake Miller a friend of yours?"

Rudi backed closer to one of the large store windows, to get out of the wind. The window displayed men's winter coats and caps, leather gloves and mittens, and overshoes. "I guessed that was it. Sure, I knew him. Poor cuss."

It was colder than ever, and snow swirled around their feet.

"No use standing out here," Rudi said. "Let's go in the store and—"

"Thanks, I'm in kinda a hurry. Somebody said you knew him better than most." The sheriff stepped to the wall, next to Rudi, and he put his hands in his coat pockets.

"I suppose so, but nobody really knew Jake. He was a funny guy."

"Well, mostly I'm interested in his background, before he came here."

"He never talked about it much. All I know is, he grew up on a farm back in Iowa. Somewhere near Storm Lake."

"That's all?"

"When he first came here, he told me he'd been kicked in the head by a mule. Knocked him koo-koo, and he was off in the belfry for a while. And one day his wife–Mable–told me that there had been some unpleasantness, but she wouldn't say what. But I found out later that Mable was a fallen woman."

"How do you know?"

"Jake told me once when he was stewed. He never mentioned it afterward. I don't think he even remembered telling me. He thought that was the reason they couldn't have kids. Hell, maybe that's what killed her. She never was too healthy."

They stood looking at the empty street; listening to the sound of the train whistle from far to the southeast.

"That's it?"

"Sorry, I knew Jake here, not back in Iowa," Rudi said. "The one to ask is Lars Nordraak. He and Jake used to be this close," Rudi held up his crossed index and middle finger. "Early on, that is. They grew apart in later years though, but Lars could—"

"Lars is in the hospital in a coma."

"A coma? What happened?"

"Nils Anderson was helping him with his windmill, and he dropped a wrench on Lars' head. From the top of the tower. Thirty feet." The sheriff's mouth twitched. "They don't know if Nordraak's gonna make it."

"Lord! Poor Lars." Rudi sat down on the wooden bench in front of the window, without brushing off the snow.

"Yeah." Sheriff Smith stomped his feet to get his circulation going.

"I gotta go and see—" Rudi started.

"Is there anyone else who knew Jake?"

"Um, yeah, you might wanna talk to Nils. They got to be pretty good friends, till Nils really started hitting the bottle."

The sheriff wrote down the name.

"I suppose Nils is really on the sauce now, after the accident," Rudi said.

"Sometimes you get more out of 'em when they're three sheets to the wind than when they're sober."

"What'd he die of?" Rudi asked. "Jake, I mean. What happened to him?"

"Dunno yet. May never know. To tell the truth, I don't think our coroner could find the cause of death if Miller had been shot with a bow and arrow."

———————

Jake stopped at the outhouse behind the church. He dismounted and held onto his mare's mane as his knees buckled from the cold. When he could stand, he took the bottle of Old Crow from his coat pocket, unscrewed the cap, and took a long draught.

None of it was nearly as frightening as he had feared. In fact it was easy, and not altogether because of the whiskey. More than easy. He was elated.

Jake set his bottle on the ground, turned the mare toward home, removed her bridle, and slapped her on the rump. She jumped ahead a few steps, then stopped. Jake took off his coat, whapped her with it, shouted, and she trotted off. She stopped on the first hill, looked back, then continued home. Jake regretted that he hadn't even named her.

Might as well get on with it. Jake took the bridle and his coat into the outhouse and threw them in, so he couldn't change his mind. Then he took off his cap and gloves and tossed them in too. No turning back now he chuckled, amused at the image of himself crawling down into the toilet hole to retrieve his clothes. He went outside and laughed out loud. There, dammit. Ha! He'd wanted to laugh like that for a long time.

No, definitely not the booze. He'd felt euphoric for weeks.

Jake lurched toward Mable's grave.

———————

"Poor old Jake."

Sheriff Smith had found Nils Anderson in The Palace. Nils' large nose and ears were buff red in the gloom of the bar, and his eyes were colorless over his mug as he took another drink.

"You won't have one?" Nils asked. He wiped his lips with his sleeve.

"No, thanks. Can we talk over there for a minute?" The sheriff pointed at a table in back, away from everyone.

"Sure."

There were only two other patrons; an old man with long, greasy-looking brownish hair that hung down past his shoulders, and a muscular, middle-aged man who looked like a blacksmith. They were at opposite ends of the bar. The bartender, a wiry, nervous type, was washing beer mugs.

Nils and Sheriff Smith sat, and the sheriff crossed his arms and leaned forward with his elbows on the table. "They say you knew him pretty well."

"Pretty well? We were neighbors." Nils gulped the last of his beer and sat looking at the empty mug. Sheriff Smith signaled for another, and Nils brightened. "Thanks. I'm trying to screw my courage up enough to go and see Lars Nordraak in the hospital. I was helping him with his well, and I dropped a wrench on his head—"

"Nordraak is still out cold. What I'm trying to find out is, was there someone after Jake Miller? Someone from his past?"

"After him?"

"Gunning for him."

It was warm enough in the bar for one of one of last-year's flies to buzz out of a crack in the wall.

"Still out cold?" Nils quavered. "Jeez, I didn't mean tuh—"

"What about Miller?"

Nils took a huge gulp of his new beer, then he belched. "That's hard tuh say. He never talked much about before he came here. But come to think of it, once he did mention something . . . Yeah, something about having to live with it for the rest of his life. Damned if I know what it was though. I was pretty pickled," Nils winced sheepishly, "but I do remember asking him, and he changed the subject."

Nils skimmed a bit of foam–and something solid–from his beer with one finger, and flung it to the floor. He took another long drink, and belched again.

"What else?"

"Huh. Not much. He was a real prize. A decent feller, but extraordinary. Kinda' a nuisance. Always talking about philosophy and stuff like that. Usually he seemed pretty normal, but other times he should'a been locked up. Mable–his wife–she was nice. Quite a looker, too. A real bearcat. Built. Yuh should'a seen the bazooms on her. How she got stuck with him I'll never know, but I heard she was nothing but a harlot when they met. Maybe they were made for each other. Anyhoo, when she died, he got worse."

Nils put his mug down firmly, to emphasize the seriousness of what he was to say next. He put his finger alongside his nose. "I think he fogged somebody, and someone was after him for it."

Sheriff Smith snapped the last-year fly off the table with his thumb and middle finger. "Why do you think that?"

Somebody came in the front door.

"He was always lookin' over his shoulder, like he was on the lam. Edgy all the time, and down in the dumps. An' he never went back tuh Iowa." Nils peered deep into his beer, as one would gaze into a crystal ball. "He was a peculiar one alright." Nils started. "Oh-oh, here comes Goofy Grimswold. He's building an arc. He can't work on it in the winter, so he—"

"Excuse me, sir."

The sheriff raised one eyebrow ever so slightly.

"Walter Grimswold." He shook hands with the sheriff. "I hope you don't think I have nose trouble, but would you perchance be talking about poor Jake Miller?"

"That's right. What about him?"

"Amiable enough, but crazy as a tick. I used to see him walking around his farm at night, and . . . ."

Jake fell, and he had to crawl the rest of the way. He was in a state of rapture. Only one disappointment: that he hadn't figured everything out sooner.

Claiborne Edwards–a large, gray, bulldog of a man–exited his outhouse as Sheriff Smith got out of his car.

Claiborne pulled up his bib overalls. "Howdy, Sheriff!" he growled and barked at the same time. "Damn, a guy could freeze his ass off! Edna's been pestering me for indoor plumbing, but I keep putting it off. It's like why fix the roof if it isn't raining? Why install an indoor toilet if it isn't winter? But then winter comes, and—"

"I'm here about Jake Miller."

"Jake? What about him?"

"What kind of a guy was he?"

"Let's go inside. My butt is already froze, and—"

"This will only take a minute."

"Huh. Claiborne went to the leeward side of the house, out of the wind and snow. A cow mooed loudly and urgently from inside the barn thirty yards away, and a dog barked from somewhere. The snow thickened.

"What about Miller?" Sheriff Smith asked again. "Some say he was unbalanced."

"Unbalanced?"

"Yes. Unbalanced and despondent most of the time."

"Hell no! Who said that? High strung I guess, but not unbalanced. On the contrary, Jake was one of the most level-headed guys I ever knew! And despondent? Hell no to that too! Oh, he was down when his wife died, but who wouldn't be? He snapped out of it."

Sheriff Smith took out his cigarette papers and caressed them between his thumb and index finger. Then he put them back into his shirt pocket without trying to roll one in the wind. "Are we talking about the same Jake Miller? Some think he was totally off."

"Crazy? Well, I suppose it depends on who you talk to. Jake was real smart–maybe a little too smart for his own good–and if you couldn't keep up with him you'd think he was half-baked. But if you were sharp enough to follow what he was saying, he made perfect sense. That's the trouble, most folks around here aren't—"

"They say he was a melancholiac."

A dark-red, almost-purple, boxlike, Essex Terraplane went by, its laboring engine muffled by the snow.

"Melancholiac? Why, not at all! He just had a strange sense of humor, and people misunderstood him, and I suppose they found him a bit aggravating. One of the funniest guys I ever knew though! Boy did he know a lot of jokes. There was the one about the fox and the raccoon. The fox was out looking for mice, when he met the raccoon. The raccoon asked . . . ."

"Close friend? Not at all."
"Well, friend then," Sheriff Smith grumped.
"I wouldn't call it that either."
"Well what in blazes would you call it then? You sat on a bench on Main Street with him and Walter Grimswold for years."
Ichabod Klopper rubbed his jowls, and his wandering eye rolled from side to side, then up, and it stayed there. "That doesn't mean we were friends," he said in his thick German accent. "In fact I really didn't like him all that much. I was just lonely."

CHAPTER SEVENTY-ONE

On the following afternoon, Sheriff Smith found Dr. Hirshmann in the stable behind his house, grooming his horses.

"Come in, Sheriff. What can I do for you?" Dr. Hirshmann put down his brush and sat on a wooden crate beside the stall from which he had just exited. He invited his visitor to sit on a bench alongside the wall.

The huge stable was better than most people's homes, with its thick, log walls, concrete floor, and large windows. The stall floors were covered with fresh straw, and the mows were full of hay. In one corner there was a work area, and opposite–on the other side of the main door–was a saddle room.

"I need some information," the sheriff said.

One of the horses had evacuated, and steam ascended from the manure into the cold air.

"About Jake Miller, no doubt," Dr. Hirshmann said. "I was going to contact you. I'm retired, but his case was . . . well, too interesting to pass up."

"How did you come to know him?"

"We met one day while walking. He was an affable sort. We struck up a conversation, and there were many conversations after that. He was uneducated, yet quite intelligent, but there was something about him. I realized he was troubled. My professional interest was piqued, and I felt sorry for him. I believed I could help. Around here they call me a head doctor, but if I may say, I have a considerable international reputation in the field of hypnotherapy."

"What can you tell me about Miller? From what I've heard, he was a strange bird."

"Very." Dr. Hirshmann took a silver cigarette case from his shirt pocket and held it out.

"No, thanks."

The doctor selected a cigarette. It was long, and the paper was brown. He pulled out a lighter. After he had lit his cigarette, he leaned back against a support post and blew smoke toward the rafters.

"He was one of my failures, Sheriff. I worked with him for months, to no avail. Indeed, it seemed like the longer we were together, the worse he got. Guilt, hallucinations, . . . Finally he stopped coming." Dr. Hirshmann took another puff, holding the cigarette between his thumb and first two fingers. "There was something in his past. Something terrible, but even under hypnosis he would tell me nothing. The last time I saw him he became so uneasy he came out of his hypnotic state, and he was restive for hours. I was reluctant to let him leave until he had calmed down. He accused me of prying, and all sorts of other terrible things, then he left, and I didn't see him until a month later. He was paranoid about me revealing his case to others."

"And in all that time, you learned nothing?"

"Very little. Whatever the ghost in his past, his reaction to it was unique in my experience. And I have had much experience."

As the sheriff found his way out, he heard Dr. Hirshmann mumble something about an unsound mind, and being much vexed.

When Stuart Simpson came out of the church, Sheriff Smith took him aside. The sky was overcast, and it was cold.

"Yes, I knew Jake," Stuart said.

"Somebody said you and he were friends."

"Friends. Hm. I suppose he considered me a friend. Mostly I was his banker." Stuart was small, dark, and perpetually nervous. He had on a black suit and a matching overcoat.

They waited while the pallbearers slid Jake's casket into the hearse. Only a few mourners exited the church, and they all got in their cars and left.

"Did he do much business with you?"

"He applied for a few loans."

"Any problems?"

"No, not at all, because whenever we approved a loan, he backed out. Never did follow through. One time he wanted money for a new car, but as usual he changed his mind, and he drove his flivver for another five years."

"Why?"

"He lost his farm once. He got it back, but he never trusted bankers after that. Not even me."

"Ever talk to him about anything other than banking?"

"Religion and philosophy sometimes. Mostly he talked and I listened."

"How was he before he died?"

"How was he? How do you mean?"

"You think he killed himself?"

"I don't know. I hadn't seen much of him over the last couple of years."

They watched the hearse pull away. Only two cars followed.

Stuart continued. "About five years ago I was pretty worried about him. He was going on about people hanging themselves. He knew all about it: how much of a drop you need, and so on. But nothing happened. Then somebody said he tried to hang himself last year, but that could'a been the usual gossip. Anyway, isn't it all over now? No wife, no kids, no relatives—"

"There may be something in his past that has to be cleared up."

It began to snow, and both men pulled up their collars.

"That was a long time ago," Stuart said.

"Nevertheless, did he ever say anything about before he came here?"

"No. Why?"

"Like someone was after him?"

"After him? No, I . . . Well, I dunno. Now that you mention it, he always seemed to get kind of agitated around strangers. I remember once we were in front of the bank in Charity, and an out-of-state car pulled up. He got real nervous and went home. I mean, real nervous. All sweaty, and he started shaking. Yeah, and there were other times too. But I never knew why."

It was snowing heavier, and everyone else had left.

"You think someone did him in and dumped the body on his wife's grave?" Stuart asked. "Good heavens!"

"I dunno what to think. I may have to send a few telegrams."

CHAPTER SEVENTY-TWO

Dr. Hirshmann stood in the middle of his sitting room as Sheriff Smith entered. The room was warm and comfortable, with the aroma of incense and tea, and the underlying smell of burning coal.

"Sorry to bother you again," the sheriff said.

They shook hands.

"Not at all. I was hoping you would be back. I trust you've solved the mystery?"

The sheriff raised one eyebrow slightly.

"Small-town gossip from my hired man," Dr. Hirshmann said. He smiled as he seated the sheriff in the armchair in which Jake had lost his most terrible battle. "A bit of brandy, Sheriff?" He gestured at a bottle and some glasses on an end table.

"No, thanks."

Dr. Hirshmann pulled a chair closer to the sheriff and sat down. "I expect that once you got to the bottom of it, it wasn't so very complicated and mysterious as—"

"I sent some telegraphs, and I even made some telephone calls. People who knew Miller back in Iowa."

"And?"

"About the worst they could say was that he was a boozer, and that he was kinda' off. And some said he was as normal as you or me."

"Really? The ones who said he was off. What did they mean?"

"Just kinda nutty. Always talkin' about philosophy and stuff. Then not long before he came here, a mule kicked him in the head, and he really went off his beam. After a few days he got back to normal, but apparently normal wasn't too good."

"Didn't he get into some kind of trouble?"

"A retired barkeep said that Miller liked to gamble, and somebody might'a been after him for gambling debts, but nothing big. And he got into a saloon fight. Apparently it wasn't much of a fight. Maybe it wasn't a fight at all. Some of the regulars thought the other guy–Barker–fell down and hit his head. Others thought he passed out because he was as boiled as an owl. They were both polluted, and nobody knows. Anyways, Barker was out for a while. They had Miller in jail overnight, sleeping it off, and when they released him the next day, he ran off with some Jezebel. I think he married the Jezebel. His wife, Mable." Sheriff Smith wiped the drooping ends of his mustache with his fingers. "Far as anyone can remember, Miller never was back."

"That wouldn't account for—"

"The guy he got in the fight with–Barker–is still kicking."

Dr. Hirshmann slumped and looked past Sheriff Smith at the metronome on top of his desk. "I must have missed something. It was obvious that Jake was suffering from deep . . . ."

The sheriff fidgeted while Dr. Hirshmann talked on.

". . . and I stick to my diagnosis that he was deeply . . . ."

Sheriff Smith glanced around the room. He focused on the medical books in the corner.

". . . so there has to be something more," Dr. Hirshmann concluded.

"Nope. I talked to near a dozen people, and it was always the same. Just your average drunk. Anyway, I'm not interested in what made him tick, I only wanna know what happened."

"A drunk? He had tapered off the drinking. The police didn't have anything else?"

"No. When all is said and done, I'm beginning to think all there was in his past was a little chicanery of some sort. Or maybe he thought he had killed the guy in the bar, and lit out because of that."

Sweat formed on Dr. Hirshmann's forehead. He reached for the brandy bottle and half-filled a glass.

Sheriff Smith took an empty whiskey bottle from his pocket and held it up. "The grave diggers who were burying Miller next to his wife found this."

"He got drunk and froze to death?"

"Maybe he wanted to freeze to death. The coroner said he couldn't find anything wrong with him, other than a little booze."

"In all my years I never . . . I should have done more."

"Don't take it personal. Nothing you or anyone else could have done." The sheriff put on his hat. "I have to get going."

As Sheriff Smith left, Dr. Hirshmann took his glass in both hands and drank. When he was finished, he poured another, and he sat staring at the metronome.

———————

The hands dropped Jake, and he felt his Wheel of Life stop. As he fell back on Mable's grave, he knew that dying wasn't hard. It was trying to live a life of reality, in the here and now–despite all of his haunts and hallucinations–that had been hard.

The snow continued to fall, and the people continued to talk, but Jake couldn't distinguish them. He prayed yet again, and as he did, a brightness illuminated the cemetery. He rolled his eyes to his left side and looked up to see a point of light that became larger and brighter as it descended. He felt himself leave his body and float toward the Light.

"Jake. I've been waiting for you." From the Light, Mable materialized. She was smiling.

Jake reached for her. "You're beautiful," he said. "Like when we were married."

"You are too."

"No, I'm . . ." He looked down at his body. He was sprawled face up, and the snow was covering him again. Someone threw a coat over him. The white rabbit stood in the nearby field, watching.

"Your suffering is over, Jake." Mable took his hand. "Come, drink with me from the river Lethe–the water that will make us forget our earthly life–then we'll cross to the Elysian Plain."

"The Elysian Plain? But that's not your concept of—"

"Heaven, then? Nirvana? Lars Nordraak and his ancestors would probably prefer Valhalla. Others Zion, or Olympus. The Indians believed that there was a 'Great Mystery' that breathed a spirit into them, and when they died, that spirit was freed, and it pervaded nature. That was their vision of heaven. What difference what we call it?"

"I wish I had known all that when I was young!"

"Come," Mable said.

"But I've got to tell Lars Nordraak, and—"

"He'll have to find out for himself."

As the light enveloped him, and lifted him, Jake looked down and caught one last glimpse of his mortal form.

www.ingramcontent.com/pod-product-compliance
Lightning Source LLC
Chambersburg PA
CBHW050014180626
46810CB00002B/405